The Understudy

ALSO BY DAVID NICHOLLS

Starter for Ten

DAVID NICHOLLS

The Understudy

HODDER &
STOUGHTON

First published in Great Britain in 2005 by Hodder and Stoughton
A division of Hodder Headline
This edition published in 2005

A Hodder and Stoughton Book

3 5 7 9 10 8 6 4 2

A CIP catalogue record for this title is available from the British Library

ISBN Hardback 0 340 83873 6
ISBN Trade Paperback 0 340 73488 4

Typeset in Sabon by Palimpsest Book Production Limited,
Polmont, Stirlingshire

Printed and bound by
Clays Ltd, St Ives plc

Hodder Headline's policy is to use papers that are natural, renewable and
recyclable products and made from wood grown in sustainable forests. The
logging and manufacturing processes are expected to conform to the
environmental regulations of the country of origin.

Hodder and Stoughton Ltd
A division of Hodder Headline
338 Euston Road
London NW1 3BH

To Roanna Benn, Matthew Warchus and
Hannah Weaver, for the breaks.

No! I am not Prince Hamlet, nor was meant to be:
Am an attendant lord, one that will do
To swell a progress, start a scene or two,
Advise the prince; no doubt an easy tool,
Deferential, glad to be of use,
Politic, cautious, and meticulous;
Full of high sentence, but a bit obtuse;
At times, indeed, almost ridiculous –
Almost, at times, the Fool . . .

T. S. Eliot
The Love Song of J. Alfred Prufrock

Learn your lines and don't bump into the furniture.
Spencer Tracy

Act One

WAITING TO GO ON

– That's not real life, lad. That's just pretending.
– But 'real life' *is* how well you pretend, isn't it? You.
Me. Everybody in the world . . .

Jack Rosenthal
Ready When You Are, Mr McGill

SUNSET BOULEVARD

CHIEF   INSPECTOR   GARRETT
(CONT.)
. . . or I'll have you back directing
traffic faster than you can say disci-
plinary action.

INSPECTOR SUMMERS
But he's just toying with us, sir, like
a cat with a—

CHIEF INSPECTOR GARRETT
I repeat - Don't. Make It. Personal. I
want a result, and I want it yesterday,
or you're off this case, Summers.
(SNOW goes to speak)
I mean it. Now get out of here - the
both of you.

INT. MORTUARY. DAY

BOB 'BONES' THOMPSON, the forensic pathologist, sickly complexion, ghoulish sense of
humour, stands over the semi-naked body of a
YOUNG MAN, early thirties, his bloated body
lying cold and dead on the mortuary slab, in
the early stages of decomposition - WPC SNOW
is clutching a handkerchief to her mouth.

3

INSPECTOR SUMMERS
So - fill me in, Thompson. How long
d'you think he's been dead for?

THOMPSON
Hard to say. From the stink on him, I
think it's fair to say he's not the
freshest fish on the slab . . .

INSPECTOR SUMMERS
(not smiling)
Clock's ticking, Bones . . .

THOMPSON
OK, well, judging from the decay, the
bloating and the skin discoloration,
I'd say . . . he's been in the water a
week or so, give or take a day.
Initial examination suggests strangula-
tion. By the ligature marks round the
neck, I'd say the killer used a thick,
coarse rope, or a chain maybe . . .

DI SUMMERS
A chain? Christ, the poor bastard . . .

WPC SNOW
Who found the body?

(SUMMERS shoots her a look - 'I ask
the questions round here . . .')

```
                THOMPSON
        Some old dear out walking the dog.
        Nice lady, 82 years old. I think it's
        safe to assume you should be looking
        elsewhere for your serial ki—
```

'Hang on a second ... Nope – nope, sorry, everyone, we're going to have to stop.'

'Why, what's up?' snapped Detective Inspector Summers.

'We've got flaring.'

'On the lens?'

'Dead guy's nostrils. You can see him breathing. We're going to have to go again.'

'Oh, for crying out loud ...'

'Sorry! Sorry, sorry, everyone,' said the DEAD YOUNG MAN, sitting up and folding his arms self-consciously across his blue-painted chest.

Whilst the crew reset, the director, a long-faced, troubled man with an unconvincing baseball cap pushed far back on a reflective forehead, dragged both hands down his face and sighed. Hauling himself from his canvas chair, he strode over to the DEAD YOUNG MAN and knelt matily next to the mortuary slab.

'Right, so, Lazarus, tell me – is there a problem?'

'No, Chris, it's all good for me ...'

'Because – how can I say this – at present, you're doing a little too much.'

'Yeah, sorry about that.'

The director peered at his watch, and rubbed the red indentations left by his baseball cap. 'Because it's getting on for two thirty and ... what's your name, again?'

'Stephen, Stephen McQueen. With a P-H.'

'No relation?'

'No relation.'

'Well, Stephen with a P-H, it's getting on for two thirty, and we haven't even started on the autopsy . . .'

'Yes, of course. It's just, you know, with the lights and nerves and everything . . .'

'It's not as if you have to *perform*, all you have to do is bloody lie there.'

'I realise that, Chris, it's just it's tricky, you know, not to visibly breathe, for that long.'

'No one's asking you not to breathe . . .'

'No, I realise that,' said Stephen, contriving a chummy laugh.

'. . . just don't lie there taking bloody great gulps like you've just run the two hundred metres, OK?'

'OK.'

'And don't grimace. Just give me something . . . neutral.'

'OK. Neutral. But apart from that . . . ?'

'Apart from that, you're doing *terrific* work, really.'

'And d'you think we'll be done by six? It's just I've got to be—'

'Well, that's up to you, isn't it, Steve?' said the director, resettling the cap, stalking back to his canvas chair. 'Oh, and, Steve?' he shouted across the set. 'Please don't hold your belly in – you're *meant* to be bloated.'

'Bloated. OK, bloated.'

'Right, places, everyone,' shouted the first AD and Stephen settled once again on his marble slab, adjusted the damp underwear, closed his eyes, and did his best to pretend to be dead.

The secret of truly great screen acting is to do as little as possible, and this is never more important than when playing an inanimate object.

In a professional career lasting eleven years, Stephen C. McQueen had played six corpses now, each of them carefully thought through and subtly delineated, each of them skilfully conveying the pathos of being other than alive. Keen not to get typecast, he had downplayed this on his CV, allocating the various corpses intriguing, charismatic leading-man names like MAX or OLIVER rather than the more accurate, less evocative BODY or VICTIM. But word had obviously got round the industry – no one did nothing at all quite like Stephen C. McQueen. If you wanted someone to be pulled from the Grand Union Canal at dawn, or lie slack, broken and uncomplaining across the bonnet of a car, or slump prone at the bottom of a muddy First World War trench, then this was the man. His very first job after leaving drama school had been RENT BOY 2 in *Vice City*, a hard-hitting post-watershed crime show. One line –

```
            RENT BOY 2
            (Geordie accent)
        Why-ay, ya lookin' fah a good time,
        mista?
```

– then a long, hot afternoon spent with his arm dangling out of a black bin liner. Of course at thirty-two, his Rent Boy days were some way behind him now, but Stephen C. McQueen could still usually past muster as most other remains.

But for some reason, today his technique was letting him down. This was a shame, because *Summers and Snow* was a TV institution, and in a few months upwards of nine million people would settle down in front of the telly on a Sunday night, to see him swiftly strangled, then lying here, inert, in a stranger's underwear. You'd be hard-pushed to call it a *break* as such, but if the director liked what he did, or didn't do, if he got on with his co-stars, they might use him again, to play someone who walked about, moved his face, spoke aloud. First Rule of Showbiz – it's not what you know, it's who you know. Stay professional. Be positive. Be committed. Always have a motivation. The trick is to *impress*. Always ensure that people *like* you, at least until you're famous enough for it not to matter any more.

Waiting for the next take, Stephen sat up straight on the cold slab, and stretched his arms behind his back till he felt his shoulders crack – important not to stiffen up, important to keep limber. He glanced round the set, in the hope of striking up a conversation with his fellow actors. Craggy, Stern, Ex-Alcoholic Loner Detective Inspector Tony Summers and Perky, Independent-Minded WPC Sally Snow were in a tight little huddle some way off, sipping tea from plastic cups and confidently eating all the best biscuits. Stephen had always nursed a bit of a crush on Abigail Edwards, the actress playing WPC Snow, and had even worked out a throwaway little joke he could use in conversation, about his role. 'It's a living, Abi!' he would quip self-deprecatingly out of the side of his mouth in between takes, then raise a mouldy eyebrow, and she'd laugh, eyes sparkling, and perhaps they'd swap numbers at the end of filming, go for a drink or something. But the opportunity had never arisen. In between takes she'd barely acknowledged him, and clearly in Abigail Edwards' eyes, he might as well be, well – dead.

A cheery make-up artist appeared by Stephen's side, spritzed him with water and dabbed his face and lips with vaseline. Was her name Deborah? Another Rule of Showbiz – always, *always* call everyone by their name . . .

'So how do I look, Deborah?' he asked

'It's Janet. You look gorgeous! Funny old job this, isn't it?'

'Still – it's a living!' he quipped, but Janet was already back in her canvas chair.

'Quick as you can please, people,' barked the first AD, and Stephen lay back down on the mortuary slab, like a large, wet fish.

Keep still.

Don't let them see you breathe.

Remember – you are dead.

My motivation is not to be alive.

Acting is not *re-acting.*

The C in Stephen C. McQueen, incidentally, was there at the insistence of his agent, to prevent any confusion with the international movie star.

It was not a mistake that anyone had yet made.

The New Romantic

Lucky Lucy Chatterton makes eyes at the hot young actor who's setting London's glittering West End – and Hollywood – on fire.

There was only one response when I told female friends I was about to interview Josh Harper – Sheer, Unadulterated Envy. 'Lucky old you,' they sighed. 'Any chance of getting his phone number?' Sitting opposite him in an exclusive West End members' club, it's easy to see why.

Still only 28, Josh Harper is Britain's hottest, and prettiest, young actor. Recently voted the 12th Sexiest Man in the World by readers of a well-known women's magazine, he shot to fame four years ago when he became the youngest actor ever to win a BAFTA for his heart-breaking performance as Clarence, the mentally handicapped young man waging a battle with terminal disease, in acclaimed TV drama *Seize the Day*. Since then he's had huge success on stage as a sexually charged Romeo, and on the silver screen as a psychotic, cross-dressing gangster in ultra-violent Brit-Crime flick *Stiletto*, while still finding time to save the world in futuristic thriller *TomorrowCrime*. Christmas sees the release of his biggest movie yet, big-budget Hollywood sci-fi adventure *Mercury Rain*, but at present he's resisting the siren call of Hollywood, to play another dashing rake, Lord Byron, in the critically acclaimed West End show *Mad, Bad and Dangerous To Know*.

'It's Byron's life, told through his own words – his letters, poems and journals,' he says, sipping his double espresso, and looking at me with those unnervingly clear blue eyes. 'It's an amazing story. In a way, Byron was the first rock star – international fame, women throwing themselves at him – but he was really radical too, and really into politics, just like me. All of that, plus he was bisexual, had an incestuous relationship with his sister, *and* a club foot. A wild and crazy guy!'

Does he identify with the character in any way? I ask.

'What, apart from the club foot?' he laughs. 'Well, we're both passionate, I suppose. And I'm really into politics, especially the environment. I'm a happily married man, of course. And my sister's great, but, you know – there are limits!' Josh Harper throws his head back and laughs again, a warm, big-hearted guffaw. At the next table, two women look across at us. Is that envy I see in their eyes?

He goes on to tell me about how he likes to mix theatre with bigger-budget, commercial work. Hollywood still holds a fascination for Josh, though he's not about to move there full time just yet. '*Mercury Rain* was great fun – running about in space suits, waving guns around – but with those big sci-fi things, most of the time you're acting to thin air, so they can stick the special effects in later. Still, I hope it's a bit more sophisticated and intelligent than most of those kinds of movies. It's basically the old Anglo-Saxon poem *Beowulf*, but set in deep space. Also, what's great about those big event films is that financially they allow me to do the stuff I really love – live theatre, like *Mad, Bad* . . . or small, independent films. Fame and celebrity, they're great if you want a restaurant table, but they're not the reason I got into this. I love the sweat and smell of *real* acting.'

So will he be doing any more big Hollywood movies?

'Of course! What can I say – I just love blowing stuff up!!! And, yes, there have been offers, but nothing I can talk about. And I don't think I could ever live in LA full time – I love my beer, fags and footy too much!'

So was it true about the James Bond rumours? Josh looks bashful.

'Only a rumour, I'm afraid. My people have talked to their people, but it's still just a pipe dream. And, anyway, I'm way too young. But one day maybe. Of course I'd love to play Bond – there isn't an actor in the world who wouldn't want to play Bond.'

The publicist is tapping her watch now, and there's only time for a few quick-fire questions. Who or what is the greatest love of your life? I ask.

'My wife, of course,' he replies unhesitatingly, his eyes lighting up. Josh has been married to Nora Harper, an ex-singer, for two years now. Sorry, ladies!

'And how often do you have sex?' I ask, pushing my luck a little. Thankfully, Josh just laughs.

'If it's not a personal question?!? As often as we possibly can.'

'How do you relax?'

'See above!'

'When and where were you happiest?'

'See above!!'

'Favourite smell?'

He ponders for a moment. 'Either new-mown grass or the top of a new-born baby's head . . .'

'Favourite movie?'

'*The Empire Strikes Back.*'

'And what's your favourite word?'

He thinks for a moment. 'One my wife taught me – Uxorious.'

....

. . . and Stephen C. McQueen thought this might perhaps be a good time to stop reading. He tossed the newspaper back on to the train seat opposite. What was it with the smell of a new-born baby's head anyway? Josh wasn't even a father. Whose head had he been smelling? From the seat opposite, the photo of Josh grinned up at him, immaculately stubbled, hands running through his hair, shirt unbuttoned to the waist. Stephen turned the photo face down, and went back to looking out of the train window, at the tower blocks and terraces of Stockwell and Vauxhall sliding by.

Stephen caught sight of his reflection in the window, and thought about how he might interpret the role of James Bond. True, he had yet to be approached about the part, but by way of a private audition, he raised one eyebrow, gave himself a suave little James Bond smile, and tried, very hard, to picture himself in a white tuxedo, standing at a roulette wheel surrounded by beautiful, dangerous women.

He had a momentary vision of himself as CONTROL ROOM TECHNICIAN 4, stumbling backwards through a sugar-glass window into the submarine dock below, his lab coat on fire.

THE NEARLY CV

Stephen C. McQueen had two CVs.

Alongside the real-life résumé of all the things he had actually achieved, there was the Nearly CV. This was the good-luck version of his life, the one where the close shaves and the near misses and the second choices had all worked out; the version where he hadn't been knocked off his bike on the way to that audition, or come down with shingles during the first week of rehearsal; the one where they hadn't decided to give the role to that bastard off the telly.

This extraordinary phantom career began with Stephen almost-but-not-quite winning huge praise for his show-stealing Malcolm in *Macbeth* in Sheffield, then consequently very nearly giving his heart-breaking Biff in *Death of a Salesman* on a nationwide tour. Soon afterwards, the hypothetical reviews that he would probably have received for his might-have-been King Richard II had to be read to be believed. Diversifying into television, he had come oh-so-close to winning the nation's hearts as cheeky, unorthodox lawyer Todd Francis in hit TV series *Justice for All*, and a number of successful film roles, both here and abroad, had quite conceivably followed.

Unfortunately, all these great triumphs had taken place in other, imaginary worlds, and there were strict professional rules about submitting your parallel-universe résumé. This unwillingness to take into account events in other space-time dimensions meant that Stephen was left with his real-life CV, a document that reflected both his agent's unwillingness to say no, and Stephen's extraordinary capacity, his gift almost, for bad luck. It was this real-life version of events that brought him here, to London's glittering West End.

At the age of eight, visiting London for the first time with his mum and dad, Stephen had thought Piccadilly Circus was the centre of the universe, an impossibly glamorous, alien landscape, the kind of place where, in an old British sixties musical, a dance routine might break out at any moment. That was twenty-four years ago. It had since become his place of work, and coming up from the hot, soupy air of the tube station into the damp late October evening, all Stephen saw was a particularly garish and treacherous roundabout. Nearby, an adenoidal busker was doggedly working his way through the Radiohead songbook, and the chances of a dance routine breaking out seemed very slight indeed. Stephen barely even noticed Eros these days, surely the most underwhelming landmark in the world. If he bothered to look up at all, it was only to check the digital clock under the Coca-Cola sign, to see if he was late.

19.01.

He was late. He quickened his pace.

The Hyperion Theatre stands on Shaftesbury Avenue, in between a kitchen equipment wholesalers and an All-American Steakhouse of the type found precisely nowhere in America, the kind of restaurant that always contains at least one woman weeping. Pushing and jostling his way through the crowds, still looking a little blue-grey from his own autopsy, he fitted in surprisingly well with the disorientated coach parties, the dazed and pale shop assistants struggling home, the doleful, homesick Spanish students offering him flyers for English classes. He hurried past an excessive number of bureaux de change, past the disreputable fast-food outlets that sold sticky, iridescent orange mounds of sweet-and-sour pork and 'pizza' – thick wedges of grey dough, smeared with tomato purée and candlewax cheese. Maybe he should eat something. Maybe a pepperoni slice. He glanced at the wedges, perspiring under high-wattage bulbs, the pepperoni glinting with oily red sweat. Maybe not. Maybe he should wait until after work. 19.03 now, which meant that he was technically late for the half-hour call. The theatre was in sight now and, looking east along Shaftesbury Avenue, he could see the immense billboard of Josh Harper looming above the crowds, three storeys high.

On the billboard, the 12th Sexiest Man in the World stood in a puffy white shirt open to the waist, and a pair of tight black leather breeches of questionable historical veracity. In his right hand he held a rapier with which he lunged towards the passers-by, whilst in his left hand he held a book high above his head, as if to say, 'I'll just finish this duel, then get back to writing *Don Juan*'. Across his pelvis were scrawled the words *Mad, Bad and Dangerous to Know* in an extravagantly loopy hand, designed to denote literary class and historical authenticity. 'A tour de force! Josh Harper *is* Lord Byron,' proclaimed the billboard, the italicised 'is' settling the argument once and for all. '*Strictly Limited* Season!' Three months ago, back in August, when he'd first seen the billboard, Stephen had amused himself by imagining that 'Strictly Limited' referred to Josh Harper's abilities as an actor, but he wasn't sure if anyone else would find this observation funny, or accurate, and besides, there was no one to tell it to.

Stephen glanced once more at his watch: four minutes past now, nine minutes late, very unprofessional, unforgivable for the understudy. Still, he might get away with it, as long as Donna wasn't at stagedoor. He hurried unseen past the huddle of autograph hunters waiting for Josh – eight today, not a bad score—

'Ten minutes late, Mr McQueen,' said Donna, standing at stagedoor. Donna was the stage manager, a short, wide woman with a large, blunt face, like a painted shoe-box, brittle ex-Goth hair, and the surly demeanour of an embittered games teacher. Permanently dressed in regulation faded black denim,

Quba Sails Southwold
96 High Street, Southwold, IP18 6DP
VAT reg : 164091614
Phone: 01502 725394   02 SEP 2024

Goods   Qty   Cost

VIVCA S/S VISCOSE STRIPE TEE Blue/White
                               1   15.00

Total Cost   15.00

Cash   20.00
Change   5.00

Staff Isobel H SWOLD

Receipt 01 16 TR1194825 Timed at 11:53

(NET 12.50, VAT 2.50)

Thank you for your custom.

any failure to meet the original promotional
requirements, as a result of returning the product.

For hygiene reasons, swimwear must be tried on
over your underwear and returned with hygiene
strips in place. Swimwear can only be returned if
purchased full price.

 www.quba.com

QUBA & Cº.

BRITISH NAUTICAL HERITAGE

Salcombe, Devon

Quba & Co are happy to refund or exchange your full
price items within 30 days of purchase with a valid
proof of purchase. We will only refund or exchange
items that are unworn and unwashed with original
labels and in a re-sellable condition.

**Sale items can be exchanged only within 14 days,
accompanied by a valid proof of purchase.**

If you have purchased products as part of a promotional
offer or discount, the refund will be adjusted to reflect

she carried the regulation big bunch of keys, which she now twirled round on her finger like a six-shooter.

'Phew!' said Stephen. 'It's like Piccadilly Circus out there!'

'Doesn't get any funnier, Stephen.'

'Sorry, Donna, it's the tube . . .'

'Not an acceptable excuse,' grumbled Donna, dialling her mobile.

'You're cheerful today, what's up with you?'

'He's not here,' said Kenny, the doorkeeper, from behind his desk.

'He's not here? Who's not here?'

'*He's* not here,' scowled Donna.

'Josh?'

'Yes, Josh.'

'Josh isn't here?'

'Josh isn't here.'

Stephen became aware of the sound of the blood in his head.

'But it's nearly curtain-up, Donna!'

'Yes, I'm aware of that.'

'Well – well, have you phoned him?'

'*Brilliant* idea,' said Donna, taking her phone away from her ear and waggling it at him. She licked her lips, pushed her shaggy fringe out of her eyes, readying herself to leave a message for the man himself, and for a brief moment she precisely resembled a fourteen-year-old girl about to ask a boy if he wanted to go ice-skating with her.

'Josh, sweetheart, it's your Aunty Donna here at the theatre. You're late, young man! I'll have to put you across my knee,' she mooned saucily into the air, tweaking the studs in her ear lobes. 'Anyway, we're *very* worried about you. Hopefully you'll walk through the door any second now, but if not, give us a call. Otherwise, we'll have to send young *Stephen* on . . .'

Stephen stood nearby, unhearing, rocking backwards and forwards slightly on the balls of his feet, making the high, humming noise he made in times of stress. Here it is then, he thought. Finally – the Big Break. After all, this had never happened before. The 12th Sexiest Man in the World was *always* on time. Until this moment, Stephen had been quietly accepting of his fate, doomed to shadow not just the most successful, most popular, arguably the most talented young actor of his generation, but also the healthiest and luckiest. No matter what glamorous debauch he'd been to the night before, no matter what time he'd stumbled out of some Soho drinking den or premiere party, Josh would be there, 18.50 on the dot, signing autographs at stagedoor, flirting with the Wardrobe Department, dimpling his cheeks, tossing his hair. Josh Harper was invincible. If, God forbid, someone shot him, he'd almost certainly smile, and reveal the bullet gripped daintily between his large white teeth.

But not today. Whilst Donna cooed on to Josh's voice mail, Stephen was imagining a number of lurid scenarios –

Josh Harper tumbling down the treacherous cast-iron spiral staircase of his luxurious warehouse apartment . . .

Josh Harper struggling to pull his shattered leg from beneath the faulty home gymnasium, the phone lying just inches away . . .

Josh Harper clutching his belly and sliding beneath the blond-wood table of the exclusive sushi restaurant, his handsome face a virulent green . . .

Josh Harper smiling bravely as plucky paramedics race to extract him from the wheels of a runaway number 19 bus . . .

'*I . . . I can't . . . can't feel my toes . . .*'

'*Not to worry, sir, Mr Harper, we'll have you out in just a mo.*'

'*But you don't understand, I've got to be at the theatre in five minutes.*'

'*Sorry, but the only theatre you'll be seeing tonight is the operating theatre . . .*'

'Right, Stephen,' sighed Donna, looking at her watch, and

thinking the unthinkable, 'we'd better get you in costume then. Just in case.'

Stephen was barely aware of the journey down the corridor to the number-one dressing room. He had a vague floating sensation, as if Donna were pushing him on a gurney. So, this is how it is, he thought, this is what good luck feels like. Though by no means a spiteful man, Stephen had been fantasising about just such a glorious catastrophe, six days a week, twice on Saturdays and Wednesdays, for the last three months now. When Stephen told Josh to break a leg, he meant it: break in two places, compound fractures, please. This was, after all, the harsh algebra of the understudy's job – for Stephen to succeed, Josh would have to suffer; an incapacitating disease, or a flesh wound of some sort, something in between flu and a mild impaling, something to take him down for between, say, forty-eight and seventy-two hours. Just long enough for Stephen to do the show tonight, refine his performance for tomorrow, get Terence the director back in, the casting people, the film producers, maybe even a critic or two, maybe discreetly call some other, better agents, the real high-fliers. The snap of an Achilles tendon, the wet pop of an appendix, a spleen even, were all that separated Stephen from the chance to turn his life around.

They were in Josh's dressing room now, Stephen pulling off his coat and shoes, Debs from wardrobe standing by, holding the costume, laundered and pristine, as Stephen started to undress. Donna was on the phone to Stagedoor. 'No sign of him yet? . . . Right, we'll give it five minutes, then we'll make an announcement . . . He's here, getting ready . . . Yes, I know . . . Ok, well, keep me posted . . .'

Thank God, thought Stephen, he's not okay.

Debs from Wardrobe held out Byron's leather breeches, and Stephen took them solemnly, and started to pull them on. He had never boxed professionally, and was unlikely ever to take it up, but he imagined that this is what it felt like before a big fight: the reverence, the sense of ceremony. He tried to clear his head, to find some kind of calm, focused place, but in his mind's eye he was already picturing the curtain call . . .

Lights fade to black at the end of the show, and a hush falls over the audience. Moments pass. Then the applause breaks like thunder, great rolling waves of it. Donna and rest of the team stand in the wings, big, beefy, moist-eyed stagehands with tears in their eyes applauding, pushing a modest Stephen C. McQueen reluctantly back on to the stage. Then the roar of the audience in his ears as they rise as one, bunches of flowers skidding across the stage to his feet. Great waves of love and respect and validation hit him, nearly knocking him off his feet. Shielding his eyes against the spotlight, he squints out into the audience, and spots the faces of the people he loves – Alison, his ex-wife; Sophie, his daughter; his parents; his friends – all grinning and laughing, screaming and shouting. He catches his ex-wife's eye, wide with new-found admiration and respect – 'You were right all along,' she seems to be saying. 'You were right to hold out, you were right not to give up. You are an actor of rare and exquisite depth and talent, and if you believe in something strongly enough, dreams really do come . . .

'Fuck me, bollocks, shit, hi people, sorrysorrysorry I'm late . . .'

. . . and panting, and tossing his hair, the 12th Sexiest Man in the World tumbled into the dressing room, entering, as always, as if someone had just thrown him a stick.

Stephen stopped putting on his leather trousers.

'Josh! You were about to give your Aunty Donna a heart attack!' beamed Donna, skipping to the door and tousling his tremendous hair. 'Mr McQueen here was just about to go and put your cozzy on.'

'Sorry, Steve mate,' Josh pouted apologetically, head cocked to one side. 'You must have thought it was your big break come at last, I expect.'

'Well, you know . . .'

Josh rubbed his arm in matey consolation. 'Well, not today, I'm afraid, Steve, my friend. Not today . . .'

Stephen forced something that approximated the shape of a smile, and started to climb out of the leather trousers. It was like landing on the moon, and being asked if you wouldn't mind staying behind and watching the capsule.

'So what is your excuse then, you bad boy?' Donna scolded Josh indulgently.

'No excuse, just had a bit of a personal situation on the home front, if you know what I mean.'

Stephen handed the leather trousers back to Bev, who smiled sympathetically and rehung the costume on the rail, ready for its rightful owner. Stephen saw that Donna was now sitting on his own pair of trousers.

'Excuse me, Donna . . .' said Stephen, standing a little behind her.

'Well, Josh, you're a very, *very* naughty boy,' mooned Donna, enthralled.

'I know, I know, I know!' said Josh, taking Donna's large hands and gallantly kissing the knuckles. 'Tell you what, you can come round and spank me after the show.'

'*could I just get my trous . . . ?*' said Stephen.

'I might take you up on that.'

'And so you should.'

'*You're sitting on my . . .*'

'I will then.'

'Come to the dressing room.'

'*. . . if you could just . . .*'

'I'm looking forward to it.'

'*. . . just let me . . .*'

'. . . Not as much as I am. Bring a bottle! And a friend!'

'. . . Oooh, saucy boy . . .'

'Do you think I could get my trousers please, guys?' said Stephen, grabbing them, and tugging. Donna stood, glaring at him for breaking the spell. A moment passed.

'Well, I'd better get the old make-up on!' said Josh, tossing his locks. 'Can't keep the people waiting,' and he held Donna's head between two hands like a basketball, kissed it with a loud 'mmmmmmoi', and settled in front of his mirror.

'*Shestooduponthebalconyinexplicablymimickinghimhic-cupingandamicablywelcominghimin* . . .'

In the corridor, Donna scowled at Stephen. 'You look awful, by the way,' she said. 'Your face is completely grey.'

Stephen rubbed his hairline and examined his fingertips for traces of make-up; small smudges of mackerel blue and grey. He couldn't tell Donna he'd been moonlighting. 'Just a little bit . . . glandy, that's all,' he said, rubbing either side of his jawline with his fingertips to prove the point.

'Honestly, Stephen, you're *always* ill. If it's not your glands, it's pleurisy, or gastric *flu*, or your misplaced bloody *coc*cyx,' she said, then stomped off to get ready for curtain-up, her prison-warder's keys rattling against her hip as she went.

Stephen stood for a moment and watched her go. Once again, he was left with the sneaking suspicion that understudying someone like Josh Harper was a little like being a life jacket on a jumbo jet: everyone is pleased that you're there, but God forbid they should actually have to *use* you.

THE MAN IN THE BLACK
WOOL/LYCRA-MIX UNITARD

Stephen C. McQueen loved acting. Some people are passionate about football, or the three-minute pop song, or clothes, or food, or vintage steam engines, but Stephen loved watching actors. All the years spent gazing at movies on telly in the afternoon, curtains closed against the summer sun, or in the front row of the local flea-pit cinema, had taken their toll, and while other teenagers had had pictures of footballers or pop stars on their walls, Stephen had pictures of people who pretended.

Over the years William Shatner, Doug McClure, Peter Cushing and Jon Pertwee had lost their seats in the pantheon, to be replaced by Al Pacino, Dustin Hoffman, Paul Newman and Laurence Olivier. Years passed, and he'd begun to notice girls – in this case, Julie Christie, Jean Seberg and Eva Marie Saint, occasionally going behind their backs with a succession of Bond girls.

And now here Stephen was himself, pretending for a living and, when the opportunities arose, he loved this too. Of course, he was aware that, as a profession, actors had any number of faults, most of them beginning with the prefix 'self-', and that there were times when he felt embarrassed, ashamed even, to be connected with such a silly, frivolous, fantastical world. But he also felt that there was a kind of integrity there in the very best performances, a kind of skill, an art even. Yes, actors could be vain and pretentious, precious and pompous, sentimental and shallow, affected and lazy and arrogant, but it needn't be that way, need it? He thought of Alec Guinness, silhouetted in the doorway in *The Ladykillers*, or the tremendous slow-dawning smile that lights up Shirley MacLaine's face at the end of *The Apartment*, or Brando and Steiger in the back of the car in *On the Waterfront*, or Peter Sellers in *Dr Strangelove* or Walter Matthau in pretty much anything, and he'd become inspired all over again. That ability to make complete strangers double up with laughter, or squirm with anxiety, or clench their fists in indignation, or scream, or weep, or wince, or sigh, just through the act of *pretending* – well, if you can do that and get paid for it, then surely that had to be the best job in the world.

As for celebrity, he had no desire to be famous, or at least not globally famous like Josh Harper. He had no expectation of seeing himself on a fridge magnet or a happy-meal. He did not want his old cigarette butts sold on eBay, had no pressing need for the best tables in restaurants, no secret desire to be photographed with a telephoto lens looking paunchy in trunks on someone's private island. Fame only interested him as an inevitable and not entirely unpleasant side effect of doing good work. All he wanted was fully employed fame. Nod-of-recognition fame.

Which made it all the more frustrating to be stuck in an acting job that involved virtually no acting whatsoever.

Stephen headed away from Josh's dressing room, back along the corridor painted two shades of glossy dark green sometimes in the fifties, giving it an old-fashioned, institutional feel, like a ritzy TB sanatorium. He received consolatory nods and never-minds from Debs from Wardrobe, Chrissy the ASM, Sam the lighting guy.

'Nearly, mate, nearly,' said Michael the DSM, consolingly. 'Maybe next time, eh?'

'Maybe next time.'

He pushed through a heavy fire door, and headed upstairs. Halfway up the underlit stairwell, he passed Maxine Cole's dressing room, nearer the stage than his and therefore superior. Fresh out of college, and straight into the small but memorable role of 'Venetian Whore', Maxine sat, wearing a white towelling dressing gown and an elaborate early nineteenth-century wig, her small, hard, pretty features all bunched in the centre of a board perma-tanned face, under high-arched doll's eyebrows. Her feet, in black lace-up boots, were up on the dressing table as she sat listening to *The Ultimate Chick-Flick Album in the World Ever* on her portable stereo, and reading *Heat* magazine with an almost religious intensity.

'Hey, Maxine!' said Stephen chirpily. 'Did you hear about all the excitement?'

'Excite me,' mumbled Maxine.

'Number twelve has only just arrived. A couple more minutes and I'd have been on.'

'Oh, yeah?' said Maxine, wholly consumed by an article about which actresses wore thongs, which favoured big pants. 'Why was he late then?'

'Don't know – trouble in paradise, apparently.'

'Really?' Maxine said, dragging her gaze up from the magazine. Nothing illuminated Maxine's life quite like marital discord, especially if it involved someone she knew, or someone famous, or ideally both. 'What did he say?'

'Not much, but he didn't get here till five minutes ago. Strictly speaking, according to Equity rules, I could have gone on.'

'Yeah, I'd have *loved* to see you tell him that, Steve. "Sorry, Josh, d'you mind sitting this one out . . ."'

'Still – one day, eh, Maxy? One day it'll be our turn.'

Maxine snuffled and turned the page. Clearly, she hated it when he lumped the two of them together. For one thing, she was actually visible on stage, and spoke, and moved around, and did some *proper* acting with Josh each night, in a number of small but significant roles. She appeared in silhouette in an up-stage doorway as Byron's beloved half-sister, Augusta Leigh,

and when Byron recited, 'She Walks In Beauty, Like The Night
. . .', it was Maxine's job to actually walk, in beauty, like the
night. Of course, the role of 'Venetian Whore' consisted primarily of lying partially naked on a four-poster bed whilst Lord
Byron wrote *Don Juan* using her buttocks as a desk, but at
least people noticed her; you could hear them, the men, shifting
in their seats, sitting upright. She had lines too, in jabbering
Italian, largely for comic effect, but still, a speaking part was
a speaking part. On the poster outside, she got an '. . . and
introducing . . .' credit. Yes, Maxine Cole was One To Watch,
she was an Exciting Fresh Young Talent, she was the Girl From
the Jalapeno-Cheese Tortilla-Chip Commercial ('To dip or not
to dip – that is the question'). Stephen, on the other hand, was
a Good Company Member – not a bad thing in itself, but no
more remarkable than a Safe Pair of Hands, a Reliable Little
Run-Around, a Comfy Pair of Shoes.

That Tannoy crackled and buzzed. 'Ladies and Gentlemen,
this is your five-minute call. Five minutes, please,' and Maxine
started rubbing expensive skin lotion into her long, creosote-
tanned legs. It was a little like watching someone lovingly oil
a gun, and Stephen discreetly turned and trudged up the rest
of the stairs to his dressing room, at the very top.

Olivier, Richardson, Gielgud, Guinness, Burton had all
climbed these stairs at one time or another, and the tiny dressing
room to which Stephen now ascended marked the location of
what had once been Dame Peggy Ashcroft's shoe cupboard.
The smell of the greasepaint and the roar of the crowd never
really permeated this far from the stage. Instead the roar came
from the boiler in the roof, and the smell was of cigarettes, old
newspapers, decaying carpet underlay; that charity-shop smell.
Stephen flopped in the tattered office chair in front of his mirror,
a mirror that, mockingly, actually was surrounded by light bulbs.
Only about a third of them were working, and the only other
source of light was a murky skylight, now black from soot and

pigeon shit, giving the room a subterranean atmosphere, despite being in a turret at the very top of the building. He turned the lights on, licked a cotton-wool pad, and tried to remove the last of the corpse make-up, leaving little wisps of cotton attached to the two-days' stubble. Then he lit a cigarette and sat for a while, looking in the mirror, examining his face; not out of any kind of vanity, but as a kind of professional obligation, like a truck driver checking the tread on balding tyres, wondering if he can get away with it.

It wasn't that it was a *bad* face as such – he had, after all, been cast as an Emergency Byron – but it had a soft, neutral, hard-to-recall quality, a milky blankness that made him much in demand for crime reconstructions and corporate-training films, but little else, the kind of unremarkable pleasantness that rendered him invisible to bartenders, bus drivers and casting directors. In the unlikely event of a movie being made of his life, he would perhaps be played by a young Tom Courtenay or, if the action were transposed to America, someone like the young Jack Lemmon, someone with that Everyman quality. Of course, the best person for the role of Stephen C. McQueen would be Stephen C. McQueen himself, but it was unlikely that his agent would be able to get him an audition, or that he wouldn't play himself badly. That was, after all, what he had been doing for some years now.

As for his supposed resemblance to the star of the show, the best that could be said was that he looked like a smudged polaroid of Josh Harper. A smudged, black-and-white polaroid of a slightly older, plumper Josh Harper. The haircut that made Josh look like a Renaissance prince (and might perhaps even be called that – 'I'd like a "Renaissance Prince", please') somehow contrived to make Stephen look like the keyboard player in a provincial British eighties soft-metal band. His nose was a little too big, his eyes a little too small, his skin a little too pale, and it was the combination of all these small

27

deficiencies that pushed it into ordinariness, invisibility. Only a mother, or his agent perhaps, would call it truly handsome. Stephen frowned, drew on the cigarette, and ruffled his own 'Renaissance Prince' with both hands, looking forward to the day, in just eight weeks' time, when he could cut the bloody thing off.

Over the Tannoy came the low rumble of Donna's voice. 'Beginners, please. Mr Harper, this is your beginner's call.'

Stephen stretched and turned the Tannoy down. Not tonight then. No Big Break tonight. Probably just as well; he wasn't really feeling up to a Big Break. He put his fingers on his neck, felt the glands in his neck, gathered saliva in his mouth then swallowed. Maybe he *was* getting ill. He curled his tongue over in an attempt to probe the back of his throat. Tonsillitis, it felt like. He put the plastic kettle on to boil, tipped three spoons of instant coffee into a chipped mug, and ate a biscuit.

On the Tannoy, he could hear the murmur of the audience subside, as the lights went down and the sound of the music began – a synthesised string quartet playing pastiche Haydn. He sat and listened for a while, alternating biscuit and cigarette, mouthing along to the lines with Josh, marking out the moves and gestures.

```
The curtain rises to find Lord Byron sitting
at a desk, scribbling away with a quill by
the light of a candelabra. Slowly, he becomes
aware of the audience's presence – he scans
the auditorium at his leisure, smiles, speaks
in a self-mocking drawl.

        LORD BYRON
    Mad, bad and dangerous to know!
        (HE SMILES WRYLY)
```

That is what they call me in England
now, or so I am told. And it is, I
must confess, a reputation that I have
done little to assuage.
     (HE PLACES THE QUILL DOWN, PICKS UP
      THE CANDELABRA, CROSSES CENTRE-STAGE,
      LIMPING SLIGHTLY ON HIS CLUB FOOT
      (LEFT), AND SURVEYS THE AUDIENCE.)
Like all reputations it is simultaneously accurate, yet fanciful. Perhaps
you would care for another point of
view? 'Twill take but ninety minutes of
your time . . .
     (HE SMILES ONCE MORE, A SLOW,
      KNOWING GRIN.)
Or then again, perhaps not. Perhaps you
actually prefer the legend to the
truth! Truly, I would not blame you. It
is only human nature, after all . . .
     I was born in the year of Our Lord
1788 . . .

. . . and it was usually at this point in the play that a profound
and stultifying boredom kicked in.

   Stephen reached up to the volume knob on the Tannoy; like
the telescreens in *1984*, you could never turn it off completely,
but it was possible to at least get Josh's voice down to a low
tinnitus murmur. He sat and read for a while, then at 20.48
precisely, exactly as he'd done ninety-six times before, and as
he would do another forty-eight times more, Stephen wriggled
into the opaque black wool and Lycra body stocking that he
wore for his on-stage role of Ghostly Figure. Very few men,
perhaps not even Josh Harper, can carry off the opaque black
body stocking with any great style or élan. Stephen looked like

a long-dead mime, and freshly depressed, he quickly pulled the heavy black cloak over his shoulders, grabbed the white Venetian face mask and tricorn hat, and headed down the treacherous back staircase that led to stage left.

On stage, Byron was approaching his tragically premature death, of a fever caught whilst nobly aiding the cause of Greek independence, and Stephen watched as Josh re-enacted Byron's illness taking hold. He was certainly coughing up a storm tonight. But was he any good? He was, it had to be admitted, almost supernaturally handsome – a poster-face, the kind that looks equally at home protruding from a suit of armour, or a toga, or a spacesuit; feminine without being effeminate, masculine without being coarse, but with something cruel about it too, something hard about the eyes and mouth, the kind of face that could play a romantic lead or a strangely appealing Nazi. On stage, Lord Byron solemnly intoned 'We'll Go No More A-roving', and Stephen watched with an uncomfortable but all-too-familiar mix of professional admiration, and a low, dull throb of envy in the pit of his stomach.

Then the red light in the wings changed to green, his cue to enter, and Stephen rolled his shoulders, cleared his throat and stepped out on to the stage. There was a time when walking on stage in front of a theatre full of people might have given him a little thrill, but frankly, this late into a long run, there was more adrenalin in trying to cross Shaftesbury Avenue. Besides, the lighting was deliberately murky, there was a lot of dry ice, he was a very, very long way upstage, and he was wearing a full face mask. Still, if a job's worth doing . . .

Think ghostly, he told himself. My motivation is to open the door in a ghostly manner.

He did so, then made a deep, sombre bow as Josh turned and walked past him, his eyes fixed straight ahead.

Now close the door, but not too fast, he thought, and slowly closed the door. He stood perfectly still as the stage lights faded on a slow ten count, then as soon as the applause began, turned and walked swiftly off stage, so as not to get in Josh's way. And that was it – walk on (ghostly), open door (slowly), bow (sombrely), close door (slowly), walk off (quickly). Room for interpretation was slight. An old theatrical saying has it that there is no such thing as a small part. This was that small part.

As always Josh Harper was waiting in the wings, eyes wide with elation, grinning and sweating like an action hero.

'Hey, Stevearoony, mate,' he shouted above the roar of the audience, dropping into his natural voice, a soft, semi-authentic cockney. This was another of Josh's not entirely endearing qualities – a congenital inability to call anyone by their chosen name, so that Donna became 'The Madonnster', Michael the DSM became 'Mickey the Big D', Maxine was 'Maximillius'. At some point Stephen had been designated 'Stevearoony', 'The Stevester', 'Bullitt' or, perhaps most annoying of all, 'Stephanie'. There seemed every possibility that if Josh were to meet, say, the Dalai Lama or Nelson Mandela, that he would address them as the Dalaroony Lamster and Nelsony Mandoly. And they probably wouldn't mind.

'. . . *really* sorry about getting your hopes up earlier, Steve. You know, about going on.'

'Oh, that's OK, Josh. Nature of the job . . .'

'More! More! Encore!' shouted the audience. Maxine was on stage, taking a token solo bow, but it was Josh they were screaming for.

'No, it's not OK, Steve, it's fuckin' unforgivable, and unprofessional too.' He grabbed Stephen tight by the shoulder. 'Listen, just to make it up to you, what are you doing Sunday night?'

'Nothing. Why?'

'It's just I'm having this big party, and I wondered if you were available?'

'More! More! Bravo!'

'Bear with us a sec, will you?' Josh sighed, then almost

reluctantly, as if bowing to rapturous applause were a chore, like taking the bins out, he turned, executed a gymnastic little hop-and-skip and scampered from the wings back out into the burning white light of the stage. Stephen watched as Josh flopped forward from the waist, and hung there, head and hands dangling limply to the floor, as if to emphasise just how completely and utterly ex-*haust*-ing the whole damn thing had been. But Stephen's mind was elsewhere. A party. Josh Harper's party. A famous person's party. He didn't really approve of fame, of course, and consciously tried not to be influenced or impressed by it, but still, a proper, genuine, fashionable party, full of successful, attractive, influential, beautiful people. *And he'd been invited.*

'Bravo! More!' shouted the audience.

Josh was back by his side. 'Quite a big crowd, seven onwards – what d'you think? I'd really appreciate it . . .'

'Sounds good to me, Josh.'

'More, more, encore . . .' shouted the audience.

'Goodly good, mate! I'll text you my address,' and he simulated some dainty, two-thumbed texting on a little mimed mobile phone; another of his gifts – a prodigious and gifted mime, always conjuring objects out of thin air: a waggled pint, a finger-and-thumb phone, a ball kicked into the back of the net. 'Oh, and it's suit and tie, by the way! And don't tell the others, Maxine or Donna or anyone else. I see enough of that lot as it is. Just our little secret, yeah?'

I'm the only one he has invited, thought Stephen, glowing.

'Sure, Josh, it's our secret.'

'Bravo! Encore! Encore . . .' The applause was starting to dip a little, but was still enthusiastic enough to justify another curtain call, if Josh could be bothered to take it.

'What d'you reckon? Think I can squeeze one more out of them?' asked Josh, grinning.

'Go for it!' said Stephen, now full of goodwill for his old

pal. Josh turned and strolled slowly out on to the stage, wiping his forehead with the sleeve of his sweat-soaked puffy shirt, and the audience's applause swelled once more as he stood at the front of the stage, looking around slowly, up into the gods and down at the stalls, applauding the audience back, thanking them, flattering them.

Standing invisible in the wings, perspiring into his black unitard, Stephen C. McQueen looked down at his own hands and found, to his surprise, that he was applauding too.

KITCHEN-SINK DRAMA

As a teenager, falling in love with old British movies of the fifties and sixties on telly, Stephen had always been fascinated by the notion of 'the bedsit'. He liked to imagine himself, in black-and-white, as an Albert Finney type, living in shabby-romantic furnished rooms overlooking the railway lines at 2/6 a week, where he'd smoke Woodbines, listen to trad jazz and bang angrily at his typewriter, whilst Julie Christie padded around wearing one of his old shirts. That's the life for me. One day – the teenage Stephen had thought, captivated – one day, *I'll* have my very own bedsit, little suspecting that this was the only one of his fantasies that was destined to come true.

The estate agents hadn't actually called it a bedsit, of course. They called it a 'studio', implying that you could either live in it or record your new album there, the choice was yours. The 'studio' was situated in a drab, nameless area between Battersea and Wandsworth, the kind of neighbourhood where every lamp-post is garlanded with a rusting bike frame. A small row of shops contained all the necessary local amenities: a chink-y, an off-y, a laundry, a scurvy-inducing Warsaw-Pact grocers called Price£avers, where a packet of Weetabix cost £3.92, and a terri-fying pub, the Lady Macbeth, a floodlit Maximum Security Wing that had unaccountably been issued with a drinks licence.

Stephen's epic journey home involved the tube to Victoria, changing at Green Park, an overland train to Clapham Junction, then a lurching 'Hoppa' bus and a brisk, nerve-jangling fifteen-minute walk, past Chicken Cottage, Chicken Village and World of Chicken'n'Ribs, then on to Idaho Fried Chicken, Idaho being the last remaining US state to be granted its own South London fried-chicken franchise. There he ran the gauntlet of the feral children, who stood in the doorway and hailed his nightly return with hearty cries of 'wanker/tosser/twat'. He unlocked the anonymous, flaking mustard-coloured front door, and the smell of questionable fried poultry accompanied him up the narrow grey stairs.

On the first-floor landing, he was pounced on by Mrs Dollis, his neighbour, a tiny, aggressive elderly lady with a startling selection of random teeth, as if her gums had been pebble-dashed. She bobbed her head suddenly out from her doorway, turning the first-floor landing into Stephen's own personal ghost train.

'Foxes have been at the bins again,' she grumbled.

'Have they, Mrs Dollis?'

'There's chicken skin all over the floor. 'S disgusting.'

'Well, isn't that the shop's responsibility?'

'It's not mine, that's for sure'

'I'll sort it in the morning, Mrs Dollis, OK?'

She groaned at this, as if Stephen had somehow been engaged in a secret programme training foxes to get at the bins, then disappeared, and Stephen continued up the stairs to his flat. He double-locked the door, and lowered the ageing blinds, slightly too small for the window, against the sodium glare of the streetlights outside.

There were two furnished rooms. The first, the aforementioned bedsitting room, was just about large enough to swing a cat in, and it was fair to say that there had been times when, had a cat been to hand, Stephen would almost certainly have swung it. Without much expectation, he pressed the button on the answering machine, an ageing flesh-coloured model with a special in-built 'gloat' feature. In a strange, sardonic intonation it informed him, 'You (obviously) have (only) *ONE* new message.'

He pressed Play.

'Hello, Dad. It's Sophie here . . .'

Stephen grinned. 'Hey, hiya, Sophs,' he said to himself, in a sentimental, slightly dopey voice that would have embarrassed Sophie had she been there to hear it. She continued, in her formal phone voice, like a junior speaking clock.

'This is just to say that I am very much looking forward to seeing you next week, and . . . and that's all, really. Mum is here. She wants a word . . .'

A word. Stephen frowned, and instinctively stepped back a little from the answering machine. There was a rustle, as the phone changed hands, then his ex-wife came on, speaking low with her soft Yorkshire accent.

'Hello there. Obviously you're on stage at the moment, giving your all, then it'll be back to Dame Judi Dench's gaff for a game of Pictionary and some songs from the shows or something, but don't forget – Monday. Hope you've got something nice planned this time, not just the movies again.' Then, in a lower voice, 'And just so you're pre-warned, Colin's taken half term off, so he may well be here as well . . .'

Stephen bared his teeth, waved his fist at the answering machine.

'. . . so no fighting, verbal or otherwise. Try and be *nice* to each other. For Sophie's sake. Please?'

Stephen pressed delete with a little more venom than absolutely necessary, then continued wrinkling his nose, baring his teeth, kicking things, but not too hard, as he went next door to the kitchenette, with its emphasis on '-ette'. Here a small Formica table fought for lino space with a sink unit, a water heater that roared like a jet engine, and an homicidal gas cooker. Despite Stephen's constant endeavour to keep the place clean and fresh, this room had a strange fermenting smell, like the inside of a child's lunch-box. The origins of the smell remained obscure – there was no fridge at present, the last fridge having recently committed suicide, or perhaps been murdered by the oven. In the meantime, he managed by keeping milk for tea on the windowledge, which would do fine for now. The studio was not really designed for large-scale entertaining; it was designed for solitary drinking, consuming fast food and weeping.

Still baring his teeth at no one, he went into the bathroom or, more accurately, the 'shower room', where a toilet, a wash basin and a temperamental shower unit were so close together that it would be technically possible to have a shower and brush his teeth whilst still sitting on the toilet. There he peed angrily, simultaneously leaning across and searching the bathroom cabinet for some left-over antibiotics to fend off his impending tonsillitis. In a perfectly understandable fit of insanity, the previous owner had painted the bathroom a deep blood-red gloss, and one day, when he could face it, Stephen had resolved to set upon the epic task of painting it over with something less oppressive: eight coats of magnolia perhaps. Until then, it was a little like showering in a crime scene.

Of course, there were limits to what a new coat of paint could achieve. The flat, he had to admit, had been a terrible, terrible mistake. He had bought it in an emergency, during the insane booze and grief-blurred weeks after the end of his marriage, as a place where he could be alone and clear his head – a bolt hole, a stopgap, a temporary solution, just until the dust settled and life got better again. In time, perhaps, he'd smarten it up, turn it into a hip, cool and compact bachelor pad, and with this in mind he'd kitted it out with the Holy Trinity of grown men living alone: the games console, the broadband connection and the DVD player. And here he had sat most evenings, watching old movies and drinking too much, trying not to phone Alison: The overriding soundtrack of this period was the pop of a fork piercing the film seal of a ready-meal, and the lesson that he'd learnt was harsh but clear – never invest in property when drunk and/or clinically depressed. Slowly, the months turned to years, two years now, and here he still was, shipwrecked and fridgeless. Miss Havisham with PlayStation 2.

Still, no point dwelling on it. Keep optimistic. Keep cheerful. His luck was bound to change soon. He found the mystery antibiotics: huge, ancient yellow and black things, like hornets. In the divorce, Alison had granted him custody of all the left-over pharmaceuticals. He couldn't remember quite what they were originally for, but an antibiotic was an antibiotic. Returning to the kitchen, he poured himself a beaker of red wine, swallowed one of the pills and, already feeling better, he decided to watch a movie. In the living room, he pulled his most valuable possession out from under the bed; the Toshiba TX 500 digital video projector.

Of course, there's no match for the true cinema experience, but the previous Christmas Stephen had unexpectedly made a little extra money from a low-budget educational DVD he'd appeared in – *Sammy the Squirrel Sings Favourite Nursery Rhymes* – in which he'd played the eponymous squirrel. It had been a personal and professional low point, but the reward was the digital video projector which, when connected to his DVD player, projected movies, 8 foot by 6 foot, and only slightly blurred, on the wall, turning his bedsit into a private screening room. If it wasn't quite the true cinema experience, it was pretty close, and all that was missing was the smell of popcorn, the rustle of sweet wrappers, and the presence of a single other human being.

The white wall opposite the sofa served as his makeshift screen. Three large framed film posters, *Serpico*, *Vertigo* and *The Godfather Part II*, brought a little bit of Hollywood to South-West London. He took these down, leant them carefully against the wall, then balanced a pile of books on a kitchen chair, plugged the DVD player into the projector, and turned it on. The room was immediately illuminated with an eerie, almost nuclear blue-white glow.

He turned to the rows of DVDs and videos. Of his own work for the screen, he owned an episode of *Emergency Ward* on video (the non-speaking, all-wheezing role of Asthmatic Cycle Courier), his poignant, doomed Rent Boy 2 in *Vice City*, a small role in a seemingly endless short film, and an Open University mathematics programme in which he'd played a Quadratic Equation. He also owned a complimentary DVD of *Sammy the Squirrel Sings Favourite Nursery Rhymes* – no director's commentary but with six cut scenes and singalong captions – which he kept hidden at the back of his wardrobe, still in its Cellophane, under a pile of jumpers. He did not feel like watching any of these. Instead he contemplated *Manhattan*, *Midnight Cowboy* and *A Bout de Souffle*, before deciding that, yes, he was in a *North by Northwest* state of mind. Cary Grant *and* James Mason, together.

He poured some more wine, watched the first few scenes, the bachelor and ladies' man out and about in '50s Manhattan, and decided that Cary Grant was definitely the way to go for Josh's party. Projected on his own mental cinema screen, he imagined himself at Josh's penthouse apartment, dressed in an immaculately tailored lounge suit, brimming martini glass held at the rim in a way that was elegant without being effeminate, at the centre of a circle of other party guests, the women, heads cocked, lips slightly parted, the men standing respectfully, deferentially, a little further away, all of them listening intently to his every word. Rather frustratingly, he had no idea what he might be saying, but he knew that when he reached the end of his monologue, the group would rear backwards in a great gale of admiring laughter.

And he imagined his good friend and mentor Josh Harper watching from the other side of the room, smiling approvingly, raising his martini glass in tribute, welcoming him into his world, and Stephen returned the smile, and toasted him back.

Like most people living in any great city, Stephen had the constant, nagging suspicion that everyone was having a much, much better time than he was.

Heading home each night on the bus, he'd see people with bottles in their hands, and convince himself that they were off somewhere extraordinary: a party on a boat on the Thames or in a swimming pool or a railway arch somewhere – places where toilet cubicles were only ever used for having sex, or taking drugs, or having sex while taking drugs. He would pass restaurants and observe couples holding hands, or gangs of pals bellowing happy birthday and unwrapping presents or chinking their glasses or laughing at a private joke. Newspapers and magazines taunted him daily, with all the things he could fail to do, all the gifted, interesting, attractive people he would fail to meet at parties in places he could never hope to live. What, he wondered, was the point of being told that Shoreditch was the New Primrose Hill, Bermondsey the New Ladbroke Grove, when you lived in a strange, nameless region between Wandsworth and Battersea, the New Nowhere? On each and every day of the week there were exhibitions and first nights and salsa workshops and poetry readings and political meetings and power yoga classes and firework displays and concerts of experimental music and exciting new-wave dim-sum restaurants and big-room trance for a shirts-off, up-for-it crowd, all of which you could fail to experience. For Stephen, London was less a city that never slept, more a city that got a good nine hours.

But that wasn't the case tonight. Tonight he was going to take his chances and actually leave the flat, and face the world again, and take his rightful place in the fashionable, fast-beating heart of things. It was the beginning of a new age, a new Stephen C. McQueen. There'd be no more standing on the outside, face pressed up against the glass. Josh was beckoning him in and never again would his evenings be accompanied by the pop of a fork piercing the film seal of a ready-meal. Riding up in the elevator at Chalk Farm tube station, he checked his reflection, undid his tie another half-inch, ruffled his hair and, by way of a little social warm-up, assumed the facial expression he intended to use when bantering with beautiful women. Forced to acknowledge that, all things considered, he looked comparatively good, he winked raffishly, popped an antibiotic just for the sheer decadent hell of it, then suppressed the gag reflex as it adhered to the back of his throat. Then, stepping out into the night, he consulted the page that he'd recklessly torn from his A to Z, and headed off to a famous person's wild party.

It is, he thought, extremely important that things go well tonight. It is extremely important that I try and perform well.

Stephen rang the bell on the high, wire-topped sheet-metal gate that protected this converted warehouse from the wilds of Primrose Hill; high-tech security was clearly a big priority for Josh, and Stephen thought there was every chance he might have to have his retina scanned. Eventually, the lock clicked open. Nothing special from the outside, thought Stephen, crossing the expanse of rain-drenched tarmac that acted as a moat in front of the long, low, red-brick building. But why was it so quiet? Perhaps the wild party hadn't got wild yet. Or perhaps it was a bad party. Perhaps Josh Harper was actually having a *bad* party, like other, normal people – eight or nine embarrassed strangers sitting round in silence, eating dry-roasted peanuts out of cereal bowls, maybe even watching tele-

vision, before drifting off at ten thirty. Wouldn't that be . . .
just *fantastic*?

Stephen found the front door, another industrial steel-clad
number, like the door of a vault, and cleared his throat, adjusted
his tie and ruffled his hair one last time, and made sure that he
was centred, focused and breathing from his diaphragm before
pressing the button on the video phone. Josh's face appeared
for a moment, gratifyingly distorted in the fish-eye lens.

'Hey, it's only Steve McQueen!' he shouted into the mike.
'The Cooler King . . .'

'Heeeyy there, Josh!' Stephen grimaced, utilising a strange
American 'game-show host' voice that seemed to spring from
nowhere, and which he resolved he would on no account ever
use again. He brandished the bottle of champagne at the lens,
as if this would in some way guarantee admission. *My motivation is to be cool. Remember, Cary Grant. Elegant, suave,
but also quietly capable of killing a man.*

'Come on up, Big Guy – first floor,' said Josh.

Big guy. Where the hell did that come from? thought Stephen.
Is he implying that I'm fat or something? He entered the bare
concrete stairwell, with its tangle of mountain bikes, clomped
up the iron stairway to yet another metal-plated door where
Josh stood, waiting for him. Despite the prescribed dress code,
he wasn't wearing a dark suit and tie. Instead he had on a beautifully tailored crisp white shirt, untucked at the waist and
unbuttoned to below his pecs, so prominent as to almost consti-
tute cleavage, worn with a tightly cut suit jacket and baggy,
low-slung jeans, and bare feet, an outfit that trod the line
between being either the height of cool, or its precise opposite.
In his right hand he held a brimming martini glass held at the
rim in a way that was elegant without being effeminate.

'Wotcha, Bullitt,' he drawled, an unlit cigarette dangling from
his mouth. With a shudder of foreboding, Stephen noticed that
Josh was carrying a pair of bongos.

'Hello there, Birthday Boy!' chirruped Stephen, reminding himself he was pleased to be there, brandishing the champagne that had been warming up nicely in his tight hand.

Josh took the bottle, politely, but with a fleeting look of bemusement and distaste, as if Stephen had just handed him his prosthetic limb. 'Oh. Champagne! Smart! Thanks, mate,' he said, seemingly embarrassed. 'Let me show you round,' and with one hand on his back, he ushered Stephen in through the vault door, closing it behind him with an industrial clang. Then drawing his arm expansively around the room, he proclaimed, 'Welcome – to My World . . .'

Stephen immediately noticed two things about Josh's World.

First, it was immense; like a domesticated nightclub, and easily large enough to play five-a-side in, a fact emphasised by a football in the corner of the room, a basketball hoop and some chin-up bars mounted on the wall. The high roof was composed of white-painted girders and reinforced glass running the length of the apartment. A spiral staircase reached up to a raised level, screened off with discreet, translucent fabric walls, which he assumed contained some sort of tasteful erotic pleasure dome. Artfully mismatched furniture – modishly kitsch old cracked leather G-plans, salvaged bar stools, and brittle antique Queen Anne chairs – were distributed around the football pitch in little clusters, perfectly chosen to facilitate social interaction, and if not all of the furniture was entirely in good taste, then the bad taste items were clearly the right kind of bad taste. The flooring was some kind of expensive seamless black rubber, as if the whole flat were somehow slightly kinky, and at the far end of the room, two Charles Eames chairs reclined in front of a massive flat plasma TV screen, currently displaying a frozen PlayStation game, a computer-generated footballer paused in mid-kick. Neat piles of imported American comics were stacked along the walls, scale models of the *Millennium Falcon*, R2D2 and an X-Wing Fighter acting as paperweights. Clearly, at an age when Josh might be expected to put away childish things, he had instead decided to invest heavily in them. An electric guitar and a drum kit lurked in the corner, like a dark threat, next to a DJ mixing desk, and the slow, discreet boom-tsch of generic chill-out music pulsed from huge hi-fi speakers perched high on metal stands.

The second thing Stephen noticed about Josh's world was that there were no other guests.

'Oh God, I'm *really* early, aren't I?' laughed Stephen, now very far from chilled out.

'No, no, not at all. If anything you're a little late. Still, gives you plenty of time to meet the others.'

Josh padded across the factory floor, pausing halfway to nonchalantly drop the bottle of champagne into one of three old-fashioned metal dustbins. Stephen felt slighted for a moment, but glanced into the dustbins as he passed, and saw that they were full of ice and perhaps another thirty bottles of champagne and vodka. Shop-bought ice. Stephen had never seen quite so much shop-bought ice.

'So what d'you think of the old place?'

'It's amazing. What was it before?'

'Disused umbrella factory. I just prefer found spaces to houses, you know? I looked at hundreds of places before I found this – banana warehouses, carpet depositories, deconsecrated churches, disused swimming pools, libraries and schools. I even looked at this old abattoir in Whitechapel, but it really smelt of, you know, death. So we ended up here. Not much, but it's home.'

At the far end of the room they turned into a screened-off industrial-style kitchen area, where three neat, clean, good-looking men with product in their hair were standing round, variously taking glasses out of cardboard boxes, laying out strips of pale smoked salmon like gold leaf, breaking up more bags of ice with a small silver hammer. All three wore immaculate, identical black suits and ties, suits very much like Stephen's own.

'Guys, this is the famous –' a little paradiddle fanfare on the bongos – 'Steeeeeve McQueen!' said Josh to deferential mirth. 'He's going to be helping you out today. Steve, this is Sam, John, and, sorry, I've forgotten your name . . .'

'Adam,' said Adam.

'As in don't-know-you-from!' joshed Josh, and Adam gave a smile like ice-cubes cracking. 'Right, got it – Adam. OK, guys, this is my good mate Steve!' All three turned and smiled their professional caterer smiles – 'Hi, Steve, hello there, any relation?, pleased to meet you Steve, loved you in *Bullitt*, Steve' – but Stephen couldn't hear them because he was still trying to process the information, still trying to make sure that his conclusion was correct. It took a while, but finally the monstrous reality of the situation took firm shape in his mind.

I.

I am not a guest.

I have not been invited to this party as a friend.

I have been asked along as a waiter.

I am staff.

I.

I brought a bottle.

But Josh was speaking now, Josh his employer, saying something about people arriving in half an hour or so, which was plenty of time, and did he want to bartend or take food round or carve the Serrano ham off the bone or just collect coats or maybe they could take it in turns and was he any good at shucking oysters, but Stephen couldn't take any of this in because of the sound of the blood ringing in his ears, so instead he asked . . .

'Is there a toilet I can use quickly?'

'Sure. Use it slowly if you want!' quipped Josh, and one of the waiters obliged him with a £15-an-hour snort of mirth. 'Other side of the room, on your left.'

'Thank you very much,' Stephen managed, very formally, and

turned and walked stiffly across the room, as if he'd just learnt how, stopping only when he was about twelve inches away from the wall. There was no sign of a door. He looked both ways along the length of the wall. Nope, definitely no door. He desperately needed to be on the other side of a door right now, any door at all, but there was definitely no door here. He contemplated kicking himself a door, but the walls looked too solid, so he worked out a form of smile, practised it facing the wall, nailed it in place, then headed back to the kitchen, where Josh was showing one of the caterers, Adam perhaps, the correct way to open an oyster.

'. . . and hold the shell *flat* in your hand . . .'

'Hi there, Josh . . . ?'

'. . . so you don't lose the precious juices . . .'

'Josh, sorry, I can't . . .'

'That's the best bit about an oyster, the juices . . .'

'Hi there, Josh – JOSH!'

'Mr McQueen?'

'I can't seem to find the toilet.'

'It's a concealed door – if you look carefully, you'll see the . . .' Josh sighed, gave up on the oyster, hocked it impatiently into Adam's hand, precious juices and all, and led Stephen out of the kitchen. As he left, Stephen glanced back, just in time to see Adam clutching the oyster shucker by the handle as if contemplating embedding it in the top of Josh's head.

Josh, meanwhile, had his arm round Stephen's shoulder, pointing at the wall opposite. 'There – you see that rectangle?' and sure enough, Stephen could make out the faint outline of a door 'That's the bog. Hidden doors, you see? Like in an old castle or something. Cool, isn't it?'

'Amazing,' said Stephen, taking care not to move his face too much, in case it collapsed.

'*Should* be amazing – it cost me a fucking fortune . . .' Josh said, then headed back to the kitchen. 'Just push it gently, and it should swing open . . .'

Stephen pushed the edge of the door and sure enough, it swung open with a futuristic pneumatic hiss. Once safely inside, he turned, locked the door, stood with his head resting against it, and let out a long, high, demented hum, the kind of noise you hear in hospital dramas, when a life-support machine is turned off. The bathroom was L-shaped, large and chic, gun-metal and black, lit only by a host of tea-lights and a jasmine-scented candle, and it wasn't until she gave a little artificial cough that Stephen realised there was someone else there.

An attractive woman with cropped black hair, in a knee-length, tight-fitting black dress, sat on the bidet with her legs crossed, smoking a cigarette.

'Everything OK there?' she asked with an American accent.

Stephen stopped humming. 'Oh, I'm sorry, I didn't realise . . .' he stammered, pointedly looking up at the ceiling.

''S OK, I'm not doing anything . . . intimate' said the woman nonchalantly, and Stephen glanced discreetly down at her crossed legs, just to check. No, she didn't appear to be doing anything intimate, just sitting quietly on the bidet, by herself, smoking. 'Amazingly, this is the only comfortable chair in this place.' The accent was American; New York perhaps. Her eyes were very dark, her mouth wide and red, and Stephen recognised her, from a brief conversation at the first-night party, as Josh's wife, Nora. 'You're one of the waiters, right?'

'Sort of.'

'Well, surely you know if you're a guest or a waiter . . . ?' she said, drawing hard on the cigarette.

'Yeah, you'd think so, wouldn't you?' Nora looked confused. He decided to change the subject. 'Should I leave you . . . ?' he asked, sensing that he'd somehow stumbled upon her hiding place.

'No, 's OK,' she said brightly, standing, and with one finger deftly wiping something from the corner of one eye. 'It's all

yours! Go crazy!' Then she lifted the toilet lid, tossed the cigarette in, listened to it sizzle, then turned to Stephen.

'Can I ask you something?'

'Go on.'

'What do you think of this dress?' She stood up straight with
her shoulders back, held the dress at her hips, and tugged so
that it pulled tight against her body. 'Josh says it makes me
look fat.'

'He did? Fat?'

'Well, he didn't say "fat," of course. The actual precise word
he chose was "lush", but he meant fat. You think I should go
and change?'

'Not at all. I think you look great,' said Stephen, because
she did.

'"Great" as in "great-big", right?'

'Great as in fantastic.'

'Great as in fantastic,' she repeated, mimicking his accent.
'Well, thank you kindly, you're a real gent.'

Stephen had a powerful weakness for Americans doing
English accents, and surprised himself by smiling. Nora smiled
back, a little anxiously perhaps, and with her eyes, which
appeared slightly red, averted to the ground. 'By the way, you
do realise you were making a weird little noise, don't you?'

'When?'

'Just now.'

'I was?'

'Uh-huh – a kind of hum. Like this.' And she closed her eyes
tight and made the noise.

'Yeah, I do that sometimes, apparently. It's a nerves thing.'

'And does it help?'

'Oh, not really.'

'Shame, I was going to give it a try. But why should you be
nervous? You're a professional, aren't you?'

'Yes, yes. I suppose I am.'

'Well, there you go. At least you're being paid to be here.' And her eyes flicked past him to the door that he leant against. He stepped to one side to open it for her, but found that it had somehow jammed shut. He pulled hard on the door handle three or four times.

'You might want to unlock it first maybe?'

He unlocked it.

'OK, here I go . . .' she said, and took a deep breath, the kind you might take before dropping through a hole in the ice, swallowed hard, and stepped out into the main room, leaving Stephen alone.

He waited a moment, then quickly locked the door again, and took Mrs Harper's place on the bidet, sitting down heavily on it. He lit a cigarette, attempting to inhale its whole length in one breath, then closed his eyes and pressed his eyelids hard with the tips of his fingers, until white bursts of light started to form, and tried to imagine what Cary Grant would do in these exact circumstances.

He was finding it hard to imagine Cary Grant in these exact circumstances.

It wasn't so much the waiter-ing. He'd been a waiter many times before, and fully expected to be a waiter again, and really didn't mind – it was part of the job, after all. What particularly irked him about the situation was spending twenty-five quid on a bottle of champagne as a gift for a supposed friend, then being expected to serve that very same champagne to strangers, then wash up their glasses. He thought back to that night, standing in the wings, trying to work out how the terrible mistake had come about. What were Josh's words exactly? 'Are you available . . .' ? 'Suit-and-tie job'? 'I'd really appreciate it'? Obviously, the simple truth was that Josh had just been too embarrassed to use the word 'waiter'. What Stephen had taken to be the hand of friendship was actually just passing him a full ashtray.

Far away in the distance, he heard the pop of a fork piercing the film seal on the top of a ready-meal.

He thought seriously about climbing out of the window, but it was too high and too small, and simply admitting the mistake would just push the humiliation one stage further – he imagined Josh's embarrassed, pitying look. No, clearly the only mature, sensible thing to do was feign acute illness. Do some acting – that was his trade, after all. He started flicking through the mental medical dictionary he kept at hand for such emergencies: angina – no, beri-beri – no, cholera – no. A stroke was too extreme, tonsillitis too mild, irritable bowel syndrome too intimate. Was there a quick and easy way to make your own lung collapse? He settled on that all-rounder food poisoning – perfectly plausible, as he did in fact feel like throwing up. He put his hand on his stomach, clutching it as if he'd just been shot in the guts, bent over slightly, practised his queasy face in the mirror, swallowed another rogue antibiotic, flushed the toilet unnecessarily, and stepped out into the room.

The music was louder now, generic cocktail-bar dance music, and Josh was hunched over the DJ decks, bobbing slightly, eyes screwed shut and the tip of his tongue protruding, one cup of the headphones pressed to his ear, as he concentrated on mixing seamlessly between two apparently identical records.

'Josh, I—'

'Heeeeeeey! Stephanie, Stevearoony, the Stevester,' Josh jabbered away like some beautifully coutured village idiot, 'I just wanted to say massive cheers for doing this,' he shouted, coming out from behind the desks, and putting his arm round Stephen's shoulder 'It's just I hate having a party and having to worry about filling people's glasses and tidying up and all that crap.'

''S alright, really, I just—'

'And strictly between me and you, *these* guys –' he nodded towards the trio of caterers in the kitchen – 'well, they've all got a bit of an attitude, if you know what I mean, like they're too fuckin' good for it or something. Plus the fact that they're bloody expensive, so it'd be nice to for the money to go to someone I know, if you see what I mean. And I expect you've done this kind of thing before, haven't you? Catering?'

'Yeah, yeah, Josh,' he said, taking the dusty bubble-pack of mystery antibiotics out of his pocket, for use as a prop. 'It's just I'm feeling a bit—'

'And you know your cocktails? A bit of basic mixology, yeah? I mean, not the fancy stuff, but vodka martinis, margaritas, all that shit.'

'Oh, yeah, sure, but—'

'Well, why don't you bartend then, to start-off with anyway, and we'll call it, what, ten, no, fifteen squid an hour, yeah?' He was holding Stephen by the shoulders now, his face just inches away, looking at him intently with his expensive blue eyes, as if about to kiss him, and Stephen realised that if he brought his head down hard and fast enough, he could quite easily break Josh's nose.

He thought about the money he'd spent on the bottle of champagne, his impending unemployment, the mortgage on that hellhole, his lack of a fridge, his daughter's Christmas present. He made some calculations in his head, fifteen times six hours, fifteen times seven maybe . . .

'Fifteen quid's *way* too much,' he said finally.

'Rubbish. You're easily worth that!' said Josh, lightly punching the top of Stephen's arms, and despite himself, Stephen actually felt flattered – yes, he *was* definitely worth at least fifteen squid an hour. 'Besides, you've got to give something back, haven't you?' said Josh.

'OK, then,' said Stephen, finally.

'Goodly good! Give us a hand with these fairylights, would you?' he barked, padding off.

At the far end of the room, across great expanses of poured

black rubber flooring and funky furniture, Stephen could see Nora Harper, lying on a distressed leather sofa, leafing through a magazine, a bottle of beer in her hand, which she raised and tipped towards him, giving him a little wave with her fingers, and a smile. At least he thought she was smiling; at these kinds of distances it was hard to tell.

'FASTEN YOUR SEATBELTS. IT'S GOING TO BE A BUMPY NIGHT.'

And half an hour later, the cool people started to arrive.

They were actors mainly, mostly in their mid-twenties to early thirties, faces Stephen recognised off the telly, from high-end, top-of-the-range period dramas or edgy new-wave sit-coms and sketch shows, or the smarter commercials; the Cute, Feisty Girl who is Britain's Biggest Hollywood Hope, a couple of sharply dressed violent-but-lovable Brit-Flick Gangsters, the Unconventional Campaigning Lawyer with the Complicated Love Life, and enough Charismatic-But-Troubled Surgeons, Hunky Doctors and Perky Nurses to staff a small rural hospital, ideally in the 1950s. The 28th and 64th Sexiest Women in the World were there, along with the 15th Most Talented Man Under Thirty and the 8th and 14th Most Powerful People in Comedy, whilst over on the low Italian sofa, the latest Heathcliff was flirting with the most recent Jane Eyre as Nicholas Nickleby looked on.

There were the TV and theatre producers too, the directors and casting agents, people that Stephen had been regularly sending the same letter to for eleven years now: 'Dear X, I understand that you will soon be casting a production of Y, and I believe I would be ideal for the role of Z, please find enclosed my CV, an 8 by 10 photograph and a self-addressed envelope, I look forward to meeting you, etc, etc.'. And here Stephen was, actually meeting them at last, or if not *meeting* them as such, at least offering them nibbles and a napkin to catch the crumbs. Initially he had worried that he might be recognised – 'Weren't you the young man who wrote to me in

1996, asking to be considered for the role of Peer Gynt?' – but realised soon enough that nothing rendered a person invisible quite so effectively as a large white china plate of chicken satay.

Elsewhere, keeping themselves to themselves, were a sprinkling of young aristocrats, heirs and heiresses, entrepreneurs, the militantly trendy: trim, shiny, young men and women with familiar surnames and honey-coloured October tans whom he recognised from the diary pages, those flash-lit party-round-up photos that Stephen sometimes found himself scrutinising with a kind of masochistic curiosity – people who seemed to have a champagne flute fused permanently to the tips of their fingers. They wore vintage silk dresses, beautifully cut suit jackets and artfully faded low-slung jeans that threatened to fall down around their ankles, and were only pegged up by finely sculpted hipbones, prominent from a diet of canapés. Unfailingly polite, they smiled and thanked Stephen for their champagne refills in strange, slurred, absent voices, cultivated somewhere between Shropshire and a Shoreditch market stall. There were a handful of models too, recognisable from controversially explicit billboard campaigns and men's style mag photo shoots, outlandishly attractive women whose names escaped him but whose breasts and buttocks he was disconcertingly familiar with; women in thrift-shop dresses and Top Shop jewellery, hair greased and slicked down in all different directions, as if they'd felt an obligation to look as downbeat as possible, because otherwise it just wouldn't be fair.

And there were children too: actor/model/child children, funkily dressed little moppets in tailored dungarees, cheekily asking for sips of champagne, and sprawling on all fours over the buffet table, their elbows in the organic smoked salmon. Stephen found himself serving champagne to a decorously pregnant woman, an elegant and serene dark beauty in a bosomy low-cut black dress with a bump so high, so round and perfect that you might almost imagine it had been surgically augmented.

Other guests had gathered round to stroke it, and it was such an appealing bump that, if he hadn't been holding a tray of honey-mustard sausages, Stephen would have liked to stroke it too. He suspected that this might have thrown her.

Stephen thought back to Alison's pregnancy: nine long bad-tempered months of unemployment in a shared basement flat in Camberwell. He had tried to convince himself that this period had been 'challenging but magical', but his abiding memory was of damp clothes failing to dry on a lukewarm storage-heater, and of Alison, bloated, angry and silently resentful, padding round in grey tracksuit bottoms, eating Bran Flakes straight out of the box as part of an on-going battle with constipation. But apart from the neat, petite bump, the dark woman at the party was as thin and graceful as a musical annotation. Stephen stood for a moment, staring at her, lost in these thoughts, until the pregnant women and her group of friends stopped talking and turned to look at him.

Quickly, he hurried off to get the Sea Breeze 'with some actual *booze* in it this time', that had been ordered by a very drunk and belligerent Wacky TV Comedian. 'Will Swap Sex For Drugs' read the retro-style slogan on the T-shirt under his suit jacket, a slogan that had the advantage of being both humorous and literally true.

Josh, meanwhile, looked around at the party he'd created, and saw that it was goodly good. He lolloped around with his long white shirt undone, calling Michaels Micksters and Johns Johnaroony, distributing beatific smiles and self-deprecating anecdotes, performing magic tricks, hoisting the funky little moppets on to his shoulders, dimpling his cheeks at their delighted mothers. At one point, Stephen actually spotted him in the act of sniffing a baby's head. He seemed to be everywhere at once, and everywhere he went people had their photographs taken with him with the cameras on their mobile phones, to prove that they were actually there, that they actually knew him.

'How you doing mate, alright?' he asked, winking, cocking and firing his imaginary gun at Stephen as he headed out to the kitchen area. Stephen was carrying a tray of goat's cheese tartlets, so was unable to fire back.

In the kitchen, he shook up the Sea Breeze, filled a glass to the brim, then drank the remains straight from the cocktail shaker, and tried to trick himself into believing he was having a good time. Maybe he actually preferred to be the wry, ironic below-stairs observer, and maybe the glasses he was loading into the dishwasher were half full rather than half empty. Certainly the booze was helping – since the party started he'd been drinking fairly indiscriminately from beer bottles and champagne glasses, and was now experiencing a pleasant, woozy Sunday night glow. He peeled the Parma ham from a stick of out-of-season asparagus and ate it slowly, leaning against the zinc worktops as Adam, clearly the ringleader, ferociously lobbed oranges into some kind of industrial juicer, as if they were grenades.

'. . . the little *bitch* actually asked me to get rid of her *chew*ing gum for her, actually *put* it in my hand, because she was too bloody bone *idle* to do it herself, like I was her bloody *skivvy* or something . . .'

'So did you?'

'Did I *hell*. Talentless little *cow*. Did you *see* her in that *last* film? Oh my *God*, that was *the* worst film I've *ever* seen in my *life* . . .'

'Everything fine in here?' said Nora Harper, glass in hand, leaning a little unsteadily in the doorway.

'Yes, thanks,' they all chirruped in unison.

'And, guys? If you want to take a break, then go ahead. I'm sure the guests can fend for themselves for a while . . .' She smiled a small, uneasy smile directly at Stephen, who suddenly remembered that the Wacky TV Comedian was waiting for his drink. He hurried back out towards the party, but Nora placed her hand lightly on his arm as he passed.

'Is that for anyone in particular?' she said, glancing at the cocktail.

'It's for . . .' and he nodded towards the drunk comedian, who at that precise moment was belching wackily into his fist and stubbing his cigarette out on the rubber floor, grinding it out with the tip of his trainer.

'Hey, YOU!' Nora shouted across the room like a New York cop. Fifteen people looked over, and the comedian pointed to himself sheepishly. 'Yeah, you – you know what an ashtray is?' He nodded dumbly. 'Know how to use one?' He nodded again. People were starting to snigger now, and he was summoning up the trademark wacky expression that could usually be relied on to get him off the hook, but Nora wasn't finished yet. 'And pick that thing up.' He glanced down at the butt on the floor. 'You heard me – pick it up.' And the man had no choice but to bend over, meekly pick up the cigarette butt and drop it into his jacket pocket.

Nora turned back to Stephen. 'Tell me, what do British people see in that guy?'

'I think people find him wacky.'

'Yeah, so wacky you want to kick him in the eye. May I?' she asked, taking the drink from Stephen's hand. 'Care for one yourself? Here, we can share this . . .' and she passed him back the drink. He took a sip, and they stood for a moment in silence, as she scrutinised his face through narrowed eyes, just long enough for him to start to feel uncomfortable.

'I should probably clear some more glasses . . .'

But she stopped him, placing her hand lightly on his shoulder once more. 'Something's bugging me – haven't we met before?' she said. 'I mean somewhere other than in the bathroom?'

'I think you might have seen me at the theatre.'

'The theatre?'

'And we spoke, very briefly, at the first-night party. I sort of work with your husband.'

'You're the one of the stage manager guys, right?'

'No, I'm an actor, well, an understudy at the moment. Your husband's understudy, in fact.'

'Want me to push him downstairs for you?' she dead-panned. 'Make it look like an accident? They're spiral stairs, the police would never know.'

'Maybe one day.'

'Or we could hire someone to do it – go fifty/fifty.'

'I'll let you know.' Once more, he felt he should get back to work.

'So what else do you do?'

'What *else*? OK, well you know that bit at the end, when Byron walks off to his death, and this Ghostly Figure opens the door for him? I am that Ghostly Figure.'

'The guy in the mask!'

'That's me.'

'I'm sorry, I should have recognised you!'

'Well, I am wearing a mask, so—'

'No, but still, you do it so well. What's the secret?'

'Practice. An hour every morning. Open-close, open-close, close-open, open-close . . .' She laughed, a warm, throaty laugh, and Stephen felt a little glow of satisfaction, and for a moment his waiter's uniform reverted to just being a really nice suit.

'And my husband – how is he to work with?'

'Well, I don't really work *with* him as such, but he's great, really, really . . .' There was a moment's hesitation as he looked for a word more eloquent than 'great'; '. . . full of energy.'

'He's certainly full of *something*. I'm sorry . . . what's your name again?'

'Stephen,' adding, almost as a test, 'Stephen McQueen.'

'Well, Stephen,' she said, passing the test, 'I probably shouldn't say this, but . . . don't you mind? My husband asking you to . . . what I'm trying to say is, he hasn't by any chance been a complete asshole, has he?'

'Not at all. Well, a little maybe. But it's OK, I've done this kind of thing before. I don't mind.' And at this moment, he really didn't mind. It was, after all, the first time he'd had actual eye contact for the last three hours, the first time he'd been treated like a human being rather than a swing bin or drinks dispenser, and he was enjoying talking to this wry, elegant, slightly severe woman, leaning unsteadily against the doorway. They both surveyed the party. The 12th Sexiest Man in the World stood in the centre of the room, wearing sunglasses, a cigarette dangling louchely from his lip, juggling satsumas, much to the delight of the 28th and 64th Sexiest Women in the World. Even from a purely statistical point of view, it was impressive.

'My beloved husband,' drawled Nora, sipping her drink. 'I love him very much, and he's certainly easy on the eye, but I do sometimes feel as if I've somehow married this . . . gifted child.' She sighed, then forced a smile. 'I'm sorry, I shouldn't be mean about him, but we've just had this terrible row.'

'Nothing too serious, I hope.'

'No, just . . . a stupid argument.'

'So you're not enjoying the party then?'

'Two hundred coked-up egomaniacs, treading asparagus into the rugs and asking me who I am? I hope it never ends.'

They both turned and looked round the party. The last of the children had been evacuated to a safe place now, joints were being rolled on glass-topped tables, and all of a sudden, a very, very long queue of people snaked along the wall to the concealed toilet door. All around the room plates piled high with tiny sausages and mushroom tartlets and skewers of rare roast lamb sat untouched, and the voices in the room had definitely become more strident and intense. 'I's and 'me's, 'wow's and 'fuck's bounced off the high, plain walls; people were not so much talking as rubbing conversation in each other's faces.

'I have some, by the way. If you're interested . . .' said Nora conspiratorially, her hand on his forearm.

'What?'

'Cocaine. I find it helps to make these things a little easier,' and she pinched her nostrils together, sniffed quietly, swallowed; the first unattractive thing she had done all evening. Stephen couldn't help feeling a little disappointed; no wonder she was talking to him so intently. She'd probably talk to *anyone*.

'Not while I'm on duty,' said Stephen, feeling that their moment had passed. 'I'd better go . . .'

Once again, she placed her hand on his arm. 'Hey, have you seen the roof?' she said, widening her eyes. 'The view's amazing. Come on – I'll show you.'

'But don't you think I ought to—'

'Stephen, I'm sorry, you don't seem to understand. If I hear one more showbiz anecdote, then I will start to scream, and there's no guarantee I will ever stop.' And she slotted one arm through his, grabbed a bottle of champagne with the other, walked him out of the kitchen, and over to the glass-stepped spiral staircase that led up to the roof.

'Quick, before they find where I've hidden the bongos . . .'

They climbed the stairs, a little unsteadily, and just as they reached the door that opened up into the night air, a particularly full-throated, flamboyant, vibrato-rich chorus of 'Happy Birthday' broke out from the room below. Nora looked over her shoulder, smiling conspiratorially at Stephen, and waved her bottle in the direction of the party below.

'You know how you can tell they're all actors?

'Go on.'

'Because every damn one of them is *harmonising*.'

TWO CIGARETTES AT ONCE

The long low flat roof of the old umbrella factory had been turned into some sort of minimalist urban garden, expensively decked and sparsely planted, and lit with strings of all-weather bulbs that transformed the fine drizzle into a special effect. Stephen turned the collar up on his suit jacket, and folded his arms tight across his chest. He'd never been on a transatlantic ocean liner, just the Isle of Wight ferry, but he had a vague notion that this was what it might feel like to stand at the railings and contemplate the wake behind you. What was that corny old film with Bette Davis in, set on the ocean liner? Where someone – Paul Henreid is it, or Fredric March? – lights the two cigarettes he holds in his mouth, and passes one to Bette Davis. He had cigarettes in his pocket, he could try that if he wanted to. Feeling woozy and reckless, he decided to give it a go.

'What in *God's* name are you doing?' said Nora.

'Sorry?'

'You smoke them *two at a time?*'

'One's for you,' and he took one from his mouth, and offered it to her. Nora stared at it. 'Sorry, did you not . . . ?'

'Thank you. Very suave. If a tad unhygienic.' She placed the cigarette in her mouth, a little gingerly, he thought. 'Josh keeps on at me to give up. Says it'll make me look *old*, an idea which clearly *appals* him. I had been trying those nicotine patches, but I had to wear so many of the things that naked I looked like a quilt.'

The word 'naked' hung in the night air for a moment. He

tried to concentrate on the view. The sodium lights of the King's Cross redevelopment glowed in the distance, and once again, the occasion seemed to demand a certain mode of behaviour, and conversation – wry and witty, world-weary and elegant; David Niven perhaps.

'So – what did you get Josh for his birthday?' he asked, more prosaically than he'd intended.

'Oh – a new iPod,' she sighed. 'Original, huh? I've been trying to resist, but he wore me down. So I got him a new iPod and told him to just shut the fuck up about it. It was either that or a goddamn samurai sword.'

'Still, what d'you get the man who's got everything?'

'Well, everything *Star Wars*-related, anyway.'

He laughed, and glanced sideways at her. Her face, beneath the glossy black fringe, was round and pale, split with a large red mouth, placed, somewhat lopsidedly under a small, neat nose, slightly pink now in the autumn air. Her teeth were large, not quite as white and regular as he expected for an American, and there was a small chip in the enamel on one of the front teeth, a smudge of lipstick on the other; something about her make-up made Stephen think of a child sitting at her mother's dressing table. Her skin was pale, with a slight, not-unpleasant oily sheen around what he believed was called the T-zone, and small amounts of make-up could be seen clumping in the lines of her eyes, which were green, dark and heavy-lidded, and quite beautiful. Although at present she was fairly drunk, or drugged, or both, her natural expression seemed to be a kind of pouty amusement, a slightly stern, sleepy look, as if she had woken a little sulky from an afternoon nap. She leant lazily on the ocean liner railing, brushing her short fringe across her forehead with her fingertips, drawing occasionally on her cigarette, and once again Stephen thought of an old film, something starring Carole Lombard or the young Shirley MacLaine maybe, an effect heightened by the dress she wore, black, plain, old-fashioned, a little too small for her slightly – what was Josh's word? – *lush* body, shiny with wear on the shoulders and bottom. He found himself wondering what it would be like to put his hand in the warm curve at the small of her back, lean over and kiss her, when she turned suddenly to look at him, eyebrows raised questioningly.

For something to say, he blurted out: 'Amazing apartment!' In the spirit of transatlantic communication he'd attempted the word 'apartment', and almost gotten away with it.

'You really think so?' she frowned, instantly making Stephen question if he did really think so. 'I *hate* it. It's like this men's magazine bachelor pad. Every morning I wake up and feel like asking if there's a toothbrush I can borrow, and then I remember I actually *live* here. I mean, what's wrong with having *rooms*, for chrissake? Josh likes to say that he put the funk into "functional". Personally I think he just put the ass into "embarrassing", but hey, what do I know?'

Stephen laughed. 'So why did you buy it?'

'Oh, I didn't, Josh did, just before we got married. Technically, I'm just the lodger. Most of my stuff's still in storage in the States. It's not exactly to my taste, but you know what they say: a house is not a home without a skateboard ramp.'

'You should see mine. What a *dump* . . .'

'You live alone?'

'Uh-huh.'

'Single?'

'Recently divorced.'

'A little young to be divorced, aren't you?'

'I'm precocious.'

Nora laughed, and Stephen felt a quick jab of delight watching her laugh, then there was another pause, as she drew hard on her cigarette.

'So why did you get divorced?'

'Ah . . .'

'If it's not a personal question.'

'Well, let me see . . .'

'Let me guess – she beat you up?'

'No. Well, not physically.'

Nora winced. 'Hey, you're not going to hurl yourself off the roof, are you?'

'No.'

'Because I'd hate to be responsible for the death of a guest. Well, *certain* guests, anyway . . .'

'Except I'm not a guest.'

'Even so. It's none of my business. I apologise. Change subject – OK, tell me, why the hell do you do this ridiculous job?'

'You mean acting or catering?'

'Well, catering isn't a ridiculous job, so . . .'

'You say what you think, don't you?'

'Stephen, between you and me, I've possibly had a little too much to drink.'

'Well, I do it because I love it. Even if it is ridiculous. When I'm actually doing it, I love it. The bits in between aren't great.'

'So why do it then?' she asked – a little more harshly than necessary, he thought. It was a conversation he'd had innumerable times, usually with concerned elderly relatives at Christmas, and he never enjoyed it.

'Don't know; overactive imagination? Watched too many movies growing up, I suppose.'

'A lot of people watched the moon landings too, but they didn't all try and become astronauts.'

'No, but you know how it is – you do a couple of plays at school . . .'

'You went to the theatre a lot?'

'Not really. I was *in* plays, but I didn't really go to the theatre at all, only panto. The Isle of Wight doesn't really have a West End. Well, it does, but it's called Ventnor.' Nora looked blank. 'So I liked acting in plays, but I always preferred watching movies.'

'Me too! You know, I'm probably not meant to say this – Josh thinks it's some kind of blasphemy or something – but I can't *stand* going to the the-atre. Every time Josh hobbles out on that stage on his orthopaedic shoe and starts talking in that weird, crazy, warbly voice he puts on, I just want to burst out laughing. I just want to shout out, "Talk *properly*!" Don't you agree?'

'No comment,' Stephen smiled, and looked back out at the view.

'So which do you prefer, acting in theatre or movies?'

'Difficult to say.' He could, of course, come out with the party line about preferring the immediate response of a theatre audience, but his main screen experience came from playing the title role in *Sammy the Squirrel Sings Nursery Rhymes*, and he suspected that this fell outside of what is generally meant by 'movies'. He decided to change the subject. 'How about you? What do you do?'

'What do I *do*? Well, that's a very good question. When I met Josh, I was a waitress in this bar in Brooklyn.'

'Is that where you're from?'

'Brooklyn? Yeah, well, no, no, New Jersey. My family's from Jersey, which is near New York but not, if you know what I mean. Anyway, that's how we met, in a bar. A humble waitress brings Josh Harper his club sandwich, and the rest is showbiz history. All of this . . .' she swept her arm across the view '. . . is like the world's greatest tip.' She took a long swig from the bottle of champagne she held by her side, holding it by the neck, as if it were a beer bottle, then passed it to Stephen, adding, almost as an afterthought – 'Oh, and I once had a hit single too. Way back in the mists of time.'

'Really?'

'Uh-huh. Well, I say "hit". Number a hundred and two in the Billboard chart in 1996.'

'That's fantastic.'

'Well, not *fantastic*,' she insisted, though Stephen was being entirely sincere. Nora was the kind of woman who particularly suited a low-slung bass. 'What did you sound like?'

'Oh, you know, the usual – jangly, sub-Joni Mitchell college-radio stuff. Music To Comfort-Eat By. We were called Nora Schulz and the New Barbarians, if you can believe that. I was being cloned by the record company as the new Alanis Morissette. I was like Alanis Morissette's stunt double. If she ever fell backwards off her stool, the record company were going to parachute me in to take her place. God knows why – I don't even particularly *like* Alanis Morissette. Ironic, don't you think?'

'Nora Schulz and the New Barbarians. Great name.'

'Trips off the tongue, doesn't it? I can't think why we weren't bigger. Of course, the record company wanted me to change it to something more Waspy, ideally Malanis Florissette, something like that. They thought we'd sell more that way, but I stuck to my artistic principles, and I stayed Nora Schulz, and well, the rest is rock-and-roll history. Number a hundred and two with a bullet.'

'And what was the song called?'

'You mean you don't remember?'

'Remind me.'

'Trust me, you won't have heard of it.'

'Tell me anyway.'

'I'm not proud of this . . .'

'Go on.'

'It was called,' and she winced, 'oh God – it was called . . . "Love Junkie".'

Stephen winced too. 'Great title.'

'Isn't it? And the kids *love* those drugs metaphors. And any song that rhymes junkie with monkey, funky and flunky has got to be a hit, right?'

'You know, I think I *have* heard of you.'

'Liar.'

'So why did you give it up?'

'I didn't. It gave me up. Besides, the few connections I have are in the States, and Josh needs to be here for his work. He's at that *crucial* stage in his career, or so he keeps telling me. So we've decided to put it on hold. Temporarily, of course. In the meantime, I've been writing a little.'

'What sort of things?'

'The usual, stories, a screenplay or two.'

'Sounds interesting.'

'Not really. I mean everyone *writes*, don't they? If you went down to that party, went up to someone and asked them how the *writing* was going, not one of them would say, "What writing?".'

'Have you shown anyone anything?'

'No . . .'

'Well, you should.'

She drew hard on her cigarette, and gave him a stern look. '*Why* should I?'

'Well, because I think it's important to persevere with these things.'

'"Hold on to your dreams?"'

'No, but to have ambitions. To find the thing that you love doing, and do it to the best of your abilities.' He glanced across at her, to see if he'd got away with this. There were, at least, no outward signs of gagging. 'And also because I imagine you would be really good.'

She curled a lip dismissively. 'That's just something *nice* to say. How could you *possibly* know that?'

Stephen felt slighted. He was perfectly capable of making blandly soothing remarks to people, but this hadn't been one of them. 'From the way you talk. You just seem as if you would be. A good writer, I mean. That's all.'

She dipped her head a little, a sort of apology, and took the bottle of champagne from his hand. 'Thank you, Stephen.' Then she took a long swig, wiped a drop of champagne from the tip of her chin with the back of her hand, then quickly sucked the drop from her finger, the whole gesture striking him as wonderfully deft and cool.

Shortly after the break-up of his marriage, when he'd pulled himself together enough to leave the flat, Stephen had started to notice that he had developed an unnerving ability to make women need the toilet. He'd be at a party, and at a certain point, usually when he mentioned the recent divorce, they'd touch his arm lightly and say, 'Will you excuse me? I must go for a pee,' and he would realise, once again, that he was, in fact, The Human Diuretic, a super-hero with extremely specialised powers. Usually, he didn't mind too much; the divorce had leached him of any romantic instincts, and he'd managed to avoid casual, loveless sexual encounters with disconcerting ease. But even so, he was surprised, and a little unnerved, to realise how much he wanted Nora to stay here with him. He felt the pressure of her elbow against his on the railing. *Put your hand in the warm curve at the small of her back, lean over and . . .*

'D'you want to know what Josh and I just argued about?'

'Only if you want to tell me.'

'OK, well, we're getting ready for the party, and we'd just, you know, made out, and everything was fine, and he lay there and leant over, with his dopey, constipated romantic-lead face, his close-up face, and said that I was . . .' she gave a little shudder '. . . I was *the wind beneath his wings.*'

'Ah.'

'. . . Like I'd be *pleased*, as if this was the fulfilment of some great ambition, to be somebody else's *wind*? Anyway . . . then we had this big shouting match and, oh, I don't know. It was so stupid . . .' For something to do, she tossed her cigarette over the railing of the ocean liner, following its trajectory with her eyes. 'Well, screw him, anyway. Josh Harper can make his own damn wind . . .'

'Oi-oi-oi, what's going on here then?' a voice boomed across the rooftops. They both turned round to see a madly grinning Josh at the other end of the roof, his arms outstretched, a glass in each hand. Tottering a little behind him was a young woman in a variation on a dress: two rectangles of black leather, tied at the side with leather string that pressed into her bare flesh, advertising her lack of underwear, and making her appear elaborately trussed. She was clearly very drunk, and struggling to stay upright in high heels on the wet decking.

'We're having a private conversation, Josh – go away!' drawled Nora.

'But Bullitt's meant to be working. Bullitt, you complete *skiver*!' he said, his arm around Stephen's shoulder, waggling his finger jokily under Stephen's nose. 'I don't pay you fifteen squid an hour to stand around chatting up my missus.'

'Screw you, Josh,' murmured Nora, taking a cigarette from Stephen's packet.

'Whooooooh!' Josh and the girl laughed conspiratorially, and for a moment Stephen felt the same crackle of tension he'd felt in the school playground, just before a fight broke out.

'Hey! Hey, hey, hey!' said Josh, draping his arm over Nora's shoulder now. 'I'm just joking, my love. Steve can do whatever he wants – we're all mates, aren't we?' and he planted a wet, boozy, matey kiss on Stephen's cheek and blew a small raspberry on Nora's bare neck. Clearly finding the raspberry less sensual than Josh might have hoped, Nora wriggled free. He grabbed hold of her waist. 'Tell me – how is my favourite girl?'

'Don't know, Josh – who is your favourite girl?'

'You are, of course. Hey, you missed me cutting my cake!'

'I did? Well, I'm sure someone videoed it.'

'They did actually.'

'Well, there you go – the moment lives on,' drawled Nora, and even through the blur of booze, a momentary look of sincere hurt passed over Josh's face.

Standing a little way off, the girl in the black leather patches stumbled and swore.

'I'm sorry, I am soooo rude,' shouted Josh. 'Everyone, this is . . .' His mouth hung open slack, searching for the name.

'Yasmin,' said the girl, swaying back and forwards, trapped by her heels in the wet decking. 'Yasmin with a Y.'

'Y indeed,' murmured Nora, crossing one arm across her chest, and placing the cigarette in the centre of her mouth like a blowpipe. 'Yasmin, shouldn't you put some clothes on, sweetheart? You'll catch your *death* . . .'

By way of diversion, Josh tightened his grip round Stephen and Nora's shoulders. 'So! What were you two talking about then – not *me*, I hope.'

'You know, you really must stop automatically assuming that people are talking about *you*, Josh,' murmured Nora, attempting to shrug off Josh's arm.

'I don't!'

'There are *other* topics of conversation, you know.'

'I know, I know! I was joking!' said Josh, his arms raised in surrender. 'Christ, Nora, why d'you have to give me such a hard time? I said I was sorry, didn't I?' They all stood in silence for a moment, listening to the insistent thump of the party beneath them.

'Oh, sodding hell,' muttered Yasmin, bending ungainly at the knee now, struggling to wrench her strappy high heel from the decking without spilling her cocktail. 'It's fucking *freez*ing up here. I'm going back in.' Stephen noticed Nora eye the back of her head, and tighten her grip on the neck of the bottle, which she held at her side, like a cudgel.

'So who's *Yasmin*, Josh?' hissed Nora.

'I dunno – she's a dancer or something.'

'A dancer! Ballet? Jazz? Table?'

'Funny, Nora, very funny.'

'I think I'd better head down too,' mumbled Stephen, but

Nora and Josh didn't seem to hear. Instead they stood now, eyes locked, Josh holding Nora tight by the top of her arms, as if to prevent her leaping over the railing. Walking away, he could hear them speaking in low, urgent voices.

'So how come this complete stranger is at your birthday?'

'She's not a stranger, she's a . . . friend of a friend or something.'

'*Girl*friend of a friend?'

'I don't know, do I? I was just trying to be sociable, you know, *pleasant*, instead of just moping about and scowling at everyone.'

'And is that why you were bringing her up on the roof? So you could be *pleasant* to each other?'

'No, to show her the view! Exactly the same as you and Steve.'

'Well, not *exactly* the same, Josh.'

'Why not the same?'

'Because at no point was I going to unbutton his fly with my teeth . . .'

'Oh, for Christ's sake, Nora, not *this* again. Why can't you just believe that I love you?'

'You don't make it very easy, Josh.'

'Come here, Nora.'

'No, Josh.'

'Please . . . ?'

Without looking back, Stephen held on to the stair-rail and descended back into the party, and from the room below came the terrible sound of bongos.

In retrospect, Stephen realised, he should never have left Nora. If he'd shinned down a drainpipe and gone home, or even jammed his hands deep into his pockets and hurled himself on to the tarmac below, the evening might still have held one or two pleasant memories. But instead, he had decided to return to the party, as one might return to an unexploded firework, and from the moment he returned to the party, he was doomed.

Descending the spiral staircase seemed to take a great deal more concentration than climbing it – the glass steps made it seem as if he was stepping into air, and they felt disconcertingly spongy and yielding beneath his feet. Adam from the caterers, was waiting at the bottom, angrily banging the ash out of ashtrays into a champagne bucket.

'And where the hell have *you* been?' he snapped.

'Just talking,' mumbled Stephen, his tongue suddenly far too big for his mouth. 'Josh said it was OK.'

Adam tutted and narrowed his eyes. '"Josh said, Josh said . . ." Just because you know the boss, superstar, you're still just a waiter.'

Stephen snarled at Adam's back, then went to get another tray of drinks from the kitchen, downing in one a glass of red wine, cowboy-style.

When a large number of people have been drinking steadily for several hours, there's sometimes a wonderful moment when everyone simultaneously reaches a state of almost perfect conviviality: relaxed, affectionate, curious, attractive, amicable and open. This perfect social moment had been achieved, for perhaps a minute and a half, then left behind, many, many hours ago. The party had mutated into something new and terrible now – drinks had been spilt, thongs had ridden up into view, the expensive hi-fi speakers had been blown but were still thumping and buzzing. Voices were raised – frequently funny voices, and names weren't so much being dropped as hurled. A huddle of groovy, stubbly boys (wearing T-shirts that read 'dislexic' and 'your point is . . . ?') were standing round the mixing desk, competitively shuffling their iPods, and the music had entered its ironic-pop phase. People were Vogueing ironically, crunching broken glass to powder underfoot, or they were hunched together in tight little groups, shouting and flirting aggressively. The whole room resembled a convention for drunk, deaf nymphomaniacs, and Stephen rolled invisibly through the crowd in the protective glass bubble of service, smiling blandly, keeping discreetly out of the camera-phone photos, pouring drinks and picking up abandoned half-full glasses, each one containing a lipstick-smeared cigarette butt. He found himself handing drinks to a tiny young woman in a spaghetti-strap dress, who was shouting up to a tall, thin, flamboyantly dressed man with a neat goatee that looked glued on, visibly perspiring under a tweedy fisherman's hat; a mildly famous young actor who'd had some success playing snide, supercilious bastards.

'. . . I mean telly's OK, it pays the bills,' said the woman, chewing gum as if her jaw had been motorised '. . . but theatre's my first love. It's soooo much more exciting, that one-on-one feeling, that sense that anything can happen. I tell you, I'd give up *Summers and Snow* in a flash – in a bloody *flash* – for a chance to do a funky little new play . . .'

Stephen peered at the woman more closely and, yes, it was his old colleague, TV's perky, independent-minded WPC Sally Snow, a.k.a. Abigail Edwards. Taking a glass from his tray, she caught his eye and gave what Stephen mistakenly took to be a smile of amiable recognition.

'Evenin' all!' he said cheerily, bending humorously at the knee.

WPC Sally Snow wrinkled her nose. 'I'm sorry, do we . . . ?'

'We've acted together!'

'Oh. Oh. Have we?'

'Uh-huh. Last week, remember? Here's a clue.' And he rolled his eyes up into his head, let his tongue loll out to the side. Abigail and the goateed man looked blank. 'I was the Dead Guy? The killer's fourth victim? On the mortuary slab? You fainted when the pathologist removed my lungs, remember?'

'Oh, right, right. Of course! You're Dead Guy.'

Silence.

'The name's Stephen, Stephen McQueen. With a P-H *not* the famous one!' he jabbered, thinking he might as well get it in first.

'Obviously not,' drawled the man with the stuck-on beard, proving that his snide professional persona wasn't much of a stretch, and Stephen had a sudden urge to tear his goatee off, or at least to enjoy trying.

'So – you probably didn't recognise me with my clothes on!' he said, turning to Abigail, but a burst of Van Halen's 'Jump' obscured the remark.

'*What* did you say?' drawled the perspiring man, looking down at him from under drooping eyelids. Even through the mist of booze, Stephen realised the remark had been a mistake. He didn't want to repeat his mistake, but saw no alternative.

'I said, she probably didn't recognise me with my clothes on!'

'*What?*' said the man again, his hand cupped to his ear.

Working on the principle that a remark gets funnier the more it is repeated, Stephen said, 'She probably didn't recognise me with my clothes on.'

'We can't *hear* you.'

'I said, she probably, she probably didn't, I said she probably didn't—'

'Speak up, please.'

'I said, she probably didn't recognise me—'

'One more time . . .'

'I just said that she probably—'

'Again?'

'She probably didn't—'

. . . and Abigail Edwards put a sympathetic hand on his forearm, as she were visiting a fan in hospital. 'We *can* hear you. Ignore him. He's just *teasing* you.'

Oh, right, I see. Well, in that case, maybe he'd like to just go fuck himself? thought Stephen, before noticing the expression on their faces, and realising that he'd actually said it too. The three of them stood, saying nothing, the man smirking and sniggering through his nose, invulnerable, Abigail biting her lip and glancing around the room, and it occurred to Stephen that if the building were any higher than two storeys, he would definitely follow Van Halen's advice, and go ahead, and jump.

'Will you excuse us, we've got to . . .' said Abigail finally, not even bothering to finish her excuse. 'Come on . . .' and WPC Sally Snow grabbed the goateed man, and tugged him away, as if taking him into custody. As he left, the man placed his empty glass onto Stephen's tray.

'More washing-up for you, I'm afraid.' He grinned, winked, turned and left.

Stephen stood for a moment, rocking back and forwards slightly. Any last traces of boozy bonhomie he'd salvaged from Nora had evaporated now. He felt unwell. No, worse than unwell. He felt . . . damned. This was *Hell*. And Hell was not just other people, it was specifically *these* other people. He became aware that the glasses on his tray were starting to chink together dangerously, as in the early stages of an earthquake . . .

'Excuse me? Hello . . . ?'

. . . and that someone was speaking to him . . .

'Hello there? Anybody hoooo-oooome?'

. . . an extremely small, astoundingly beautiful young woman, one of the Hot Young Brits Currently Turning Heads In Hollywood, was frowning up at him from some distance below, sucking a lollipop. 'The Bitch is Back' said the curly writing on her T-shirt. Stephen read this, and smiled, and then felt a sudden urgent need to emphasise that he was reading her T-shirt, rather than staring at her breasts.

'"The Bitch is Back!"' he said aloud, delighted to have defused what might otherwise have been a potentially embarrassing moment.

'Yes, yes, alright, very clever, now listen – we've spilt some red wine,' said the Hot Young Brit, pulling the lollipop from her mouth and waggling it at him. 'Could you get some salt, please? If it's not too much *trouble*?'

'Absolutely. Salt,' and unthinkingly he handed the tray of dirty glasses down to her, which she took instinctively, then stood and looked at in confusion, holding it at arm's length, as if she'd been handed the head of John the Baptist.

'Exceeeuse me!' she drawled, but Stephen was gone, heading directly away from the kitchen and the salt, and seeking refuge, for the second time that night, in the toilet.

Miraculously, there was no queue, presumably because everyone was too far gone to find the thing, and with huge relief, Stephen locked the door behind him. The bathroom was a very different place from the rubber-and-gun-metal showroom he'd hidden in five, no, God help him, six hours ago. Even above the heady scent of the Diptyque candles you could smell the drugs and the asparagus wee. He sighed and leant over the toilet, his arms outstretched before him, as if about to be frisked.

Did it have to be like this? Weren't drunk actors meant to be lovable? Wild, carousing, boozy testosterone-fuelled men, Burton, or Harris, or Flynn or his own namesake; big-hearted, irresponsible forces of nature, filling rooms with convulsive laughter, their wild, irrepressible, boozy charm melting the hearts of beautiful women. It seemed unlikely Stephen would be melting any hearts tonight. Clinging to the cistern, Stephen wasn't even entirely sure that he was capable of peeing effectively, and he remembered, far, far too late, that 'lovable drunk' lay just outside of his range. Booze didn't make him anarchic or funny or daring or louche. It didn't make him irrepressible; if anything, it made him repressible. It was like some terrible self-inflicted injury, as if he'd elected to be repeatedly run over. Like any schoolboy, he knew it was a bad idea to mix grape and grain, but to go grape/grain/antibiotics/grape/grain/grain/grape/antibiotics/grain/grape/grain was beyond stupid. He decided to blame those mystery antibiotics. Even Errol Flynn knew not to drink on antibiotics.

He looked in the mirror, and tried to focus. It felt as if he was wearing his grandmother's glasses, but he could see that his face was puffy and slack, his eyelids heavy, his complexion the colour of surgical rubber, and his head felt numb and dense, as if it had been filled with cavity-wall insulation. He ran his left hand down his right arm to locate his wrist, then his wristwatch, bringing it backwards and forwards in front of his eyes to find the focal point, then struggling hard to convert the physical position of the hands into some kind of meaningful information. Drunk o'clock. He was seized by a desperate, passionate desire to be sober. He closed his eyes and made a silent deal with God: please, God, make me sober now, take me home, put me to bed, and I promise, I will never, ever drink again. But God clearly had caught the last tube, because when Stephen opened his eyes the walls and floors of the bathroom were now visibly stretching and contracting around him. He *must* sober up. What did people do in films to sober themselves up? Drink coffee, take a cold shower, get slapped. He imagined it would take very little to get himself slapped.

There was a knock at the door. 'What are you doooo-ing in there?' shouted an insinuating female voice outside.

'Dying,' he said quietly to himself, then rested his head on the mirror as the copper basin filled, then leant over to splash his face with cold water.

Halfway to the sink, he stopped. On the smeared dark marble surface next to the toiletries was a short, stubby line of a flaky white substance. *Drugs*. Someone had left some drugs behind.

Outside of the occasional joint or swig from a recreational bottle of Night Nurse, Stephen was not a big drug-user. His last encounter with cocaine had culminated in him giving a clench-jawed analysis of why his marriage had failed to a roomful of complete strangers, and since then he'd come to the conclusion that, when it came to the abject loss of self-respect, alcohol usually served the purpose just fine. But now desperate measures were required. Maybe he just needed that extra push, that little buzz, and wasn't cocaine meant to sober you up, endow you with incredible self-confidence? Perhaps if he took these drugs he could salvage the evening, and be a little more like, well, like Josh Harper.

'Whatever you're dooooing, can you hurry up, please?'

It was too much to resist. He quickly fumbled in his inside jacket pocket, found his wallet, pulled out a grubby, moist five-pound note, and rolled it as best he could into a flaccid tube, then leant over the fat little worm of waxy cocaine and inhaled sharply. He threw his head back, felt the stuff hit the back of his throat, and tasted the distinctive soapy, chemical tang as it started to dissolve. He pinched his nostrils together tight to make sure nothing escaped, then leant for a moment against the marble unit and waited for a wave of sublime, decadent elation and self-confidence to hit him. A few lumps remained, so Stephen licked his fingers, rubbed the white stuff deep into his gums, just like he'd seen in the movies, told himself that this was definitely the good stuff, the pure shit, and it was only at this point, as he surveyed the ranks of expensive grooming products arranged on the marble surface, and identified the

chemical tang as sandalwood and musk with a back note of
ammonia, that Stephen realised the waxy white substance he'd
just snorted was debris from Josh Harper's antiperspirant
deodorant.

He started to perspire. The narcotic effects of snorting a
deodorant stick, even Josh Harper's, are not well documented,
but it seemed that a sense of elation and increased self-
confidence are not among them. Coughing and spluttering, he
tried to get his head under the complicated tap fittings and
struggled to take several mouthfuls of warm tap water. But his
head wouldn't quite fit in the deep copper basin, and when he
tried to clamp his mouth to the mixer tap he simply succeeded
in painfully scraping his gums against it, and squirting hot water
down his suit. Thoughtfully someone had left a bottle of red
wine, half full, on top of the cistern, so he grabbed that, and
drank and drank until the soapy taste had gone, then slumped,
coughing and spluttering, his back against the door.

See? This is what happens when you leave the flat, he scolded
himself. You could be home by yourself now, watching an old
movie. But no, you had to go and leave the flat. Never, ever
leave your flat again . . .

And there must have been some sort of dreadful chemical
reaction with the snorted antiperspirant, and the antibiotics,
and the varied kinds of alcohol he'd consumed, because after
that things started to get very fuzzy.

He remembered wringing the water out of his tie, then struggling out of the bathroom to find the place surrounded by three
incredibly desirable women. One of them said something, the
words sounding muffled and distant, as if spoken underwater,
and the other women laughed. Stephen laughed too, in his
raffish Errol Flynn way, at how desirable they were in their
spangly dresses, like mermaids, and he said something aloud,
something about mermaids, then said it again, then speculated
on how he wished he were a merman, adding, by way of

clarification, that he was on antibiotics and had also just inhaled Josh Harper's deodorant. The women nodded, and walked round him, like you'd walk round a hole in the road, and then all went into the bathroom together. This seemed an incredibly provocative thing to do, so he tried to follow, but could no longer find the door. He had a sudden, irrational, overwhelming desire to play those bongos. Maybe if he played the bongos for the mermaids they'd let him join them. Bongos were the answer. Bongos were the key. Must. Find. Bongos.

Then he glimpsed the Hot Young Brit in 'The Bitch is Back' T-shirt, the one who'd asked him for salt, crouched over a stained rug, waggling a tub of Saxa table salt at him accusingly. He veered away, past Josh, who was saying, 'Steve McQueen, this is my mate Steve McQueen, that's his name, can you *believe* it, an actor called Steve McQueen, Steve McQUEEN . . .' and then, thank God, he saw Nora, his dear old friend and confidante Nora, lovely, smart, funny, sexy Nora, at the other side of the room, sitting on the sofa, stirring her drink with a straw, waggling her shoulders to the music in an aloof, non-committal way, looking sad and lonely and glamorous and very, very beautiful, and he decided that his new mission in life was to rescue her from this terrible place and these terrible people. She must have sensed the undeniable truth of this too, because she caught his eye and smiled. He grinned and pointed at her, the way a sailor might point spotting landfall, and she pointed back at him, arm fully extended. Stephen took this as his cue, and tumbled over, beaching himself on the sofa next to her. He made noises that he hoped resembled language, and she made some noises back, kind sympathetic noises, and then, fantastically to his mind, felt his forehead with the back of her hand, like a nurse.

Soon afterwards, Stephen found himself lying in his overcoat, on top of a great pile of other coats in what must have been the bedroom, whilst Nora called a cab, or an ambulance, or an undertaker, he didn't much mind which. Through the pile of coats he could feel the bed pulsing in time with the music, and when he peered around he realised that the walls and ceiling were pulsing too, exactly like the rubber walls of the bathroom. His stomach contracted suddenly, and vomiting on every single guests' coat at once suddenly seemed a very real possibility, so he hauled himself upright, and searched for a point to focus on – a nifty little trick he'd picked up in a jazz-dance class – and settled on a reproduction full-size white Storm Trooper helmet from *Star Wars*. Like a toddler, he allowed gravity to take him over to the mantelpiece, and picked up the shiny white fibre-glass helmet, which stood next to what seemed like a fairly comprehensive collection of *Star Wars* figurines, not boxed, but still in excellent condition. The inside of the helmet was lined with scrappy yellowing foam, and smelt a little musty. Might it be nearly thirty years old? Might it be – my God – an *original*? There are few, if any, men of Stephen's generation who can resist wearing a genuine, original Storm Trooper's helmet, and accordingly he lowered it reverently onto his head, like a crown, and nearly gagged at the sudden stuffiness, the distant aroma of a stuntman's egg-and-chips breath from 1977. From somewhere within the hot, dense fudge of his brain came the instruction 'Don't spew in the Storm Trooper's helmet', and he hurriedly took it off again.

And putting it back on the mantelpiece, he suddenly became aware of what Josh was using as a helmet-stand.

A British Academy of Film and Television Arts Award. Best Actor 2000.

He picked the heavy bronze trophy up, felt the weight approvingly, nearly dropped it, then scanned the room for a mirror, just out of curiosity, just to see what he looked like holding an award.

He decided that he looked superb, and entirely natural, and that he'd have looked even better had it not been awarded to someone else entirely. Swaying a little now, he attempted to swing the trophy up to arm's length in front of him. 'Ladies'n' Gendlemen of th'Academy, than' you all f'votin' f'me, and I'd jus' like to say a big than' you, if I may, to my old pal and understudy Josh Harper . . .'

It was at this precise moment that Nora Harper returned with news that the cab had arrived, and with an almost super-natural speed and grace, Stephen deftly tucked the award under his overcoat, clamping it tightly under his armpit.

And after that, everything got very vague indeed.

Fade to black.

Act Two

THE TITLE ROLE

'I don't see you just folding balloons in joints. You're going to be folding balloons in . . . colleges and universities.'

Woody Allen
Broadway Danny Rose

The first thing Stephen saw when he cranked open his eyes on Monday morning was the man's face on the pillow next to him. Classically handsome, a little like Josh Harper's – flat-nosed and strong-jawed, and framed with short, curly Renaissance Prince hair, it stared back impassively at Stephen with its one unseeing eye, perched upright on a marble block pedestal, engraved with the words 'Best Actor 2000'.

Stephen squealed, and scrambled to the wall side of the bed as far from the face as possible, tugging the duvet with him. The face teetered for a second, then fell backwards on to the floor, landing with a thud, like a severed head. Stephen lay frozen for a moment or too, just long enough to work out where he was and what he'd seen, then crawled to the edge of the bed and peered over, hoping, praying that he'd imagined it. There it was again, next to a spilt glass of water, the heroic bronze face, just like Josh's, looking up at him, the corners of his mouth turned up in an almost imperceptible grin.

A memory bubbled up like swamp gas, of a long, hallucinatory cab ride home, of finding the award jammed under his coat, where he'd hidden it from Nora . . .

He had accidentally stolen an award.

He must get rid of it. He contemplated wrapping it in a bin-liner and throwing it in the Thames. But it's hard to throw anything in the Thames without someone seeing you, and what if someone called the police, or some freak tide washed it up? What if someone checked it for fingerprints? Prison. It took very little for Stephen to become convinced that he was going to prison. He pictured himself in prison uniform, a long period in remand, a distressing visit from his ex-wife, being sucked into the seedy world of smack, getting shivved in the communal showers . . .

Of course, he was being paranoid. No one goes to prison for stealing Best Actor awards. best just to keep hold of the thing, pick a moment, sometime when the heat had died down, and smuggle it into the theatre, and leave it at stagedoor. Maybe with an anonymous apology, composed of letters cut from old newspapers. In the meantime he decided to wrap the head in a blanket, and stash it at the back of the wardrobe, along with his complimentary DVD of *Sammy the Squirrel Sings Favourite Nursery Rhymes.*

With a sudden surge of shame, he realised that he was going to be late picking up his daughter. Quickly pulling on his coat, he plunged his hands in his pockets to check for the keys, and immediately squealed and yanked them out again. The insides were warm and wet, and appeared to be full of some kind of soft matter. It was like plunging his hand into guts, but he took a deep breath, gingerly reaching in again, and pulled out a moist, disintegrating burgundy napkin, full of mashed-up canapés – miniature quiches, cocktail sausages tacky with mustard and honey, something that may once have been a devil-on-horseback, now dismounted. The buffet. He'd accidentally stolen the buffet. Had anyone seen him stealing the buffet? Had Nora? A BAFTA, the buffet, what else might he have stolen? *Cash?* He reached into his pocket again, and felt something made from hard plastic that seemed to bend as he squeezed. He pulled his hand out slowly. A six-inch pose-able figurine of Han Solo, in his costume from *The Empire Strikes Back*, daubed in what looked like satay sauce. A BAFTA, the buffet, a *Star Wars* figurine; for the first time he understood the full meaning of the phrase 'toe-curling'. He could feel them straining against his scuffed trainers. He shook his head, opened his eyes wide.

I must put last night behind me.

I must not let Sophie down.

I must concentrate.

I must be at my best for Sophie.

My aim and objective is to show Sophie and Alison that I am a good, responsible, loving, successful father.

As quickly as possible, he stuffed the stolen buffet deep into the bin, washed his hands, splashed his face, shaved, all the time feeling his brain, bruised and sore, rolling around in his head like an orange in a shoe-box. He changed his clothes to something clean and smart, an ironed shirt, sensible trousers, a proper jacket, proper shoes. He swallowed two aspirins, gargled with TCP to fend off the tonsillitis, put his coat back on and stepped out into the street, hopefully to some degree a new man.

HARRISON FORD AND THE
BREAKFAST ROOM OF DOOM

Shortly after the birth of his daughter, Stephen had indulged in the orgy of solemn philosophical speculation that inevitably accompanies new fatherhood. What, he worried, will happen to my family if I'm not around to look after them? How will they manage if I'm not always there? Now, seven years later, he had his answer.

They were actually managing fantastically well.

Sophie now lived with Alison and her new husband, Colin, an investment banker, in a comfortable Victorian house conveniently near Barnes Common. The house, or home, had five bedrooms, a large garden with a gazebo and a modernist water feature, and two shiny new cars in the front drive. Detached, red brick, with large sash windows and a smoking chimney, it was the kind of house a child would draw; after all, how do you draw a bedsit?

Standing at the door, Stephen glanced down to his left at the neat row of green wellies by the doormat, arranged in descending order of size, like the Three Bears. He rang the doorbell, and tried not to feel like a salesman.

The door was opened, as he knew it would be, by Colin. He was wearing his various shades of moss-and-lichen-coloured catalogue casual sportswear, stretched unappealingly over the broad, doughy physique of a public school rugby player turned occasional golfer, and once again Stephen felt the sharp thrill of unambiguous, guilt-free hatred. Colin, meanwhile, offered up that self-satisfied smile on his big, pink rugby-captain face, the collar of his polo shirt turned up in irreverent celebration of the holidays, his cheeks so rosy they might have just been freshly rouged. Or slapped. That was how Stephen liked to imagine it anyway; slapped, very hard, simultaneously, with table tennis paddles.

'Steve!'

'Colin!'

'We wondered if you were coming.'

'Well – here I am.'

'Well – good to see you!' he lied. 'I'll let the young lady know!' Colin turned and shouted into the depths of the house. 'Sophie, Steve's here!'

Pause.

'So, come in,' said Colin, opening the door just wide enough for Stephen to squeeze through. He wondered whether he should wipe his feet, then decided against it. That'll teach him. He followed Colin through towards the kitchen, but was stopped in his tracks by Sophie barrelling into him at high speed from the living room. She wrapped her arms tightly round his neck, her legs around his waist as if clinging to a tree, squeezing all the air out of him.

'Hey – where did you come from?' he gasped, kissing her forehead.

'Why are you wearing those clothes?' she said, peering down the short length of her small nose.

'What clothes?'

'Nice clothes.'

'Hey, I always wear nice clothes.'

Sophie just frowned.

'Well, I knew I was seeing you, so I got dressed up specially!'

She frowned harder. 'No you didn't, silly.' Then, her face brightening, 'Have you got a job interview?' she asked.

Stephen paused just for a second, before saying, levelly, 'No, Sophie, because I've already got a job, thank you very much.'

'I know, but a *proper* job.'

'Get down now, dumpling,' said Colin, diplomatically. 'I think you're a little bit heavy for poor old Steve.' Colin was one of those men who seem to carry around an invisible wet towel to flick at people. Stephen heard it snap, and once again felt the hot flush of hatred.

'No, she's not! You're not too heavy for me, are you, princess? You're light as a feather!' and with some difficulty, he extended his arms to full length and locked them at the elbows, so that Sophie's forehead clunked noisily against the lampshade.

'Could you please put me down now, please?' asked Sophie quietly.

Struggling to suppress a groan, Stephen lowered her to the floor.

'All ready and raring to go then, Sophie?' asked Colin, rubbing her bruised head.

'I'm nearly ready.'

'Well, run up and get your coat on,' he said, pushing her towards the staircase. They stood in the hall in silence, listening to her clomp upstairs, and Stephen passed the time by wondering if he could have Colin in a fight. Certainly, Colin had the edge in body weight, but Stephen had the motivation. Especially if he were armed with, say, a cricket bat. Or a samurai sword . . .

'Hey, listen,' whispered Colin, 'we've been meaning to ask – what are you getting you-know-who for Christmas?'

'I don't know yet. Why, what are you getting her?' Her own house maybe? Stephen wondered. A small island perhaps?

'A piano,' whispered Colin, and Stephen felt the wet towel snap near his ear.

'But haven't you already got one?' said Stephen, remembering the old upright that he and Alison had bought from a junk shop ten years ago.

'That old pub piano? It's unplayable. No, we thought we'd invest in a baby grand or something. I wanted to tell you, just in case you wanted to, I don't know, chip in for the piano stool or some sheet-music or something.'

Snap went the towel . . .

'Actually – I've sort of got something special planned for Sophie,' Stephen improvised.

'Oh – right. OK, well, if you've got it covered . . .'

'Oh, I have.'

'Right. Well. Great.'

And that was that. They both stood in silence, leaning against opposite walls of the hall, like mismatched wrestlers. Colin broke first. 'Right, well, the Lady of the Manor is in the breakfast room, if you want to say hi.'

'O-K,' Stephen said, and followed the burble of Radio 4 in the direction of the breakfast room, whatever the hell *that* was.

He found his ex-wife standing precariously on a stepladder, hanging curtains, her back to him. He stood in the doorway and watched her silently for a moment, and found himself wondering how he'd ever managed to get away with marrying her. She had certainly transformed from the lippy, dungaree-wearing rolly-smoking pint-drinker that he'd married eight years ago at Camden Registry Office. Small, healthy and neat, dressed in expensively casual clothes, her hair expensively dishevelled, she looked like a TV Commercial Mum now, the perky, wise, sexy mum with a contemporary edge, tucking her pretty daughter up in bed, before returning to the dinner party to hand expensive mints to attractive professional friends. She'd absolutely clean up, he thought, if she hadn't given up acting for recruitment consultancy.

'I was told to ask for the Lady of the Manor.'

'That'll be me then.'

'Need a hand?'

'Hi, Stephen. No, I'm fine. With you in a second,' she said, her breath a little strained with the effort of holding her arms above her head. Her voice was soft and bright, with the trace of a Yorkshire accent, which, like the meaningless Celtic symbol tattooed on her hip, faded a little year by year. She was wearing jeans and a jumper in some kind of expensive creamy wool, tugged up at the elbows, and Stephen found himself regarding the light downy hair on the small of her back, the two inches of expensive-looking underwear peeking over the edge of her expensive-looking jeans. Was it wrong to look yearningly at your ex-wife's underwear, he wondered. After all, they'd been together for nearly eight years, happy for seven–six at least – they'd had a child together. They had made love hundreds, maybe thousands, no, OK, hundreds of times; surely it was only natural for him to look at her this way? In the end he decided that, whilst it wasn't exactly *wrong* as such, it was undoubtedly pretty futile.

'What are you doing anyway?'

'Just putting up the winter curtains,' she said. *Winter* curtains – they had different curtains for different times of the year. Amazing. 'Have you boys been chatting?' she asked hopefully.

'Uh-huh,' mumbled Stephen.

'What about?'

'I was just asking him why he always keeps the collars of his shirts turned up.'

'Stephen . . .'

'Is it just a look? You know, a fashion choice . . .'

'I *love* this tone of voice, Stephen, really I do.'

'. . . and isn't that difficult for you? I mean, don't you want to reach over and just turn them down?'

'D'you want to wait outside?'

'No.'

'Well, pack it in then,' she said, smiling just a little as she came down and kissed him lightly on the cheek, the platonic kiss that they'd been working on for two years now. 'What's that funny smell?' She wrinkled her nose, sniffed his neck. 'TCP? Run out of after-shave?'

'It's a new antibacterial after-shave. "Destiny" by SmithKline Beecham.'

'You're not ill *again?*'

'Oh, you know, just a little glandy. I think it might be tonsillitis.'

She tutted in a matronly way, then stood back at arm's length to get a better look. Since the divorce, she'd developed an irritating tendency to scrutinise him in this cosseting manner, as if he were an evacuee.

'You've ironed a shirt.'

'That's right.'

'You're wearing proper shoes.'

'Is that allowed?'

'Of course. I just thought, what with your gypsy lifestyle and all. It's like you're on your way to the magistrates' court.'

'Thank you.'

'Job interview, is it?'

Stephen sighed. 'No. And anyway, I've got a job, remember? Till Christmas, anyway . . .'

'You look tired, though. Wild night?'

'You could say that.'

'Anywhere special? Movie premiere, awards ceremony?'

Stung now, Stephen put on the modest tone that inevitably ended up sounding cocky, and said, 'Oh, you know – just Josh Harper's birthday party.'

'Josh *Harper's* birthday party! Whoooooo-ooooh! 'Ark at you, with your fancy showbiz pals!' Alison's accent tended to make a comeback when she was being sardonic. 'So where was the party then?'

'At his apartment, of course,' mumbled Stephen.

'Not his house, not his flat, his *apartment*. Which is where?'

'Oh, up Primrose Hill way.'

'Up Primrose Hill way! 'Course it is. Meet anyone nice amongst the showbiz community? Any *ladies?*' she leered suggestively, a little ironic twinkle in her eye. The question irritated him, partly because it made him feel like a teenager, but primarily because it cost her so little to ask it. The unfortunate fact was that Stephen still loved his wife – ex-wife – still ached with it, would be very happy to still be married to her, would marry her again, right now, here, in the breakfast room with the winter curtains, if he possibly could. It was only in recent months that he'd managed to contrive a practicable, day-to-day method of living without her, and the fact that she'd clearly be delighted to get him off her hands caused him a shiver of sadness. It reminded him of what he already knew – that if he told Alison that he'd met someone else, and they were very much in love, her response wouldn't be jealousy or regret, but relief, *glee* even, the sort of unseemly glee you might feel in off-loading a house that you knew was subsiding.

'Go on, spill the beans,' she winked and nudged him. 'Is there a new *special* friend?'

'Could we change the subject, d'you think?' he said eventually.

'OK, what time are you bringing Sophie back?' she said, climbing back on the top of the stepladder and straightening the curtains.

'Not late. Five-ish.'

'Good, because she's got homework to do.'

'Homework?'

'Yes, homework'

'*School* homework?'

'As opposed to . . . ?'

'What *subject*?'

'I don't know. French, I think.'

'But she's seven, Alison!'

'So?'

'Seven-year-olds can't speak French.'

'French seven-year-olds can.'

'So what kind of school gives a seven-year-old homework?'

'I don't know, Stephen, a *good* school?' she said, and even though he loved her very much, Stephen was seized with a momentary desire to kick the stepladder over. There were two clear courses of action open to them, to change the subject and keep things civil, or to have a futile row.

'Oh, a *private* school, you mean?'

'Oh, here we go,' she sighed, stepping down off the ladder once more. 'Not this again. Stephen, I'd *love* nothing more than to have a sixth-form debate about private education, but there's not much point, is there? I mean, we're not suddenly going to take Sophie out of a good school, and put her in a crap school, just because of your political principles.'

'They used to be your principles too, as I recall.'

'Well, it's much easier to have principles when you don't have a child of school age.'

'I *do* have a child of school age, it's just I still have the principles.'

'Yeah, well, I changed my mind.'

'So did *you* change your mind, or did Colin change your mind for you?'

'Stephen, *no one* changes my mind for me,' she snapped back, eyes narrowed, and silently acknowledging this to be true, Stephen attempted a different tack.

'I just sort of naïvely imagined I might have some say in my own daughter's education.'

'You did have a say, and we listened to it, and took a different view. Besides, what do you care? It's not as if we're asking you to *pay* for it!' Alison said this with only the trace of a sneer, but still enough of a sneer to make her now look ashamed. She turned and stared out of the window. Stephen could feel it looming between them – The Row. They were going to have The Row again, and there was nothing he could do to stop it. Best to just get it over with.

'Meaning what?' he said.

'Nothing.'

'Meaning if I got a proper job . . .'

'No.'

'. . . if I stopped daydreaming, stopped wasting my time . . .'

'I didn't say that, did I?'

'I'm not going to give up now, Alison.'

'I know! And I didn't ask you to. You're free now, you can do what you want. I just sometimes think you might be happier . . .'

'. . . if I just gave up?'

'Yes, fuck it! Give up! Sell out! Surrender! Join the real world!'

'And is this Alison the recruitment consultant speaking?'

'No, it's Alison your *friend*. You're capable of so much more, Stephen.'

'That's not the point. It's like the other day, Josh almost didn't turn up for the show. I was actually stood in the wings in his costume, more or less. Two more, one more minute and I'd have been on stage, playing the lead role.'

'You are *never* going to play the lead role, Stephen. These sudden, amazing reversals of fortune, they *never* happen. Most people learn this stuff just from living – why is it taking you so long?'

'But it *does* happen; it happens all the time!'

'Not to you, Stephen, those things never happen to *you*. And even if they did, what then?'

'Well – it would be a break, wouldn't it? A change, an opportunity to show what I can do, the start of something . . .'

'And this lucky break, what if it never, ever comes? What if you wait and wait and wait, and nothing happens, and you end up with nothing?'

'That's not going to happen . . .'

'. . . You can't build your life on the possibility that Josh Harper's going to get struck by lightning, it's just not realistic.'

'OK, maybe not, but you know what it's like in this business. There are loads of actors whose careers don't take off until they're much older.'

'Yes, but like *who*, Stephen?'

He remembered the Han Solo figure in his pocket. 'Harrison Ford didn't make it till he was thirty-six!' And even as the words left his mouth he realised it was not the right thing to say. Maybe she'd pretend she hadn't heard it.

'Oh, for crying out loud . . .'

'What?'

'You're *not* Harrison Ford . . .'

'I know! That's not what I meant.'

'. . . and you don't live in the Hollywood Hills, Steve, you live in Battersea borders.'

'I know that! I'm just saying . . .' Stephen paused, just for a second. Aware that his argument was crumbling, he decided to do the only sensible, mature thing, and create an elaborate, unsustainable lie. 'Look, if you must know, I'm waiting to hear about something right now, as a matter of fact. Something big.'

'What?'

'A . . . movie. The lead. The lead role in a movie.'

'The lead role in a movie?'

'Uh-huh. A big-budget American thing. Romantic comedy. I can't say too much about it at this stage. But it's a big role. The title role, in fact.'

Alison narrowed her eyes, and shook her head sceptically. 'The title role?'

'Uh-huh. The title role.'

'And what's it called?'

'It's called . . . can't remember.'

'You can't remember the title?'

Impro! Think of a name, just any simple name, any plausible-sounding man's name . . .

'It's called *John . . . Johnson. Johnny Johnson.*'

'*Johnny Johnson . . .*'

97

'It's a working title.'

'I see. And why you?'

'What d'you mean, why me?'

'I mean, why cast you? Why not cast, I don't know, Josh Harper or someone?'

'They want a fresh face.'

'A *fresh* face?'

'An unfamiliar face.'

Sceptically, she examined Stephen's unfamiliar face. 'And it's a *romantic comedy*, you say?'

'Not *so* hard to believe, is it?'

'The comedy I can see, but the romance . . .'

'Alison . . .'

'So what's it about then, this "romantic comedy"?'

'You know, the usual. Transatlantic, culture-clash thing. It's about this English guy who falls in love with a feisty American woman.' He was warming to his subject now, growing into the lie, casting the female role in his head, even visualising individual scenes, the cute meet, the first kiss, but Alison still looked sceptical. 'It's much better than it sounds. Like I said, I can't really say too much at this stage. I don't want to jinx it.'

'So you haven't *got* the part?'

'Not . . . definitely,' he said, fumbling behind him for an escape route.

Alison sniffed, turned her back. 'Oh, I see . . .'

'But I'm heavy-pencilled!'

Alison spun round to face him. 'Stephen, you've been bloody heavy-pencilled all your life!'

'Hello, there . . . ?' asked Colin, sliding into the room as if on casters.

'For Christ's sake, Colin!' snapped Alison, deploying the Yorkshire accent. 'We're having a *private* conversation.'

'I realise that. I just wondered if maybe you could keep your voices down a little, that's all,' and he nodded towards the door.

At the end of the hallway, now dressed in a yellow vinyl mackintosh and carrying a small rucksack tightly in her hand, Sophie stood patiently, staring intently at the floor, as if by not looking up she might prevent herself from hearing.

'Just coming, sweetheart,' Stephen shouted down the hall in his best cheery voice. Then he took a deep breath, attempted a smile at Alison, who was biting her thumbnail and raised one hand back. Then as quickly as he could, he squeezed past Colin in the doorway, took Sophie by the hand and left the house.

'*Il pleut*,' said Sophie.

'Il pleut,' repeated Stephen.

Sophie had only ever seen her father's flat once. The visit had not been a success for either of them. Sophie had come round on a rainy Saturday afternoon, and together they had played a brutally melancholic game of *Cluedo* that had been scarcely less distressing than witnessing a real-life murder, in the study, with a candlestick. The visit had come during a particularly dark time in the divorce process, the daytime-drinking months, his Miss Havisham period, and even now he would shiver at the possibility that he might be guilty of having scared his own daughter. Certainly Sophie must have said something to Alison, because shortly afterwards it had been diplomatically suggested that maybe they'd like to go on 'day-trips' instead. He had reluctantly decided not to push for further overnight visits, at least not until he'd brought some sense of order to his life.

Consequently today they found themselves walking hand in hand down Richmond High Street on a Monday morning in light drizzle, looking for somewhere where they could drink soft drinks and talk until the cinema opened. These outings weren't uncomfortable as such, but Stephen's delight at seeing his daughter was always tempered by a vague feeling of restlessness and displacement. It was as if they'd lost their keys, and were waiting for someone to come home and let them in.

'*Il neige*,' said Sophie.

'What's that then?'

'It's snowing.'

'*Il neige?*'

'*Il neige.*'

'*Il neige.*'

'*Très bon. Très, très bon, mon père.*'

'*Merci beaucoup, mon chérie.*'

'It's "*ma*", not "*mon*". Girls are feminine, remember?'

'God – vaguely.'

They walked past Burger King. Stephen was aware that Colin violently disapproved of Sophie eating fast food, and whilst usually this would have been recommendation enough, Stephen found the combination of strip-lighting and urban grooves too bruising for his present state.

'So – where shall we go then?' he asked Sophie.

'Don't mind.'

'Well, what do you feel like eating?'

'I like sushi,' said Sophie, showing off.

'You don't like sushi.'

'Yes I do,' she said, but without much conviction.

'You're meant to be a *child*, Sophie; children don't like sushi. Not even Japanese children.'

'Well, *I* do. Sushi *and* sashimi.'

'So when did you have sushi then?'

'In Waitrose yesterday. Colin gave me some of his.' Typical bloody Colin, he thought; dangling raw tuna from his fat pink fingers into my daughter's mouth in Waitrose, explaining what wasabi is, making her taste a little, laughing when she pulls a face.

'What did Colin give you then?' he said, struggling to maintain a neutral tone.

'I told you – sushi. It's raw fish on rice, whereas sashimi—'

'I know what it is, Madame Butterfly. I meant what *kind* of fish was it?'

'Don't know, just pink fish.'

'Well, we're not having sushi, I'm afraid. I'm exercising some parental authority.'

''S OK. I didn't like it that much anyway.'

'No, me neither. Bleeeeeuch, raw fish,' he said, pulling a disgusted face, and they walked a little further down the High Street, seeing who could pull the most disgusted face, and make the most disgusted noise, Sophie hanging off his elbow with her whole body weight, and for a moment Stephen felt as if he'd won a little victory over Colin, and big houses on Barnes Common, and sushi for the under-eights.

As usual, they ended in Pizza Express, with all the others. While Sophie told a long and complicated story that he didn't understand about a friend from school he'd never heard of, Stephen debated whether he should order any wine. He badly needed something to take the edge off last night's hangover, but he didn't want Sophie to think he was drinking again, or smoking either. He imagined the cross-examination when she got home. 'And what did Daddy have for lunch, Sophie?' 'Daddy had a bottle of wine and twenty Marlboro Reds.' It wasn't that he was exactly fearful of his daughter – though she did seem an unnaturally shrewd, serious and intimidating little girl, more so since she'd started going to that new school – it was just that her behaviour bore no relation to Stephen's own memories of childhood. He would have been more than happy for her to get food on her clothes, to eat ketchup from the sachet, to turn her nose up at anything green. But instead she sat upright in her chair, gave her own vegetarian order to the waitress, clearly and confidently and with a little polite thank-you-very-much smile, unfolded her napkin carefully and placed it neatly on her lap. She sliced her pizza into trigonometrically precise one-twelfth wedges, chewed it methodically, pronounced it 'excellent'. She behaved with such easy sophistication and self-confidence that if Stephen had been bold enough to order a bottle of wine, the waitress would probably have asked Sophie to taste it. It was like going on an outing with an ambassador to the UN.

'So how are you doing at this posh new school then, Sophs?'

'Oh, OK. I'm good at art and writing, but my maths is a bit below par.'

A bit below *what*? A golfing term. One of Colin's golfing terms. 'I shouldn't worry, Sophs, I was always rubbish at maths too,' he said, trying to strike up some kind of allegiance.

'I didn't say I was *rubbish* at it. I'm just not fulfilling my potential, that's all,' corrected Sophie. Stephen's hand went instinctively to his cigarettes, nestling in his pocket next to Han Solo.

'How about sport? D'you like sport?'

''S OK. I like hockey, but I find netball banal.'

'You find netball *what*?'

'Banal. It means—'

'I know what banal means, Soph. What about the piano? How's your piano coming along?'

'Piano's boooooooring' she said. Well, thank God, thought Stephen, a normal response. Still, better toe the line.

'Yeah, well, it's boring now, but you'll be glad of it when you're older.' My God, not the you'll-be-glad-when-you're-older speech – sometimes he bored himself, really he did. 'I used to have piano lessons, and I always wish I'd kept it up.'

'What's a heavy pencil?' said Sophie, suddenly.

Stephen stopped chewing. 'Where did you get that?'

'When you were talking to Mum. You said you were heavy-pencilled, and she said you were *always* heavy-pencilled. Except she swore.'

'Heavy-pencilled means . . . that was a private conversation, Soph.'

'Why were you shouting then?'

'It means that I *might* have got a job. In a movie.'

'And when's it coming out?' she said, her eyes wide.

'What?'

'The movie, the one you're heavy-pencilled for?'

A deep sense of unease rose in him. It was one thing to lie to your ex-wife, out of self-defence, but there was something unforgivable about repeating the fib, the lie, to your daughter. He opened his mouth, closed it, leant forward in his seat. 'Look, this movie, it's not definite, it's a possibility, a very, very slight possibility. It's best if you just forget about it, OK?'

'What kind of film is it anyway?'

Well, Sophie, it's a non-existent one . . .

'It's a . . . a romantic comedy.'

'What's one of those?'

'A romantic comedy is a story where one person's unhappy, and then they meet and fall in love with another unhappy person, but they can't get together and be happy because of the obstacles—'

'What obstacles?'

'I don't know – she's married to some big film star or something. Anyway, there's lots of obstacles in their way, but in the end they overcome the obstacles and become boyfriend and girlfriend and everyone's happy.'

'And is that what happens in your film?'

'It's not *my* film, Sophie. I probably haven't even got the part. I almost certainly haven't got it. In fact, let's forget about it . . .'

'Do you have a girlfriend?'

'Please, let's forget about the film, eh, Sophie?'

'Not in the film. In real life.'

Stephen touched the cigarette packet longingly with the tips of his fingers.

'Why d'you want to know?'

'No reason. I am just making conversation.'

'Why, has your mum said something to you?' he asked, but

the words came out wrong, and he sounded a little more bad-tempered than he'd intended.

'Noooo,' she said defensively, with an upward inflection.

'So why's everyone so interested all of a sudden?'

Sophie said nothing.

'Well, the answer is no, I haven't got a girlfriend, not in the film, and not in real life, alright?' There was a moment's awkward silence, the kind of awkward hiatus that really ought not to occur in a conversation with a child. Sophie filled it by taking a drink from her glass, even though the juice was long gone. The ice cubes rattled noisily against her lip.

'I only asked a question,' she added, finally.

'I know, I know, Sophs . . .' He reached across, tucked her hair back behind her ear, and kept his hand on the back of her neck. Did he imagine it, or did she stiffen a little? Why did this always happen, he wondered. Sophie was the only unambiguously good thing he'd ever achieved, and he wanted very much to cast himself as a mad-cap life-force, an irreverent, impoverished but lovably eccentric alternative to her boorish, mirthless stepfather. He wanted to be larger than life, even if in reality he felt slightly smaller. Clearly Sophie was not convinced; she could sense the strain. The performance wasn't working. He took his hand away from her head.

'I don't mind what you ask me, Sophs. You can ask me anything you want. It's just it's quite a personal question, that's all. I mean, have *you* got a boyfriend?'

'No-oooo. But that's not the same.'

'Why isn't it the same?'

'Well,' she said, slowly, in her parental tone, 'mainly because I'm only seven years old.'

And Stephen had to admit, it was a fair point.

. . . but the undoubted star of the show is Stephen McQue-
en. His performance of the Cowardly Lion is really, really
good, and and got lots of laughs from the audience. With
songs and laughter a-plenty, *The Wizard of Oz* is definitely an very good play, and I would highly reccommend
it to most people, but it is Stephen's performance of the
Lion that really makes this play a Rrrrrrrrrrroaring Success!

So wrote Kevin Chandler, theatre critic for Shanklin St Mary's
Comprehensive School's *Termly Times* student newspaper of
Stephen's 1986 performance. The *Shanklin and Sandown
Advertiser* concurred, calling him 'a star in the making, just like
his namesake, the American film star Steve McQueen!' It was,
everyone agreed, a fantastic performance; he was, in Kevin's
evocative phrase, 'really, really good'. At the last-night party,
Beverley Slater, his Dorothy, and generally considered by pundits
to be *way* out of his league, led him behind the humanities huts,
and as he stood there, shivering in the December night, one
hand placed gingerly in Beverley's bolero, head spinning with
applause and lust and contraband cider, his mind was made up.
Clearly, a career in show business was a sure-fire gateway to
social status, artistic fulfilment, critical acclaim and barely
comprehensible sexual adventures with beautiful women, women
even more glamorous, and fascinating, gorgeous and complex
than Beverley Slater. The only real dilemma would be how to
balance theatre work with his Hollywood commitments. He had
the dizzying sensation that he wasn't in Kansas any more.

He was, however, still on the Isle of Wight; a nice enough place to grow up but from a show business point of view, he might as well have been on Alcatraz. Over the Christmas holidays, Stephen decided to radically rethink his long-term career options. A career in computer-programming lost its previous heady splendour, and he took up GCSE drama instead, the local equivalent of running off and joining a circus. To his parents, who ran a newsagents and were engaged in a tireless life-long crusade against young shoplifters, he might just as well have announced that he had decided to drop computer studies in favour of crack and prostitution.

Over the next few years he grew and developed as an actor. He bought a lot of candles, and tried to read by them. For a brief, regrettable period, he took to wearing his jumper knotted around his neck. He started carrying a small bottle of water around with him, and observing and imitating people he saw on buses, once nearly getting beaten up in the process. He watched *Amadeus* six times. At seventeen, in tribute to James Dean, he took up smoking and driving badly, bought a number of oppressively tight black polo-necks, and a long flowing overcoat, which he wore, collar up, all year round, turning Shanklin High Street into his very own Boulevard of Broken Dreams. He devoured a second-hand copy of Stanislavsky's *An Actor Prepares*, and began to work hard on his affectations. Performing a scene from *Look Back in Anger* at college, he employed The Method, and managed to stay quite snippy and miffed for several weeks, ruining several family meals in the process.

Right up until he started applying for drama schools, his parents hoped that he'd have a change of heart, do something more vocational, more structured. But it was no use trying to persuade Stephen; the words of the critics still sang loud in his ears: 'A Rrrrrrrrrrroaring Success,' proclaimed the *Termly Times*. 'A glowing future in acting awaits the talented Master

McQueen,' screamed the *Sandown and Shanklin Advertiser*. In retrospect, it was perhaps an almost perfect example of why you should never believe your own reviews.

Even now, some fourteen years later, watching a sparsely attended half-term matinée screening of *The Wizard of Oz* at the Richmond Repertory Cinema, Stephen couldn't help thinking back to his own acclaimed interpretation, and wishing that Sophie had seen that performance. A video tape of the show did exist, in his parents' loft, but theatrical magic rarely comes across on the small screen, and besides, it was Betamax. He reached into his pocket for another fizzy cola bottle, and settled a little lower in his seat.

Sophie, meanwhile, was doing her best to communicate that she found the film inappropriately babyish and unmagical: swinging her legs extravagantly, kicking the back of the empty seat in front, exhaling loudly through her nose during the soppy scenes, making facetious groans all through 'Somewhere Over the Rainbow'. During the winged monkey attack, she'd slipped off to the toilet, and not returned. Stephen was too engrossed to notice at first, but when he eventually realised that she'd been gone for at least ten minutes, he leapt from his seat and stumbled up the aisle to look for her.

On the way, he cursed his inability to judge these days properly. She seemed to be growing up so quickly and, seeing her so briefly and intermittently, it had become impossible to spot the small increments of change, to notice the point at which she'd stopped liking *The Wizard of Oz* and started to worry about whether he had a girlfriend. Watching her grow was like a jerky stop-motion film: with every week that passed something small but significant had changed, something had been lost. Was she drinking coffee? Buying pop music? What was on the walls of her bedroom now? Did she want her ears pierced or not? This multitude of small gaps in his knowledge accumulated, until he didn't know how to pitch his behaviour any

more. He felt himself coming across as awkward, or patronising, or self-conscious, or banal, or, worst of all, slightly creepy,
fearful and strange, as if he'd abducted her for the afternoon.
She was slipping away from him, just as Alison had, and there
seemed to plausible way to prevent it.

He found her sitting in the lobby, swinging her legs, reading
her Jacqueline Wilson novel, and clearly identifying with it.

'There you are! I was just getting worried about you. What
are you doing?'

'Just reading.'

'Well, d'you want to come back in? We're missing it.'

'Don't mind.'

'It's those monkeys with wings, isn't it? That bit always
freaks me out too. Look –' and he held out one violently shaking
hand.

'It's not that,' she scowled.

'Bit too banal for you, is it?'

'A little bit banal.'

'So d'you want to go? Are you bored?'

'Don't know,' she said, unable to look at her father. She was
pouting now, and staring at the floor. Not on the verge of tears,
but just clearly terribly sad. This happened a lot on his days
out with Sophie. Things would start well, with hugs and silly
games and larking about, but gradually she'd lose her enthusiasm for him, and the fun would dwindle away, like a toy
winding down. Stephen remembered what it was like, that
terrible heavy sorrow you feel as a child, and knew that, short
of producing a pony, or a baby grand, there and then in the
cinema lobby, there was little he could do to shift it. He wanted
desperately to try, though, so he crossed to her, held the top of
her head with both hands and kissed it, then knelt down in
front of her, and held her gently by both shoulders.

'The thing is, Sophs, I know it's only a silly film for little
kids, and I'm a big, proper grown-up who should have grown

out of all that stuff, but if I don't find out if they get back to Kansas, then there's no way I'm going to be able to sleep tonight. So come back in with me, and we'll watch the end of the film, and then we can go absolutely anywhere you like, and do absolutely *anything* you like. Alright?'

Sophie looked up at her father through her fringe, then down at the floor. Smiling with her lips shut tight, she said, 'I think – if you don't mind – I think that I would like to go home now.'

It was only with a great deal of conscious effort that he managed not to alter the expression on his face.

'O-K then! I'll take you home.'

Travelling back into town on the train, Stephen realised that he would have to find a way to make his daughter proud of him.

There had been some successes before, of course – his Benvolio in *Romeo and Juliet*; that interesting new play; a not-so-bad-considering production of *Godspell*; a fringe production of *The Caretaker* back in '97, other little sips at success. Unfortunately, Sophie had been unable to share in these moments, and the only performance she had ever seen her father give was his tragic, doomed Asthmatic Cycle Courier in *Emergency Ward*, which had made her cry uncontrollably, though not for the right reasons. In all his other work for the screen he had been dead or dressed as a squirrel, and now he worried that maybe Sophie thought his career was something he had made up, a complicated conspiracy between Alison and Stephen, to explain where he got to in the evenings. He had a sudden horror that Sophie might grow up and never see him doing anything wonderful, or even just good. Surely he had to represent something more to his daughter than two legs of a piano stool.

Something had to be done, and urgently, but how to go about this remained a mystery. The title role in *Johnny Johnson* would be perfect, of course, but was also a figment of his imagination, and so unlikely to come off. All he needed was a major role that wasn't a lie, a Best Actor Award that wasn't stolen. Perhaps if Josh were sick tonight . . . Perhaps if something terrible had happened at the party . . . What if he had drunk too much, or there'd been some terrible skateboard pile-up,

he'd choked on a smoked almond, or been beaten up by his
own caterers . . . ?

Josh was standing outside the stagedoor, jauntily signing
autographs for a trio of Japanese students, grinning away,
laughing and joking, in overenunciated English. After the monu-
mental eight-hour *faux pas* of the party, Stephen decided the
best thing to do was keep his head down, and slip by unseen.

'Hey, Steve – hold on, will you?' shouted Josh, gave a solemn
little cod-oriental bow to his new friends, said 'sayonara' with
a Japanese accent, then bounded over.

He knows, thought Stephen. He knows I stole his BAFTA.
My motivation now is not to reveal that I stole his BAFTA.

'I ruv Japanese girls, don't you? Vell-y sexy, velly, velly sexy.
How are you today, rou *naughty* boy?' Josh barked in his ear,
draping his arm over his shoulder, causing all the muscles in
Stephen's neck and face to contract simultaneously; a gang-
ster's hug, like the one Al Pacino gives John Cazale in *The
Godfather Part II*. 'I know it was you, Fredo . . .'

*He knows. He can smell his own buffet on me. He can sense
his Han Solo in my pocket. He definitely knows . . .*

Joined at the shoulders, they squeezed, with some difficulty,
through the stagedoor.

'. . . feering a riddle bit tender, are rou? A riddle bit lough?'

Stephen wondered how long Josh was going to keep the accent
up for. Often when Josh discovered a comedy voice, there was
a very real possibility of it going on for several days.

'Oh, I'm alright. Little bit worse for wear, I suppose . . .'

'Come on up to my dressing room, we'll have a little chat,
yeah?'

Josh Harper's large, comfortable dressing room was situated
at the front of the theatre, just behind the massive billboard, so
that he could experience the pleasing sensation of looking down
at the rumble of Shaftesbury Avenue from between his own
massive thighs. There were semi-fresh flowers in a vase, a shiny

new private kettle, a set of weights, a day bed on which Josh could recharge his animal magnetism between matinées and evening shows. There was even a complete working set of high-wattage pearly light bulbs round the massive mirror, which was partially obscured by all the hundreds of good-luck postcards – Van Goghs and Cézannes and pictures of Burton and Olivier by way of comparison, Blu-Tacked to the mirror, as required by strict Equity by-laws. Bottles of room-temperature champagne and a thick pile of play and movie scripts humbly awaited his attention, next to a Cellophane-wrapped basket of scale-size muffins with a gift card attached. Josh nodded towards the basket.

'From the movie studio. Fancy one? They'll only go stale, and I can't eat them, I'll get fat,' he said, somehow managing to imply that, for Stephen, that particular battle had long since been lost.

'No, I'm alright, thanks.'

'Steve, can I just ask – what do you think of my teeth?' asked Josh, making Stephen jump by leaning in suddenly, and baring them.

'Sorry?'

'My teeth – d'you think I need them done? Be honest now . . .' and, like a horse-trader, he pulled his lips out of the way with two index fingers. It was a toothpaste commercial.

'I think they're lovely,' said Stephen. *Lovely? You called his teeth 'lovely', you little freak. Where did 'lovely' come from?*

'D'you really think so?' Josh asked, putting them away. 'My agent wants me to get them whitened, or capped, or something. For "the movies". Can you believe it? She knows I *hate* all that showbiz Hollywood bullshit.'

'So are you going to do it?'

'Oh, yeah, probably. Hey, maybe you should get yours done too. Not that there's anything wrong with your teeth or anything, but it *is* tax deductible. I could talk to my guy, see how much it would cost you.'

Stephen's mouth puckered involuntarily, keeping the offending teeth well out of sight.

'Hey, make yourself comfy.' Josh nodded towards the day bed, flicked on the kettle, then sat astride the swivel chair and swung it round to face Stephen, his head on his folded arms, cocked at a questioning angle, an unsettling combination of the macho and the effeminate. No man looks good astride a chair, thought Stephen. It was like being ruthlessly interrogated by a member of the touring company of *Chicago*.

'So – what time did you get in?'

'God, can't remember. Three?'

'You didn't throw up in the cab, did you . . .'

'I think I'd remember that.'

'. . . 'cause you were pretty out-of-it, you know?'

'I was aware of that.'

'Apparently you told a certain someone to go fuck himself.'

'Yeah, that rings a bell. Sorry about that.'

''S alright, he probably deserved it. Still – great crack, wasn't it? Great crack . . .'

'You smoked *crack*?' said Stephen, impressed, despite himself.

Josh slipped into a top-o'-the-morning accent – 'No, you know great *craic*, great *craic*.'

'Oh, right, yes. Great craic!'

'Aren't my friends a*maz*ing? You got to talk to them, yeah? I mean, it wasn't all work, was it? Didn't look like it. Anyway – I haven't been to bed yet. I am absolutely *wasted* today, man. Completely wasted.' He didn't look wasted. If anything, he looked even better than usual – peachy and glowing and healthy; a slightly sweaty plastic sheen perhaps, like a mannequin, but otherwise absolutely ready for his close-up. But then he always looked like this; it would come as no surprise to discover that Josh Harper had a Dorian Gray-style portrait in the converted loft of his loft apartment, the difference being that the portrait looked fantastic too. 'Shame you had to work, mate,' he said, adding meaningfully, 'for *some* of it, anyway. Oh, which reminds me . . .' He reached into his back pocket.

There's a standard moment in any film featuring a prostitute as a central character: the awkward-and-degrading-handing-over-of-the-money scene.

'. . . there you go, my friend – one hundred squid-ders exactement.'

'That's way too much.'

'No, go on – take it.'

'I can't. Anyway, I didn't *do* anything for the last two hours, except abuse your guests.'

'Go on – take it. I'm earning *way* more than you, so it's only fair. Practical socialism, isn't it?' He waggled the wad of twenties under his nose, and even Stephen had to admire the way Josh could pass condescension off as political integrity. He palmed the money, quickly crumpling it into his pocket.

'So, you met the lovely Nozza then!' said Josh, in an attempt to clear the air.

'Who's Noz— Oh, you mean *Nora*.'

'Uh-huh. Fan*tas*tic, isn't she?'

'Absolutely.'

'A truly beautiful woman.'

'She's very attractive . . .'

'And *incredibly* sexy too,' closing his eyes, shaking his head slightly.

'Yes,' was all Stephen could think of to say.

Josh opened his eyes. 'Sorry, that's a naff thing to say, I know, but she just is.'

'No, I can imagine,' said Stephen, who could imagine, and had imagined. 'Very, very funny too.'

Josh smiled sadly, breathed out through his nose. 'What sarcastic, you mean?'

'No, you know – feisty.'

'What, because she gives me a hard time?'

'No, I just mean—'

''S alright, I deserve it most of the time. Problem is, she's just so much smarter than me, you know?'

'I'm sure she's not.'

'Trust me, she is. *Much* smarter. I do all this . . . stupid stuff, say the wrong thing, do the wrong thing and . . . well, I know I'm not up to the job. But I worship her, you know, Steve? I really do, whatever she thinks. I just wish she'd trust me, that's all.'

Stephen wasn't sure what to say to this, so stood in silence, nodding sagely, listening to the squeak of Josh's swivel chair as he moved it side to side with the tips of his toes.

'Anyway, she *loved* you,' said Josh, eventually.

'Nora? Did she?' said Stephen, delighted.

'Yeah. She said you were the only person there she could have a decent conversation with. She *hates* my mates usually. Absolutely *hates* 'em. 'Specially the girls. She'll be in later; you should come and say hi.'

'OK. Alright, I will.' Stephen heaved himself up from the day bed. 'See you later – have a good show, yeah?'

'Yeah – you too, mate.'

You too – that's a laugh, thought Stephen, opening the door to leave.

'Did she talk about me, by the way?' Josh asked it as an afterthought, but the look on his face was that of an anxious schoolboy. What did he want to hear, Stephen wondered.

'No. Not really. I mean, only good things. Why?'

'Just . . . no reason, no reason . . .'

He closed the door and was about to leave, when Josh called again – 'Oh, Steve!' He opened the door again. Josh was still sitting astride the chair, lighting a cigarette now. 'One other thing?'

'Go on.'

'I can't find my Best Actor Award.'

Time to do some acting. Pretend. Do your 'Innocent' face. Furrow your brow, let your mouth hang open a little, raise the pitch of your voice . . .

'What d'you mean?'

'My Best Actor Award – some wanker stole it from my bedroom.'

Innocent. Think innocent. You are innocent. Maybe chuckle a little bit as you say . . .

'Why-hy-hy would anyone do that?'

'I don't know, Steve.' He folded his arms, gripping his own biceps. 'Jealousy, I suppose, or spite. You didn't see anyone with it, did you?'

'No. No, no, I didn't, no.' *Too many 'no's. Keep it real, keep it grounded . . .*

'I mean, it's just a stupid hunk of metal, awards don't actually *mean* anything, and I hate all that showbiz bullshit, but I just don't like to think one of my real mates would do that. Unless it was the cleaners, of course . . .' and an idea could be seen forming behind his eyes '. . . or one of the bloody caterers.'

'I'm sure it's not one of them.' *Too confident, too certain . . .*

'Why not? They were in and out of that bedroom all night.'

'It's probably still at home, or it's a joke, just a stupid joke, someone pissed and mucking about. You'll get it back, it'll turn up.' *Too much dialogue. Stop talking. Remember, less is more . . .*

'Yeah, well, funny kind of joke. I'm just glad they didn't nick my original Storm Trooper's helmet.'

'You've got an original Storm Trooper's helmet?' *Incredulity – nice touch.*

'Yeah, original 1977. Only fifty still in existence. Worth a fortune too. Almost as much as my complete set of *Star Wars* figures.' In his pocket, Stephen felt Han Solo kick him hard in the hip. Josh sniffed, spun the chair back round to face the mirror, pulled his lips apart, and returned to the vexed issue of his lovely teeth.

Stephen backed out, and closed the door softly behind him.

In films, when a character has managed to get away with something, they signal their relief to the audience by leaning with their back against the door, their hand still on the door-knob, looking up at the ceiling, and exhaling audibly, perhaps making a noise that sounds like 'pheeeew!'.

And even though there was no audience, that is exactly what Stephen did.

He hid Han Solo on top of the wardrobe.

At 8.48 precisely, as he'd done exactly ninety-nine times before, and as he would do another forty-five times more, Stephen left his dressing room, went down to stand in the wings and watch Josh's performance. Tonight, standing in his usual spot, he saw Nora and once more felt a little jolt of pleasure. He tapped her lightly on the shoulder, and she turned and gave a startled yelp, perfectly understandable, given the combination of mask and body stocking, but just loud enough for Maxine to scowl across at them from the stage-right wings. Stephen sucked his belly in, lifted the mask up, mouthed a 'sorry', and smiled reassuringly at Nora. She smiled back, a big, crooked smile, seemingly genuinely pleased to see him, then took his hand and tugged him further back into the wings to talk.

'Nice leotard, my man,' she whispered.

'Technically it's a unitard.' In the name of decency, Stephen pulled the cloak tight around him. 'It's meant to make me look sinister.'

'Like you wouldn't *believe* . . .'

'Well, thank you.'

'I thought that whole underwear-as-outerwear thing was over. And yet here you are . . .'

'You like it?'

'Like it? I *love* it! Very easy on the eye. Awfully *snug*, isn't it?' she grinned. 'Button gusset?'

'No, you sort of climb into it.'

'Lycra? Spandex?'

'Lycra-mix. I'm one of the few men in London who can really carry off a Lycra-mix unitard.'

'Oh, I think *I'll* be the judge of that . . .' she said, and there was a light-hearted tussle as she tugged at the cloak. 'Is it backless? Let me see . . .'

Meanwhile on stage, in the throes of mortal fever, Lord Byron was giving a particularly passionate dying speech.

'That's my cue.'

'Don't go,' she giggled, holding on to the cloak.

'I've got to go!'

'Just stay here – let Josh open his own damn door.'

Stephen's cue light was green. He summoned up a stern, professional face.

'I'm *serious*, Nora.'

'But I must talk to you.'

'OK,' said Stephen, delighted. 'OK, in my dressing room . . .'

'I'll see you up there.'

'Fine, fine,' he whispered, pulling his mask down, straightening his face.

'Knock 'em dead, superstar,' she whispered, pushing him onto the stage.

As he walked menacingly across the back of the stage to open the door, the Ghostly Figure struggled to suppress a smile, but thankfully it was too dark for any of the audience to notice, and besides, he was wearing a mask.

Back in his attic dressing room, Stephen extricated himself from the catsuit with canine grace, then, when Nora didn't arrive, took a few moments to have a good long look at his teeth. They'd always seemed perfectly adequate before, but now, after comparing them with Josh's, they seemed particularly gnarled and smoky, like the keys on a pub piano. After an unhappy ten minutes spent prodding and scraping with a bent safety pin, he resigned himself to the fact that Nora wasn't coming.

Just as he was pulling on his coat, she stumbled in, carrying her coat and an exquisite bouquet of red roses.

'Mind if I come in?'

'Please – step into my office.'

'Hey, they've really got you tucked away up here, haven't they? Sorry it took so long. Josh urgently needed his ego massaged. Unless someone tells him how amazing he is every twenty-five minutes, his heart stops beating.'

'So you watched the whole show then?'

'God, no! Why would I wanna do *that*? Still, Josh doesn't need to know that, does he?' She lowered her voice. 'Tell me, d'you think this play's actually any *good*?'

'Well, it's not really a *play*, as such. I mean, it's not that dramatic.'

'No, I got that . . .'

'But with the right performer. Someone charismatic, like Josh . . .'

'Or you.'

'Or me.'

'I thought you were *electric* tonight, by the way.'

'Thanks very much. That's because you were watching.'

There was a moment's pause, as the remark wafted around the small room, and they both wondered where it had come from and what it might have meant.

They smiled at each other, and Nora said, 'So . . . how are you today?'

'OK. I have some mystery bruises that I can't quite place, but I'm not too bad. Listen, I have a vague memory of you putting me in a cab last night.'

'Pouring you into a cab.'

'Sorry about that. I'd been taking these antibiotics, you see, and clearly you're not meant to drink on them.' It sounded a little puny, put like this, but too late, he'd said it now.

'Antibiotics, eh? You rascal. And I thought maybe you were just a lousy drunk.'

'Yeah, well, I am that too. Some people get charismatic and funny and seductive when they're drunk. I just weep and pee on the toilet seat.'

'Now, *there's* a winning combination.' She smiled her staggering smile, and Stephen noticed once more the lines that formed in the corner of her eyes, how fantastic they were. 'Don't worry. We were all as bad as each other, really. In fact, that's why I was looking for you; I'm sorry for being such a pissy old witch last night.'

'You weren't.'

'Oh, I was. Screaming at Josh in public like that. *Very* attractive. I'd blame it on the drugs and the booze, but it's all just my fault really – I never know when to stop. And I *hate* Josh's parties. After you left, that's when it got *really* gruesome – the back-rubs started.'

'Did you get a back-rub?'

'Are you kidding? I'd break their fuckin' fingers. And of course they found the bongos! And that was it, everyone high as kites, jamming and bellowing about their favourite *sex*ual positions till six in the morning. I tell you, when some pretty little thing you've never met before starts giving your husband a massage and bellowing that she only really likes it from behind, then you *know* it's time to call it a night.'

'Who was doing that?'

'Oh, some cute little hussy in a strappy dress – they all look the same after a while. Anyway, the point is, compared to most of the people there you were an angel. A burbling, incoherent angel, but still an angel.'

'I put my coat on this morning, and my pockets were full of canapés.'

Nora laughed. 'That's OK. They were only going to be thrown out anyway. Did you eat them?'

'I'd already sat on them in the cab so they weren't at their best.'

'Ni-ice. Reeee-ally nice.'

'I think there's some of that smoked salmon tucked right down in the left-hand pocket.'

'I'll pass, thanks.'

There was a silence, and they both suddenly become aware how small the attic room was. Now would have been a good time for Stephen to slip into his suave Cary Grant persona, flirting on the train with Eva Marie Saint in *North by Northwest*, or perhaps a more affable Jimmy Stewart type, in *The Philadelphia Story*. But Stephen suspected that it was hard to will yourself charismatic; he might as well try and will himself invisible. Instead he became acutely aware of the black body stocking hanging on the back of the door behind her, like some terrible skin that he had shed. For want of something to do with her spare hand, Nora twisted her short fringe between her fingers.

'Anyway, you'll be pleased to know that Josh and I have kissed and made up. French-kissed, in Josh's case. I just wanted to come by and thank you for being such good company, and for refereeing between me and Josh,' and still holding the bunch of flowers, she reached out and squeezed Stephen's hand.

'It was a pleasure,' said Stephen, taking the roses from her, and looking round the room. 'I'm afraid, I don't have a vase or anything . . .'

Nora stood looking at her empty hand. 'Actually, I'm sorry, the flowers, they're not for you.'

'Right, I see . . .'

'They're for me, from Josh . . .'

'Of course they are.'

'. . . though you can have them if you want.'

'No, don't be silly, they're yours,' and he managed, with some difficulty, to press the flowers back into her hand. After some resistance, she took them.

'By the way, it's pronounced v*ay*se,' she said, with a smile.

'"V*ay*se." I'll try and remember.'

'As in tom*a*yto.'

'NOR-A!' projected Josh from the bottom of the stairs.

'Hey. I should go,' said Nora, pulling on her coat. 'Josh is taking me out to some insanely expensive Japanese restaurant, then we've got to go home and pull up all the floorboards, in case his award's under there or something. Honestly, the way he goes on, anyone would think they'd kidnapped a *child*. But I just wanted to say it was nice to meet you properly. So. See you round, yeah?'

'Hope so,' said Stephen.

'Bye then.'

'Bye.'

'Nora! I'm waiting, sweetheart,' called Josh, from the bottom of the stairs.

'He's worried his sushi will get cold,' said Nora. 'See ya.'

'Bye.'

She smiled once more, and closed the door, and it occurred to Stephen that he would almost certainly never see her again – not properly anyway – maybe just a brief, formal goodbye at the last-night party. He felt all the air go out of his body, and slumped down in his chair.

'But listen –' said Nora, appearing once again in the doorway – 'we should meet for coffee sometime. Josh is getting his teeth whitened or his dimples syringed or his head shrunk or something, so I'm by myself most days.'

'We could go to the movies one afternoon.'

'Movies in the afternoon. I *love* that. I'll get your number from Josh and give you a call.'

'Here you are!' said Josh, appearing in the doorway behind, scooping his arms around her waist, just beneath her breasts, pressing his cheek next to hers. 'Come on love, we'll be late.'

'Hey, maybe Stephen could join us!' said Nora, without much conviction.

'Not tonight – I want you all to myself,' and he tightened

his grip, lifting her slightly into the air. Nora twisted her head round and kissed him, a please-put-me-down-now kiss, then they both stood and turned back to Stephen, both grinning, as if standing on a red carpet waiting to have their photograph taken.

A moment. Then –

'So. See you, mate,' said Josh.

'See you, Josh.'

'Bye, Steve,' said Nora.

'Bye, Nora.'

And they were gone.

Stephen waited briefly, then silently followed them out, standing on the landing with his back to the door in silence, listening to the sound of their kissing and their voices echoing in the stairwell.

'So, what were you two talking about?' he heard Josh say.

'About *you*, my love . . .' The sound of another kiss, then: 'We only ever talk about *you*.'

'I didn't mean—'

'I know, I know . . .'

'Come here,' said Josh, then something muffled, that Stephen presumed was 'I love you.'

'You too, sweetheart. I love you too.'

. . . And Stephen stood silently, listening to them leave, hoping very hard that he wasn't about to fall in love with Nora Harper.

Act Three

THE AMAZING ADVENTURES OF NORA SCHULZ

'Some people take, some people get took . . .'

Billy Wilder and I. A. L. Diamond
The Apartment

NEW YORK, NEW YORK

Nora Schulz was seven years into her career as a professional waitress when Josh Harper snapped his fingers at her for the first, and last, time.

Much is said and written about the perils of achieving success too early, but Nora couldn't help feeling that early failure was no great shakes either. After their assault on the lower reaches of the Billboard chart, Nora Schulz and the New Barbarians took a new direction to harder-edged, more experimental material, which in turn led in the direction of the bargain bins, internal wrangling, and an acrimonious break-up. Taking comfort from the fact that she was still only twenty-three, Nora had picked herself up, swallowed her pride, and pragmatically decided to look for a restaurant job, just for a few months, just to tide her over while she wrote new material and found a new record deal.

Her first job was in Raw!, a terrifying eat-as-much-as-you-can sushi restaurant in the West Village, with a kitchen that smelt like a rock-pool, and a chef who somehow managed to make tuna actually taste like the chicken of the sea. Then came Dolce Vita, a chic Italian restaurant-cum-money-laundering operation where she'd stared, nightly, over a tundra of empty white tablecloths. This was followed by a fanatical macrobiotic vegan place called Radish – less a restaurant, more a brutal totalitarian regime – where music, alcohol, salt-cellars and pleasure were all strictly proscribed, and pallid, sick-looking customers picked silently over their beetroot carpaccio before leaving, too weak to tip. This was followed by eighteen morbidly

unhappy months in an up-scale mid-town cigar bar, Old
Havana, where she'd been ogled nightly by boozy young
executives in identical Banana Republic high-waisted pleated
trousers, pulled up snug against their crotches by wide, gaudy
suspenders. Although incredibly lucrative, revolution came to
Old Havana when she punched a customer for trying to slide
a twenty-dollar bill down her blouse. The cigar he'd been
smoking at the time had exploded gratifyingly over his face,
exactly as in a Warner Brothers cartoon, but the brief feeling
of elation was swiftly followed by redundancy and burnt
knuckles.

A short spell working as a masseuse in Central Park came
to an end after people complained that she pressed way too
hard, and a short, desperate period of unemployment had
followed. Her music career, the reason she'd moved to
Manhattan in the first place, had diminished to little more than
a hobby – a Sunday night residence, accompanied on guitar by
the nicest of the New Barbarians, in an arty West Village bar,
where customers competed to shout over their unusual, acoustic
jazz version of 'Smells Like Teen Spirit'. By now, Nora was seriously contemplating admitting defeat and returning to live with
her divorced mother and two younger brothers in their small
apartment under the Newark flight path.

Then, at the last moment, she landed a job at Bobs, an unpre-
tentious neighbourhood bar and restaurant in the Cobble Hill
section of Brooklyn, and had fallen in love with the place,
moving to the area to be nearer her work. It was everything a
restaurant job could be. The food was good and reasonably
priced, and customers tipped accordingly. The owner, Bob, was
charming and benign, the cooks were clean and friendly, washed
their hands after going to the toilet, and were relatively drug
free. No one stormed out halfway through their shift, no one
hurled abuse or bread rolls at her in the kitchen, no one locked
her in the meat fridge as a practical joke, no one stole from

her locker. Shifts were flexible, allowing her to do the occasional gig elsewhere if, and when, she got the chance. People remembered each other's birthdays. As waitressing jobs go, it was the Holy Grail. And that was the problem. It was all too easy.

Because the rest of her life was a disaster. Her most recent boyfriend, Owen, an almost catatonically slothful and bitter wannabe screenwriter she had met at the restaurant, had become writer-in-residence on her futon. There he'd lie, fully clothed, all day, with food debris in his scrappy beard, reading and rereading a book, *Screenwriting Made Simple*, over and over again, with no apparent outward sign of it being made simple. His days were broken up with occasional raiding expeditions on Nora's fridge, or to the local video store, where he rented movies solely so that he could eat vast quantities of salty snacks and give a long, tooth-numbing commentary: '. . .This is what they call the inciting incident . . . conflict, conflict . . . ah – the B-story begins! . . . Hey, here comes that Second-act Confrontation . . .'

But if, as *Screenwriting Made Simple* claimed, character really was action, then Owen was someone with virtually no character at all. The relationship had become sexless, loveless, almost entirely without affection, and was sustained solely by Owen's inability to pay his own rent, and Nora's morbid fear of being alone. Her doctor had prescribed her Prozac, which she'd started taking somewhat reluctantly, her guilt and anxiety about being on medication fighting with the advertised sense of contentment. The months sloped by, and turned to years, and nothing changed. She started to drink more, to comfort-eat and put on weight, to smoke too much of the dope she bought off the busboys. She turned thirty, and for her birthday Owen bought her a DVD box set of the *Alien* movies and some disconcertingly crude lingerie in the wrong size, a lurid tangle of elastic and scarlet PVC straps and buckles, the kind of thing more usually worn by women who dance in cages. Nora was not a cage-dancing kind of girl, and she had hurriedly stashed the thing in the back of her drawer. Sexual activity had petered out some months before anyway, and most nights were now spent lying awake on the futon that had started to smell indelibly of Owen, her head woolly after too much red wine and Tylenol PM, woozily contemplating whether to stove his skull in with his laptop, or strangle him with the lingerie.

Her own career, always a long shot at the best of times, had started to seem fanciful and futile. New York was bulging with attractive women with pleasant jazz-folk voices and bossa nova versions of 'Big Yellow Taxi'. It wasn't even as if she could dance or act; in a city where almost every waitress was a so-called triple threat, Nora was merely a single threat, and not a particularly threatening one at that. At twenty-three she'd been a singer who did some occasional waitressing; then, at twenty-seven a waitress who did some occasional singing; and finally, at thirty, a fully fledged waitress. Ambition and self-confidence had started to leach away, replaced by envy and self-pity, and more and more she'd started to avoid going home in the evenings. Owen would be there, in the small overheated room, deconstructing an action movie through a mouthful of pistachios, and she'd get sarcastic, and snipe at him, and they'd argue, and she'd feel angry, and ashamed at herself for not telling him just to get out.

In search of some other creative outlet, she picked up his copy of *Screenwriting Made Simple*, read it, digested it, and started to sit up late, smoking and making tentative notes – dialogue she'd heard from the guys in the restaurant, stories from her days in the band, bits of family mythology, pages and pages of it, all scrawled in a woozy long hand in the early hours of the morning. Reading these back the next day, straining to be objective, she began to suspect that maybe they weren't so bad, and maybe there was something else she could do after all. Then the next time she tried to write, the page would remain resolutely blank, and this new ambition would suddenly seem as impractical and futile as all the others.

That long cold winter, waking up late in the morning with another hangover, and the warm pretzel-scented breath on her face of a man she'd long since ceased to care for, it had become clear to Nora that she was numb with loneliness. Her luck would have to change. Something good would have to happen, and it would have to happen soon.

Then, in April, Josh Harper walked into her restaurant and ordered the club sandwich.

THE MAN OF THE YEAR AWARDS

He had come to America after his big break, playing Clarence, the terminally ill, mentally handicapped, disabled hero of *Seize the Day*, a TV movie that got an unexpected cinema release, confirmed his potential, toured the festivals and won him his BAFTA. The reviews had been glowing, superlative, and the TV, film and theatre offers had been pouring in. He had put in the hours too, flirting ruthlessly with journalists in hotel bars, and had had any number of weak-kneed articles written about him as result – crude passes disguised as journalism: those amazing eyes, that lop-sided smile, the down-to-earth unaffected charm, the sex appeal that he apparently oozed without intending to. He had modelled the new season men's suits in the weekend supplements, and got to keep them after-wards. He'd invested in property. He'd been invited to a maga-zine's Man of the Year awards, and though he hadn't actually been named *the* Man of the Year, he'd at least met the Man of the Year, and snorted coke with him, ironically enough, in the disabled toilets. Suddenly he had acquired two agents and a manager, a publicist, an architect, an accountant, a financial adviser; he had People. He was a person who needed People.

Off-beat, ultra-violent transvestite gangster drama *Stiletto* followed, then the raffish anti-hero in a BBC costume drama in which, according to the *Radio Times*, he 'set the ladies' hearts a-racing'. Seeking to broaden his range and appeal, he had accepted the second-lead in *TomorrowCrime*, a big American commercial movie, in which he was to give his portrayal of Otto Dax, a Wise-Cracking Rookie Cop With

Principles At War With The Corrupt Authorities In Megapolis 4, a role he referred to either as 'just a bit of fun' or 'the most appalling sell-out', depending on who he was talking to. Best of all, on the flight over to LA, he'd flown first class – no, not even first class – *premiere* class, 'first' in French, courtesy of the studio. As he accepted his third glass of complimentary champagne from the air hostess (noticeably prettier than those in economy), and surveyed the vast, indecent savannahs of almost empty space from his reclining chair, it felt as if some wonderful mistake had been made. Better still, on opening the in-flight magazine, he discovered an article, 'Mad about the Boy; Why Hollywood's Going Crazy For Josh Harper'. No wonder people were staring. He lifted the glass of champagne to his lips, and saw that the air hostess had written a phone number on his coaster. The flight from London to Los Angeles takes twelve hours and, for Josh, it wasn't nearly long enough.

After two weeks on the Evian trail in LA, it was back to New York, to see new friends and, in theory, work on his accent for the movie. Coming into Bob's late one night, drunk and a little stoned, he'd made the potentially mortal error of snapping his fingers to gain his waitress's attention. The ensuing tirade had been so vituperative, so sharp and funny that Josh had had no choice but to apologise profusely, to buy her a drink, then another, to stare at her as she tried to work, then tip her ostentatiously. After the place had closed and everyone else had left, he helped her refill the salt-cellars and the ketchup bottles, and put the chairs on the table, all the time stealing little glances at her. Then, once everything had been put away, they slid into a booth and talked.

As was her nature, Nora had been sceptical at first. She didn't particularly care for English people, especially not the young, supposedly hip ones who came into the bar most evenings and brayed. She disliked the patronising, superior attitude, the complacent belief that just being English was remarkable enough in itself, as if Shakespeare and The Beatles had done all the work for them. And, no, she did *not* care for the accent, which always sounded nasal, snide and brittle to her. She hated the political self-righteousness, and their absolute conviction that the English were the only people in the world who could be left wing, or use irony. Nora had been deploying irony to great effect for the last twenty-five years, thank you very much, and didn't need lessons in it, least of all from a nation that couldn't even pronounce the word properly. When it first became clear that Josh was not only English, but an English actor, it was all she could do not to tumble bodily through the fire exit. If ever there was a word that set off alarms for Nora, it was 'Actor'; only 'Juggler' and 'Firearms Enthusiast' held more dread.

But in this instance, Nora had decided to give Josh the benefit of the doubt, a decision made somewhat easier by the fact that he was, by some considerable way, the most attractive human being she had ever seen in her life. She had to stop herself bursting into laughter, he was so beautiful. He was a walking, talking billboard; absurd blue eyes, full lips and flawless, seemingly poreless skin, as if he'd been air-brushed, but not effeminate, or preening or, God forbid, groomed. Not only was he beautiful, and undeniably sexy, but he was funny and charming too, if a little gauche and puppyish. He listened to her with unnerving attentiveness, a steady, incisive gaze that teetered on the edge of being stagey, perhaps a little overdone. He laughed at her stories, he made all the right encouraging noises about her fumbled singing career whilst being suitably self-effacing and wry about his own; he seemed genuinely bemused by all that was happening to him, refreshingly modest about what he called his stupid good luck. He was almost absurdly gentleman-like and charming, like something from an old black-and-white British movie, yet not at all meek or sexless; quite the opposite in fact. And yet the charm, the attentiveness, didn't seem like an act, or if it was an act, it was so accomplished and convincing that she was perfectly happy to accept it as the real thing.

They discovered that they were from similar backgrounds – boisterous but affectionate upper-working-class families, where you had to shout to make yourself heard. When the bottle of whisky they were draining made them too woozy to talk properly, they switched to coffee, and before they knew it, it was starting to get light outside. So at six in the morning Nora locked up the restaurant, and they walked down to Brooklyn Heights and over Brooklyn Bridge into Lower Manhattan. This was exactly the kind of cutesy, self-consciously romantic behaviour that Nora usually liked to sneer at, and accordingly she did sneer a little as they crossed the bridge, hand in hand, but without really meaning it this time. It made a change, after all. On her first date with Owen, he had taken her to a Mexican restaurant in the late afternoon, so that they could catch the two-burritos-for-the-price-of-one happy hour, then on to *Stomp!*, which had given her a migraine. She hadn't minded at the time, or not too much. Romance embarrassed her, and Owen was just being practical, even if the rest of the evening was a little gassier than a girl looks for on a first date.

They arrived back at Josh's hotel, just as the rest of the city was struggling to work. There they'd fallen asleep in T-shirts and underwear on the freshly made bed, curled up facing each other like parentheses. They awoke three hours later, both thick-mouthed and a little self-conscious, and whilst Josh was in the bathroom, Nora drank a large glass of cold water, then another, then used the hotel phone to call her apartment. Owen was still asleep, only noticing that Nora hadn't come home when the phone had woken him. It was not a particularly long or tender conversation. Nora simply suggested that he put his pants on, pack his stuff, and got the hell out of there, and to take his *Alien* DVDs with him while he was at it.

Then she lay back on the huge bed for a moment, curled up

on her side, looking out the hotel window at the office building opposite, trying very, very hard to conjure up something that felt like sadness or regret. When this proved impossible, she started to laugh quietly to herself. Then, feeling much better, lighter and happier, she sat up, took the rest of her clothes off, went into the bathroom, pulled back the shower curtain and kissed Josh Harper.

They didn't leave the hotel room for three days. By the following September, they were married, and Nora Schulz had become Nora Schulz-Harper.

'. . . and that's how we met. More than two years ago now. It's a very touching story, don't you think? Still, I expect Josh has already told you about it. He tells every damn *journalist* he ever talks to – "How I met my wife, the plucky waitress, and rescued her from a life of mindless drudgery." It's even on his official website . . .'

They were sitting drinking gritty, bitter cappuccinos and eating partially defrosted cheesecake in The Acropolis, an original 'fifties greasy spoon on a side street off Shaftesbury Avenue. Their initial intention had been to go to the movies, but they couldn't find anything that they hadn't already seen, or that wasn't composed entirely of CGI, so had gone and sat in a café instead. There they'd drunk enough coffee to start to feel sick and shaky, and had talked and talked, or rather Nora had. Stephen didn't mind, though. He found himself liking her even more now they were both sober. She was funny and bright, dry and self-mocking and smart and sexy and . . . what was the point? Clearly she loved him. Why else would she talk about him all the time? In the spirit of self-protection, he had decided to concentrate on Nora's flaws, but was having trouble actually spotting any.

'And you got married? Just like that?'

'Well, not just like that. He wooed me pretty ruthlessly. Champagne, presents, first-class transatlantic flights. Josh is a great believer in the magical power of florists. For months I couldn't step out of the apartment without kicking a black orchid. You know Josh; he doesn't do those things by halves.'

'Sounds romantic.'

'Oh, it was. But not corny-romantic, you know? It was wild too. I mean, for the first six months we were drunk or high or having sex pretty much *all* the time. What I remember of it was wonderful.'

'He really adores you, doesn't he?'

'Does he?' she said, lighting up, despite herself. 'I don't know . . .'

'Of course he does. He worships you.'

'Well, being worshipped is all very nice, but we deities still enjoy a little conversation every now and then, you know? Something other than, "Do you think my teeth need fixing?"' She smiled, and sucked on her dessertspoon, then patted the back of Stephen's hand with it. 'Hey, how about you? How did you meet your wife, ex-wife?'

'Alison. Oh, college.'

'Ah – high-school sweethearts. Love at first sight?'

'Not really – not on her part, anyway. More a long, slow, methodical campaign.'

'You wore her down.'

'I wore her down.'

'You stalked her.'

'But tenderly.'

'I'm sure. So what went wrong?'

'You want the long version, or the short?'

'Do long. Unless it's *really* long. If I slump face down in my cheesecake, you should maybe think about winding it up.'

Stephen put the cold coffee to his lips, changed his mind, put it down again.

'I think she just got fed up, really, waiting for a break. When we first got together we thought we'd be OK – you know, an adventure, poor but happy. Then after Sophie was born, it turned out we were just poor. Not that Sophie was a bad thing – she wasn't, she was great, is great, best thing I've ever done by far,

and she probably kept us together longer than we would have
without her. But it just stopped being any . . . fun, that's all.
Worrying all the time, doing crappy temp jobs, eating toast
and bickering. At one point I used to – I've never told anyone
this – I used to pretend I had interviews, fictional auditions for
big parts in made-up movies, go out and sit in a café, tell her
I'd been heavy-pencilled, then make up an excuse for not getting
it, like they wanted someone taller or something.' The confes-
sion was a little fresher than he could reveal, but he hoped Nora
would reassure him.

'Wow. That *is* pretty pathetic,' she sighed, and shook her
head.

'Isn't it.'

'Still, if you will do this ridiculous job . . .'

'I know, I know. Anyway, in the end, she just got bored. You
know how it is – the intoxicating aphrodisiac that is failure.'

'It's not failure. It's postponed success. We're just late developers, you and me.'

'Yes, well, too late for Alison, anyway. She got this temping
job in the City, and made herself invaluable, of course, and
started to enjoy it, and work late, and the next thing I knew
she's having it off with her boss in a boutique hotel, and that's
it really. She's a recruitment consultant now. Lives in a big fuck-
off mansion in Barnes. *Very* happy. Happy, happy, happy, happy,
happy.'

'But at least you're not bitter.'

'At least I'm not bitter.'

'And is that the long version?'

'Did you want it longer?'

'I don't mind, really.'

'I think that's quite enough.'

Nora stirred her coffee. 'So – you seeing anyone?'

'God, no.'

'But don't you get a little . . . ?'

'Not really. I read a lot, watch a lot of movies, I have broadband, cable. I have a high-resolution video projector, surround sound. I'm like this high-tech monk. Really, it's a lot of fun.'

'And what d'you think about her?'

'Who? My ex-wife? I don't. Well, that's not true. I try not to think about her.'

'But you still love her?'

'Sort of. I miss Sophie, though.'

'Your daughter?'

'My daughter.'

There was a moment's silence, the first of the afternoon, and Stephen attempted to fill it by crushing a grain of sugar against the Formica table with his thumbnail.

'Well – I'm sure you'll learn to love again,' Nora said finally, and nudged his hand with her own.

He looked up at her. 'That's what I'm afraid of.'

She smiled, and there was another pause as they searched for something to say.

Nora shifted uneasily in her seat. 'Jesus – listen to us. Let's try and do something *fun*, shall we? Burn off some of this caffeine.'

Stephen had seen, on average, five movies a week since he was five years old. This was on top of a certain number of plays, and too much television drama, but it was the films that had stayed with him. He'd witnessed any number of phenomena not usually found in his own particular region of the Isle of Wight: exploding planets and melting faces, lesbian vampires and Viking burials. Movies had taught him a huge number of skills too, some more practical than others. He had learnt how to kiss, how to make French toast, how to hot-wire a car and hide the dirt from an escape tunnel. He had learnt that property developers were generally evil, and that taking a cop off a case because he's got too personally involved doesn't mean he won't end up solving the case. He also felt that he stood a pretty good chance of landing a jumbo jet, assembling a sniper's rifle, and stitching and cauterising his own wound.

Not all of the things he'd learnt from films had proved quite so helpful. On his first driving lesson, he'd had to be physically prevented from constantly waggling the steering wheel from side to side. He had witnessed an intimidating number of female orgasms, many more than he could ever hope to be responsible for. In romantic comedies, he had seen a thousand last-minute declarations of love at airports, or train stations, usually in the rain or snow, declarations that had proved rather more persuasive than his own real-life attempts. Arriving in London at nineteen, he did exactly what he'd seen actors do when hailing a cab – raise right arm, step out into street, shout, loud, on an upward inflexion, 'Tax-I!' – and been laughed at by passers-by because of this. Two weeks into his professional training, sleeping with a woman for the first time (Samantha Colman, his fight partner from an erotically charged stage-combat class), he utilised a devastating little erotic trick he'd picked up from an old Stewart Granger movie – kissing his way up from the hand, and then foot, in little staccato pecks; a technique that Samantha Colman later said made her feel like an ear of sweetcorn.

In all the most intense and intimate experiences of his life, he couldn't help comparing them with how actors had simulated similar moments: his ecstasy at the birth of his daughter, say, or his grief at the news of the premature death of a school-friend, yelping for joy when Alison agreed to marry him, or the smile he'd worn on his wedding day. That's not to say any of his responses were any less sincere. It was just that, consciously or otherwise, he was always comparing his behaviour with how he had seen actors respond, hoping that it might somehow match up. Life seemed to be at its best, its truest and most intense when it most resembled life as simulated on screen: full of jump cuts and slow motion, snappy exit lines and gentle fades to black.

And this was what he most enjoyed about being with Nora. She made him feel smarter and funnier, more complicated, less shabby and mundane than he suspected he really was. She made him feel well cast, and in a central role too, rather than the understudy of some phantom other self. Not the *lead* role as such – impossible, with Josh around – but not quite a walk-on part either; nothing showy or heroic, but at least someone sympathetic, someone you wouldn't want to see blown up, or sucked through an airlock into deep space, or devoured by piranhas. More than just human remains.

In this particular sequence, they were marching out into the winter afternoon, striding through west Soho, her arm slid through his.

'By the way, after our conversation at the party, you'll be pleased to know I've been writing again.'

'You have? What on?'

'Oh, just this movie idea I've been thinking about for a while now. It's set in Jersey in the eighties – about this band getting together, then splitting up. It's OK, I think. Funny.'

'I'm sure it is. That's fantastic. I'm really pleased.'

'Well, you were so encouraging –' and she squeezed his arm with her own – 'and it's not like I don't have the time.'

They ended up in an amusement arcade on Old Compton Street, where Nora insisted Stephen join her on one of those dance-step machines, and as he stood next to her, stomping out a dance routine on the illuminated dance floor, he had a sudden anxiety that Nora might be one of those kooky, free-spirit types, the kind of irreverent life-force who, in the imaginary romantic comedy currently playing in his head, turns the hero's narrow life upside down, etc., etc. The acid test for free-spirited kooki-ness is to show the subject a field of fresh snow; if they flop on their backs and make snow-angels, then the test is positive. In the absence of snow, Stephen resolved to keep an eye open for other tell-tale kookiness indicators: a propensity for wacky hats, zany mismatched socks, leaf-kicking, a disproportionate enthusiasm for karaoke, kite-flying and light-hearted shop-lifting; the whole Holly Golightly act.

It wasn't that he found these qualities unattractive – quite the opposite, in fact; before she became a recruitment consultant, Alison had displayed kooky, free-spirited tenden-cies too, and had certainly turned his narrow life upside down, etc., etc., for a few years, anyway. It was just that he was also aware that in real life, romantic-comedy behaviour could wear pretty thin, pretty quickly. There was something a little self-conscious and unsustainable about this kind of thing, some-thing of a performance – having fun, but also being aware of having 'fun'.

'You can really dance, Mr McQueen,' Nora shouted, breathless, over a synthesised cover of 'Get Down On It'.

'Three years of tap,' he replied, then, feeling a powerful need to recover at least a small vestige of his masculinity, he went to look round the arcade for something to punch, shoot or drive.

He spotted it tucked away at the back of the arcade, where old arcade games go to die – *TomorrowCrime*, the first-person shoot-em-up based on Josh Harper's box-office hit of two years past. On the screen, a plausible computerised rendition of Josh, in the role of wise-cracking rookie cop Otto Dax, in his long black leather overcoat, was gunning down murderous cyborg assassins in Megapolis 4.

Nora and Stephen looked at each other, eyes wide.

'Wanna play?'

'Of course,' said Stephen, droppng a coin in the slot, drawing and aiming the large red plastic handgun.

'You know what I think?' chipped in Josh, as Otto Dax, from the game's speakers.

'Tell me, Josh darling?' said Nora.

'I think it's time we kicked some cyborg ass.'

It soon transpired that kicking cyborg ass was not one of Stephen's special skills. Even with Nora urging him on, there were, in Otto's words, just too damn many of them, and before a minute was up, the computerised Josh was clutching his chest, buckling at the knees and slumping to the floor. 'Ah well – who wants to live for ever?' groaned Otto Dax, with his dying breath.

'So – how does it feel?' asked Nora, her hand on his back.

'What?'

'Being my husband?'

'It feels . . . OK,' said Stephen, blowing the imaginary smoke from the end of his make-believe firearm, and putting it back into its slot.

Late that afternoon, Nora and Stephen walked slowly back towards the theatre. The challenge, clearly, would be getting there without remarking on the giant billboard of Josh, looming over Shaftesbury Avenue, but it's quite hard to walk past a thirty-foot likeness of your husband in tight leather trousers and say nothing at all. Nora stopped on the corner of Wardour Street opposite, and peered up at him.

'That thing freaks me out every time,' she said, wincing. 'It's like having God looking down at you or something.'

'God in a puffy white blouse.'

'God with pecs and abs. God with gym membership.'

'Apparently, on a clear day, you can see his nipples from the London Eye.'

Nora laughed. 'What I wouldn't give sometimes for an aerosol can and a stepladder. Just so you know, that bulge in his breeches has definitely been air-brushed in.'

'Really?'

'Oh, yeah, definitely. Josh probably bribed the poster guys.' And here Nora slipped into a very approximate impersonation of Josh. '"Bigger! Oi blahdy wan' the bleedin' fing bigger!" What's funny?'

'I love hearing Americans do bad English accents, that's all.'

'Shut your bleedin' face.'

They crossed Wardour Street and stood at the stagedoor.

'So – d'you want to come up and see if Josh is around?'

'No, I think we've had quite enough Josh this afternoon. Send him my love. And we must do this again soon, yeah?'

'I'd like that very much,' Stephen said, and realised that he'd very much like to kiss her too, and leant over towards her, but suddenly became aware of thirty feet of Josh lowering over them, rapier pointed at the back of his head, so ended up just rubbing his cheek against hers. It felt like a consolatory gesture, the kind of thing you'd share with a strange aunt at a funeral, and she stiffened a little, and headed off briskly towards the tube.

Stephen signed in at stagedoor, and headed to Josh's dressing room. He had resolved to tell him about the afternoon straight away; not that he was falling in love with his wife, of course, but the fact that he'd seen her; best keep things honest, out in the open, emphasise the platonic. He stopped on the stairs outside Josh's dressing room, heard loud classical music playing, knocked lightly, then pushed the door open.

In classic farce, there are two standard comic responses to coming into a room and seeing something you shouldn't – the double take, and the long dead-pan stare. Stephen opted for the latter. It was, after all, taking him a few moments to untangle the precise circumstances in the room, which limb belonged where. Maxine was sitting astride a chair facing away from Stephen in the direction of the window, with one leg up on the desk. She was completely naked, apart from the high lace-up boots she wore for her part in the play, and it seemed from where Stephen was standing that she had grown another pair of legs. The illusion would have been complete, were it not for the fact that the third and fourth legs were noticeably more muscular and hairy than her own, with the feet and knees twisted in the opposite direction. It soon became apparent that these legs belonged to Josh. His face was buried fairly deep in Maxine's chest, but the rest of him was just about visible in the full-length mirror that had been removed from the wall and leant against the day bed for the participants' viewing pleasure.

Standing frozen in the doorway, it occurred to Stephen that, a) apart from a carefully suppressed childhood memory of his parents on a camping holiday in Brittany, he had never actually seen two other adults engaged in sexual intercourse, and that, b) all-in-all, this was actually a very good thing. It was all just too crudely biological, too messy and intimate and ungainly, like watching someone floss another person's teeth. He was acutely aware of his non-participation and, as if on cue, just to make the situation as explicit and distressing as possible, Stephen became aware of Maxine's words.

In a low, breathless whisper she was insisting, with an Italian accent, 'Oh, Lord-a Byron, you're-a soooo good-a . . .'

To which Lord-a Byron responded, 'You feel so *hot*, Consuela . . .'

. . . and Stephen realised that they were having sex *in-character*, that this was Method Sex, to classical music. Given the historical context, Josh's use of the word 'hot' seemed a little anachronistic, and wasn't Consuela a Spanish name? He thought it would be churlish to point this out, and decided instead to back discreetly out of the room. But as he reached for the door handle, the chair, which had been used to ineffectually jam it shut, skittered across the wooden floor and clattered to the ground, the top of the chair now acting as a very effective doorjamb, locking him in the room, which now seemed very, very small.

With some apparent reluctance, Josh extricated his face from Maxine's chest and, remarkably, instead of looking straight at Stephen, looked in the mirror first, at himself, tossed his hair, then looked at Stephen, and even the shock of seeing someone else in the room wasn't quite enough to wipe the grin off his face.

'Hi, guys,' said Stephen.

Without quite keeping her hips still, Maxine turned her head to look at Stephen too, with a basilisk glare. The small room was quiet, except for the sound of breathing, the steady creaking of the swivel chair and the orchestral music on the CD player, now rising to a lush, dramatic climax, which Stephen suddenly recognised as the soundtrack to *The Lord of the Rings*.

He watched as a dirty smirk started to form on Maxine's face.

'It's our warm-up!' she said, and started to laugh, and then Josh laughed too, a lewd, low chuckle, before he caught his breath, straightened his face, and said, in a low voice, very slowly and distinctly . . .

'For fuck's sake, Stephanie. Shut the door behind you.'

THE PHANTOM OF THE OPERA

INT.THEATRE.NIGHT
C/U An upright piano is suspended from a rope, swaying, the rope dangerously frayed, chafing against a metal bar or

No, hang on. Start again . . .

the rope is being cut with a large knife, by an UNSEEN ASSAILANT wearing a black cloak and sinister white mask. WE CUT TO —

JOSH HARPER, 29, devilishly handsome, on stage performing his climactic speech, unaware of his impending doom. CUT TO —

— the rope again. C/U on the fibres snapping one by one as, down below, Josh approaches the speech's climax.

Extreme C/U on the final thread as it stretches and ultimately snaps, and the piano plummets. Josh hears the sudden snap and rush of the rope running through the pulley. *Crash Zoom* into the startled expression on Josh's face, CUT TO the gasps of horror from the audience, the booming atonal chord as the

```
piano hits, extreme C/U of a WOMAN
screaming, then back to C/U of Josh's
arm in his puffy white shirt,
protruding from beneath the debris, the
fingers twitching uselessly as a pool
of blood starts to trickle from beneath
the remains of the piano. Above the
screams, a sinister, vengeful laugh can
be heard. as we CUT TO - THE GHOSTLY
FIGURE. A twisted, leather-gloved hand
reaches up to the white mask, which he
now removes, revealing the disfigured,
hate-twisted features of
```

'Mr McQueen!' hissed the voice from the stage-left Tannoy. 'Once again, this is your cue, Mr McQueen. McQueen, you're on!'

Quickly Stephen pulled his mask down over his face and trotted, a little less supernaturally than usual, through the gloom at the back of the stage, to stand at the door and wait impatiently for Josh to get on with it and die. He did his bit – open door (slowly), bow (sombrely), close door (slowly), walk-off (quickly) – though perhaps with a little less grace and commitment this time.

Josh was waiting for him in the wings, grinning.

'Hey there, Bullitt!' he shouted over the applause, biting his lower lip in his version of cheeky remorse. 'Sorry about that whole sexual intercourse business earlier. Want to go for a drink after? Talk things through . . .'

'Josh, it's really none of my business,' said Stephen, scowling somewhat ineffectively behind his mask.

'Let me give my side of the story, yeah? Clear the air?' The applause surged as the lights came up on an empty stage. 'Look, I've got to go and do this, but I'll come and get you afters. Give me five, yeah?' and Josh did his absurd little hop-and-skip backwards, then trotted out to the front of the stage as the applause swelled, and the mores and bravos started, and he gave his 'I am ex-*haus*-ted' flop forwards.

Stephen pulled the mask up on to the top of his head and watched. 'Don't clap!' he wanted to shout. 'Don't applaud him. He's a buffoon, a preening, narcissistic, arrogant, puffy-shirt-wearing fool. Do *not* applaud this man. He is definitely *not* a nice man. This is a man who has sex to *The Lord of the Rings* soundtrack.'

As if any of this would have made the slightest difference.

As he stomped up the stairs back to his dressing room, Donna, the company manager, pounced.

'So, Mr McQueen, what was all *that* about?'

'Sorry, wasn't concentrating.'

'For God's sake, Steve, all you have to do is bow to Josh and open a flipping door. It's not much to ask, is it?' she said, squeezing past him. 'A monkey could do it, if we could find one with an Equity card.'

Maxine stood waiting outside his dressing room.

'Any chance of a quick word?'

She followed him in, and leant with her back against the closed door, biting her lip, a Film Noir *femme fatale* from just outside Basingstoke, and it was perfectly possible to imagine a tiny silver pistol in the pocket of her fluffy white dressing gown. Or an ice pick, perhaps.

'I know what you think, Steve,' she purred

'What do I think, Max?'

'You must think I'm a real flirt.'

Stephen turned, to see whether she could be serious. It wasn't true to say that Maxine was entirely devoid of principles. She tried, wherever convenient, to buy dolphin-friendly tuna, and had unshakeable convictions about, say, the wearing of tights with mules, or navy blue with brown, but these aside, Maxine was pretty much free of any values whatsoever. Consequently, she was clearly struggling to maintain her approximation of a guilty expression. The corners of her mouth were visibly fighting not to turn up, the smirk of a toddler who has just taken great pleasure in deliberately wetting herself.

'"Flirting" doesn't really cover it, though, does it, Max?'

'No, I suppose not. Still, if you'd *knocked* on the door, Stephen, instead of bursting in like that—'

'I did knock!'

'Not a *proper* knock, though. What's the point of knocking if you don't want anyone to hear it?'

'Well, if you'd turned *The Lord of the Rings* soundtrack down maybe . . .'

'How long were you stood there, anyway?'

'No time at all.'

'Still, having a good old butcher's, though, weren't you?'

'No!' he said, struggling not to sound defensive.

'Mouth open, eyes out on stalks. I mean, anyone else would have just walked out and shut the door . . .'

'Hey, Cons*ue*la—'

'. . . not stood there for fifteen minutes, lapping it all up.'

'I can't—'

'I'm surprised you didn't pop home and get your camera.'

'I don't believe this.'

'What?'

'You expecting *me* to apologise!'

'Well, *I'm* certainly not going to apologise! It's only sex – phenomenal sex, as a matter of fact – but I haven't done anything *wrong*.'

'And what if it had been Nora who'd walked in?'

'It wasn't, though.'

'She was stood outside on the street, Maxine.'

'Josh says she never calls by uninvited, she always phones first. It's one of their boundaries.'

'Well, that's handy for you.'

'Honestly, Steve, I can't believe you're turning this into some big deal. It's not even like it's this great marriage or anything. Josh tells me all about her; she's weird, if you ask me. I mean, you've met her, Steve – don't you think she's weird?'

'No! She's just quite . . . intense.'

'"Intense" is just the arty word for "loony". Josh reckons she's schizophrenic or manic-depressive or something.'

'Rubbish.'

'It's not rubbish! It's true. She's on medication and every-thing. *And* she's got a drink problem. Josh is always getting home and finding her drunk.'

'So does that make it better or worse?'

'What?'

'You and Number Twelve having this . . . thing. Does it make it better or worse if Nora's unhappy?'

He watched Maxine's face contort as she struggled with the dilemma. 'It makes it . . . God, that's *so* like you, Stephen.'

'What is?'

'Making it into a whole big right-and-wrong thing.' She sat on the edge of the dressing table, gathering the dressing gown over her thighs, slowly organising her features into an expression entitled Compassionate Remorse. He could see the facial muscles straining to keep it in place, like guy ropes.

'I'd like to get changed now, Maxine,' said Stephen, beginning his nightly tussle with his hosiery, in the hope it would drive her from the room.

'So. Are you going to snitch on us then?'

'Who to?'

'You know – the newspapers. Or her.'

His mobile phone started to ring. He glanced at the display – Nora. 'If you don't mind, Maxine . . .'

'Who's that? Is that her?'

'Close the door behind you?'

Maxine pulled a face, and reluctantly backed out. Stephen waited one more ring, then picked up.

'Hey, superstar!' said Nora.

'Hi! Hi, how are you?'

'Oh, alright. Good show? Knock 'em dead, did you?'

'Well, you know . . .' and the mobile phone slipped from his shoulder and nested in his gusset. He scrambled to retrieve it. 'Sorry about that – I've got my legs caught up in this bloody body stocking.'

'Well now, *there's* an image to conjure with,' said Nora, sniggering, and there was a brief silence, presumbaly while she conjured with it.

'I can feel you mentally dressing me,' he said, and there was a fantastic bark of laughter down the phone. He waited until she had finished, then said, 'So – where are you? What are you doing?'

'Oh, you know, another thrilling night; hanging out by myself, watching the World Darts Championship. Now *that's* what I call a Great British Sport. Sport of Kings. Someone could clutch their chest and drop dead at any moment – it's electrifying . . .' Her voice was low, and a little husky and he pictured her lying alone on the sofa in front of that huge TV screen, bored, a little drunk perhaps. The conversation certainly had the aimless, mumbled quality of the late-night, drunken phone call; he recognised the type, having made a few himself.

Josh knocked and entered simultaneously, causing Stephen to redouble his effort at extracting his feet from the awful, sinister tangle of black Lycra.

'Oh, sorry, mate, shall I wait outside?' he said, hand clamped tight over his eyes.

'No, 's alright, come in,' said Stephen, draping his overcoat over his exposed lap.

'Who's that?' asked Nora, on the phone. 'One of your groupies?'

He glanced over at Josh, standing in the doorway, engrossed in writing a text message. 'Josh,' he whispered.

'Yeah, he said he was taking you on the town with him tonight, is that right?'

'I think so, yes.'

'Well, behave yourselves. Send him home in one piece. Don't wind up in some crack den or brothel or something. Well, *you* can do what you want, obviously, but don't let Josh . . .'

'I won't.'

'Remind him he's a happily married man.'

'Oh, I will.'

'And, Stephen?'

'Yeah?'

'I just wanted to say it was good to see you this afternoon. I don't actually have too many friends over here, ones who aren't Josh's cronies, anyway, and, well, it's just good to occasionally spend time with someone who doesn't want to screw my husband.' Stephen laughed through his nose, and clambered into his trousers. 'Or *do* you?' mumbled Nora.

Stephen glanced at Josh, who was leaning in the doorway with his mobile clutched to his chest, texting someone in quick squirrel-like gestures, biting his lip in concentration.

'He's not my type,' said Stephen.

'No, mine neither.' Nora laughed quietly. 'So. Soon, yeah?'

'Hope so.'

'Me too. OK, pass me over, will you?' Stephen lobbed the phone to Josh who, with some irritation, stopped texting for a moment.

'Hi there, beautiful . . . I won't . . . I won't . . . 'Course I won't . . . I will . . . Love you too . . . Yeah, if you're awake . . . I look forward to it. See you.' Josh hung up Stephen's mobile with one hand, sent his own text message with the other, chucked the mobile back to Stephen without looking, and whilst Stephen retrieved it off the floor, said, 'Right then – let's hit the town!'

There are few places more uncomfortable to stand than just behind a man signing autographs.

For a start, Stephen found it hard to know what to do with his face, or hands, conspicuously unencumbered as they were with pen or paper. He opted for deferential patience – an indulgent half-smile, hands behind back, the kind of posture adopted by someone standing near royalty.

Josh, meanwhile, had adopted his after-show voice, a slightly husky, given-my-all growl, his cockney accent on full. As was his habit, he was also still wearing just a tiny bit of make-up.

'Who shall I make it out to?' he asked the bobble-hatted lady that Stephen had noticed here several times before.

'To Carol.'

'"To . . . Carol . . ."' murmured Josh, as if speaking the words made it easier to write them. '"Loads . . . of . . . love . . . Josh . . . x . . . x . . . x."'

'Could you sign it to Kevin?' said a wizened young man in aviator shades from deep inside a parka.

'Hey, I tell you whose autograph you should get, Kevin,' said Josh, nodding towards Stephen. 'This gentleman here is *Steve McQueen*.'

Oh God, thought Stephen, here it comes . . .

'Not *the* Steve McQueen?' said Kevin.

. . . And there it is.

'With a P-H,' said Stephen.

'Steve's in the show!' said Josh.

'I didn't see you,' said Kevin, sceptically.

'Well, it's just a cough and a spit—'

'Except the spit got cut!' chipped in Josh. Kevin laughed obediently, and Stephen felt stung into justifying himself.

'And I understudy Josh too.'

'Yeah, if I get hit by a bus, he signs my autographs for me. Right, sorry, folks, ain't you got homes to go to?' Josh shouted humorously. 'Got to run, sorry, bye now, see ya,' he apologised, backing away, hands outstretched, then did one of his trademark high-diver hop-and-turns and started sprinting up Wardour Street, Stephen following close behind, his reluctant bodyguard. Going anywhere in public with Josh was always a strange experience. Stephen watched the mouths fall open as Josh approached, heard the whispers of recognition that he left in his wake. In response, Josh had perfected a cheery, matey nod, a polite but professional yes-I-am-who-you-think-I-am smile, simultaneously amiable and excluding, which he tossed out left and right as they marched on through the crowds.

'Autographs! What's *that* about, hey?' said Josh over his shoulder. 'Who the hell hangs around in the rain collecting autographs?'

'It's proof, though, isn't it? A little bit of fame, a little bit of success and glamour to carry around with you. It's the nearest most people get to it.'

'But they don't even bother to see the play, a lot of them! They're loonies, Steve, I tell you – complete and utter nutters.'

'I don't know about that . . .'

'Yeah, well, that's easy for you to say, you don't have them hassling you every night.' And then realising that this might possibly be misinterpreted as conceit, Josh struggled to perform a U-turn towards humility. 'I mean, I'd understand it if I was, I don't know, Jack Nicholson or someone. When I met Jack Nicholson in LA, of course I asked him for his autograph, but that's because it was Jack bloody Nicholson! But me? I'm just *me* – why would they want *my* autograph?'

'Absolutely no idea,' murmured Stephen, in all sincerity.

They barged north into Soho, ignoring the stares and shouts of recognition from the people they passed, the pissed-up after-office crowd, the herds of rickshaws, the underdressed blue-veined women in the doorways of the clip joints near Brewer Street, offering Josh freebies. Heading up the alley towards Berwick Street, a gang of lairy office boys on a big night out spotted Josh, one of them shouting, 'Oi, Harper, you wwwwwwanker!' and Stephen found himself wondering if a fight might break out, and if Josh, who had trained extensively in martial arts for *Mercury Rain*, might be tempted to try out a few moves, and might perhaps find those moves wanting in a street-fight situation, against a bar stool, say, or a bottle and four pissed-up blokes from Catford.

But Josh ignored the remark, and they strode on in silence until they reached a fashion wholesalers just north of Berwick Street market, and a discreet reinforced black door that Stephen had never noticed before. Josh pressed the buzzer.

'I thought we'd go here, if you don't mind. It's nothing spesh, but it gets us out of Cow Town for a while, yeah? And we can really talk properly, get to know each other a little better.'

'Yeah, alright,' smiled Stephen. Clearly the important thing was not to get seduced. Let him do the talking, but don't get taken in. *My motivation is not to get conned by Josh Harper . . .*

The door was opened by a fantastically cool, hard-looking woman, black hair slicked back, like a particularly striking android. On seeing Josh she flung her arms apart, narrowly missing Stephen's jugular with the edge of her clipboard, and threw herself onto Josh.

'Hello, you bee-autiful man,' squealed the replicant.

'Hello, you! This is my good friend, Steve McQueen.'

'Not, *the* Steve McQueen?'

'With a P-H.'

'Well, glad you could make it anyway, Steve! Come on in, come on in . . .' and she ushered them inside and down a dimly lit flight of faux-industrial stairs into the deluxe, exclusive bowels of the building.

Lounge was a subterranean candle-lit box full of leather and metal, glass and rubber; the kind of stylish, bar-of-the-future that instantly seems incredibly dated. In design, it was a fairly good approximation of the Korova Milk Bar in *A Clockwork Orange*, and with a similarly convivial, easy-going atmosphere. Instead of Droogs, the clientele was composed largely of sleek, hard-faced, willowy girls, listening to boozy, lecherous, prematurely gouty young men from the media, reclining in cream and liver-coloured leather booths, or perched uncomfortably on what used to be called, on the Isle of Wight at least, 'poufs'.

'You boys make yourselves comfortable,' said the replicant, planting another kiss on Josh's cheek. 'I'll be over in a second for your order.'

'Who was that then?' asked Stephen, after she'd left.

'Absolutely no idea. That's why I always say "hello, you" or "sweetheart" or whatever. That way you don't have to remember anyone's name.'

'Nice tip, Josh.'

'So, where shall we go then?'

'How about that banquette?' said Stephen, using the word 'banquette' for the first and, he hoped, last time, in his life.

'Cool. Lead on, Macduff!' said Josh, deftly casting himself in the larger role.

They turned and began to weave between shin-scraping glass tables, past a tablecloth-sized dance floor, flashing ironically, where a lone skinny girl danced with an aloof, narcotic stagger, as if stumbling away from a crashed car. They squeezed into the dimly lit booth in the corner. Stephen had been to exclusive private clubs like this before, and always found himself weighing the thrill of being admitted against the awfulness of the place itself: the rubber-necking, the cokey self-absorption, the physical discomfort and simmering hostility, the complete absence of human warmth and affection. Still, he supposed that this was yet another of the prices Josh paid for his fame, doomed to a lifetime of martini-holes like this.

They looked at the cocktail menu in silence, Stephen's hopes of a pint of Stella and a packet of Twiglets fading fast. They ordered Japanese beers and Spanish olives from the replicant, and sat looking out into the room, Josh biting his plump lower lip and bobbing his head slightly to the music. For something to do, Stephen bobbed along.

'What do you think?' smiled Josh, proudly. 'Bit poncey, I know, but at least we won't get hassled.' *We*. Stephen loved that 'we'.

The drinks arrived. 'So –' Josh chinked his beer against Stephen's – 'I expect you must think I'm a real tosser.'

Stephen thought it polite to at least try to argue. 'I don't know, Josh. It's just, well, I know Nora now, and we're sort of friends, and it puts me in a difficult position, that's all . . .'

'I know, I know, Steve, and I really wish I hadn't put you in that position. Me and Maxine – well, I don't know what she's said to you, but it's just about the sex, really. And I have to say, it is pretty *amaz*ing sex.'

'Yeah, so she said.'

'Did she?' said Josh, momentarily puffing up, then remembering he was meant to be ashamed, and deflating again. 'I mean, it's hardly surprising, is it? I have her lying starkers across my lap on stage every night – what am I meant to do? I'm only flesh and blood. It doesn't mean I love Nora any less.'

'Except – it sort of does, doesn't it?'

Josh considered this for a moment; sipped his beer. 'Yeah,

well, maybe a little bit less, but I do still love her. I really love, Nora. Really I do. And I would *never* do *anything* to hurt her, it's just –' he put his beer down, solemnly – 'can I be frank, Steve?'

Like 'I've got a bone to pick with you', 'Can I be frank?' always made Stephen's heart sink. The best answer, he felt, would be 'I'd rather you weren't', but instead he nodded, and said, 'Of course.'

Josh shifted sideways in his seat, and shuffled a little closer. 'The fact is, Stephen, I'm not like you. I know I'm not very bright. In fact, it's worse than that. I'm actually pretty dumb. Like when I got this part, I went out and bought all the books on Byron, just like you did – I know, I saw them in your dressing room – and I tried to read them and had to give up, because I didn't understand a word. I just left them lying around in rehearsals. Same as when I played *Romeo* – I had to sneak out and buy the bloody GCSE revision notes. Most of it I got from watching the DVD. I reckon a good fifty per cent on my Romeo was nicked off Leonardo DiCaprio. I'm so stupid, for years, I thought the Swan of Avon was an actual swan.'

Hadn't Josh used this line in an interview somewhere? Stephen was pretty sure he had, but smiled politely anyway.

'You see you're laughing at me, and I don't mind. People laughed at me when I was doing Romeo as well – all those snooty, floppy-haired bastards who went to Oxbridge, playing Angelo or Fernando or whatever, all standing round the rehearsal room holding their spears and sniggering, because this pleb was playing the part that rightfully belonged to them. People laughed at me then, same as they laugh at me now, same as you laugh at me, and Nora probably too – don't deny it, I know you do. And you're right to laugh, because the fact is, I am a deeply ignorant, shallow, foolish man. The only thing I have in my favour is this . . . this . . .'

Josh screwed up his face, gestured vaguely in the air, searching for a word that was accurate without sounding arrogant. Once again, it struck Stephen as strange that someone so graceful and expressive on stage, someone who, on a cinema screen as large as a house, he had seen save the human race on more than one occasion, could frequently be so bumptious and incoherent in real life. Seeing Josh look for the right word was like watching a toddler shuffle an immense pack of cards.

The search for the word continued for some time, before Josh settled on '. . . thing. This thing – acting. Fuck knows where it came from; at school I couldn't do anything. I was Remedial Kid, Special-Needs Boy – that's what the other kids used to sing on our way to classes.' And to the tune of 'Let It Be', he sang, '"Special needs, Special needs . . ." Thick as shit, no prospects – useless. And ugly too – I know you must think, I've always been . . .' another word-search . . . 'that I've always looked like this, but I haven't. It's only since I started acting, got a bit of confidence, got my hair cut, spent a bit of money on clothes. For the first time in my life, people actually pay attention to me, actually listen to my opinions. Radical Islam! A journalist asked me the other day what I thought of Radical Islam! I said to him, I haven't got a bloody clue, mate! All this fame stuff, I know I don't always handle it well, and I talk a lot of crap and everything, and I do stuff I shouldn't, and I can be a bit arrogant sometimes, a bit selfish. But I'm really trying to be a decent bloke, really I am.' He leant forward, tapped the side of his head with one finger. 'Every single day, when I wake up, there's this voice in my head, and it's saying, "Remember, Josh mate, you're nothing special, you don't deserve any of this, you just lucked out. This could all end at any moment, so behave. Be nice. Be decent. Be *good*."'

'But . . .' Josh leant in closer now, so as to talk man to man, a slight smile playing on his lips, '. . . I get these letters, Steve, at stagedoor, I get these letters from women, and I see them in the front rows of the stalls, looking at me, giving me, you know,

The Look, and I go to parties and I get passed these little notes
. . . check it out –' he reached into his wallet, pulled it open for
Stephen to examine – '. . . names and phone numbers, from
posh women, *famous* women, women I'd only ever seen in magazines, models, singers, actresses, society types, aristocrats . . .'
and he pulled a scrap of cigarette-packet from the confetti in
the folds of the wallet, passed it to Stephen.

'Josh – call me, you won't regret it! – Suzie P.,' it read.

'"You-won't-regret-it-*exclamation-mark*." What does that
exclamation mark *mean*, Steve? What kind of images does it
suggest? I'll tell you – that exclamation mark represents sex.
That, my friend, is dirty punctuation. And I don't even know
who Suzie P. is! Just some girl who came up to me in a club.
I'm even a gay icon, apparently. I mean, it's just *mad*. And, I
can't lie, it's wonderful too. I've got everything I've ever wanted
and I can't help it, I *love* it. I love it all! I even love being a gay
icon! And if you had it, even a taste of it, you'd love it too.
And you know what? Married or not, you'd do exactly the same
as me. Any man would.'

'Not if I was with Nora,' Stephen said instinctively, then, moder-
ating it slightly: 'Someone like Nora. I mean, Nora's amazing.'

'I know! I know she is, and I love her, I really, really love her.
Nora is far and away the most amazing thing that's ever
happened to me in my whole entire life. It's just that since I
married her, all these other amazing things have happened too.
And inevitably that means . . . opportunities. I swear, ninety,
no ninety-five per cent of the time, I am one hundred per cent
faithful. But every now and then, that voice in my head, that
Be-Good Voice? Well, it sort of . . . goes . . . very . . . quiet. The
fact is, Steve, I've discovered that it's incredibly hard to become
even a tiny bit famous without turning into a bit of a wanker.
Another beer, yeah?'

'OK.'

Josh raised his hand to the replicant, who had been staring

at him anyway. Stephen was still holding the scrap of Suzie P.'s cigarette packet. *You-won't-regret it-exclamation-mark*. He caught Josh staring at it. 'D'you want this back?' Stephen said, offering him the phone number.

Josh looked at it for a moment, then with some effort said, 'No, fuck it, you have it.'

'What am *I* going to do with it, Josh?' laughed Stephen.

'You could call her.'

'You think if *I* call her, she won't regret it?'

'You don't know till you try, mate.'

'"Hi there, Suzie? We've never met, and Josh can't make it, but it's OK, I'm his understudy . . ."'

'Alright, alright, chuck it away then.' And Stephen screwed up the piece of card, tossed it in the ashtray, where they both continued to glance at it as they waited for their drinks, like ex-smokers eyeing an open fag packet. *You-won't-regret-it-exclamation-mark*. Finally, Josh had to snatch the number out of the ashtray and set fire to it with the complimentary matches.

'You know what the real problem is, Steve?' he said, holding the burning phone number with the tip of his fingers.

'What?'

'The constant erotic possibilities. It's agony. Especially if you're stuck with a condition like mine.'

A condition? What condition? Not an . . . *illness*? 'What condition's that then?' asked Stephen, taking care to keep hope from his voice.

Josh was looking mournfully down at the ashtray now, poking the ash with the burnt match. 'Well, not a condition, an addiction more like.'

'What, cocaine?'

'No! Sex. I think I might be a sex-addict.'

Stephen choked on his laughter.

'No, seriously. It's a proper condition. You wouldn't laugh if I told I was anorexic, would you?'

'No, of course not,' said Stephen, fearing that perhaps he might.

'Well, then. It's the same thing.'

'Josh, it's *so* not the same thing.'

'No, but it's serious. Very serious. It's very, very serious. It destroys relationships, really it does. I've read all about it. It's because I'm basically insecure.'

Stephen felt laughter bubbling up. 'Josh, you're lots of things, but trust me, you are *not* insecure.'

'I am! I am *so* insecure. And consequently, I seek affirmation through sexual gratification, and that's why I'm a sex-addict.'

'That's *such* crap. We're all sex-addicts, Josh, it's just most of us never get a chance to do anything about it.'

'But this is different. I've read all about it, on the Internet,' said Josh, warming to his subject and, rather disconcertingly for Stephen, subconsciously caressing his own left pectoral. 'I'm a classic case, putting my relationship at risk through dangerous liaisons with inappropriate partners, like Maxine and . . . well, like Maxine. It's because sex is the only other thing that I'm any good at, apart from acting. It's basically down to low self-esteem.'

'You think you suffer from *low* self-esteem?'

'Absolutely! If I learnt to love myself a bit more, I wouldn't be in this situation.' Stephen felt laughter bubble again. 'And the awful thing is, all of a sudden, people keep *offering* it to me. I tell you, if I wasn't married, I'd be just appalling.'

'Yeah, but you are, aren't you? Married, I mean.'

'Yeah. You're right. I am. I *so* am,' he said with a sigh.

'So . . . what are you going to do?'

'I don't know, mate, I really don't know . . .' mused Josh, shifting his attention to his right pec now, where others might scratch their head. 'I mean, there's meetings and support groups I could go to, but I'd probably just end up shagging the other sufferers. And if the press ever found out—'

'I meant, what are you going to do about Maxine?'

'Oh, right. Well, I suppose I'll just have to exercise some self-control.' He slipped into his best version of meek contrition, sighed deeply, ruffled his hair with the fingertips of both hands. 'To be honest, I've been trying to call it a day anyway. That's why, in a weird kind of way, I'm actually *glad* you found out.' And here he leant right in, so that his face was almost touching Stephen's. 'Stephen, I'm not here to pressurise you to keep quiet. You and Nora, you're sort-of mates now, and if you really feel you have to tell her, then so be it. I'll face the music, and I won't blame you.' He licked his lips, lowered his voice. 'But what you have to know is that I really, really do love her. She's my best friend, my soul mate, she keeps my feet on the ground. I wouldn't be able to get up in the mornings without her, just wouldn't be able to function. And that's why, if you *do* decide to keep this to yourself, well,' he put his hand on Stephen's forearm, 'I'll be very, very, *very* grateful.' Then he looked into Stephen's eye, an earnest, pleading, moist-eyed look, and squeezed his arm so hard that Stephen had to fight not to wince. 'And you have no idea how grateful I can be . . .'

At this exact moment a middle-aged woman appeared over his shoulder, giggling, a little blousy and clearly more than a little drunk, and placed her hand on his back. 'Excuse me, Josh, I just wanted to say I'm a massive fan of—'

'For fuck's sake, what is *wrong* with you?' hissed Josh, with sudden, startling scorn, his teeth bared. 'We're trying to have a private conversation here! Just piss off out of it, will you?'

The woman staggered backwards, as if pushed in the face, stumbling against a chair, her mouth open, her eyes suddenly wet with shock, and Stephen watched, mortified, as she sloped back across the club, shoulders hunched over, and sat back down at her table, humiliated.

'Sorry about that,' said Josh, wiping his mouth with the back of his hand as he turned back to Stephen, grinning but with the edge of disdain still in his voice. 'I just get so . . . mad sometimes. I wouldn't mind on the street, but you'd think in a place like this, people would perhaps be just a little bit less fucking *dumb*, wouldn't you?'

Stephen looked past Josh at the woman, back at her table now, in a huddle with her friends, one of whom was simultaneously rubbing her shoulder and scowling across at Josh.

'They giving me grief?' asked Josh, his back to them.

'Uh-huh.'

'You think I was a bit harsh?'

'A little maybe.'

'Well – tough shit.'

But the moment hung in the air. Josh stared at the floor mournfully, pouting and peeling the label from his bottle, but clearly they were no longer on friendly ground, and he suddenly downed the beer, and stood up.

'Let's get out of here.'

Heads down, they were making their way to the exit, when Stephen felt Josh tug his elbow. 'Wait here a sec, Steve. I've just got to do something.'

Stephen stood and watched as Josh walked back across the club to the woman, approaching behind her, then crouching at her elbow, touching her gently on the arm. She turned and initially her look was one of hostility, fear even, but Josh just whispered intently in her ear for a minute or so, like a stage hypnotist, his head humbly bowed, and before long she was nodding, then smiling, and then, remarkably, laughing. Josh stood now, bent humbly at the waist, said something to the whole table, hands out, palms up in self-reproach, and they all laughed heartily too, and a couple of people raised their glasses to him as he said goodbye. He kissed the woman quickly on the cheek, and she blushed, put one hand to the blessed cheek, the other hand to her chest, breathlessly, and, watching from a distance, Stephen was unsure whether he should feel impressed or horrified.

'No damage done,' said Josh, at Stephen's side. 'Better be getting back to the little lady!'

AN OFFER YOU CAN'T REFUSE

Of course Stephen knew he would never tell Nora. Still, he couldn't deny that there was something appealing, flattering even, in having Josh dance attendance on him in this way. After the humiliation of the party, it felt like getting even, both for Nora and for himself, and he resolved to leave Josh dangling for a while, to keep him on his toes. At least he could feel confident that he hadn't been taken in. He hadn't been conned by Josh Harper.

On the street it had started to rain, and they stood huddled together in the doorway, keeping an eye out for black cabs. 'Oh, and by the way,' said Josh, casually, 'I've been meaning to ask you – you do know my lines, don't you?'

'That's my job, Josh.'

'And the moves? I mean, you'd be confident, being me, if you had to?'

'Absolutely. Why?'

'Nothing, I'm just saying there's a very good chance that you might have to cover for me for a couple of shows at some point, that's all.'

Stephen laughed. 'Rubbish, you're never ill.'

'No, but what I mean is, I *might* be coming down with something. In the near future.'

'Well, I've got some echinacea in my bag.'

Josh looked sombre. 'Not a cold, Steve – *seriously* ill.'

'Seriously? What is it? I mean, if you don't mind me asking . . .'

Josh looked at the floor, a choke in his voice. 'The doctor says it's . . . it's . . . skive-alitis.'

'What?'

'Skive-alitis. You know – the Lurgy? Bunk-off's disease? PlayStation Syndrome? Not now, but maybe on, say, a Wednesday and Thursday? In about a month's time, December the eighteenth or thereabouts. My Christmas present to you. Would that suit you, d'you think?'

Stephen was silent for a moment. Eventually – 'Are you . . . are you suggesting . . . ?'

'I'm not suggesting anything,' said Josh, with a stage wink.

'. . . because if they found out . . .'

'How would they find out? If I'm ill, I'm ill.'

'But the management, they'll *know*.'

'How will they know? It's not like I'm going to pretend I've lost a leg or something. It's just flu, or glandular fever or food poisoning, an iffy oyster or something. If I can cough myself to death on stage every night in front of eight hundred people, then I can convince Donna that I've got the squits. I'm an actor, remember? Lying is what I *do*.'

'Well, thanks for the offer, Josh, but I've got to say no.'

'Hang on a sec – you're telling me you don't want to play the lead role in a hit West End play?'

'No, I'd love to play it—'

'So what's the problem?'

'So, it's just that, knowing what I know, I just don't feel . . . comfortable accepting, that's all. I mean – I don't want to feel as if the two things are in some way connected, as if I've made some sort of . . . deal.'

'*Deal?*'

'Yeah – deal.'

Josh put one hand to his chest and took a few steps back in surprise, a response so stock and hackneyed that only an accomplished actor could get away with it. 'Hang on a sec, mate – you think it's a *bribe*? Is that what you're getting at?'

'Not exactly.'

'You think I'm doing it just to hush you up? Keep shtum with Nora and I'll make you a star? Christ, Steve, what do you take me for? I know you think I'm a bit of a tosser, but I didn't realise you thought I'd sink as low as that.'

'I don't think that, it's just—'

'If you must know, I've been meaning to give you a break for ages, it's just I haven't had a chance to do it. But if it really offends your *principles* so much, if you really think that's why I'm doing it – to have some kind of *hold* over you—'

'It's not that, it's just – if I'm going to get somewhere, I'd like to do it on my own merits, that's all.'

Josh laughed loud. '*Merits?* Steve, mate, you haven't *got* any merits, not as far as the public's concerned. You could be Larry bloody Olivier, and it wouldn't make any difference, not if no one gets to see you. But look, if you're really happy as the invisible man, sitting up there in that crappy dressing room, drinking tea and picking your feet, instead of showing people what you're capable of, then sure, fine, by all means, let's just forget the whole thing. But you know what the meek inherit? Fuck all, mate. Fuck. All.' Josh stepped out into the rain, and started walking north towards Oxford Street. 'Just don't expect the opportunity to come up again, that's all. Like you said, I'm never ill.'

Stephen waited a moment in the doorway, playing the old familiar scene again, on the screen in his head.

. . . the roar of the audience in his ears as they rise as one. Great waves of love and respect and validation wash over him and, shielding his eyes against the spotlight, he squints out into the auditorium, and spots the faces of Alison, his wife; of Sophie, his daughter – grinning and laughing, screaming and shouting, eyes wide with pride and delight . . .

'Josh – hold on a moment, will you?' he called, turned up the collar of his coat, and ran up Berwick Street. 'I don't want to appear ungrateful, Josh. I mean, I appreciate the offer—'

'Look, Stephen, cut to the chase. Your career – with the best will in the world you're not exactly setting the showbiz world alight, are you?'

'Well, no, but—'

'And you should be, shouldn't you? I mean, you *want* it, you *deserve* it. You're better than half those talentless clowns out there. All you need is a lucky break, am I right?'

'Well, I suppose . . .'

'And it would help for you to do a show or two? Lead role in a West End play. Invite some people along, influential people, show them what you're capable of. I could have a word with my agent, get him along, and you can invite your family. I couldn't see it, of course, but Nora could come along.'

'But surely people are only coming to see *you*?'

'No, they're coming to see the play. Like The Dane says – the play's the thing. And you're as good as me, aren't you? You must think you are, or you wouldn't do it.'

'Well . . .' Stephen glanced sideways at Josh, who was grinning back at him, 'I'm not bad.'

'Well, fuck 'em then. It's not like we're selling them shoddy goods. You're the one and only Stephen C. McQueen! With a P-H! You'll blow their fuckin' socks off.'

He stepped suddenly out into the street to hail a passing cab, and Stephen saw the cabby's smile of recognition. 'Primrose Hill, please, mate,' said Josh in full-on barrow boy, and opened the cab door.

He's serious, thought Stephen. This is it, at last, the Big Break. This is how you make your own luck. You say yes.

Say yes.

'Josh?'

Josh closed the cab door, and crossed back to Stephen. 'Well?'

'You'll end this thing with Maxine, yeah?' said Stephen.

'Of course.'

'And you'll make things alright with Nora?'

'Absolutely.'

The cabbie beeped his horn.

'Alright then,' said Stephen 'Let's do it.'

Josh put one hand on his shoulder, squeezed it hard. 'You're sure?'

'I'm sure'

'Two days, December the eighteenth and nineteenth? That's two evening shows and a matinée. Just in time for Christmas. That's another part of the deal by the way – you have got to be fucking sensational.'

'I will be.'

'OK. It's a deal.'

Josh winked, and turned to get in the cab, then stopped, turned back and said, just a little too casually, 'Oh, and just for my peace of mind, and completely unconnected, we're cool about you not saying anything about you-know-what to you-know-who?'

Stephen thought for a moment, then shrugged. 'Lips are sealed.'

'Promise?'

'Promise.'

Then just as suddenly Josh was in the cab, and driving off into the rain.

Stephen stood watching as Josh grinned at him through the back window, mimed an imaginary gun, fired it, then drove off back to Nora. Somewhere behind all his hope and elation, Stephen had the definite sensation that he had made some kind of terrible mistake.

Then he turned and walked south towards Trafalgar Square, and the Night Bus home.

Act Four

THE BIG BREAK

Sawyer, you listen to me, and you listen hard . . .
They've got to like you. *Got* to. Do you understand?
You can't fall down. You can't because your future's
in it, my future and everything all of us have is staked
on *you*. Alright, now I'm through, but you keep your
feet on the ground and your head on those shoulders of yours and go out, and, Sawyer, you're going
out a youngster but you've got to come back a star!

Rian James and James Seymour
42nd Street

THERE'S NO BUSINESS
LIKE SHOW BUSINESS

The international headquarters of the Creative Talent Agency Enterprises Limited were located on the further outskirts of London's glittering West End, in Acton to be precise, on what used to be called an industrial estate, but had now been redesignated a 'business park'. Stephen did not relish going to see his agent. Frank was always supportive and cheery, but it still felt a little like visiting an enthusiastic amateur dentist. On a day like this, as he walked across the rain-swept forecourt to the low, grey sprawl of aluminium and chipboard pre-fabs, surrounded by a razor-wire fence, the business park looked more than ever like somewhere you might try to tunnel out of.

The offices themselves occupied a compact two-room 'suite' in between a dubious travel agent's and a debt-recovery agency. A gang of big, sour, red-faced debt-collectors loitered on the stairwell, eating garage sandwiches and smoking violently, and Stephen squeezed past them sheepishly, then stood outside his agent's office, dried his damp hair with the sleeve of his overcoat, patted it down, assumed a confident, urbane, professional smile, knocked gently on the flimsy wood-veneer door and entered.

Melissa, the receptionist, stood guard at the front desk, methodically scouring the bottom of a low-fat yoghurt carton with a plastic spoon. A stationery catalogue lay open on the desk before her, a game of solitaire flickered on the yellowing computer monitor by her side

'Hi, there! I wanted to see Frank,' said Stephen, smiling and, for no apparent reason, pulling on the lobe of one ear.

Melissa glanced up momentarily from the wide selection of ring-binder files, then went back to noisily digging for sub-atomic traces of yoghurt in the bottom of the pot.

'Is it about representation?' she sighed.

'Well, not exactly . . .'

'Because we're not taking on any new clients at the moment. The books are full, but if you want to send us your photo and CV we can keep your details on file.'

'No, you don't understand, Melissa – I already *am* a client. It's me – Stephen McQueen? Frank's expecting me.'

Melissa sucked her teaspoon. 'Oh, right, of course, sorry, Stephen, I didn't recognise you.'

Well, whose fault is *that*? thought Stephen, but didn't say it. First rule of showbiz: never, ever alienate your agent. Melissa sat up straight, settled the hands-free headset back on her head, and dialled Frank's extension, a slightly redundant use of the technology, given that Frank's voice could be heard perfectly clearly through the pre-fabricated partition behind her.

'Frank?'

'I'm on the mobile, Melissa, what is it?' growled Frank from the other side of the wall.

'Just to say Steve McQueen's here to see you.'

Stephen braced himself. *Here it comes . . .*

'The famous one? Or the client?' shouted Frank.

. . . and there it is.

'The client,' smirked Melissa.

'Lovely. Tell him if he'd care to take a seat I'll see him in a minute.'

'If you'd care to take a seat, he'll see you in a minute.'

'OK, fine. And, eh, Queen of Hearts next, I think,' said Stephen, in a stab at raffishness.

'*What?*'

Stephen nodded at the game of the solitaire on the computer screen.

'Oh, I see,' mumbled Melissa, smiled for an instant, then began jabbing flamboyantly and seemingly randomly at the keyboard like a deranged concert pianist. 'If you'd like to wait over there. . . . ?'

Stephen settled on the row of seating a short distance away from Melissa, seating so low that it felt effectively like sitting on the floor, lowering himself down carefully until his knees were level with his head. Mustard-coloured foam filling peaked invitingly out of a hole in the fabric, but he fought the temptation to pick at it.

Melissa's intercom buzzed. 'Tell Steve I'll see him now,' said Frank from the other side of the partition.

'He'll see you now,' said Melissa.

'Oh, right-ee-o,' said Stephen, hauling himself up from his seat on the floor. *Right-ee-o.* Where did *that* come from? He squeezed past Melissa and headed into the inner sanctum.

The small brown office smelt of stale fags and instant coffee, and was thick with the billows of blue-grey fug emanating from Frank, late forties, a bony, elongated man with swept-back thinning hair and teeth the colour of pound coins. Even the whites of his eyes had somehow turned a bruised yellow, and he wore an almost flesh-tone polo-neck, overstretched and slack at the neck, giving him that much-sought-after slipped-goitre look. He sat twisting his chair jerkily from side to side with the nervy energy of a man who subsisted almost entirely on catering tubs of generic chicory coffee, powdered milk, room-temperature Coke, sweets and Silk Cut. On the edge of the cluttered desk, a Glade pine air-freshener made the room smell like a pine forest destroyed by fire, and next to that, a bowl of gourmet jellybeans was peppered with ash.

'Hello there, Mr McQueen, and how *are* you?' he said, balancing his current cigarette on the edge of a Coke can and offering Stephen his bony, yellow-tipped hand. Frank had the look and demeanour of an inappropriately cheerful mortician who's made an unusual sideways step into showbiz. In reality he was an ex-actor who'd had a long successful stint in a soap as a randy, bigamous greengrocer. When the greengrocer had died in a freak fork-lift truck accident, Frank had looked forward to the challenge of taking on the classics – a chance to give his Vanya perhaps, even one day his Lear – but all people could see was that randy bigamous greengrocer, and in the end he had crossed to the other side: 'Poacher-turned-gamekeeper, if you will . . .'

'Good to see you, good to see you. Sit down, sit down, help yourself to jellybeans.' Stephen gingerly sat opposite on the somewhat unstable second-best swivel-chair – again, the mustard-coloured foam peeked through the seat fabric. Don't pick. Concentrate. Be firm but friendly, professional but relaxed.

'Raining, is it?' asked Frank. Given that rain could be heard on the roof and seen through the window, 'Yes' seemed the only appropriate reply.

'So – good news, young man,' said Frank, retrieving his cigarette, and getting down to business. 'I have a little something for you here.' And he searched through the topsoil of paperwork on his desk, before retrieving a slip of paper, which he snapped tight a few times in front of Stephen's face. 'A cheque, made out to a Mr Stephen C. McQueen for the princely sum of £1762.24.'

'Really? What for?'

'*Sammy the Squirrel*. Foreign Sales. Apparently you're absolutely massive in Eastern Europe.'

'Well, that's good to know.'

'Told you it was worth it, didn't I? And it gets better. They want you back for more.'

'They do? What for?'

'The sequel. *Sammy the Squirrel 2 – If You're Happy and You Know It*.'

Stephen's good mood evaporated. It would have been

expecting too much, perhaps, for Frank to offer him the title role in the romantic comedy he'd told Alison and Sophie all about. That had, after all, been a figment of his imagination. But Sammy? Again? It was like being told that he'd have to go back to prison.

'And d'you think it's going to be on one of those sequels that's actually better than the original?'

'Didn't you say you wanted to work, Steve? Well, you ask, and Frank provides. Think of it as an opportunity to revisit a much-loved role.'

'And what does the part entail?'

''Bout two grand.'

'No, I mean, what does the role involve?'

'I don't know, the usual – singing songs with your Woodland Pals, holding a big acorn . . .'

'But have you seen a script?'

'Not yet. I don't think I can get you script approval or anything, but they were very keen to have you back.'

'Alright, Frank, I'll give it some thought.'

'Could get you noticed.'

'Only by pre-schoolers, Frank.'

'Hey, film directors have children too, Steve. And the money's not bad. A grand and a half plus potential residuals . . . ?'

'I'll think about it, Frank.'

'What's to think about?'

'I'd just rather do something new, that's all.'

'This is new!'

'What's new about it?'

'Well, the first one was about numbers, whereas this one focuses on the alphabet.'

'It's still skin-work, though, Frank.'

'What are you talking about? They can see your face.'

Stephen sighed and looked at the rain on the window. 'Well, like I said – I'll think about it.'

'Alright, but don't think about it too long, yeah? Winter's a quiet time of year and, like it or not, a grand and a half is not peanuts.'

'Or hazelnuts,' added Stephen.

Frank laughed and coughed at the same time. 'Hazelnuts — like it, very good. You should be on the stage, friend.' Frank's mobile started to chirrup Scott Joplin's 'The Entertainer', and he snapped it up instantly, scrutinised the display, and scowled. 'Sorry, Steve, got to get this one. Bear with me, will you?' He pressed a button, swivelled the chair through ninety degrees, put his feet on the edge of the desk, and surveyed the car park — his movie-mogul stance. 'Hello there . . . Well, I'm with a client at the moment so it's not the best time . . . Steve McQueen . . . No, not that one . . . Look, I thought we'd already gone over this . . . No, I'm not prepared to do anything before Friday . . . I don't care . . . I told you, I simply *do not* care! . . .'

If he's going to talk tough, maybe I should leave, thought Stephen, rising an inch from his chair, nodding towards the door, but Frank gestured for him to sit back down, clearly relishing the opportunity to put on a show for a client.

'No, money is *not* the issue, it's simply a question of schedule and *practicalities* . . . Tomorrow's an absolute non-starter . . . No, now listen to me, we're just going round and round in circles here —' he glanced at Stephen, shaking his head and rolling his eyes theatrically — 'Friday is my *final* offer. If you can't wait till Friday, then I'm afraid you'll just have to try elsewhere.'

Maybe Frank's not so bad after all, thought Stephen, feeling guilty. The truth was, he'd been planning to invite Josh's high-powered agent along to his forthcoming Big Break, hopefully jump ship soon after, then break the news to Frank — 'I think we should be free to see other people.' But maybe Frank was OK. This is, after all, what you want from an agent: tough talk, fearlessness, loyalty, an unwillingness to compromise on behalf of his clients . . .

'I'm sorry, no, that's my final offer. Alright then, Friday it is
... About four o'clock? And, Mum? I'll need someone else
there to help me get the fridge down the stairs ... Well, I can't
do it by myself, can I? Well, ask the neighbours. Ask whatsis-
name next door. Look, Mum, I've got a client here with me
... No one you'd know ... Alright, see you Friday.' And he
hung up.

'Sorry about that,' said Frank, once again rifling through the
papers on his desk – the casting breakdowns, letters from
prospective clients, pages torn from *The Stage*. 'Mum's got this
new fridge coming on Thursday, and Argos are refusing to take
the old one away. Can't blame them really; I wouldn't touch it
with a bargepole. I'm surprised it hasn't walked out the flat all
by itself. And she's on the fourth floor with no lift, don't know
what she expects me to do – drop it down the stairwell or something. Hey, I don't suppose you know anyone who needs a fridge,
do you? It'll need bleaching.'

'Well, I do . . .'

'Frank's eyes lit up at the opportunity to help a client. 'You
do?'

'. . . but I haven't really got the space for it.'

Frank stopped rustling papers. 'You don't have a *fridge*?'

'Not at the moment.'

'So what do you use instead?'

'Oh, the windowsill.'

'Bloody hell, Stephen, we really do need to get *you* some
work!' he said, and started sprinkling ash on his desk with a
renewed sense of purpose.

It can't be good to smoke so much in such a small room,
thought Stephen. Frank was clearly being kippered slowly by
Silk Cut. If he were to die suddenly – not impossible, given
that he did his weekly shop in a nearby garage – then there
was a very good chance that he'd keep.

'Right, what have we got here. Nope . . . nope . . . nope . . .

Ah, here we go – there's a billboard commercial here. For floor cleaner. Blokey-types wanted, could be nice money. You can do blokey, can't you? Want me to put you up for it?'

Stephen pictured himself on a billboard, mop in hand; imagined Sophie seeing it, on her way home from school, with a group of her posh schoolfriends – 'That's my dad up there, the one in the pinny . . .'

'Don't think so, Frank.'

'It's extremely quiet out there at the mo . . .'

'I know, I know. But, well, that's modelling, Frank. I'd sort of hoped for something where I, you know, moved, spoke and stuff.'

'Can you speak Russian?'

'Not as such.'

'Pity. Nice job, next week, playing some Cossack or other. They need fluent Russian. You could always learn, I suppose.'

'Not before next week, though.'

'No, no, probably not.' Back to the papers, digging into the substrata now – 'Nope . . . nope . . . nope . . . Here we are – *Raisin in the Sun*, Dundee Rep?'

'No.'

'Why not? If you're not prepared to travel, Steve . . .'

'It's not that, it's just, well, I'd need to be black.'

It was the *Vagina Monologues* farrago all over again. Frank read the casting breakdown, his lips moving, then looked back up at Stephen just to check that black definitely lay outside his range, sighed, as if this were in some indefinable way Stephen's fault, then went back to his papers.

'"Actor/Singer/Dancers required for *Fear!* A musical version of Bertolt Brecht's *Fears and Misery in the Third Reich*." No actual wages, as such—'

'I really need to be earning, Frank.'

'OK, how about this then: "Theatre Folk! An exciting new educational theatre company, kids' show about dental hygiene, touring schools in the Fens, starts January. *Nothing But The Tooth*." Pun, you see? Money's not great, but the per diems are sensational. You'd be playing someone called, let me see – Tommy Tartar. Don't fancy it?'

'"Tommy Tartar"?'

'Right, we can forget *that* then,' said Frank, irritated now. He tossed the papers back on his desk, blew a long plume smoke through his thin nose, leant back in his chair till it squeaked dangerously. 'You know the best thing you could do for your career, Steve?'

'Go on.'

Frank glanced over his shoulder and beneath his desk for eavesdroppers or surveillance equipment, and in a very serious voice, intoned, 'Kill Josh Harper.'

Stephen laughed.

'I'm serious. What you have to remember, Stephen, is that it's a very, very thin line between huge success and utter failure. You know, even to this day, I remember you in that production of *Godspell*. Your performance is burnt on my retina.' Stephen winced, unable to think of anything worse to have burnt on a retina. 'You've got talent to burn, all you need is exposure. You take over from Josh, even if it's just for a couple of shows, and I'll get the best people in – casting directors, TV people – and you, my friend, you will be flying. Like a . . .' he searched the smoky air of the small office '. . . like an eagle.'

'Well, it's funny you should say that, Frank,' said Stephen, in a low voice.

'What?'

Stephen also glanced over his shoulder, checked beneath his desk, and in a low voice intoned, 'Well . . . what are you doing round about the eighteenth of December?'

THE 'F' WORD

'Can I ask you something?'

'Of course.'

'We're friends, aren't we? I mean, I know we haven't known each other too long, but I like to think we're sort of friends . . .'

'I think so.'

'So you'd tell me the truth? If I asked you something personal?'

'Absolutely.'

'So I can trust you?'

'You can trust me.'

'Is Josh having an affair?' asked Nora.

The conversation took place one afternoon, a week after the deal had been agreed. Stephen and Nora were walking back over Waterloo Bridge late in the afternoon, away from the National Film Theatre, where they'd just been to see a revival of *Double Indemnity*. Stephen had seen it maybe ten times before, but it wasn't until he'd sat and watched it with Nora at his side, their elbows touching, both wrist-deep in the same immense bag of Revels, that he'd become fully aware of the film's clammy sexual tension, and found himself idly wondering how comprehensively insured Josh was. In case, you know, he had an accident or something . . .

Afterwards, walking across the bridge, they talked about their favourite actors.

'Cary Grant, of course . . .' said Nora.

'And Jimmy Stewart.'

'Cary's better.'

'Burton, Olivier?'

'A little heavy for my taste. I haven't really seen that much.'

'How about Hepburn?'

'Not Audrey. Katharine's great, but Audrey's too skinny and sweet.'

'I admire Katharine, but I don't think I'd want to actually, you know, *go out* with her.'

'With Audrey you'd stand a chance.'

'But what would I tell Julie Christie?'

'I loved Jane Fonda. That's who I wanted to be. Jane Fonda in *Cat Ballou*, or *Walk on the Wild Side*. Jane Fonda in a lumber-jack shirt.'

'You know who I think my all-time favourite is?' said Stephen. 'John Cazale.'

'Don't know him.'

'Yes, you do – John Cazale. He played Fredo, the weak brother, in *The Godfather I* and *II*. That bit – "I know it was you, Fredo. You broke my heart." He was engaged to Meryl Streep and died of cancer, really young, forty or something, and he only ever made five films, that's all, just five, *all* of them nominated for Best Film, every film he was in, a Best Film, and he's brilliant in all of them. Even when he's not saying anything, even when he's in a scene with Pacino or De Niro or whoever, he's the only one you watch. When he dies in *Godfather II* you can't even see his face, and he's still heart-breaking.'

'Exactly like you as Ghostly Figure.'

'*Exactly* like that. Anyway, that's why you do it. Not to be famous, just to be *good*. To do good work. Find the thing you really love doing, and do it to the best of your ability.'

'And is there some kind of time limit on this? A deadline.'

'There would be if I could do something else.'

'That's bullshit, Steve – everyone can do something else.' Nora said this with perhaps a little too much venom, and they both walked in silence for a while.

Stephen, a little stung, spoke first. 'Actually, my agent just gave me some good news.'

'Oh, yeah?'

'I just got a new acting job.'

'That's great! A play?'

'A film. Just a low-budget, indie thing. I'm filming next week, actually.' In order to lend conviction to his story, he was thinking of *Sammy the Squirrel 2 – If You're Happy and You Know It*, and whilst this was perhaps stretching the definition of 'movie', at least it wasn't an out-and-out lie. He had decided that he was doing far too much lying these days. He really ought to try to stop lying.

'What's it called, this movie?'

'*Dark Obsession*. It's a sort of a crime-drama thing. I play this jaded, cynical, police-marksman-guy. Called Sammy. Nothing special, just the usual macho bullshit. It'll probably never even get a cinema release,' he said, confident that, in this instance at least, he had truth on his side.

They crossed the Strand and found a dark, deserted backstreet pub in Covent Garden, away from the main tourist traps, and squeezed in next to each other on a red velvet bench, drinking double gin and tonics.

'D'you mind me asking you something?'

'Go on?'

'You won't be offended?'

'I might be.'

'OK, well – wasn't it a little . . . mean of your parents?'

'What?'

'To call you . . . ?'

'Ah.'

'You see, you do mind.'

'No, no, it's fine. It wasn't meant maliciously, it was just my maternal grandfather was called Stephen, and he died shortly before I was born, so it was a sort of tribute. And I suppose it wouldn't have been such a problem if I'd gone into computers, like I was meant to. It wouldn't have seemed quite so . . .'

'Ironic.'

'Ironic.'

They were silent a moment.

'Steve McQueen was amazing,' said Nora.

'I always preferred Newman.'

'But you know who I really loved? Walter Matthau. Now *he* was sexy. And for years I had a weird thing about Dick Van Dyke too, but only ever as a chimney sweep. I had this recurring fantasy about him climbing into my room late at night, all sooty, leaning his, you know, chimney-sweeping equipment in the corner. And, God, Danny Kaye too. Me and Danny Kaye in a big apartment on the Upper East Side, hanging out, practising tongue-twisters. Talk about barking up the wrong tree.'

'And now here you are – married to a real-life film star,' said Stephen.

'I know. How the hell did *that* happen? Sometimes I wonder if I might have been better off with Danny Kaye.' She laughed, and glanced at Stephen, then leant forward and sipped her drink. There was a brief silence, the kind that invites a question.

'Everything OK?' asked Stephen.

'I suppose so,' sighed Nora, then sat back in her seat. 'I shouldn't complain. I mean he's a really sweet guy and incredibly generous and everything, even if he does call me "Nozza". He makes me laugh, and he supports this whole writing thing, and puts up with me when I'm in one of my moods. And the sex is still pretty sensational, of course.'

'Yes, you said.'

'Did I? Sorry. Still, he's definitely changed since he became, you know . . . the *f-word*.'

'In what way?'

'You sure you don't mind talking about this?'

'Not at all.'

'OK, well for one thing, he's suddenly become unbelievably vain. At home, I've had to cover the reflective surfaces, otherwise he'd never leave the apartment. Ever since he was named "Twelfth Sexiest Man in the World", it's been out of control.'

'That's what we call him at work – Number Twelve.'

'Who's "we"?'

Best not mention Maxine.

'Maxine and I.'

'Maxine?'

Hold your nerve, hold steady . . .

'The girl in the play.'

'The slutty one?'

'Well—'

'Number Twelve – he loves that! He pretends not to, but sometimes I think he's going to buy himself a rifle and a ski mask, track down the other eleven and Take. Them. Out. And he's started to buy these crazy kitsch clothes, you know the kind of thing – big collars, crazy colours, this dark blue velour suit. Velour beyond the call of duty, I call it. Then there's his black *leather* shirt, and these . . . these . . .' she swallowed hard, '. . . *suede* underpants,' and gave a little stage-shudder. 'Just think, Steve – cows *died*. I swear, sometimes we go out to a premiere or something, and I feel like this librarian who's somehow married a pimp. And – this one sends me *crazy* – if he sees someone wearing something he likes, he doesn't say "Where's that from?", he says "Who's that by?". "Who's that *by*?" – like it's some work of art or something. "Well, it's *by* Marks and Spencers, you dope." The other day I caught him trying to get something for *free* for this premiere. Can you imagine? He starts earning all this money and all of a sudden he thinks that entitles him to *free* clothes. What kind of crazy logic is that? Or crazy morality, come to that. Hey, you have to promise not to tell him I told you any of this.'

'Of course not.'

'And you don't think I'm being bitchy?'

'Well, yeah, a little, but I don't mind.'

'Alright then, what else?' She clapped her hands together. 'OK – he wears these annoying aviator sunglasses all the time, even around the apartment. God knows why – presumably so *I* won't hassle him for his autograph. Oh, and he won't go on public transport any more.'

'Which is fair enough, I suppose.'

'Except it's hard to feel too sorry for someone who's constantly *Googling* himself on the computer, *and* printing out the results. And he keeps logging on to his own websites too, sneaking into the chat-rooms, just to check out what the fans think – www.egomaniac.com. Oh, and he's almost constantly working out. Pretty much every time I see him he's dangling from a doorway in his suede underpants. Why he can't exercise with a few clothes on is beyond me. It's like I'm living with this buff orang-utan. No offence to your fellow professionals, Stephen, but you tell a guy that he's a gay icon before a certain age, and there's a very real possibility that he'll turn into a complete *ass*hole.'

They both smiled, picked up their drinks simultaneously, and Stephen found himself looking sideways at Nora's face, noting the lines that formed at the corner of her dark eyes when she laughed, and as he watched, the lines faded, her face straightened. 'I've never known a guy spend so much time texting, or reading texts, and his cellphone's always ringing late at night too. He won't talk in the same room as me, he just puts on this weird "professional" voice and skips out, and stands and whispers in the hall.'

'Well – that doesn't mean anything, I'm sure.'

'So who is he texting then?'

'Well, do you ask him?'

'I try not to. Or he says it's "the Coast".'

'Well, it probably is the Coast.'

'Yeah, well, you're probably right.' There was a pause, and

they sat and listened to the tinny jingle of the fruit machine. '"The *Coast*!" Can you believe that? It's like when he says "Stateside". I'm American, and even I don't call it "the Coast".'

'Maybe he means Margate,' said Stephen, hoping to lighten the mood.

'Where's Margate?'

'It's an English town. You know – on the coast.'

'Oh, right. Yeah, maybe.' Nora puffed sharply at the cigarette, wiped something invisible from her lip, thought for a moment, and then said it.

'Can I ask you something?'

'Of course'

'We're friends, aren't we? I mean, I know we haven't known each other too long, but I like to think we're sort of friends . . .'

'I think so.'

'And you'd tell me the truth? If I asked you something personal?'

'Absolutely.'

'So I can trust you?'

'You can trust me.'

'Is Josh having an affair?' asked Nora.

Of course, he could just tell her. She had a right to know, after all; Stephen didn't owe Josh anything.

Except for the deal, of course. It seemed unlikely that, if he said something now, Josh would still be inclined to go along with the deal.

'No-ho-ho,' said Stephen, shaking his head incredulously.

Nora narrowed her eyes. 'You're sure?'

'Absolutely.'

'And you'd tell me? If you knew something?'

'Nora, nothing's going on.'

'You promise?'

'I promise.'

'Thank you. I feel much, much better now.'

Like everyone, it seemed, Stephen was a firm believer in the benefits of detoxing.

He couldn't quite say what these toxins were, or where they'd come from, or what harm they did, but he firmly believed that there was a fixed quantity of these substances in his body, about a pint and half of the stuff maybe, white and cloudy, like sour milk. Or perhaps it was more solid, a pound and a half of buttery, oily stuff, the accumulated debris of ready-meals and bus exhausts, economy cheese and doubtful sausages. It was these toxins that were holding him back. The good news was that it was perfectly possible, if you drank oceanic quantities of water, and sweated it out again, and moved your bowels in new and extravagant ways, to get rid of them. With this in mind, and with the Big Break looming, three performances less than two weeks away, he calmly decided to turn his life around.

He stopped drinking, or at least stopped getting drunk alone. He cut down on cigarettes too, and took to drinking gallon upon gallon of liquidised fruit instead. He steamed the things he longed to fry, he ate pulses and pine-nuts and sunflower seeds and other items more usually found on bird tables. He girded his immune-system, gorging on slow-release vitamins and oily black echinacea, and any other random minerals and supplements he could find in the medicine cabinet, including some leftovers intended for pregnant women. High on life's possibilities and evening primrose oil, he ran every morning in Battersea Park until both sides ached and the breath rasped in the back of his throat, then doubled over and coughed until his ears rang. He felt terrible and fantastic at the same time.

Each night, in the quiet of his attic dressing room high above Shaftesbury Avenue, he turned the Tannoy down, ran his lines and practised his moves. The role of Lord Byron was physically and emotionally demanding and, more pressingly, also involved taking his top off for quite long periods. In order to rid his body of the slightly beanbag quality it had recently taken on, he performed endless sets of press-ups and sit-ups, chin-ups and crunches, until life started to resemble the montage training sequence from *Rocky*. Two weeks was probably not quite long enough to turn himself into a gay icon, but if he couldn't develop abs of steel, he could at least aspire to a soft metal alloy.

He also resolved to work on his charisma and animal magnetism. As an actor, Stephen C. McQueen possessed any number of qualities. He was certainly one of Britain's most punctual young actors. He was a deft mime and a competent sight-reader. He could, if a human life depended on it, jazz-dance, and at Elizabethan folk dance, few men could touch him. If, as he was frequently told, acting is really *re*acting, then he reacted like no other. Yet he was not entirely confident of his charismatic qualities, his ability to hold an audience through sheer personal magnetism, and to this end, he rather sheepishly agreed to take up Josh's offer of coaching. Instead of spending afternoons at the movies with Nora, he now came early into the theatre, strapped a sword to his belt, stood on stage and ran through scenes for Josh. If this felt like switching sides, he tried not to dwell on it.

'Mad, Bad and Dangerous to Know (*smile wryly*). That is what they call me in England now. Or so I am—'

'STOP,' shouted Josh, slumped in his seat in Row K, his legs draped over the chair in front. 'Go back to the beginning.'

'Mad, Bad and Dangerous to Know (*smile wryly*). That is—'

'No, go back again.'

'Mad, Bad—'

'Again!'

Stephen squinted out into the auditorium. 'Can I ask why?'

'Sorry, Steve, but I just don't believe it.'

'What don't you believe?'

'Any of it. I don't believe a word.' Josh took a swig from the obligatory small bottle of water, leant forward, and put his head on the seat in front. 'You're meant to be *Lord Byron*, Steve. You're meant to be a great lover, a rebel, a fighter. People thought Byron was the devil incarnate; convention, marriage, fidelity, all that crap meant nothing to him. He was motivated by love and passion and desire, not common sense. This is a guy that slept with his *sister*, for crying out loud . . .'

'His half-sister, technically.'

'Doesn't make it any easier, Steve.'

'So what exactly is it you're not getting?'

'I'm just not getting "mad, bad and dangerous", mate. I'm getting sensible, kind and careful, and who the fuck wants to see a play called *Sensible, Kind and Careful*?' Settling into his role as director, Josh stood now, and carried his bottle of water to the front of the auditorium, looking round fruitlessly for something to sit astride. 'Problem is, you're acting from here, Steve –' he tapped his forehead with his finger – 'from your *mind*, from your brain. You're thinking way too much. Even in Row K, I can see you thinking.' He placed his bottle of water on the edge of the stage. 'You know what you should really use instead?'

He wondered if Josh was going to suggest he use The Force.

'You know where you really should start acting *from*?'

Usually, the generic answer to this question was 'the diaphragm,' but Stephen had an awful idea what might be coming next . . .

'You should be acting from *here*.'

. . . and sure enough Josh suddenly grabbed between his own legs, taking care to use both hands. He directed the precious bundle of material at Stephen, cradling it as if it were an animal he was about to release back into the wild.

'Here, yeah?'

'Right, right, OK,' said Stephen, to a fixed point in the upper circle.

'Here, yeah Steve? Here. Here, yeah? Yeah?' insisted Josh, shaking it again, for emphasis.

'Yeah, yeah, I get it, Josh.'

'And *here* too,' and he took one hand away from his trousers, and thumped his own chest hard with his fist. 'Here, and *here* too.'

'Right. The heart, yeah?'

'Exactly. The heart. The cock and the heart. Make it your motto.'

'Right OK. The cock and the heart?'

'The cock and the heart.' With some apparent reluctance, Josh let go of his cock and his heart, and vaulted onto the edge of the stage. 'Look, close your eyes for me, will you?'

'Close my eyes?'

'Yeah, do it.' He squeezed the top of Stephen's arms tight. 'Close your eyes.'

Unsure as to whether he trusted Josh enough for a trust exercise, Stephen closed his eyes, and immediately opened them again.

Josh tutted. 'Look, I'll do it too,' he said.

They both closed their eyes.

'Now, think of someone you really want. I don't want to know who it is, but I want you to conjure up an image of this woman, her face, her body or whatever, someone you really fancy – no, more than just fancy, someone you *desire*, someone you *want*, the person you want and desire most in the whole world.'

Stephen did so.

'You got it?'

'Got it.'

'She's there?'

'She's there.'

They both stood for a moment, eyes closed, thinking hard about someone.

'OK, picture that face, think about it, then when you're ready, open your eyes and go from the top.'

Stephen did so.

'Better,' said Josh, after a while. 'Much, *much* better.'

The following Sunday was yet another seize-the-day day, the ninth in a row since Josh had made Stephen his offer. At this rate, there was a very real possibility that Stephen would seize-the-fortnight.

He decided that, as a special treat, he would take Sophie out for burgers in Soho. He was feeling flush from his catering mishap and the money that was coming his way for agreeing to do *Sammy the Squirrel 2*, so they ate at an up-scale American-style bistro, surrounded by smart, complete metropolitan families attempting the authentic brunch experience, the parents reading newspapers at the table whilst their smart, well-dressed children pushed food around their plates, bitterly regretting ordering the Eggs Benedict.

'What *is* Eggs Benedict?' asked Sophie.

'Don't call me Benedict!' replied Stephen, pretty wittily he thought, though Sophie's expression remained unchanged. 'It's this flabby poached egg in this kind of nasty, heavy yellow gloop. It's like brains on toast.'

'Can I have that then?'

'No! I just told you, Soph, it's disgusting. It sounds as if it'll be great but trust me, it's really horrible.'

'So what can I have then?'

'You can have absolutely anything you want from the menu, providing it doesn't contain too many vitamins and minerals, OK?'

'But what if I just want a salad?'

'You can't – it's the law. And no fruit juice either. And you're only allowed to have Coke if it's got a scoop of ice-cream in it.'

'That's dis*gus*ting.'

'How do you know if you haven't tried it? It's important to try the finer things in life.'

'Why are you encouraging me to make unhealthy choices?' she asked, frowning.

'I'm not, I'm just . . . I'm trying to *spoil* you, Sophs. It's good to be spoilt every now and then, and I'm sorry, but a bowl of steamed spinach isn't spoiling someone. Most kids love this stuff; they don't worry about the health implications.'

'So what are you having then?'

'I'm having salad.'

'*You're* allowed salad!'

'Because I'm trying to lose weight. I don't want to get all fat and pink like old Colin, do I?'

Sophie smiled behind her menu. 'I'll tell him you said that.'

'Go on then, tell him. I'm not scared of Colin.'

'You don't like Colin, do you?'

'What makes you say that?'

'I can just tell. You act as if you do, for my sake, but you don't.'

'I don't *dis*like him.'

'Yes you do.'

'I don't, Sophs, it's just, I just . . . it's complicated.' Stephen went back to looking at the menu.

'Well, I don't like him either,' said Sophie emphatically.

Stephen put his menu down again. 'Why don't you? Hey, he's nice to you, isn't he?'

'I suppose so.'

'So why don't you like him?'

'Because you don't.'

He leant across the table towards her. 'That's not a reason, Soph. You should like him, or try anyway. It doesn't matter what happened in the past – he's a good man, and he loves your mum, and, well, you should try and get on with him, OK?'

'OK.'

'You promise?'

'S'pose so.'

'Look, Sophs –' he frowned severely, and jutted out his lower lip as far as possible – 'I'm doing my stern face here.'

'Alright, I promise.'

'Good.' He squeezed her hand, and went back to the menu. 'Actually, that thing I said, about him being fat and pink, better not tell him. Just to be on the safe side. Promise?'

'Maaaaaybe.'

'What's French for maybe?'

'*Peut-être.*'

'Exactly. *Peut-être.* God, you're clever. And you can go crazy and have your spinach and rocket if you want, as long as you have dessert too. Pecan pie or something. Hey, you're not one of those wimpy kids who's allergic to nuts, are you?'

'I don't think so.'

'Good.'

'Suki Hodges in our class is allergic to nuts, and she ate one by accident and her head swelled up like a basketball.'

'Trust me. She's just pulling focus.'

'What's "pulling focus"?'

'You'll find out.'

'Why are you being like this?' Sophie asked, out of the blue.

'Like what?'

'Funny.'

'Funny-weird or funny-nice?'

'Funny-weird.'

'You see, I thought I was being funny-nice.'

'You are. Sort of.'

'Well, maybe it's because I'm pleased to be out with my very brilliant daughter. That's OK, isn't it?'

'S'pose so.'

The waitress arrived, and Stephen found himself flirting with her as he gave the order. The flirtation was quite subtle, he thought – just a soft, lopsided little smile, and a certain misty gaze, as if going ever-so-slightly crosseyed – but it was still enough for Sophie to roll her eyes and kick him under the table.

'Don't say anything, Sophs, but I can't help thinking our waitress is a little bit in love with me.'

'*Sooo* embarrassing,' said Sophie, in a sit-com intonation.

Then, having first extracted a solemn vow of secrecy from Sophie, he let her sip his beer, and smiled indulgently as she performed the obligatory pretending-to-be-drunk act. They talked about school, specifically recent developments in the gerbil situation. Their food arrived, the flirtation with the waitress continued, then Stephen listened patiently as Sophie told him, earnestly, and in great detail, all that she'd recently discovered about The Golden Age of the Tudors.

'And what about acting?' he asked.

'It's OK. I've joined the ASDS.'

'Who are the ASDS?'

Sophie shook her head at his ignorance. 'After School Drama Society.'

'I think I've heard of them. In fact, my agent put me up for that.'

'Stupid,' mumbled Sophie.

'Don't say "stupid", say "silly".'

'Silly then.'

'And what are you working on?'

'Oh, devised work, mainly,' said Sophie, very sombrely.

'I see – *devised* work,' said Stephen, nodding sagely. 'And do you like it? Acting, I mean.'

'I like it, but I wouldn't choose to do it professionally. Colin says it's alright when you're young, but it's not a proper job for a grown-up. He says it's undignified.'

'Quite right too.'

'So why d'you do it then?'

Stephen thought for a moment. 'D'you remember that Christmas, a couple of years ago, where you let me and Mum stick that realistic fake moustache and those big mutton-chop sideburns on you? There are photos of it, remember?'

'Ye-es,' she said, a worldy seven-year-old mortified by the childish antics of her four-year-old self.

'And you wore them all day, and made everyone laugh, even Nanny McQueen, who usually only ever laughs when people hurt themselves, and you wouldn't take them off, even when you went to bed?'

'That was just showing off.'

'Yes, but it was *good* showing off, Sophs. That is the most I have *ever* laughed in my whole life. *Ever*. I mean seriously, I thought I was going to *die* from laughing. And that was fun, wasn't it? Pretending, mucking about, making people happy – it felt good, didn't it?'

Sophie thought for a moment, her forehead wrinkled in concentration. 'I suppose so.'

'Well, that's what acting should be like. Good showing off. Now can I swap some of your chips for my salad?'

'OK then.'

At the end of lunch, Sophie belched and Stephen felt a little swell of pride.

Afterwards, feeling pleasantly nauseous and woozy, they strolled towards the National Gallery. This felt like a suitably educational-but-fun, father-daughter activity on a beautiful winter Sunday afternoon, and Stephen improvised a route through the Soho shops that didn't involve passing too much pornography. There was, however, no way of avoiding Shaftesbury Avenue, the Hyperion Theatre, and the giant billboard of Josh Harper.

Stephen felt a little wary of this at first, then remembered that, thanks to contractual stipulations, his own name would actually be in print on the posters outside the theatre. Perhaps it might be fun to show his daughter her father's name in print on a West End theatre: actual, irrefutable documentary evidence that his professional career wasn't just something he had made up. Perhaps she might actually start to feel proud of him, rather than anxious or confused, a little taste of things to come before his big break on the eighteenth. They paused for a moment in front of the huge black-and-white photographs of Josh that wallpapered the outside of the building.

'JOSH HARPER BESTRIDES THE STAGE LIKE A MIGHTY COLOSSUS . . .'

'This is simply acting at its very finest.
Harper is clearly the natural heir to Olivier
and Burton. Catch this extraordinary
talent while you still can . . .'

'*Harper* owns *the stage, prowling it like
a tremendous, lithe young panther.
Make no mistake, ladies, Mr Harper really
is sex-on-legs . . .*'

JOSH HARPER

STARS IN

"*Mad, Bad and Dangerous to Know. . .*"

WRITTEN AND DIRECTED BY Terence Blackheath
AND INTRODUCING Maxine Cole

WITH

Stephen C. McQueen

The poster suddenly seemed to Stephen like a vindictive optician's chart.

'Hm. And what's the play about?' asked Sophie, in her best classroom voice.

'It's about this man called Byron, who was a famous poet, and a lord, and who had lots of adventures, and was very popular with the ladies, just like me with that waitress back there. Look – there's my name . . .' he said, crouching down and pointing at the floor. 'If anything bad happens to *this* guy –' he straightened, pointed at a photo of Josh, his finger in the centre of his forehead – 'if he's sick or a piano falls on him or anything, then I get to take his place.'

'Why are you called Stephen C. McQueen?'

'It's so people don't confuse me with the legendary American movie star.'

'Does that happen?'

'No. No, it doesn't, Sophie.'

'So why aren't you in any of these photos?'

'I am – that's me, there.'

'Where?'

'At the back . . .'

'*Where?*'

'There!'

'Why's it so smoky?'

'It's dry ice. It's to make me seem mysterious.'

'Is that why you can't see your face?'

'Exactly. It's to make me look ghostly, give me an air of intrigue and mystery. You know – spooky, like the grim-reaper, leading Byron on to his death . . .'

'So he is your friend then?' she asked, pointing at a large black-and-white photo of Josh, perspiring prettily in high-contrast close-up.

'Uh-huh. I mean not a really good friend, not a *best* friend or anything, but we go out for a drink and stuff.' Oh, and I'm in love with his wife, he thought, but said, 'And I know his wife quite well – she's really nice. And he invited me to his birthday party, so . . .'

'He's quite attractive, isn't he?'

'Attractive?'

Sophie looked thoughtful. 'You know – handsome.'

'Oh God. *Et tu, Sophie*.'

'Is that French?'

'Sort of.'

'So can I come and see him? And meet him afterwards?'

'Well, it's a bit old for you, and a bit boring, to be honest. But if, in a couple of weeks or so, December the eighteenth or thereabouts, if something happens to Josh, if he gets, I don't know, gastric flu or food poisoning or something, then you might get a phone call out of the blue, and you and your mum might have to rush to the theatre, and watch *me* play the main part instead. Wouldn't that be exciting?'

Sophie seemed a little unsure about the prospect. 'I suppose so. But could I get his autograph, d'you think?'

For the first time, Stephen felt the day lurch out of his control.

'What d'you want his autograph for?'

'I told the girls at school you were his best friend, and they said I was a liar, so I need proof.'

Don't argue. Just keep moving, thought Stephen.

'I'm sure an autograph can be arranged.'

They crossed Shaftesbury Avenue, through Chinatown, where they gawped at strange, red alien meats hanging in the steamy windows, and Stephen pointed out the clatter of the mah jong tiles in upstairs rooms. Then they hurried across Leicester Square, before the sound of panpipes and the sight of silver-painted living statues could make Stephen feel too depressed, to the National Gallery.

Certain environments – parks in autumn, deserted beaches at sunset, skating rinks, anywhere with snow, all of them inevitably tend to inspire kooky, free-spirited movie behaviour. Galleries in particular are prone to this kind of stuff, and that afternoon with Sophie, Stephen allowed himself to succumb. There was a great deal of arm swinging whilst holding hands, a lot of jokey comments about the paintings, speculation about who was saying what to whom, a lot of giggling. It wasn't so much an activity as a sequence, but Stephen felt funny and happy and pleasant to be with, and realised that, for the first time in a very long while, he and Sophie were actually having fun.

Once it had got dark, they walked across the Thames to Waterloo Station arm in arm, and joined the day-trippers and pre-Christmas Sunday shoppers on the train home to Barnes, Sophie falling instantly asleep in the crook of his arm. As the train crawled past the shell of Battersea Power Station, his mobile rang, and with his left hand he carefully extricated it from his coat without waking her. He saw Nora's name on the phone's display and smiled.

'Hello, stranger!' said Nora.

'Hi, there.'

'I was starting to wonder if you've been avoiding me.'

'Of course not,' Stephen whispered.

'Hey – have I called at a bad time?' said Nora.

'No, this is fine . . .'

'It's just every time I call, you seem to be getting in or out of a pair of pantyhose.'

'Never on the Sabbath. I'm on the train, with Sophie.'

'You're on a date?'

'Sophie, my daughter.'

'Sophie, of course.'

'She's asleep.'

'OK, well, I'll be quick. It's just I've been looking through my diary and I find that I have absolutely nothing in my life to look forward to, so I wondered if you felt like going to the movies sometime? Or coming round here, after a show? Josh has just bought this new wide-screen TV for the bedroom. It's so he can watch all his own movies, naked *and* lying down. Why don't you come round and see it – the TV that is, not Josh naked – we don't have to watch a Josh Harper movie, of course, and it would give my life some purpose.' She lowered her voice a little. 'I haven't seen you for a while, and I've sort of missed you.'

Had she?

'Yeah, you too,' whispered Stephen.

'So – what are we going to do about it?'

He could pretend to be busy, of course. After all, where was the pleasure in sitting around, acting as platonic confidant, listening to her talk on and on about him, when all he really wanted to do was lean across and kiss her? Hadn't he been trying to give that up? Clearly there was only misery and frustration to be had there. He pictured her face.

'I'd love to see you,' whispered Stephen.

'OK, well –' she hesitated for a moment, as if she had something more to say '– well, let's talk tomorrow?'

'Tomorrow.'

'OK, tomorrow.'

'Tomorrow, then'

'OK, bye.' He hung up the phone, and looked out of the window at the Wandsworth terraces, and caught his reflection in the mirror, smiling.

'Who was that?' asked Sophie, without opening her eyes.

'I thought you were asleep.'

'I was pretending. Who was that?'

'None of your beeswax.'

'Don't say beeswax, it's stupid.'

'None of your business, then. And don't say "stupid", say "silly".'

'*Silly*, then.' Sophie shifted to look up at him, her eyes half open. 'Was it a *girl*?'

'It might have been.'

'I think it was your *girl*friend,' she said, with a playground snigger.

'Why would it be my girlfriend?'

'Because you were talking like this . . .' and she bunched her mouth up into a tight little moue, rolled her eyes up in her head, and in a high, lilting voice cooed, '"Hellooooo there, *lov*ely to talk to you, I'd *loooove* to seeeee you, mmmmoi!"'

Stephen laughed. 'I did *not* talk like that, and it's none of your business, and anyway, Nelly, it was a *private* conversation.' Sophie settled once again into the crook of his arm, closing her eyes. 'Just out of interest, what if she was my girlfriend?' he asked, brushing her fringe across her forehead. 'You wouldn't mind, would you?'

'I suppose not. As long as she's really nice,' murmured Sophie, and yawned a stage-yawn, signalling the conversation was at an end.

She is, he thought. That's the whole problem.

'Is it safe?' whispered Stephen.

'Yes, it's safe,' replied Alison. 'Come in.'

Colin was out at a rugby-team reunion when they arrived back, and wasn't expected home till late. Stephen said good-night to Sophie, gratified by the hug he received, and pleased that Alison had seen it, then waited in one of the three reception rooms while Alison put her to bed.

He poured wine into a heavy crystal goblet that felt like a prop, perched on the edge of a low-slung sofa and immediately slid down into its depths. It stank of expensive leather. He looked around the immaculate room, and wondered at how far Alison had come from the basement flat in Camberwell where the three of them had lived less than three years ago, hemmed in by mismatched MDF furniture, empty wine bottles, posters in cheap clip-frames, ashtrays and burnt-out night-lights. Now, squeaking and sliding on the meaty brown sofa he felt shifty and illicit, as if he'd accidentally been locked overnight in Heal's furniture department. Retro-jazz burbled inoffensively from overdesigned hi-fidelity speakers, the kind of innocuous easy-listening anti-music Alison would have snarled at when they first met, and he knew immediately, with absolute certainty, that somewhere in the house there would be at least one, possibly two, copies of *Buena Vista Social Club*. Clearly she'd discovered a talent for interior design too: every object in the room – the heavy wineglasses, the modernist candlesticks, the dark-wood photo-frames, the up-lighters and down-lighters, the paperweights untroubled by paper – everything felt as if it had come from a particularly ambitious and cohesive wedding list.

On a low lacquered black and Chinese-red coffee-table at Stephen's side, in amongst the scented candles and the chronological back copies of *Vogue* and *The Economist* and *World of Interiors*, stood a wedding photo in a silver photo-frame – one of those artfully informal wedding snaps that attempt to convey what a very, very special day it had really, really been – a whole gang of well-groomed prematurely wealthy young people crammed, whooping, into the frame. He peered closely at Colin, noting the wedding-morning razor burn, the way the meaty head bulged over his ridiculous winged collar, as if being slowly garrotted by his own pink silk bow-tie, and for some reason, Stephen thought of his childhood space-hopper. An equally ruddy banker, wearing little sunglasses and a humorous kilt, presumably the nominal Best Man, gurned over his shoulder, whilst Alison, in a low-cut silver-grey dress was smiling with what Stephen imagined, hoped, was a satirical glint in her eye. In the foreground, Sophie peered through her fringe at the camera, the bouquet clutched in front of her face, as if hiding from these people. Clearly a very, very special day. It had been a notable day for Stephen too, the first time in his life he'd managed to get through a whole bottle of vodka by himself, along with eighty cigarettes and an emotionally disorientating quadruple bill of *A Room with a View*, *Moonraker*, *Deliverance* and *The Texas Chainsaw Massacre* on the DVD projector. No photographs were taken of that particular day. In fact, it suddenly occurred to Stephen that he hadn't taken a single photograph of anything for the last three years. When he'd been with Alison, they'd seemed to take pictures of the most innocuous things – of Sophie asleep on the sofa, or Alison reading; he still had the photographs. These days, he wasn't even sure where he kept the camera.

He tried not to read too much into this. Absently, he necked his glass of wine in one go, then peered closely at the photo of his ex-wife, looking beautiful and only slightly hard. She really was an amazing woman. How the hell had he managed to foul *that* up?

'Put the light *out*, Sophie. I mean it,' shouted Alison from the hallway. Stephen hurriedly put the photo back, and grabbed a magazine as an alibi as Alison entered the room, smiling, about to speak . . .

'*World of Interiors*! I can't believe you subscribe to this aspirational, bourgeois rubbish.' Stephen could hear his own voice in his head; how unappealing and hectoring it sounded, that absurd, pompous use of the word 'bourgeois'. But the stupid wedding photo, and the awful fact of Alison's presence in it, and how lovely she looked, had all combined to make him sulky and petulant and, yes, envious. 'What is this appeal in drooling over pictures of other people's houses?'

'God, you know, you're *so* right, Steve, and I wouldn't look at it usually, it's just there's a big article in there about bedsits this month, so . . .'

They both glanced at each other, then looked away. Alison pushed her hair back off her face, sighed and frowned, and on the Scandinavian hi-fi speakers, someone way too young started to croon their way through. 'I've Got You Under My Skin'.

'Actually, technically it's not a bedsit, it's a studio.'

'Sorry – studio.' She sighed, looked up at the ceiling, scratched her head. 'It's nice, isn't it? Just being able to meet up and chat away like this?'

'Start again then?'

'Yeah. OK. Let's start again.' She poured herself a glass of wine, returned the wedding photo to its usual place, and patted Stephen affectionately on the knee, managing, once again, to give the impression that she knew absolutely everything. Then she sank into the sofa next to him. 'I was *about* to say Sophie said she had a nice time today.'

'You sound surprised.'

'I'm not surprised. She always has a nice time with you, she loves seeing you, you know that. Just some times she has more fun than others, that's all.'

'Yeah, it was fun.'

'She said you might have a *girl*friend too,' she said, nudging him, that familiar little jeer in her voice.

'Don't start.'

'What?!'

'Talking to me like I'm a twelve-year-old. It sounds like you're going to tell me how babies are made.'

'Well, I'm curious – go on, spill the beans . . .'

'Maybe,' said Stephen, aware of the almost criminal inaccuracy of the impression he was giving. 'There's sort of someone, but there are . . . complications.'

'Not *another* hermaphrodite?'

'As good as. She's married.'

'Really? You dark horse! Who's she married to?'

The 12th Sexiest Man in the World, he thought, but things were still a little too raw for his ex-wife to play the role of best friend and confidante, so instead he said 'Oh – no one you know.'

'Well, you don't want to let a little thing like a marriage get in your way.'

It was too obvious an opportunity to miss. 'After all, you didn't, did you?'

They looked at each other for some time.

'Walked right into that one, didn't I?'

'Uh-huh.'

She nudged his foot with her own, bumped her shoulder matily against his.

'Change the subject?'

'Alright. Let's change the subject.'

Alison put her hand on his knee, and used it as leverage to slide off the leather sofa. 'Stay there, I'll go and get some more wine.'

Within half an hour, they were fairly drunk. For the first time since the divorce, something of the old ease and affection had returned, and they both recognised this, and sought to sustain it by drinking more.

'Any news about Johnny Johnson?'

'Who's Johnny Johnson?'

'You know, your title role, your transatlantic romantic comedy?'

'Oh, the *movie*? No, no news.'

'But you're still heavy-pencilled?'

'I'm still heavy-pencilled.'

'And the *theatre*?'

'D'you have to say it like that?'

'Like what?'

'"The *theatre*."'

'Sorry. How is it, though, you old *gypsy*, you?' She reached across to ruffle his hair, and he caught her hand and held it.

''S alright. Hey, if I were ever to get a chance to go on, you'd come and see me, wouldn't you?'

''Course I would.'

'Even if it was at short notice, even if you had to drop everything at the last minute?'

''Course I'd come. But it's not very likely, is it?'

Yes, it is, it's definite, he wanted to say – December the eighteenth. 'Still, got to hold on to your dreams, haven't you?'

'Dreams.' She nudged him with her foot. ''Ark at you, Judy Garland.'

'Ambitions, then.'

'Yeah, well, it's fine having dreams, as long as they're not unrealistic.'

'Yeah, but then what's the point of realistic dreams?'

'Wise words, Steve,' she murmured. 'Not sure what they mean, but still, wise words. Hey, you haven't got a fag, have you?'

'I thought you'd stopped.'

'I have.'

'Well, is it really a good idea . . . ?'

'Come on, give us one, before Gruppenführer Colin comes back.'

Stephen reached into his pocket, and laughed as she snatched the packet out of his hand. There was a certain guilty, furtive, vaguely sexual pleasure in the ritual of lighting his ex-wife's cigarette for her, watching as she drew the smoke into her mouth with her eyes closed tight, then gave a low, dirty laugh of delight as she fell back onto the sofa, let the smoke curl slowly out of her mouth and up into the air. Smoking was a filthy, disgusting habit, of course, in no way cool or glamorous or sexy, as all those movies seemed to suggest. If, and when, he caught his daughter smoking, he had a long, harsh preprepared speech ready about bad breath and addiction and cancer, but still, there was no denying that it was appealing in a way that, say, eating a stick of celery never would be. There's a beautiful piece of acting in *In the Mood for Love* where Maggie Cheung's character conjures up the memory of her lost lover by lighting one of his cigarettes, and whilst Stephen found it hard to feel that strongly about a pack of twenty Marlboro, he was undoubtedly susceptible to the imagery. In movies there are no overflowing ashtrays, no yellow-tipped fingers or woollen tongues. And Alison was definitely one of life's great smokers, like Lauren Bacall say, or Rita Hayworth or Anne Bancroft. The only other woman who had this talent for making every cigarette seem post-coital was Nora Harper.

The two of them started to get a little muddled in his mind. He realised that he liked, or loved, the same things in both of them: the wryness and irreverence, the occasional ferocity, the casual elegance, the fact that they were both smarter and harder and sharper than he was. He loved spending time with them, despite the inevitable frustration involved, and he loved hearing them laugh, loved the sense that their laughter was hard-earned. He found both of them almost unbearably desirable. He also realised that, quite coincidentally, they were both entirely unavailable.

Alison reached for her wineglass, lay back on the sofa, her feet nestling disconcertingly near Stephen's groin, and he noticed that she was wearing something very un-Alison, something that he thought might be defined as pop-socks. Was she flirting? She was definitely flirting. Stephen began to feel almost a little Byronic.

'D'you remember that last job I had?' she said. 'In that stupid bloody film.'

'Sexy Air Hostess.'

'Not even Sexy Air Hostess One; Sexy Air Hostess Number *Four*. One line of dialogue – "Complimentary *nuts*, sir?" – and three days spent freezing my arse off in that stupid costume, blouse undone to there, and my tits hanging out, in a warehouse in Borehamwood, saying it over and over again – "Complimentary *nuts*, sir, complimentary *nuts*, sir" – while some drooling cameraman stuck his lens up my little skirt. And we'd just found out I was pregnant with Sophie, and I thought, right, that's it, bollocks to this, I've had enough. I mean I used to love it, when I was younger, when you and me first got together. But I thought it would be . . . different, you know? I thought it would be worthwhile in some way, and would make people's lives better, and I'd meet all these brilliant, creative people, be part of a community, and play fantastic parts, and do great, hard-hitting, political TV plays that millions of people would watch and talk about, and be entertained, and inspired, and moved by. And *changed* by. And then all of a sudden, you're doing it, actually getting paid for it, that thing you've always dreamed of, and it's *nothing* like that, nothing at all. No fun, no satisfaction, no control. It's like this completely different job – saying "complimentary *nuts*, sir?" all day, with my boobs hanging out. I felt like I'd been conned – years of hassle and waste and envy and anxiety, for *this*? Just to play bimbo air hostesses and murdered prostitutes and strippers. And that's why giving up was so easy. 'Cause most of the time, the job was about being made to look like a fucking idiot,' and she took a long swig of her wine, before adding accusingly, 'by *men*, mainly.'

'You were a very sexy air-hostess, though,' said Stephen, now feeling fuzzy-headed and flirty.

'Aw, gee . . .' she murmured, and exhaled a long plume of smoke. 'A dream fulfilled.'

'No, it's true.'

'Yeah, well, *Colin* obviously appreciates it,' she sniggered through her nose, hiding her face in her glass.

'What d'you mean?'

She gave him a sideways look, and a grin. 'Well . . . we've got a copy on video, yeah? And when I'm out, he has a sneaky watch.'

'You're joking.'

'It's true. I can tell, 'cause he keeps putting it back in a different place, the silly sod. Unless he's got a thing about Sexy Air Hostess One, of course.'

'Well, that's flattering, isn't it?'

'I did film it, what, eight years ago. I'd rather he showed a little more interest in the contemporary model, to be honest.'

'Well, I *still* think you're amazing.'

'Don't flirt with your ex-wife, Steve. It's not on.'

'So I'm wasting my time?'

'Absolutely. I love you loads, Steve, you know that,' she said, and Stephen noted once again how the addition of the word 'loads', like 'lots' and 'tons', rendered the three words that preceded it entirely innocuous. 'And if things had worked out differently . . .' She arched her back on the sofa, took a drag of the cigarette and stretched her arms up above her head. 'But,

well, I'm with Colin now and I do love him. God knows why
– he's a pompous old bastard sometimes.'

'Can I ask you something?' said Stephen, pouring more wine.

She peered down at him, along the length of her body, and
narrowed her eyes. 'Go on.'

'You promise not to get angry?'

'Nope.'

'OK.' Deep breath. 'What the hell do you see in him?'

'Colin?' Alison laughed a little drily, screwed up her face,
then sat up suddenly, and locked her arms around her knees.
'I tell you what it is. It's like cars.'

'Cars.'

'Cars. When you're young, you want something wacky and
fun, a yellow 2CV, or a crappy old mini or something, and you
don't mind if it breaks down, or if people laugh at you, because
you still can't believe that you're *allowed* to drive. You'll drive
*any*thing. Then you get a bit older and maybe you want something a bit flasher, not expensive necessarily, but a bit zippy and
cool and dangerous, something that everybody else wants. And
then I suppose, with me, I just got to the age where what I
really wanted was just a big, heavy, expensive old BMW.
Something that makes you feel . . . safe.'

'And that's Colin? Colin's the Beamer.'

'Colin's the Beamer.'

'Well, he's certainly roomy.'

'See – I sound shallow now, don't I?'

'Uh-huh. So, what was I then? The yellow 2CV?'

'God, no. You were my VW Golf.'

'One point eight?'

'One point six diesel engine.'

'Economical . . .'

'Navy blue, but with leather interiors. And one of those natty
little sun-roofs.'

'I don't know whether to be pleased or appalled.'

'Be pleased. Lovely little car, that. Lot of women would kill for a little blue VW.'

'You think so?'

'And I'm speaking here as the one previous careful lady-owner.' There was a small silence while they sat and looked at each other, then, out of the blue, she leant further forward and took his hand.

'I don't think we see enough of you.'

'Who?'

'Me and Sophie. I mean, I'm not suggesting we all go on some family caravaning holiday or anything, but we'd like to see you more. We miss you. Especially Sophs. You know, if you wanted her to stay over, or to go away somewhere . . .'

'And what's bought this on?'

'Nothing. Just you seem . . . better.'

'Better?'

'Not so sad.'

'Well, you know – I did go a bit nuts back then.'

'I know you did, and that was my fault, and I'm sorry. But you *are* better, yeah?'

Stephen felt his head get hot. 'Getting there.'

'And has that got anything to do with this mystery married woman?'

'Don't know. Maybe.'

'You think something might happen?'

'Not sure.'

'But you're heavy-pencilled?'

'Not heavy. Medium-pencilled.'

'A 2B.'

Stephen's pun-reflex kicked in. '2B or—'

'Stop!' said Alison, grabbing his arm in an unspoken '. . . or I'll kill you.'

Stephen closed his eyes tight. 'Fight it, fight it, fight it . . .'

'I do love you, you know,' said Alison, and Stephen opened

221

his eyes. 'Not like I used to, not in the same way, I mean, but I really do.'

'Yeah, well – you too.'

'Well – that's nice to know,' and, with half a smile, 'I'll bear it in mind.'

'Do,' said Stephen, and they heard the sound of a key in the lock. 'It's the Beamer.'

'Right on bloody cue,' murmured Alison, stubbing out the cigarette.

'Ali? Is someone smoking?' shouted Colin from the hallway.

'In fact, I think you're still absolutely amazing . . .'

'Pack that in now,' whispered Alison, removing her feet from Stephen's lap.

'Do we have to?'

'I can smell smo-oke,' shouted Colin.

'Yes, we do,' hissed Alison, curling her legs up beneath, brushing the ash from her lap. Red-faced and maybe a little drunk too, Colin loomed in the doorway, like a strict but fair head-boy.

'Hi there!' said Alison and Stephen simultaneously.

'Oh – hello there, Steve. Where's Sophie?' said Colin, somehow contriving to make it sound like 'what have you done with Sophie?'.

'She's upstairs, smoking,' said Alison. 'Stephen bought her her first pack of fags. He's been teaching her, haven't you, Stephen?'

'Uh-huh.' But all the fun and flirtatiousness had gone, and Stephen was now trying to work out the quickest way to leave the house.

'Right. I see,' said Colin, with his space-hopper grin, as he crossed over and picked up the second empty bottle of wine by the open neck, as if it were forensic evidence 'Goodness! Are you both *pissed*?'

'Just a little, my love,' Alison said affectionately, taking

Colin's hand by the fingertips, shaking out his arm. 'Just a little.'

'Well, that's fine, just so long as you remember it's a Sunday night, and it's a school-day tomorrow.'

'I know what day of the bloody week it is, Colin,' snarled Alison, throwing his arm away from her. 'And I'm thirty-one years old, I don't have *school*-days.'

And shortly afterwards, Stephen left to get the bus home.

He got back late that night, woozy, elated and flirtatious, and resisted the temptation to pour himself one last drink, partly because of the calories in a glass of wine, and partly because, there's ultimately very little satisfaction to be had in flirting with yourself. He had an intense desire to talk to Nora. Maybe he should call Nora. Maybe not.

Instead, he sat at the small desk that overlooked the back yard of Idaho Fried Chicken. In a pile of postcards on his desk was a first-night card from Josh Harper, written way back in July. He'd meant to throw the thing away, but had been prevented by a shabby notion that it might one day be used to impress someone. If Josh's career went according to plan, it might even be worth something.

Scrawled on the back of the postcard, in fat, loopy blue biro, it read:

> *To Stephen – thanks for the support, mate. Hope you get your Big Break soon, and get to show* me *how it's done. Break a leg. Or break MY leg! Ha Ha!!! Loads of love, your mate, Josh Harper!*

He leant the card upright on the desk in front of him, then took a pen, and on the back of an old phone bill, practised Josh's signature ten times, squinting in the light, like the Donald Pleasence character in *The Great Escape*. It wasn't bad – not exactly a perfect forgery, but it would do for his purposes. He took a copy of the theatre programme from the small pile he kept in his desk drawer, and opened it to the full-page, black-and-white photo of Josh near the front, all cheekbones and perspiration, slightly parted lips and blazing eyes. He took one last look at Josh's signature on the postcard then, speaking the words in Josh's voice, and with as much of a flourish as he could manage he wrote –

> *To the lovely Miss Sophie McQueen,*
> *Big love and kisses*
> *Josh Harper XXX*

He compared Josh's handwriting with the original. Not too bad. On the front cover of the programme, with a different pen, in his own handwriting, he wrote,

> *Hello there, princess! It was great to see you on*
> *Sunday. It's always great to see you, of course,*
> *but it was particularly great. Didn't you think so?*
> *I thought so. Anyway, look at page 4! A*
> *FAMOUS ACTOR'S AUTOGRAPH! Hope this*
> *does the job at school. And remember, I love you*
> *very, very, VERY much.*
> *Dad.*

Then he put the programme into an envelope, wrote Sophie's name and address in a slurred hand, and put it by the door, to send later in the week. Then he turned on the DVD projector, put on one of his favourite movies, *Sweet Smell of Success*, turned off the light, and watched as the bare wall opposite shuddered into life in black and white, and soon fell asleep in the flickering light.

THE BIG WHITE BED

Stephen and Nora lay together on a bed as wide and white as cinema screen. It was one in the morning, and Nora was wiping the tears from her eye with the back of her hand.

On the wide-screen television at the end of the bed, the credits were rolling on *The Philadelphia Story*. It had been Nora's suggestion, and Stephen had gone along with it, without quite remembering how woozily romantic the film was. Watching it late at night on Josh's huge immense television, in Josh's bedroom, felt unbearably suggestive. He wasn't aware of the existence of a film called *Stephen Is In Love with Nora*, but perhaps only that would have been more pertinent. The long, drunken wooing scene between Jimmy Stewart and Katharine Hepburn seemed particularly eloquent and apt. He wondered if Nora had felt the same thing too, but judging by the vast quantities of hummus and pitta bread that she was eating, the emotion that she mainly felt was peckish.

'Now *that* is an amazing film,' said Nora, twisting round and crawling the considerable distance down to the far end of the bed to turn the DVD player off. 'Anyone who prefers *High Society* to *The Philadelphia Story* is *insane*,' she said, leaning over the edge of the bed for the second bottle of wine. 'Excuse me for sticking my fat behind in your face.' She was wearing an oversized white dressing gown of the kind more usually found in upmarket hotels, and the whole bedroom had that modern hotel-room atmosphere, albeit a room that had been fitted out with a set of dumbbells, a pogo stick and a scale-model of the *Millennium Falcon*. Josh had had friends in to see the show,

225

and had promised to join them as soon as he could, but the film was over now, and it was assumed that he had probably ended up in some private club. From the chest of drawers, Josh's original Storm Trooper helmet glared at Stephen accusingly. The old helmet-stand, the BAFTA, still lay at the back of Stephen's wardrobe, wrapped in a blanket.

'You know what I *really* hate?' said Nora, clambering back up the bed to Stephen.

'Go on.'

'Special effects. What's special about special effects? Even when they're amazing, it's like watching a big, dumb cartoon. It's just embarrassing, sitting in a cinema with all these supposed adults, all leaping up and down watching a kid's movie. Whatever happened to movies with *people* in? Human beings.' She lay on her side, facing him now, her head resting on her hand. 'It's like these auditions Josh keeps going for, where they want him to be a killer cyborg, or the cop-of-the-future, or half-man half-terrapin. What's the point? He's throwing his talent away – after all, it's not like anyone's going to be watching him *act*.'

'D'you tell him this?'

'Yeah, but he just says that I don't understand the grand world-conquering master-plan that is his career. Besides, Josh *loves* all that comic-book stuff. He pretends he doesn't, but he does. I've seen him weep, actually *weep* like a baby, when Han Solo gets carbon-frozen in *Empire Strikes Back*.'

'Well, it's a very powerful moment.'

'Yeah, for an eleven-year-old maybe. Actually, I think the idea quite appeals to Josh. He doesn't want to be buried or cremated, he wants to be carbon-frozen. Has he told you the latest, by the way?' She took a sip of the red wine, and Stephen braced himself once more for someone else's good news. 'They want him to be the new Superman.'

'Well, it was bound to happen eventually. Superman, James Bond or Jesus.'

'Except he'd only agree to play Jesus if he could be armed.'

'He shoots first, forgives later.'

Nora slipped into her passable Josh impersonation, 'The thing is, I just think the character could be a bit more pro-active, 's all . . .' then laughed, and pulled herself upright against the pillows. 'I'm amazed he hasn't told you about Superman. It's meant to be top secret, of course, but he's telling just about everyone he knows. People he brushes up against. Apparently, if the studio can get their heads around casting a cock-er-ney Superman, the part's his. God knows what *that*'ll do to his ego; he already thinks he can leap build-ings in a single bound. I caught him in the bathroom the other day with his hair waxed into a little kiss-curl, doing this –' she pulled a determined frown, and put her clenched fist at arm's length in front of her – 'in the mirror. I asked him what he was doing. He said he was *stretching*.' They both laughed. 'Don't know where I can get my hands on some kryptonite, do you?'

In a manner of speaking, Stephen was in possession of kryp-tonite himself, but nothing he could actually tell her about it. It wouldn't have been fair; after all, Josh had promised he'd change.

'Serves me right, I suppose,' she continued.

'What for?'

'For marrying a man who collects toys and calls me Nozza.'

He pulled himself upright, leant against the pillows next to Nora.

'How is it going?' he asked, unsure of what he wanted the answer to be.

'With Josh? OK. Fine. Why d'you ask?'

'I just wondered if there was any change.'

'Why should there be any change?'

'I just thought maybe . . .'

'I don't know, Steve.' Nora sighed, and flipped on her side

to face him. 'Sometimes I get the feeling he wishes he'd married someone a bit more red-carpet-friendly, that's all.'

'That's ridiculous.'

'It's true.'

'What makes you think that?'

'Just the way he ... reads magazines, or looks around a party, like he's choosing from a menu – "Shall I have that? Or that? Or I could have that ...". Not just women either, men too; he's a collector. He turns his attention on you, and that's it. He's got so much happening in his life, and I've got so little happening in mine ...'

'At the moment.'

'At the moment, and I wouldn't be surprised if he was, you know, disappointed.'

'With what?'

Nora shrugged. 'With me, sometimes.'

'How could anyone ever be disappointed with you?' He had said it without thinking first, and Nora glanced at him sideways, and frowned.

'Don't be sappy, Stephen.'

'No, I mean it.'

She turned once more to look at him, with a slightly stern smile. 'Are you flirting with me, Mr McQueen?'

'Don't be ridiculous,' he mumbled.

She pouted jokily, her chin on her chest. 'I'd like to think it maybe wasn't quite *so* ridiculous.' She looked at him without moving her head, just out of the corner of her eye, frowning slightly, the ghost of a smile on her lips. And here it was, a chance to be reckless, to say something impetuous, provocative, to be the protagonist, not the understudy; make a move, say what you feel, like Jimmy Stewart in *The Philadelphia Story*. Even if she turned him down, or slapped him, at least it would be some kind of action, some kind of change or forward movement. Remember Josh's motto? He put his glass down carefully on the hard flat mattress, put his hands behind him, and hoisted himself further up the bed so that his face was level with Nora.

'Oh, Stephen . . .' she sighed.

'Nora . . .'

'I think you may have just sat in my hummus.'

Stephen lifted his left buttock to remove the plate of hummus, and in doing so deftly kicked over the glass of wine.

'Oh, Jesus . . .'

'It's OK.'

'I don't believe it, I'm so clumsy.'

'Really, it's fine. I just need to get these sheets off before it soaks . . .'

'Here, let me help.'

'Please, Stephen,' said Nora, with just a trace of irritation, 'I can do it.'

Shortly afterwards he stood in silence in the utility room, waiting for his cab to arrive. The last time he'd been in this particular room it was to fill the dishwasher with dirty glasses, and he couldn't help feeling that he was already a little more familiar with Josh Harper's white goods than he wanted. Yet here he was again, watching as Nora knelt and pushed the bedding into the washing machine.

'So sorry about that.'

''S OK, these things happen.'

He heard the click of the front door.

'We're through here, Josh!' called Nora, closing the washing machine door and standing.

'Hello, beautiful,' barked Superman, barrelling over, through the kitchen and into the back room, grabbing her so hard that she had to hold on to the washing machine for support, then kissing her once hard on the mouth, then again. It was a slightly lewd, open-mouthed kiss, the kind of kiss you can actually *hear*, even over the sound of a hot-wash cycle, the kind of kiss more usually seen at a fairground, behind the waltzers. A kiss that makes a point.

'What was that for, lover-boy?' said Nora, coming up for air, glancing at Stephen, embarrassed.

'Does there have to be reason?' said Josh, clearly a little drunk.

'No, it's just I think maybe I lost a filling,' and she looked over at Stephen and laughed, and he did his best to laugh back.

'Steve doesn't mind, do you, Steve?'

'Don't mind at all,' said Stephen, minding more than he could possibly say.

SUPERMAN VS. SAMMY THE SQUIRREL

EXT. WOODLAND POND. DAY

SAMMY THE SQUIRREL sits in a rowing boat on the lake (we'll blue-screen this). In the boat is a birthday cake he has made. ('Happy Birthday Olivia' must be written on it – BIG letters please, props!) He notices the children at home . . .

> SAMMY THE SQUIRREL
> Hello there, boys and girls! I'm off to see Olivia the Owl. It's her birthday today, you see, and I want to take her this extra special chocolate cake I made her as a present –
> > (INDICATE THE CAKE – AD-LIB HOW
> > NICE IT LOOKS, ETC.)
> Trouble is, she lives in a big old oak tree right on the other side of the lake. The only way to get there is to row.
> > (HE STARTS TO ROW AGAIN)
> Phew! By my tail and whiskers, it's very hard work, this rowing. Very huffy puffy work indeed! I wish there was some way to make it easier . . .
> > (THINKS!)

I know - how about singing a song - a
song about rowing! Can you think of
one? I know a song about rowing -
maybe if you know it, you can sing
along with me? By my furry tail,
doesn't that sound fun!!!!
   (PRE-RECORD MUSIC UP - HE STARTS TO
   SING)
Row, row, row your boat/Gently
Down the stream/Merrily etc. etc.
etc.
Continue ad-lib . . .

Stephen sat in his dressing room, from teeth resting on his
bottom lip, unconsciously slipping into character. He looked
at the page for some time, wondering if there was some way
to memorise the words without having to actually read them.
Perhaps he could absorb them through his fingertips. It wasn't
that he minded doing kids' stuff –he actually quite enjoyed
it – but it brought back bad memories of the dark, depressed
period just after the divorce became official, and the four
long, grim days in an under-heated warehouse in Mill Hill,
dressed in an eczema-inducing squirrel suit, singing about
the wheels on the bus going round and round, and round,
and round . . .

He shivered, leant back and rolled his shoulders, as if physically shrugging something off, then went back to learning his
lines. At 8.48 precisely, as he'd done exactly one hundred and
twenty-two times before, and as he would do another twenty-
two times more – or nineteen times, if you allowed for his three
performances as Byron – he headed down the treacherous back
staircase that led to stage left, to watch from the wings. He
walked on (ghostly), opened door (slowly), bowed (sombrely),
closed door (slowly), walked off (quickly) – and was about to

slide off back to the dressing room, when Josh tugged on his cape.

'Hey, come and see me afters, will you? I need to ask you a big favour.'

'Actually, I really ought to—'

'Two minutes, yeah?' And without waiting for an answer, Josh did his high-diver's hop-and-skip and went back out for his curtain call.

After the show, Stephen knocked at Josh's door, heard an affirmative grunt over the sound of very loud hip-hop, and went in.

Josh lay stretched out on the floor face down, wearing only his underpants, moaning, and for one terrible/wonderful moment Stephen thought he had hurt himself, had fallen over, and was struggling to get up, then collapsing again. He was just about to ask if he could help, when it become clear that Josh was in fact performing elaborate press-ups, launching himself up into the air with a grunt, and clapping in between each one, like an unnaturally toned performing seal.

'Oh – I'm sorry, I'll go . . .' Stephen said, backing out the door.

'Hey (clap) there! (clap) Come (clap) in! (clap) Sit (clap) down . . .'

Stephen settled into the swivel chair at the dressing table, nearly putting his elbow into the four fat slugs of cocaine that were lined up on a CD cover, Public Enemy's *Fear of a Black Planet*. A rolled-up twenty-pound note and a platinum credit card lay along side, next to a bottle of champagne and a *Les Miserables* souvenir mug.

'Tuck (clap) in (clap), Stephanie (clap) . . .'

It wasn't a good idea, of course, not with another ten hours under hot studio lights staring him in the face. But there it was, a gift from Josh. Stephanie tucked in, winced, then drank warm champagne from the *Les Miserables* mug.

'D'you want to see something really funny?' giggled Josh, pulling himself to his feet, and pulling his trousers on.

'What?' said Stephen, blinking hard, pinching his nose.

'I mean *really* funny.'

'Go on.'

'You're not to tell anyone I showed you this, alright?' Josh pulled open the drawer of his dressing table, reached beneath a pile of scripts, and pulled out a Jiffy bag. 'And you've got to promise not to take the piss.' Grinning and giggling, he reached into the bag, and pulled out a garishly coloured rectangle of cardboard, which he turned round slowly, like a conjurer. In a bubble of clear plastic was a small plastic doll.

'Josh Harper is proud to present (drum noise) my . . . very own . . . action figure!'

'Oh . . . my . . . God!' laughed Stephen, in spite of himself, snatching the toy from Josh's hand. Against a black background, in raised metallic capitals were the words *Mercury Rain*, and a photograph of Josh in futuristic military garb, a space rifle clasped across his chest. Stephen felt his jaw tighten, and began to hear the blood in his head.

'Lieutenant Virgil Solomon – Planetary Expedition Force!' barked Josh. 'That's me! All the way from a sweat-shop in Taiwan. Gangs of twelve-year-olds, painting my hair on for seventy-five cents a day. It's appalling, really,' he added, unable to suppress his glee in the face of global exploitation. Stephen peered closely at the action figure's face – there was a vague resemblance, he supposed, but not much; two little blobs of cornflower blue for the eyes, but a fat nose and thick neck, slicked black hair and a little crimson scar on one cheek.

'Where'd the scar come from?'

'Fighting huge mantis-like creatures,' said Josh, buttoning up a beautiful, fresh white shirt.

Stephen peered closer. 'Bloody hell – you're ugly,' he laughed.

'I know! Look how fat they've made me too – big fat bloody great porker. Do you think they've made me look fat?'

'No, not really.'

'Seriously, though . . .' said Josh, rubbing his abs for reassurance.

'A little bit fat, maybe.'

'I knew it! Those Taiwanese bastards. I should sue!'

'Still, they do say being turned into an action figure adds ten pounds.' Josh tried to snatch the toy from Stephen's hand, and for a moment they resembled two eight-year-old boys, friends almost, bickering in a playground.

'I want to open it!' whined Stephen, enjoying himself more than he really ought.

'Well, you can't. I'm worth more in my original packaging. Go and buy one if you want one.'

'So apart from being pose-able, do you actually *do* anything?'

'What, like fire a rocket or something? Nah.' He pinched his nostrils together, snorted, swallowed. 'My utility belt glows in the dark, but apart from that, sod all. Though I do have my very own hover chopper, retailing at £17.99.'

'And do any of your clothes come off?'

'Not unless I have another couple of these,' Josh giggled, nodding at the remaining lines of cocaine, and Stephen became aware of the need to say something quickly.

'So – a BAFTA, your very own action figure . . .'

'Yeah, life's sweet, isn't it? Except I still can't find that bloody BAFTA.'

There was a moment's silence. Stephen couldn't feel his teeth any more, and had become aware of the sound of his heart beating against his chest. Could Josh hear it, he wondered. And why had he asked him here anyway? Surely not just to show off his action figure. Out of friendship? Were they friends now, or did he just want someone to watch him do his press-ups?

'Listen, Steve, here's the thing –' Josh turned the music down, settled astride his swivel chair again, crossed his arms, gripped and squeezed his own biceps, and Stephen felt the first shiver of anxiety – 'I've told Nora that you and me are going out for a drink after the show tonight.'

'Did you? Right, well, that would be cool, Josh, but actually, I'd better not stay out too late. What with the eighteenth coming up and everything . . .' In fact, the shadow of the big red squirrel was looming, but there was no reason for Josh to know that.

'No, no, 's alright, I don't want to go either, it's just I sort of needed, well – an alibi.'

'An alibi?'

Josh snapped his teeth together a couple of times, and started to examine the tips of his fingers. 'I'm sort of having a drink with someone, you see. At that club we went to.'

'Josh . . .'

'It's not what you think it is, Steve. It's just to talk. The thing is, this certain someone, this woman, she's a friend of mine and, well, she's only decided she's gone and fallen in *love* with me.' He wrinkled his nose and groaned at the inconvenience, as you might groan at finding out a goldfish had died. 'She's getting pretty serious about it too, texting me all the time, sending me letters and everything, so I said I'd go and meet her for a drink and talk about it, try and calm her down before she gets all Fatal Attraction. And that's why, if Nora asks, I just need you to tell her you were with me.'

'But there's nothing going on, with this other woman?'

'Nothing.'

'You're sure, Josh?'

'Absolutely.'

'Because I know we've got a deal but—'

'Not a deal.'

'An . . . arrangement then.'

'It's nothing to do with that.'

'But I wouldn't feel comfortable if I thought . . .'

'I completely understand . . .'

'. . . if I thought I was just creating a, a diversion for you.'

'I know. And you're not.'

There was a knock at the dressing-room door. Josh leapt quickly to his feet and opened it a small way, leaning out into the corridor. Stephen could hear voices, low and urgent, and Josh gave a small nod in Stephen's direction, indicating that they should be careful what they say. The woman leaned in to follow the direction of Josh's nod, and that's when Stephen saw her, Abigail Edwards, TV's WPC Sally Snow, his co-star from *Summers and Snow*.

'Hello, there,' said Abigail, peering into the room, smiling politely.

'Hello,' said Stephen, as coldly as he could muster.

'Don't I know you from somewhere?'

'Maybe.'

'I know – aren't you Dead Guy?'

'That's right,' said Stephen, quietly. 'I'm Dead Guy.'

'Steve was one of the waiters at my party, remember?'

'That's right, I remember now. You told my best friend to go fuck himself.'

'That's me.'

And then there seemed to be nothing else to say.

'So I'll see you there in ten, yeah?' said Josh.

'OK, lover, don't keep me waiting,' murmured Abigail, then kissed Josh on the cheek. Then putting on a fake smile, leaned in and said, 'Nice to see you again, Dead Guy,' then was gone.

Josh closed the door. 'Aren't our police wonderful?'

'Your new lover, Josh?'

'Absolutely not,' he said, with a smile, a smirk. 'What makes you say that?'

'She just called you "lover".'

'So? Loads of people call me lover.'

'I'm sure they do.'

'Alright – we've got together maybe once or twice.'

'Josh!'

'But I swear, I didn't enjoy it . . .' and he laughed out loud, and hunched back over the cocaine, sniffing hard, then pressing both his eyes with the heal of his hand. 'Ay caramba!' he gasped, and swigged from the mug of champagne. 'I don't know what it is, Steve. Maybe it's the uniform . . .'

But Stephen was on his feet now, reaching for his coat.

'You know your problem, Josh?'

'What?'

'All cock, no heart.'

'Oh, come on, don't get like that, Steve.'

'Like what?'

'Like my bloody mum. I'm only human, mate, I'm only flesh and blood.'

'Yeah, so you keep saying.'

'And, anyway, you know what they say – it doesn't count if you're on location.'

Stephen sighed. 'You're not on location, Josh.'

'No, but as good as,' and he pushed the cocaine towards Stephen. 'You sure you don't want any more of this?'

'You've no idea what you've got, have you?'

'What d'you mean?'

'Nora. You've no idea what she's worth, how lucky you are . . .'

'Course I do! That's why I'm seeing Abi tonight, to knock it on the head.'

'And then what?'

'What d'you mean?'

'I mean, who's next? Maxine, her, God knows who else – who's next to get that special Josh Harper treatment?'

'Hey, you can love someone without actually being *faithful* to them, Steve,' he said, then to his credit, looked just a tiny bit shamefaced. 'Alright, I admit, maybe we got married a bit quickly, and maybe I'm not ready for that level of commitment. But I worship Nora, really I do. She's smart and she's funny and I like having her around.' His eyes were misting up now, getting rheumy and moist, and he was speaking his dialogue in his best 'emotional' voice, slightly cracked and wavering, and Stephen wondered if he was going to go the whole hog, and actually start to cry. 'Nora's my rock, Steve. She's my Northern Star. She's . . .' and he paused, searching for his next line.

'The wind beneath your wings?' prompted Stephen.

'Yeah. Yeah, if you like. Is that really such a bad thing?'

Stephen reached for the door handle.

'And anyway, we had a deal. You cover for me with Nora, and you get your big break, remember?' said Josh.

'That wasn't the deal, Josh.'

'Wasn't it? Because it sounds fair enough to me. Hey, still – if you want to forget about the eighteenth, then that's fine by me. But you know me; I'm very, very rarely ill. It's unlikely a chance like this will come up again.'

And suddenly Stephen realised that a piano was never, ever going to fall on Josh Harper. Not unless someone pushed it.

Stephen sighed, and closed the door. 'You promise you'll finish it?'

'I promise'

'Tonight?'

'Absolutely.'

'No excuses, no sneaking back to her flat?'

'Scout's honour,' said Josh, holding his hand up.

'OK, then,' said Stephen, very quietly.

'What?'

'I said . . . I said all right.'

'So you'll cover for me?'

'Yes, Josh. Yes, I'll cover for you.'

By the time they stepped outside, the autograph hunters had given up hope, and disappeared off into the night, and they stood for a moment on Wardour Street. Josh grabbed Stephen's hand with both his, and squeezed something into his palm.

'There you go – present for you,' he said, grinning expectantly.

Stephen looked down at the small effigy of Lieutenant Virgil Solomon of the Planetary Expedition Force, then back at Josh's grinning face, and wondered how far up his nostril it might be possible to jam the action figure.

'I don't know what to say,' he said, because he didn't.

'Forget about it, and thank you for – well, you know, for covering for me. I'll make it worth your while. The eighteenth, yeah? Two evenings and a matinée.' He lunged forward and gave Stephen his Superman hug, winked and turned north towards the club. 'See you tomorrow, Stephanie,' he said, over his shoulder.

'Josh?' shouted Stephen after him.

'What?'

'Could you use my proper name d'you think?' said Stephen, slowly and quietly.

Josh walked back towards him. 'What – you don't like "Stephanie"?'

'What d'you *think*, Josh?'

'But I've always called you Stephanie, ever since I've known you.'

'Yes, Josh. Yes, you have. But I don't like Stefano, or Stevesters, or Stevaroony, or Bullitt, and I definitely don't like Stephanie.'

'I'm sorry, mate. I had no idea,' he said, sincere and contrite. He punched the top of Stephen's arm, and backed away, breaking into a grin. 'See you tomorrow – *Stephanie*!!!'

Stephen smiled, lips tight together, mimed an invisible gun, pointed it at Josh's head, and pulled the trigger, and Josh laughed, mimed his head exploding, turned, and scampered away through the crowd.

It was that last 'Stephanie' that did it.

On Victoria Station, he slipped into an old-fashioned phone box, Clark Kent-style, and closed the door. He could have used his mobile phone, of course, but he was paranoid that they might track his number. He knocked aside the fast-food containers with the back of his hand, wiped the mouthpiece of the receiver on his coat, and called Directory Enquiries for the appropriate number, then dropped another coin in the slot, took a deep breath, sniffed, and dialled.

At the very last moment he decided to disguise his voice, use an accent, a Welsh accent maybe, and to put something over the receiver. In a film, this would be a white handkerchief, but all he had in his pocket was a purple Pret A Manger napkin. Quickly, he stretched it over the mouthpiece. It smelt slightly of Thousand Island Dressing. Welsh accent? Or Geordie perhaps? Cardiff or Newcastle. A voice answered the phone, and the accent crashed somewhere in between.

'Could ai speeek to your showbiz desk, please?' *Showbiz* desk? 'Showbiz'? Even in a recognisable accent, the word seemed suddenly absurd.

'I beg your pardon?'

The accent veered off towards the West Country. 'Yah showbiz dairsk?'

'Sorry, still can't hear you . . .'

He took the napkin off the mouthpiece and crossed the Irish Sea. 'Oi wood loike to spek tow the showbiz desk if I moy, please.'

'The *showbiz* desk?' asked the telephonist.

He cross-faded to his normal voice. 'You know – the gossip pages, famous people, showbiz, that kind of thing.'

'Can I ask who's calling?'

'Actually I'd sort of prefer to remain . . . anonymous.' Even his own voice, he was aware of how foolish he sounded. Surely there was some way of doing this with some dignity, and without saying the word 'showbiz' again? Maybe not. Maybe he should just hang-up . . .

Suddenly a well-spoken lady on the showbiz desk picked up. 'Hello there, Anonymous, how can I help you?'

'Hello is that the showbiz desk?' *Stop saying 'showbiz'.*

'Ye-es,' said the woman in a smooth, insinuating voice. Stephen hadn't been expecting this – he'd hoped for some cynical, raddled old geezer, not this crisply spoken, sceptical young woman.

'Hi, there. I just wondered, this is a tricky matter, but do you know the famous actor Josh Harper?'

He heard her exhale through her nose. 'We're aware of Josh Harper. What about him?'

'Hi, well, it's just, I was just in this private members' club on Berwick Street, Lounge – do you know it?'

'I know of it, ye-es.'

'Well, anyway, he was with someone, this woman, who didn't look like his wife.'

'I see.' She paused, wrote something down. 'Any idea who she was?'

'She looked vaguely familiar, the policewoman from that TV show *Summers and Snow*, is it?'

'Abigail Edwards?'

'Exactly. Abigail Edwards . . .'

There was a moment's silence. The Tannoy on Victoria Station blared out an announcement, and Stephen felt a surge of paranoia, as if this might in some way give him away.

'And how d'you know it's not just a friendly drink?' she asked, sceptical.

243

'I'm pretty sure it's more than that.'

'You're sure?'

'Absolutely.'

There was a long, uncomfortable silence. Was she writing something down, playing for time whilst they traced the call? His ears started to perspire, something he had never experienced before. Clearly he hadn't thought this through. Clearly he should just hang up . . .

'So, Mr Anonymous, do you have a name, or number or something we can call you back on? Maybe a mobile?'

'Actually, I'd rather not.'

'Because I have to tell you that we don't usually pay money for this kind of thing.'

'Oh, no, no, I don't want any money.'

'I see. Right, well, we'll look into it.'

'That's it?'

'That's it.'

'OK then – good night.'

Stephen was about to hang up.

'But before you go, can I just ask you something?' she asked, suddenly very friendly and chirpy.

'Sure, sure . . .'

'I'm sorry, I probably shouldn't say this, but I'm curious. Can I just ask – why are you doing this?'

'"Why?"'

'I mean, a grown man like you – what do you care? What's your motivation?'

It seemed a very good question, and not one Stephen was equipped to answer immediately. For Nora? Was he doing it for Nora? Did he imagine she would in some way be *pleased*?

'Is it some sort of moral crusade?' she asked. 'Public interest? Are you just settling some sort of score? Have you got something against him? A grudge or something?'

Stephen hung up the phone.

In the romantic-comedy version of his life, this would more normally be the point where he should have done something heroic, something quirky and charming, passionate and romantic, something that would make the audience roar their approval performed out of love for Nora, But try as he might, he could find precious little romance in an anonymous phone call. He stood with his head resting against the glass, ankle-deep amongst the burger boxes and discarded evening papers, and wondered if he'd ever felt lower in his life.

He reached into his pocket, and dropped Josh's action figure into the debris on the floor.

And when he stepped out of the phone box, he was still Clark Kent.

SKIN WORK

The results, the next morning, were better, and worse, than he could ever have hoped for.

Stephen was sitting in the canteen of a production facility in Twickenham, wearing a heavily padded nylon squirrel costume, an immense fibre-glass hazelnut sat on the table next to his bacon roll. Opposite him, the floor manager flicked through the paper, and that's when Stephen saw it, and groaned out loud. The floor manager looked-up.

'Any chance of me borrowing your paper?'

Immune to his animal charms, the floor manager scowled, and Stephen was forced once again to accept that playing the title role in a film didn't automatically grant him any particular authority.

'For one second? Please?'

The floor manager exhaled through his nose, handed the paper over, and left. Stephen gripped it tightly in both paws.

Just as there is no such thing as a small part, there is supposedly no such thing as bad publicity. Yet this was clearly bad publicity. Photographs of celebrity street-fights never look particularly impressive – arms seem to flail ineffectually, punches always seem to miss their mark; it always looks more playground than boxing ring – and this photograph was no exception. In many ways, it was a generic sort of snap, the kind that appears in a newspaper every day, just another famous person, eyes glazed, falling-down drunk, pressing their face into a bouncer's chest, flopping boneless out of a cab. Even so, it was strange to see a class act like Josh Harper in such a photograph, to see him losing his cool, and some way down the chart from Number 12. A smaller photograph to one side filled out the story: Abigail and Josh stepping out of the Lounge club in the rain, Abigail with her hand over one side of her face, Josh standing chivalrously in front of her, pointing at one of the paparazzi, snarling, his eyes red from the flash of the camera. Then the main photo – Josh suspended in the air over Berwick Street, one leg kicked high, a leather-bloused paparazzi tumbling backwards. 'Not Josh-ing any more,' read the head-line.

Hot young superstar Josh Harper was out on the town with a beauti-ful brunette last night. Nothing unusual there, except the woman was *not* Mrs Harper. Instead it was Abigail Edwards, star of TV's hit detective series *Summers and Snow*. 'I saw them in the club talking very intently,' said an on-looker. 'They seemed to be really getting on. But when they left the club together and he saw the cameras, he just started to completely freak out. He was swearing and lashing out like a wild animal . . .'

Inside his wild animal costume, Stephen felt all his pores open simultaneously.

'ALLO, 'ALLO, 'ALLO

'He started shouting, then tried to snatch my camera away and throw it to the ground,' said freelance photographer Terry Dwyer, who sustained cuts and bruises in the attack. 'He just went wild. I don't know what he was so angry about. It was just an innocent little snap-shot, after all . . .'

Stephen tossed the paper back onto the table, then sat with his head, his real head, in his paws.

He must have known this might happen when he made the anonymous call, but he'd blithely assumed that Josh would get away with it, as he always did, that the photographers wouldn't bother turning up, or that the photo would prove too innocuous for the newspaper to bother with. But there it was. What had he been thinking? And what about Nora? Surely she'd have seen it. Should he call her? What would Josh have told her? Would she be angry? Of course she'd be angry, she'd be devastated, destroyed, and it would all be his fault. He felt shabby and spiteful, the kind of petulant shame he hadn't felt since he was a child, and the costume wasn't helping matters either.

'Everything alright?' asked Olivia the Owl, sliding her full-English breakfast next to his.

'What? Oh, just someone I know in the papers.'

'Josh Harper! You *know* Josh Harper? Is he a friend of yours then?'

'Yeah, well, sort of . . .'

'Really?' she gasped, eyes wide. 'A *good* friend?'

'Well, not a *good* friend exactly . . .'

She swooped on the paper, peered at it gleefully. 'Josh, Josh, *Josh* – what have you been up to, you *naughty* boy? And with *her*!'

'Mr McQueen? We're ready for you now!' shouted Geoff, the director, a squat, depressed-looking man, and clearly not an animal lover. Stephen tucked the massive hazelnut under his arm, and walked through to the studio, his tail literally between his legs.

The first song in the schedule was his big solo number, 'Row, Row, Row Your Boat'. When the backing tape started up, Stephen dutifully smiled with his big buck teeth, and began pumping away on prop oars for the best part of the morning, ad-libbing squirrel-y chat to the imaginary kids at home about gosh, by his tail and whiskers, what hard work all this rowing was, all the time thinking about Nora, how she was, when he might see her, what he might do to make amends. Finally, after rowing some considerable distance, he handed over to Olivia the Owl, who was to perform a song about sizzling sausages, for reasons that didn't stand up to too much scrutiny. The last

session scheduled that morning was to involve a lot of improvised banter with local schoolchildren, and Stephen would need
as much strength as he could muster if he was to handle a
whole studio full of precocious kids, so he headed back to the
canteen, in the hope of clearing his head a little. By his tail and
whiskers, he felt awful.

The paper was still there on the canteen table, open at the
photo, smeared with buttery fingerprints now, Josh pointing
out at him accusingly from pages 5 and 6, his face contorted,
sweaty and bleached out, eyes red with the glare of the flash.
Another terrible thought – what if Josh couldn't do the show
tonight? What if he bailed out, citing 'personal difficulties'?
What if he went on some terrible self-destructive drunken
bender? Stephen had a momentary vision of a broken, red-
eyed Josh stumbling round an anonymous hotel room in his
underpants, the contents of the mini-bar emptied out onto
the bed; Josh lying unconscious in an overflowing bath-tub,
his mobile phone ringing unheeded. Cut to a theatre full of
expectant journalists, following up on the scandal, wondering
what has happened to the leading man; Stephen standing in
the wings as the lights went down, wearing Josh's costume,
the reviews the next day, newspapers spinning towards the
camera. 'Missing Star's Understudy Gets His Chance To
Shine . . .' Cut to Josh in the hotel bath again, his head sinking
slowly below the water . . .

Stephen reached into the deep marsupial pouch in the front
of his costume – zoologically inaccurate, but convenient – and
turned his mobile phone on. Instantly it began to vibrate in his
hand, like a living creature, and he came very close to hurling
it across the room. He peered at the screen – Nora's name.
Keep calm, he told himself. Just keep calm, be nice, try to help.
It's the least you can do. He put the phone to his ear, wondered
why he couldn't hear anything, pulled the red fur hood back,
then put the phone to his ear again.

'Stephen? Are you there?' she whispered, her voice low and hoarse.

'Hi there!' he said sympathetically, removing the prosthetic teeth and scampering out into the corridor.

'Oh God – you've seen it. I can tell, you've seen it. You've got that pitying tone to your voice. That poor-Nora tone. Oh God, oh God, oh God . . .'

'I've just seen it now.'

'God, I *hate* this crap, it's *so* humiliating! That slimy little creep . . .'

'I'm sure it was perfectly innocent.'

'Bull*shit* it was innocent. Josh has told me all about it, the little *prick*. Not straight away, of course. He came back at two in the morning, with these bruised knuckles, and said that he'd been *mugged*, would you believe, and there I am, mopping his brow and tending to his wounds like this complete *idiot*, until it finally seeped into his tiny brain that it was all going to be in the papers, and he confessed. I've been awake all night, watching him babble, and wring his hands, and make these pathetic excuses.'

'It must have been—'

'It's been awful, the worst, just this long, awful, terrible huge row, shouting, screaming for hours on end, throwing things . . .'

'Is he still there?'

'No, he's gone now. Would you believe it, at one point, he was trying to spin me some bullshit line about how it was all down to his lack of *self-esteem*. That's when I lost it, and threw the little prick's *Millennium Falcon* out of the window. He went out to get it and I locked the door after him and I haven't seen him for the last three hours.'

'And what did he say had happened?'

'He said this *act*ress, what's-her-name, Abigail or whatever, is ob*sessed* with him, that she se*duced* him, the poor little lamb, that he's only flesh and blood, that it was a moment of weak-

ness, blah blah blah. Basically, his defence was I can't help it if
I'm so goddamn irresistible, the arrogant little—'

'Where is he now? Is he there with you?'

'No, he's gone into hiding, at his agent's or something. And
now there are these little men with cameras hanging around
outside, and I'm scared to answer the phone. I can't even leave
the house to get more booze, and I think I might be going
crazy.'

'More booze? Is that a good idea, Nora?'

'Certainly seems that way . . .'

'It's quarter past eleven, Nora.'

'You got any better ideas?'

He should go and see her, of course. He should get out of
the stupid costume and jump in a cab now and rescue her, but
did it count as a rescue if you were responsible for the situation in the first place? Maybe he could confess – maybe; try
and convince that he had done it out of some weird, twisted
sense of devotion, tell her that he was in love with her, and
he'd fouled things up irredeemably but was there any chance,
even the slightest possibility, that she might feel something in
return? This was clearly the thing to do, but he was filming
with the precocious kids soon – a long, quite demanding semi-
improvised segment, climaxing in a rendition of 'Ten Green
Bottles'.

'Stephen – I need to ask you something.'

The register of her voice had changed, and he could tell she
was now lying down. For the second time in twenty-four hours,
he had the strange sensation of feeling his ears start to perspire.
'Go on.'

'Well, last night Josh told me he was out with you, and it
turns out he wasn't, and I just wondered – did you know
anything about all of this?'

Keep a steady nerve. Acting is reacting. Sound indignant.
'No!'

'You had no idea?'

No, too indignant. Don't protest too much. 'No . . .'

'And you haven't been covering for him, have you?'

Incredulous. Try incredulous. 'No-ho-ho!'

'Because I'd hate to think that all this stuff was happening behind my back, and everyone was just kind of . . . *laughing* at me.'

'Nora – I would never, ever do that.'

'You wouldn't?'

'I wouldn't *dare*.'

She laughed, briefly and bitterly, through her nose. 'No. No, of course you wouldn't.'

They were quiet for a moment, and Stephen thought once more about how he wasn't nearly as nice a person as he pretended to be.

'Stephen – I need to ask you a favour.'

'Of course.'

'I wondered . . . I wondered if I could come and stay with you?'

Had he just heard her correctly? He tucked his whiskers out of the way. 'Stay with me?'

'I don't really want to be here alone, with the phone ringing all the time, and photographers hanging around outside, and I thought about running back to New York for a while, but then I'll just have to explain it to everyone, which is just too humiliating to even think about, and I could always go to a hotel, I suppose, but I'll just end up swallowing the mini-bar, and, and, I don't know, it's not a good time for me to be alone. I need a friendly face, so I thought maybe I could kind of – hide away. With you? Just for a couple of days or so. D'you think that would be OK?'

Stephen tried to picture Nora Harper in his flat, and couldn't quite do it. Of course, he was flattered that she was turning to him, and thrilled at the idea of her proximity, at having her there, all to himself, if only temporarily. But try as he might, he couldn't see Nora in his studio in Battersea borders. He pictured the curling linoleum in the kitchen, the blood-red bathroom, the socks drying stiff on the storage heaters . . .

'If you don't think it's a good idea . . .' she said quietly.

'No, it's not that, it's just it's a bit of a dump, that's all. I mean, it's just very different from what you're used to. It's a bedsit, for starters – well, not a bedsit, a studio.'

'You've got a couch, haven't you? I'll sleep on the couch.' She laughed through her nose. 'Or *you* can sleep on the couch. Of course, if you're worried I'm going to jump you in the middle of the night . . . Hey, what if I promise not to force you into tearful, loveless sex?'

Stephen closed his eyes, and banged his furry red head twice against the corridor wall. 'OK, well, if you promise.'

'I won't, I swear.'

'But I don't even have a fridge, Nora. Not at the moment. I did have one, but—'

'Stephen, I don't need a fridge. I just need some company and somewhere to – clear my head, work out what me and Josh do next. I just really, really don't want to be on my own, that's all.'

Stephen gave his flat one last mental search, scanning the rooms, trying to remember if there was anything he didn't want her to see – underwear lying around, dirty dishes piled high. He wished he'd had a chance to pile some intellectual books by his bed, but no, there was nothing too bad, nothing unforgivable.

'Of course you can stay,' he said. 'Stay for as long as you want.'

'That's great – thank you, Stephen. Where are you? I'll come and see you now.'

'NOW?!'

'To get the keys. Unless you want me to kick down the door . . .'

'NO! No, no, not now.'

'Why not?'

He ran his paws over his big bushy tail. 'It's just now's not exactly the best time.'

'Oh.' She sounded disappointed 'Oh. Why? You've got some woman there or something?'

'Hardly. No, it's just I'm sort of out filming today.'

'You're filming? Of course, your movie! Your crime-thriller thing, yeah?'

'That's the one,' he mumbled, wondering why every third thing he said these days seemed to be a lie.

'Mr McQueen!' bellowed the floor manager from the doorway, '"Ten Green Bottles" please!'

'What was that?' said Nora.

'Nothing – look, I'd better go. I'm only scheduled here till five. I'll phone you later, arrange a place to meet, at six-ish. I'll give you the keys and the address, then meet you there after the show.'

'OK.'

'And, Nora, take it easy, yeah? Turn the phone off, make some coffee and go to bed, and we'll talk properly tonight. OK?'

'Sounds good.'

'This will all sort itself out, Nora, I promise you.'

'Yeah, well, we'll see . . .'

'And Nora?'

'What?'

'I'm really, really sorry.'

'Why? It's hardly your fault.'

'No, but still.'

'Well, thank you, Stephen.'

'What for?'

'For everything you've done. You're a pal, Steve. I appreciate it. Really, I do.'

And she hung up. Stephen slid down the wall and sat for a moment. There was a certain illicit pride, a shabby delight that she had turned to him in her moment of crisis, even if it was a moment of crisis that he had manufactured, but he didn't dwell on this, and besides, at the other end of the corridor he could see the local school children filing into the studio, supervised by Olivia the Owl, whom they regarded sceptically, as well they might.

When working with kids, Stephen found the best, and least embarrassing, approach was to stay resolutely in character, so he popped his prosthetic teeth back in, and did a little energising squirrel-y scamper outside the studio door, before entering and immediately seeing her.

His daughter stood to one side of the studio, talking earnestly with a friend, and Stephen slid round behind her, crouched down, placed two big red paws on her shoulders and spun her round, his face just inches away from hers.

'Surprise!' he shouted, and was immediately taken aback at just how long and loud and piercing a child's scream could be.

'What's French for "I'm sorry"?'

'Don't know. We haven't done "I'm sorry" yet.'

'Well, when you learn it, will you tell me?'

Sophie nodded solemnly.

She sat some distance away from her father in the small, smoky greenroom. With its ashtrays, plastic cups and old tabloids, it seemed a particularly grubby and inappropriate environment for a child, and Sophie clearly felt this too, sitting awkwardly on the edge of an orange stackable chair, staring blankly at the page of her book. Out of compassion, Stephen had been allowed to step out of his costume for a while, but they wouldn't have time to reapply his make-up, so he still had whiskers and a round mask of red and brown in the centre of his face. With some justification perhaps, Sophie was clearly finding it hard to look at him.

'So all those kids are from the famous After School Drama Society, yeah?'

Sophie nodded.

'And you're sure you don't want to come back with me and join the others?'

Sophie shook her head.

'Because I thought it might be a laugh, me and you, performing together for the first time. Our screen debut together. I thought it might be fun.'

'It's not *fun*,' Sophie mumbled at the floor. 'It's just stupid.'

Stephen leant forward in his chair, touched her on the knee. 'It's just pretending, Sophie. That's what I do. That's my job.'

'Well, it's a stupid job!'

'No, it isn't, Sophie. Not always,' he said quietly, adding weakly, 'And don't say "stupid", say "silly".'

Sophie glared at him, her eyes wide and red. 'But it isn't "silly", though, it's stupid! Stupid, stupid, stupid . . .'

'Sophie—'

'. . . stupid, stupid . . .'

'Sophie, don't—'

'. . . stupid, stupid, STUPID!'

The door to the greenroom opened. The floor manager showed Alison and Colin into the room, both in intimidating heavy over-coats and dark suits, and for a moment Stephen had the definite sensation that he was being visited in prison. Alison glanced momentarily at Stephen, narrowed her eyes dismissively, then held her arms out to Sophie. 'Come here, sweetheart,' she said and, head down, Sophie crossed the room into her mother's arms.

'Colin,' said Stephen.

'Stephen,' said Colin.

'I accidentally made her jump, didn't I, Sophie?'

Sophie said nothing.

'Colin, could you take Sophie and wait in the car for me for a couple of minutes?' instructed Alison, in a calm, level, profes-sional tone, and Colin took Sophie by the hand and led her out the door. She didn't look back.

'I'll phone you later, Sophie, yeah?' said Stephen, but she had already gone.

Alison came and sat in the chair Sophie had just vacated, rested her head on her hand and looked at him levelly, like his defence lawyer, or prosecution lawyer perhaps, he wasn't yet sure which. She was wearing a long, black pencil skirt, white blouse, black jacket, and it occurred to Stephen, entirely in-appropriately, that she looked very beautiful.

'So . . . looking good, Steve.'

'Thanks, Alison. You too.'

'Thank you,' and with one hand she smoothed the skirt out

along her legs. 'Just, you know, everyday office clothes. Just what most normal people wear.'

'I think . . . I think maybe I gave her a little scare.'

'So it would seem.'

'I don't know why – the character's actually meant to be lovable.'

'Maybe she was a bit . . .' she paused, searching for the word, '. . . surprised. So is this that big movie you've been telling me and Sophie all about? The transatlantic romantic comedy? The title role?'

'No, that's something else.'

'I see.'

'But I am the title role in this too. Sammy. I'm a squirrel.'

'Right. Sammy the Squirrel.'

He leant forward in his chair, ran his hands through his hair, sighed. 'I know you're not necessarily that interested, Alison, but I'm actually really, really good in this.'

'I'm sure you are, Steve.'

'In Eastern Europe I'm huge. And I'm enjoying it too, working with kids. There's nothing to be embarrassed by. You should know – you did panto, you did kids' plays.'

'Hey, I know!' Alison looked indignant. 'There's nothing wrong doing stuff for kids, not if it's what you really want to do.'

'So why aren't you taking me seriously then?'

'I don't know, Steve. Maybe it's the whiskers.'

They sat in silence for a moment, looking at each other, eyes narrowed.

'You don't think I'm any good, do you?' said Stephen, finally.

'No.'

'Well, that's certainly the impression you give, Alison. I mean, if you *do* think I'm good then why don't you support me?'

'Hold on, Stephen, sorry, but I don't think you understood me. What I meant was – no, I *don't* think you're any good.'

A moment passed.

'You don't?'

'No. No, I don't.'

Again, a moment.

'Since when?'

Alison closed her eyes. 'Never.'

'Whoa, hang on – you've *never* thought I was any good?'

Alison shrugged. 'Sorry.'

'Well . . . that's just your personal opinion.'

'No, I don't think so. I don't think it is. I think it's an objective opinion. No one thinks you're any good.'

'No one?'

'No one.'

Stephen's mouth moved, without necessarily finding any words to use. 'So, hang on, in all the years you've known me, nothing I've ever done, none of it has ever been any good. It's all been a waste, I've always been bad – is that what you're saying?'

'No, not out-and-out bad exactly, just . . . not good either. Sorry.'

'So what about *The Cherry Orchard*?'

'I didn't *love* it, Steve.'

'That episode of *Emergency Ward*?'

'Not great.'

'*Under Milk Wood*?'

'Your accent let you down a little.'

'Benvolio in *Romeo and Juliet*?'

'It's Benvolio – no one notices Benvolio.'

'You said I was the best thing in it!'

'Well, it was a very, *very* bad production, Steve.'

'So how about . . . I don't know . . . *Godspell*?'

'OK, a) that was nine years ago, b) no, you weren't that good, c) it was bloody *Godspell*, Stephen.'

'I see. So, is this you being cruel to be kind, or just being cruel?'

'I'm telling you this because I care about you.'

'Well, I'd hate to see you try and hurt me, Al,' he said, surprised, and horrified, to feel anger, hatred even, boiling up inside him, the same rage he'd felt at the end of their marriage. And struggling to keep his voice level he said, 'Sorry, Alison, but you're going to have to explain that a little more clearly.'

Alison's face softened slightly. She sighed, leant forward in her chair, so her face was close to his, her hands clasped tight together, and she spoke quietly. 'When you and I first got together, and we were all optimism and excitement and everything, you used to say this thing to me, usually when you'd had a bit to drink – you used to say that the key to happiness is to find the thing that you're absolutely best at, the thing you love the most, stick with it, no matter how hard it gets, and do it to the absolute best of your abilities. And I remember really admiring you, and fancying you and, well, actually, loving you for that.'

'But now you disagree?'

'Not at all. No, I don't disagree at all. I think that's a fine philosophy; find the thing you're good at, and do it with all your heart. But, Stephen – this isn't it. I look at you, and I don't see a man who's found the secret of happiness. Someone scared, and frustrated, and bitter, yes, but not happy. And it's because you're not living in the real world, Stephen. If you were younger, it would be fine, but you can't just wait around hoping for some miracle, for your luck to change. It doesn't work like that, only in films. You can't blame luck. Luck *doesn't* change, not unless you make it. You've got to take some control of your life. Do something sensible for once.'

'Shouldn't you go and get Sophie?'

Alison stood, and was reaching into her jacket pocket now, looking for something. 'Why don't you come and see me at the office, Stephen? At the recruitment consultants . . .'

'You're not going to give me your *business card*?'

'There are people you could talk to, people who could give you advice.'

'Please – *please* – do not offer me your business card . . .'

'You could retrain. You're good with technology, or something creative, something with kids. Kids love you.'

He stared at the card in her hand. 'No. Sorry, thanks for the offer, but no.'

The floor manager stuck his head round the door. 'Sorry, Steve, we're going to need you back in costume pretty soon.'

'OK – five minutes.'

They stood for a moment in silence, before Alison returned the card to her pocket. 'OK. Well, I'd better be going,' she said, getting up, smoothing down her skirt in a practised, professional gesture, and walking past him without quite being able to look him in the eye.

'Alison?'

Alison stopped in the doorway, and turned to him, her eyes red and wet now.

'You're wrong,' he said, in a calm, steady voice. 'I know you're used to being right, but this time you're wrong. I am good at this, really, really good, in fact, and I am going to prove it to you, to you *and* Sophie, and I'm going to make Sophie proud. And soon. Be ready, because I swear to you, it's going to happen any day now.'

Alison looked at him for a long while, shook her head and said, 'I hope you're right, Stephen. Really I do.' Then she lowered her head, turned, and closed the door behind her.

BRIEF ENCOUNTER

They arranged to meet outside the Burger King on Victoria Station at six o'clock, the place he'd called from the night before. Just like in a movie, he was returning to the scene of the crime.

Inevitably filming overran, and Stephen finally stumbled, numb, out of the studios at five thirty. Right on cue, the skies opened, fat oily drops of grey rain that stung his eyes. Drunk with power, Frank had insisted the production company hire a private car to take the film's leading man to the theatre, but Stephen couldn't find it in the car park, and by the time he threw himself bodily into the back of the people-carrier, he was soaked. He asked the driver to take him to Victoria, then slumped in the back, dripping with rain, desperately scrubbing at his face with a fistful of disintegrating toilet roll in an attempt to remove the last of the make-up that had been stencilled around the edge of his furry head-piece. Peering at his reflection in the driver's rear-view mirror, it seemed as if he had a perfectly circular strawberry birthmark in the centre of his face. He bunched the last of the toilet paper up into a small damp ball, and kept scrubbing until the clump disintegrated in his hand and crumbled onto his lap. His breathing was shallow, and his chest felt tight in what was either distress at all that had happened that day, or the onset of pleurisy.

Half an hour later, they pulled up at Victoria Station. Nora's phone was turned off, and he was terrified that he might have missed her, but as he rose to step out of the car, the driver called to him.

''Scuse me, sir?'

'Uh-huh?'

'Could I have your autograph, please?' said the driver, holding a pen out to Stephen.

Stephen stared dumbly at the pen in the driver's hand. So this is what it feels like, he thought. He'd never been recognised before, but perhaps the driver had kids who were fans of Sammy the Squirrel. Or perhaps it was his doomed Asthmatic Cycle Courier, or Man in Bank, Rent-Boy 2, Third Businessman, Mugging Victim. Perhaps Alison was wrong, and someone *had* noticed his Benvolio after all. *Could I have your autograph, please?* He looked up at the driver's expectant grin. It was the first kind thing anyone had said to him all day. Stephen smiled modestly, and settled back in his seat.

'Of course, I'd be more than happy to – who do you want it made out to?'

'Sorry, sir?'

'The autograph. Who do you want it made out to? Your kids or something?'

'Just your name, sir. It's for the invoice.'

Stephen nodded, took the pen and the clipboard, signed his name on the invoice, and hurried out to find Nora.

The idea of meeting on a train station had seemed romantic at the time, as if it might hold a melancholic black-and-white charm, like something from an old movie. But train stations have changed a great deal since then and, standing outside Burger King, Nora looked hunted and anxious. She stood with her back against the very phone box he'd called from the previous night, wearing a long heavy overcoat over a black dress, the collar turned up, her wet fringe clinging to her face as she glanced anxiously round at the crowds of damp, scowling commuters. Nearby, a school brass band played 'In the Bleak Midwinter', just to hammer the point home.

'Sorry I'm late,' Stephen gasped.

'That's fine,' said Nora, managing a smile. 'Thank you for coming.' She put one arm around his neck, and pressed her cheek against his. He had a momentary spasm of anxiety that Josh's action figure might still be nestling in the rubbish at the bottom of the phone box behind her, but thankfully he'd been swept away in the night. He turned his head to look at Nora. She seemed exhausted, her eyes red, her breath warm with whisky, and with her face inches away he could see that a small, red spot had started to form on the rim of her nostril. Stephen felt an overwhelming desire to lean in and kiss her, and was startled and delighted when Nora suddenly took his face firmly in her hands, pulling it even closer towards her, scrutinising him intently, and with a great belly flop of pleasure he realised that she was about to kiss him. Some long-buried reflex made him lick his lips quickly, in anticipation. *Put your hand in that warm place in the small of her back, lean forward and . . .*

'What the hell is wrong with your *face*?' she said.

'My face?'

'Your face. It's all brown and red.'

'Is it?' he said, rubbing it vigorously with his wet sleeve.

'You look like you've been punched repeatedly on the nose.'

'I haven't. Well, not yet anyway . . .'

'What does that mean?'

'Nothing, nothing. It's make-up,' and he started rubbing at his cheeks with the back of both hands simultaneously in a way that was at least partially still in character. 'It's for this police marksman thing I've been doing today. It's, eh, camouflage. You know, the usual macho bullshit . . .'

She peered closer and seemed to pinch something between her finger and thumb, and tug – a thick, synthetic black fibre. 'Is this . . . is this a *whisker*?'

'No-ho-ho,' he laughed mirthlessly, taking the fibre from her, dropping it on the floor. Change the subject. 'How are you feeling, anyway?'

'Oh, well, you know – considering my marriage is falling apart in the national press, I'm pretty good.'

'And have you spoken to him?'

'No. Well, briefly. I told him to go away and leave me alone, though not using those precise words.' She smiled, and there was a moment's pause. 'Hey, aren't you going to be late for the show?'

'Absolutely. So – you've got the address, here are the keys. Next train's platform 7, three minutes' time, then get a taxi from outside Clapham Junction station, yeah? Right to the door. There might be some kids hanging round, shouting abuse and stuff, but don't try and answer back, just ignore them, it's not worth it.'

'O-K.'

'D'you need money for the cab?'

'I have money.'

'And when you get there, just shut the door, put your feet up, watch an old movie or something. There's DVDs and videos on the shelf. I'll be back in, what, three, four hours. Help yourself to anything you can find, not that there *is* anything. Don't bother looking for a fridge, there isn't one. There was, but it died, and I'm getting a new one soon, but the milk's on the windowsill, and there's a fried chicken place downstairs, if you're feeling reckless. They do spare ribs too, though they're a bit of an unknown quantity, I'm afraid. In fact, I'd hold out if I were you. I'll bring you something when I come home.'

'Thanks for this, Stephen. You're a star.'

'Well, not a *star* . . .' he protested, but she looped her arms round his chest, giving him a boozily affectionate hug, and they stood there for a moment, Stephen inhaling the scent of shampoo and smoke from her wet hair, the damp wool of her overcoat. After the events of that long, terrible day, it felt blissful. He closed his eyes, and pressed his hands against her back. The school brass band were now reversing over 'Jingle Bells', and yet despite this he'd have been very happy to stay there for a while, but the station clock read 18.25.

He pressed his lips against the top of her head, and said, 'I've got to go. Any message for Josh?'

'Tell him to go screw himself.'

'And apart from that?'

'Just that.'

'OK, I'll tell him.'

She pulled away and looked up at him. 'Except don't. In fact, can you not tell Josh anything? That we've spoken, or where I'm staying tonight? It's not that I'm trying to punish him or anything – well, not *just* that. It's just I don't particularly want to see or speak to him at the moment, that's all. You know how persuasive he can be – he'll get all cow-eyed and pouty and passionate and sincere, and, well, I'd like to stay angry with him for a little longer. Let's keep it our secret.'

'OK – our secret.' Then Stephen squeezed her hands, and turned round and ran against the tide of commuters, back towards the tube station.

'You know, if there's a bigger tosser in the whole of London, then I'd like to meet him, Steve. Really, I would.'

Josh Harper sat on the edge of his day bed in his puffy white shirt, head in hands, his face pale, his eyes red and swollen; still handsome, but clearly shaken, as if he'd just returned from a disastrous cavalry charge. 'I should have listened to you. What was I thinking, Steve? What was I playing at?' He started to rap the side of his head with his fists. 'Stupid, stupid, stupid, stupid, stupid, stupid . . .'

Steve wondered if he should perhaps put his arm around him, if only to try to stop him saying 'stupid', but decided that there was a real possibility that this might feel hypocritical. Instead, he leant forward, and squeezed his knee. 'So have you spoken to her?' he said eventually.

'Only for a minute – she says she's going to stay with friends for a couple of days. God knows who – she hasn't *got* any friends, only ones she knows through me. Hey, *you* don't know where she is, do you?'

She's at home, now, at my *flat, waiting for* me . . .

'Of course I don't know,' said Stephen.

Josh looked at him intently for a moment, then took the teaspoon from the neck of last night's bottle of champagne, poured two inches into his mug, drained it in one, and winced, which is surely not the point of champagne. 'Anyway, she doesn't want to hear from me. I don't blame her, either. God, Steve, I just hope *you* never have to go through something like that.'

'Well, you know, when I got divorc—'

'Shouting, screaming, throwing things,' Josh continued. 'Crying one minute, hurling abuse the next. And when I tried to explain myself, that's when she really freaked out, smashing up my *Star Wars* things, really laying into them.'

'You didn't tell her any of that stuff you told me, though, did you, Josh?'

'What stuff?'

'You know – the sex-addiction, low self-esteem thing.'

Josh looked sheepish. 'I might have mentioned it, yeah.'

Stephen visibly winced.

'She went crazy, Steve. I wouldn't mind, but some of that stuff's twenty-five, thirty years old, antique more or less, and she was just drop-kicking it around the bedroom! My *Millennium Falcon*'s knackered, just totally fucked . . .'

'Five-minute call,' said the voice on the Tannoy. 'Mr Harper, this is your five-minute call. Five minutes, please.'

'. . . we were meant to be going on holiday too, soon as the run was finished. Two weeks in St Lucia. That's not going to happen. I'm probably not even going to be able to get my deposit back.' He reached once more for last night's champagne, poured it into his mug.

'Is that a good idea, Josh?'

'Not to mention the *Mercury Rain* premiere next Sunday! What am I going to do, Steve?'

'Take Abigail Edwards instead?' said Steve. Josh curled his lip. 'Sorry – not funny. Have you spoken to Maxine, by the way?'

'I tried, but she just threw her travel-iron at me. That's all women seem to do these days, Steve, chuck stuff at my face.' He stopped suddenly, with the mug halfway to his lips. 'You know, I wouldn't be surprised if she set the whole thing up in the first place.'

'That's completely cra-a-azy . . .' said Stephen, with his manu-factured laugh during the word 'crazy'.

'Is it? I'm not so sure. The paparazzi were definitely waiting for us when we came out.'

Keep calm. Don't sound defensive. 'You're just being paranoid. Those places always have photographers hanging round outside.'

'This one doesn't – that's why we always go there. Besides, it's exactly the kind of nasty, vindictive thing Maxine would do. 'Cept what's the point of blaming her? It's my fault. I am *so* stupid. Stupid, stupid, stupid . . .' Josh curled over, and laced his fingers behind his head, pulling down on his neck as if trying to tug himself through the floor. Stephen placed one hand on his shoulder.

'Are you OK to do the show tonight, d'you think?'

Josh looked up at him and scowled. 'Of course I am!' he snapped, shrugging Stephen's hand away 'Don't you worry, Steve mate, you'll still get your big break.'

'I didn't mean it that way.'

'Didn't you? 'Cause it sounded like you were getting ready to jump in my grave, mate.'

'Not at all.'

'Don't sweat, Stevie-boy, the deal still stands.'

'I wasn't talking about—'

'You'll still get your chance, three shows, the eighteenth onwards, just like we—'

'Josh, for once in your life, will you just shut the fuck up and listen to someone else speak?'

Josh's mouth hung open in a perfect O, as if he'd just been punched in the face, and the effect was so gratifying that Stephen wondered if it was too late to punch him too.

Confident he had Josh's attention, he continued, 'I wasn't talking about our "deal", which was never meant to be that kind of deal in the first place, if you remember. Of course you should go on and do the show tonight. I was just trying to be . . . sympathetic, that's all. I was trying to help.'

'Yeah. Of course, you're right.' Josh slumped back in his chair, ran his hands through his hair. 'Sorry, mate, it's just I'm a bit on edge, that's all.'

'Yeah, of course you are. And yes, there'll probably be some journalists out there in the audience tonight, but so what? You just go out there and do your job. That's the main thing, isn't it? Fuck 'em!'

'Exactly – fuck 'em!'

Josh took Stephen's hand and squeezed it, and Stephen put a hand on Josh's shoulder and squeezed it back, and they stood for a moment like old, old friends, mutually squeezing, until the Tannoy system hissed and crackled.

'Beginners, please. This is your beginners' call. Mr Harper, to the stage please, this is your beginners' call.'

Stephen punched the top of Josh's arm, and Josh punched Stephen right back.

One thing was immediately clear about Josh's performance that night – he was certainly giving his all. Instead of his misery ruining his performance, it was enhancing it; he was, in actor's jargon, 'using it'. There was a great deal of weeping and expressive perspiring going on, a lot of slack-jawed, moist-eyed keening, a lot of emotion trapped in the throat, so that it sounded a little like he was suppressing a burp. It seemed to be doing the trick, though. Across the stage from Stephen, Donna, the company manager, stood in the wings crying. Stephen had previously assumed that she'd been born without tear-ducts, or at least had them sealed up with gaffer tape, but there she stood, tears coursing down her cheeks, dabbing at her eyes with the edge of her black leather waistcoat. Even Maxine, the woman scorned, was at it. Consequently, even fewer people than usual noticed as Stephen's Ghostly Figure walked on (ghostly), opened door (slowly), bowed (sombrely), closed door (slowly), walked-off (quickly). Stephen could sense the tangible tension of the audience and, sure enough, there was a long, suspended moment, as Stephen and Josh stood side by side in the wings, like a spark fizzing its way along a length of fuse. When it started, it was overwhelming. Josh gave Stephen a little shrug, as if to say, *I, too, am bemused by my awesome power*, then gave his little high-diving-board hop-and-skip before trotting out onto the stage to accept once again all that was due to him.

Stephen was back in his dressing room before the applause came to an end. He pulled on his coat, walked unseen past Josh's dressing room, overflowing now with friends and well-wishers, unnoticed past the crowd at stagedoor, a dense pack of journalists, fans and autograph hunters, curious passers-by, and paparazzi looking for a return match. He pulled his coat tight around him against the cold, and, invisible once more, he hurried home, where Josh's wife was waiting for him.

DIAZEPAM

Almost immediately, he knew that something terrible had happened.

He had been standing on the street, his finger pressed hard on the doorbell, for some time. When there was still no reply, he backed out to the very edge of the kerb and shouted up at the dimly lit window, attempting to make himself heard above the sound of the traffic on the wet street. Nothing. He shouted 'Nora' again, attempting to ignore the jeers from the customers inside Idaho Fried Chicken, then stepped back into his doorway, took out his phone, dialled Nora's number, and swore under his breath when inevitably it clicked over to her messaging service. Seeing no other option, he took a deep breath and rang Mrs Dollis's bell.

Mrs Dollis stuck her head warily out of the window, like an upsetting glove puppet, a lit cigarette clamped between arthritic knuckles.

'Go 'way!'

'Hello, there!'

'I said go 'way, will you? Bloody kids.'

'Mrs Dollis, it's—'

'Piss off out of it.'

'Mrs Dollis, it's me, it's Stephen, Mr McQueen. From the top floor?'

'It's eleven o'clock!'

'I know, I'm sorry, it's just I'm locked out of my flat, Mrs Dollis.'

'No you're not.'

Stephen swore under his breath. 'Really, I am, Mrs Dollis.'

'So how come I can hear your TV through the floor?'

'That's someone else, Mrs Dollis.'

'So who's in your flat then? Not burglars . . .'

'A friend. I gave my friend my keys.'

She scowled down at him. 'You're not meant to give your keys to just anyone, you know.'

'I know that, Mrs Dollis, and I haven't. She's a good friend of mine.'

'So why won't she answer the door then? If she's such a good—'

'That's what I want to find out.'

It seemed to take an absurdly long time for Mrs Dollis to come and open the door.

'Foxes have been at the bins again . . .'

'Not now Mrs Dollis, eh?'

He squeezed past her, pounding up four flights of stairs to his floor. The door was locked. He banged hard on the plywood, his chest tight with panic now.

'Nora? Nora, it's me, are you there? Nora! Open the door . . .'

No reply, just a ribbon of flickering grey light from the gap under the door and the blare of a film soundtrack, *Some Like It Hot* he thought. He turned and hurtled back down the stairs, knocked on Mrs Dollis's door, and bounced up and down on the balls of his feet as he waited. Finally she opened the door to her flat, which smelt overpoweringly of vinegar and fried onions.

'What now?'

'I need the spare key, Mrs Dollis.'

'Why?'

'Because my friend's not opening the door.'

'Why?'

'I DON'T KNOW WHY, DO I? THAT'S WHY I NEED THE KEY!'

Mrs Dollis snarled, 'Don't take that tone with me, young man.'

'Alright, I'm sorry, I apologise, but really, I need the spare key as soon as possible.'

Mrs Dollis scowled, and finally backed into her flat to get the key, leaving Stephen to pace the hallway, frantic, running terrible paranoid fantasies about what he might find in the flat. Stock movie images played in his head –

```
- pan across to find a handwritten note
  on the mantelpiece, extreme close up of
  an empty bottle of pills rolling from a
  hand onto the floor . . .
```

He snatched the key from Mrs Dollis, turned and ran up the stairs, taking three at a time, jabbed the key into the lock and entered.

She was lying, curled up on the sofa, wearing her black dress, in the flickering grey light of the large image projected on the wall, *Some Like It Hot*, the scene on the yacht between Curtis and Monroe. Nora might conceivably have just fallen asleep, were it not for fact that she was lying on the volume button of the remote control; the soundtrack was so loud that the speakers were distorting, yet still she didn't move. Stephen gently lifted her head to retrieve the remote and pressed the mute button, then knelt in front of her, immediately smelling the whisky on her breath, noticing the empty bottle that had half-rolled under the sofa, the debris from two torn-up cigarettes on the coffee table.

'Oh God. Oh God, oh God, oh God. Nora – can you hear me? Nora – wake up . . .'

He put his face close to hers, and felt her hot, sour breath on his cheek. Her make-up was smeared round her eyes like bruises, and she smelt of sweat and booze and old perfume.

'Nora, can you hear me? If you can hear me, open your eyes.'

'Who's that?' she mumbled through sticky lips. 'Is that Josh?'

'No, Stephen – it's me, Stephen.'

'Heeey there, Stevie. What are you doing here?'

'I live here, Nora. Remember? How are you? How are you feeling?'

'Me? Never been bedder. Soooo-perb. Hey, is Joshy with you?'

'No.'

'Where's Joshy then?'

'I don't know, Nora.'

'Is he with *her*?'

'No, he's not.'

'Is he here?'

'No, he's not.'

'GOOD! GOOOOOD-DA! I never, ever want to see him again, that dirty, lying, handsome bastard . . .'

'Nora . . .'

'. . . that treacherous good-looking sonofabitch . . .'

'. . . can you sit up, d'you think Nora?'

She smiled and rolled her eyes. 'Oh, unlikely, I think.'

'But d'you think you could try?'

'Nope!'

'I really think you ought to try . . .'

'Nope!'

'Please?'

'Just lemme *sleeeeep*, will ya? I want to go back to sleep again, please . . .' And once more he saw her eyes flutter, felt her weight go dead in his arms.

'Nora, listen to me – have you taken anything? You have to tell me if you've taken any pills, any medication.'

'What for?'

'Just tell me, Nora.'

'I don't know. Just the usual . . .'

'What's the usual, Nora? Nora? Hello? Nora!' She had faded away again. He lowered her back down onto the sofa, scanned the room for her handbag, and emptied the contents onto the floor – bundles of gluey disposable tissues, lipsticks, tampons, tweezers, a toothbrush, a cork-screw, the remains of a toilet roll, a paper cocktail umbrella, a huge bunch of keys, a tiny Swiss Army penknife, a brown plastic bottle of pills, three left, rattling at the bottom. 'Diazepam' it said on the faded label. 'Avoid alcohol.' He clenched the bottle in his hand, stumbled back and knelt beside her. For no other reason than because he'd seen it in films, he gently lifted her eyelid – the iris was there, flickering, but looking normal enough, and the pupils were dilated, but he had no way of knowing if this was good or bad. Most of Stephen's emergency first aid had been gleaned from playing Asthmatic Cycle Courier in *Emergency Ward*, but he vaguely suspected that this was one of those scenarios where it might become necessary to slap someone. He placed his hand gently on her cheek, as if lining up a shot, brought it a short distance away from her, moved it in closer, then further away, then brought it down sharply.

'Owwwww! For crying out loud. . . . !' shrieked Nora, and punched him hard in the ear.

'Owww!' said Stephen

'Hey, you started it, you dirty *bast*ard,' she moaned, and tried to punch him again. Fortunately the second blow was ineffectual, and merely glanced off the top of his head. He grabbed hold of her wrists, and felt the energy going out of her body, as she fell back and closed her eyes again.

'Nora – I need to know something?'

'What is it *now*?'

'These pills, the diazepam – how many have you taken?'

'Why the hell d'you. . . . ? Oh, I get it – you think I'm trying to do myself in, is that it? Because of my broken heart over old Joshy . . .'

'I just need to know.'

'What does it say on the bottle, Doctor Steve?'

'"Take one half an hour before going to bed."'

'Well, that's exactly what I took.'

'Just one?'

'One, maybe two.'

'Maybe more than two?'

'I don't remember!' She picked up a pillow, hugged it over her face. 'Now for cryin' out loud, Stephen, just go to bed and let me sleeeep, will ya?'

Stephen tugged the pillow away from her 'You can't sleep, not just yet. Let me make you some coffee.'

'I don't *want* some coffee.'

'But you've drunk all this booze, Nora.'

'Soooo? I can handle my booze, unlike *some* people I can mention.'

'At least sit up and talk to me for a while,' and he clambered onto the sofa, put his arm around her and hoisted her into an upright position. 'Or we'll watch the movie,' and he physically directed her at the screen, the kissing scene between Monroe and Curtis. 'I think Curtis is really underrated as a comedian.'

'Steeeve McQueen,' she mumbled, her voice low and mean, digging a finger into his chest. 'Now, there's a joke. What kind of a dumb name is that anyway? Your parents must have reeeeally had it in for you, Stevie-boy . . .'

'Let's just watch the movie, yeah . . . ?' he said, his voice holding steady.

'Jeeesus, Steve, you can be a real pain in the ass sometimes, really you can . . .'

'I'm just trying to help.'

She flopped back against him now, in the crook of his arm. 'I know you are, Steve, but all this *help*ing, all this being ni-ice all the time, nice, nice, nice, nicey, nicey, nice, this whole mensch act, well, I don't mind telling ya, it can really get on a person's nerves, ya know? Really start to g-rate. In fact, to tell ya the truth, it can start to seem jus' a liddle bit crr-reepy . . .'

'You're sure you don't want that coffee?'

And Nora suddenly wrenched herself away, scrambled to the

other end of the sofa, turned and stared at him and shouted, 'DIDNCHA HEAR? I SAID NO! FOR FUCK'S SAKE, STEVE, NO WONDER YOUR FUCKIN' WIFE LEFT YA!'

For a moment or two the room was silent as they sat at opposite ends of the sofa, glaring at each other in the flickering grey light. The words had felt so like a punch, that Stephen had actually put his hand to his head, and his mouth opened and closed again, starting to form words that he had to consciously prevent himself from saying.

Nora wiped the corner of her wet mouth with the back of her hand, then let herself flop backwards onto the sofa, curling up on her side, tucking her dress under her legs, closing her eyes tight.

'Fuck you, Nora,' said Stephen, as if to himself.

'Hey. Fuck *you* too, Stevie-boy,' she said quietly, but without conviction, and curled up even tighter.

Stephen got up slowly, went into the kitchen and shut the door behind him. As a kid, when adults said 'I need a drink', he'd always wondered what they meant. Now he knew. Far too often these days, he found himself needing a drink. More than that, he found himself suddenly envious of Nora's oblivion. Perhaps if he were to get as drunk and doped as she was, these things would matter less. This suddenly seemed like not just a reasonable plan, but an absolute necessity, and to this end he took a bottle of vodka down from the cupboard, poured a good three inches into a glass, and added some warm, flat tonic water. He saw that he still had the brown bottle of pills clenched tight in his hand and without any clear idea of what this might achieve, he unscrewed the lid, popped one in his mouth, then drained the glass in one go.

He poured himself another inch of vodka.

He heard some noise from the next room, the sound of movement, then a sudden thump, the kind of noise a body might make, say, falling off a sofa. Stephen resisted the temptation to go and help, stayed where he was, emptied the glass again. Shortly afterwards came a long, pained groan, the kind of noise you might make having just fallen off a sofa, then the sound of uncertain footsteps. Nora crouched in the doorway, bracing herself between the handle and the doorframe, cigarette packet in hand, her lips wet, her face completely white except for the dark smudges around her eyes, looking like a silent movie actress.

'Hey,' said Stephen, struggling to stay stern. 'How are you feeling?'

'Just . . . awful,' she replied.

'Forget it, we all say things we don't—'

'No, I mean, I think I'm going to throw up,' she blurted, and stumbled into the red bathroom.

They both huddled in the tiny room, his hand gently rubbing her back, or brushing the wet hair from her forehead. This intimacy would at any other time have been thrilling, but any romance or tenderness was undermined by the remnants of his anger, and by Nora being sick, repeatedly and volubly, into the washbasin. This went on for some time, so long in fact that Stephen got two chairs, and squeezed them in, so that she might at least throw up in relative comfort.

They sat there largely in silence, or at least without speaking, and when at last it seemed to have come to an end, Nora finally said, in a rasping voice, 'Love what you've done to this place.'

'Thank you.'

She raised her head from the basin. 'OK – I think that's the last of it.'

'Let's hope so.'

She flopped back in her chair, smiled at him. 'Well, it's good to see, after all the shitty things that have happened today, that you and I still know how to have a good time.'

'How are you feeling?'

'Uh-oh – Doctor Steve's back.' She put her hand to her head, then to her stomach. 'I feel in-ter-esting. Don't worry, I'm not going to ask to borrow your toothbrush. I have my own, in my bag.' Stephen went to get it, taking the chairs with him, then returned and watched from the doorway as she laboriously brushed her teeth with one hand and reached for her cigarettes with the other, and thought about how she sometimes reminded him of an unusually metropolitan trawler skipper.

'D'you want a shower maybe? Freshen up a bit.'

'Maybe. Yeah, maybe.' He reached past her, and set the shower running, then went back into the living room to find some fresh clothes for her to wear. He found a clean T-shirt in a drawer, a pair of tracksuit bottoms in the laundry bag, and returned to the misty bathroom.

He was immediately reminded of the scene in *Witness*, where Harrison Ford's jaded Philly cop sees shy Amish widow Kelly McGillis bathing, and there is a shared look of intense yearning between them. There were no yearning looks in this instance, or none that he could discern anyway, because Nora was in the process of trying, and failing, to pull her dress off over her head. The dress was the same one she'd been wearing when they'd first met at Josh's party – old, black, beautiful, shiny with wear at the shoulders and bottom – but she had attempted the manoeuvre without undoing the buttons at the shoulder first, and there was a kind of louche escapologist's wriggle going on, as she stood, mottled and pale, knock-kneed in mismatched underwear and a pair of sagging black tights, attempting to yank the dress past her chin with one hand, and using the other hand, in which she held the lit cigarette, to prevent herself tumbling over into the shower stall. Suddenly feeling a little Amish, Stephen chivalrously attempted to fix his gaze on a polystyrene ceiling tile.

'Need a hand?' he said, to make his presence known.

'Someone turned the lights out, Doctor,' she giggled from within her dress.

'OK, hold on,' and he stepped forward just as she tumbled towards him, grabbing his arms by the elbows, leaning into him, and pushing him back against the wall. She stood there for a while, laughing now, her body pressed against his, as he very carefully attempted to unbutton the dress from the inside out.

'Ow! Hair, hair!'

'Stay still then.'

'I'm trying . . .'

A button popped off, and he palmed it into his hand. 'OK, I've got it – hold on,' and he bunched the dress up in both hands, pulled hard, and hoped that she didn't hear the sound of tearing fabric. After a moment she opened one smudgy eye, then the other, but didn't move away from him, in fact moved closer, and they stayed there for a moment, his hands on her bare back, damp now with steam and sweat, supporting her weight, their noses touching, her hipbone pressed hard into his belly, poised halfway between a slow dance and a brawl.

Nora started to laugh, a thick, woozy chuckle. 'Well, this is . . . *in*teresting,' she murmured, her cheek pressed against his now.

'It certainly is.'

'Care to join me?' she whispered in his ear.

His hand had somehow found its way beneath her bra strap, and her skin felt soft and warm, but her breath smelt of cigarettes, toothpaste and whisky, and something else that he didn't care to think about.

'I'd ask you to dance, but my pantyhose appear to be falling down,' she murmured.

With as much suaveness as he could muster, he reached round to the back of her thighs, grabbed the material, and tugged upwards. 'There you go.'

'Thank you kindly, young man. So – care to dance?'

'Dance? No, I think I'd better leave you to it.'

'Oh,' she pouted. 'Oh – OK. Party-pooper.'

'Maybe another time.'

'Yeah, maybe. May-be,' she grinned, and slowly winked one smeary eye.

'Shall I take that, or do you want it in the shower with you?' he said, indicating the cigarette that was currently smouldering against the plastic shower curtain.

Frowning, she brought the cigarette up to eyelevel, held it close and examined it curiously, as if someone had wedged it between her fingers without her permission. 'Maybe not,' she murmured, shrugged, placed it between her lips, then passed it to Stephen, who did the same, noting that the end was slightly damp from her mouth. Nora was staring at him intently now from under heavy eyelids, her lips slightly pouting, in a lush, boozy parody of seductiveness, and in the search for something to do, Stephen leant across and dabbled his fingers under the shower head.

'Hot?' asked Nora.

'A little hot. Want me to turn it down?'

'No, I *like* it hot.'

Stephen started making his humming noise.

'Hey, are you nervous, Doctor?'

'Why would I be nervous?'

'Your nostrils are flaring, Doctor.'

'Yeah, that happens sometimes.' He bought his hand up and pinched them together. 'Sorry.'

'Don't be sorry, Doctor – I liiiike it.' She pressed her hips harder against his, and he felt a sudden sharp pain in his groin, as if he'd walked into a table. Her eyes were closed now, her face tilted up towards his, and he realised that he could almost certainly get away with kissing her. He considered the possibility. Was kissing something you should 'get away' with? There was, it had to be acknowledged, a queasy, inebriated eroticism in the situation, and whilst this wasn't an entirely bad thing, the 'doctor' joke was irritating him, as was the sense that this addled seduction was less the manifestation of an unspoken sexual attraction, more the result of a cocktail of whisky and pills and getting even. And as for that 'I like it hot' line . . . He was, he decided, too old and too sensible to be grinding hipbones like this. With some effort, he decided not to kiss her, a decision clarified for him by Nora visibly suppressing a bilious belch, then changing colour and pushing him to one side to get to the washbasin.

'You OK?' he asked, back in doctor mode.

'I think so. I think maybe . . . maybe I should have that shower.'

'So you think you can . . . do the rest by yourself?'

'I think so. If not, I'll holler.'

'Well – you know where I am . . .'

'I know where you are,' she said, looking up from the washbasin, and giving him a queasy smile.

He smiled back, closed the door, then went and lay on the sofa, watching the DVD play out on the white wall, Monroe sitting on the piano singing, 'I'm Through With Love' with the volume on mute.

Nora reappeared fifteen minutes later, dressed in the clean T-shirt, make-up removed, mute and pale and seemingly more sober now, clutching her aching ribs. She smiled and frowned at the same time, and head down, crossed to the sofa and lay down with Stephen, curling in front of him. They lay there for some time looking at the glow of the fake coals on the electric bar fire, as the moisture from her damp hair soaked through his clothes to his skin.

'Every time I close my eyes, the room starts to spin.'

'Don't close them then.'

'But I've got to. I'm *so* tired.'

'Well, just lie here with me for a while. You'll feel better soon.'

'Soon?'

'Eventually.'

She shifted her position so that she was looking at the ceiling, her legs draped over his.

'This has got to be the worst twenty-four hours of my life.'

'Me too. Well, top five.'

She looked at him, concerned. 'Why?'

'I'll tell you another time.'

She sighed, and curled up tighter.

'What are we going to do, Steve?'

'About Josh, you mean?'

'About Josh. About everything.'

'Nothing tonight. Let's wait till morning. Talk then.'

'You think things will be better in the morning?'

'Not better. Clearer, maybe.'

'Why do you bother, Steve?' she murmured.

'With what?'

'With me. Why do you put up with it? What's in it for you?'

'I have absolutely no idea.'

Nora exhaled deeply, and closed her eyes, and Stephen leant towards her so that he could see her face. Two small crescents of toothpaste were drying in the corners of her mouth, and he had a sudden desire to wipe them away with his thumb and forefinger. She must have sensed him watching her, because she suddenly shifted position, flipping on her back and turning to face him.

'What time is it?'

'Half-two.'

'Oh God,' she groaned. 'We should try and sleep, I guess.'

'OK. You have the bed, I'll have the sofa.'

'I know I'm meant to argue, but I'm too tired.' She closed her eyes. 'Unless . . .'

'What?'

'Unless we slept together. I don't mean make out or anything. Just, you know – for warmth, whatever.'

'I can't, Nora.'

There was a pause, and after a while she murmured, 'Why not?'

He could tell her, of course, but when he looked down at her face her eyes were closed again, and her breathing had become slower and deeper, and there seemed no point in telling her while she slept. Besides, his leg had developed cramp, and was twitching disconcertingly, which he thought might undermine the moment. As if to emphasise the point, Nora had started to snore too, a surprisingly loud sawing noise. Her metropolitan trawler skipper's snore.

'Some other time then,' he said quietly.

In a film or a play, this would have been the moment where the hero would have lifted her up and carried her gently to the bed without waking her, but realistically, there was a very strong probability of braining her on the coffee table, so instead he put his hand on her head, whispered, 'Come to bed,' in her ear, and walked her over to the bed.

'Can I sleep now?' she mumbled.

'You can sleep.'

Lying fully clothed on the sofa, he pulled his overcoat up over his shoulders, took one last look at Nora, then closed his eyes and sank into a sleep so deep that it felt like an anaesthetic.

He was woken the next morning by the smell of his own armpits.

He peeled the cushion from his face, sat up and peered over at Nora. She was lying on her back, looking very pale and fragile, her mobile phone pressed to her ear. Stephen watched silently as she frowned, sighed, erased a message, listened again, frowned again, sighed again, erased again . . .

'What's up?' he asked.

'Just checking my missed calls.'

'Two of those were mine.'

'And the other forty-three?'

'Ah. How is he?'

'Well, the first five or six were apologetic, then he switched to anger, then he got kinda whiny, then defensive, abusive, and now he's being . . . yes . . . sarcastic, I think . . . hard to tell. He sounds pretty drunk or wired or something. I locked him out without his keys, so God knows where he's calling from.' She hung up the phone, slumped back onto the bed. 'He sounds in a pretty bad way. I should call him, I guess.'

'Yes, but . . . not just yet.'

'No, not just yet.' She groaned and turned over on her side to face him. 'So – I should apologise. For the bits I can remember at least. I'm sorry, I haven't been that wasted since my wedding day.'

'You don't have to apologise.'

'But I should at least try and explain. You'll have to come over here, though. I can't feel my legs.'

He stood, crossed and lay next to her on the bed.

'The thing is, I got a little blue and had a little too much to

287

drink, that's all. I was trying to drown my sorrows, and I guess I must have held their head under a little too long. I wouldn't want you to think it was anything more . . . melodramatic than that. OK?'

He took hold of her hand. 'Except it wasn't just the booze, was it?'

'I just wanted a little oblivion for a while. You can understand that, can't you?'

'I suppose so.'

'So – subject closed?'

'If you want.'

'I do.'

'OK – subject closed.'

She nudged him with her shoulder, and leant forward to look at him. 'Anything else we need to talk about?'

'What d'you mean?'

'Well, I seem to have these mysterious bruises on my hips, and I have a terrible idea that I may have got them by hurling myself at you.'

'There was a bit of that, yes.'

'Can't have been much fun for you. Some weepy, big-boned old lush slobbering all over you . . .'

'Well, usually that would have been fine, but the timing wasn't great, I suppose.'

'And did anything – you kno . . . ?'

'I helped you pull your tights up, but that was about it.'

She screwed her face up, put her fingers in her ears. 'That's a horrible word. "Tights" is a terrible word.'

'Sorry – "pantyhose".'

'"Pantyhose" is *much* better. So I guess you must have found me pretty irre*sis*tible, huh?'

'Well, yes, I do, did, but you were also a little drunk and, well, there are rules about that sort of thing. And besides, I was a little anxious that you'd throw up on me . . .'

'Oh God . . .'

'. . . and you're married, of course . . .'

'Not so's you'd notice.'

'. . . and also, to be honest, I was still a little angry with you.'

Nora winced. 'Wanna tell me why?'

'Well, you had just punched me.'

'I did?'

'Uh-huh.'

She sat up straight, took hold of his chin and scrutinised his face 'Oh my God, where?'

'Just the ear. I did slap you first, but that was for medical reasons.'

'Well, maybe I punched you for medicinal purposes.'

'I don't think so.'

'Well, I'm sorry. And for anything . . . unkind I might have said too. And thank you for resisting my wet-faced charms.' Then, in her best accent: 'You're a proper English gent.'

'Any time.'

They were silent for a moment, and lay on the bed next to each other, staring at the wall opposite. After a while, she nodded towards the framed photo on the wall. 'Your wife and daughter, huh? At least, I'm assuming it is, unless you're one of those guys who hang round maternity wards with a camera.'

'No, that's them.'

'They look great.'

'They are.'

She turned her head to look at him. 'So – what do we do now?'

'Stay here?'

'Here?' said Nora, without enthusiasm.

'I'll go now and get some food, and while I'm gone, you can phone Josh, tell him you're in a hotel and you're safe, and you'll call when you're ready. Then when I come back, we'll have a shower – separate showers – lock all the doors, turn all the phones off, I'll make us some breakfast, some coffee, and we can just, you know, hang out. Watch movies. Of course, I'll have to go out to do the show tonight, but I'll come straight back. I'll be back by ten. How does that sound?'

'Like I've been taken hostage?'

'No, it'll be like . . . we're on holiday.' He noticed her eyes flick around the room. 'OK, well, not holiday maybe. Just, you know – safe.'

'We can't just stay at home and watch old movies, Stephen.'

'I know.'

'At some point, we'll have to go out and face the real world.'

'I know that.' Feeling scolded, he got up and moved quickly towards the door, pulling his coat on. 'I'll be back in five minutes.'

'Stephen?' He turned. Nora lay on her side on the bed, looking at him 'You do know I'll have to leave you eventually, don't you?'

'Of course. But not just yet, eh?'

'OK. Not just yet.'

And Stephen turned, and left before she could change her mind.

THE BIG SPEECH

'*You do know I'll have to leave you eventually, don't you?*'

The day was dark, heavy and numbingly cold. The sky looked bruised and low, and the air had that metallic taste, as if threatening snow or a storm. Walking down the street to the arcade, Stephen C. McQueen was entirely sure of two things – that he loved Nora, and that he would have to tell her this at the next available opportunity.

He stood in the Price£avers, searching the barren shelves for groceries so startling and delicious that they might tempt her to stay, or, failing that, something with any nutritional value at all. He bought soluble aspirin, milk, a loaf of brownish bread, fizzy water, and two Mars Bars, and thought about what else he might do to persuade her to stay, to get her to see past the crappy flat and the stalled career, to see the potential rather than the raw materials. To somehow make her swap an unfaithful success for a passionate failure.

He would have to make a big speech.

In a movie, of course, this speech would have come entirely naturally, fluent, unforced, unpremeditated. Passionate, eloquent, clinically effective declarations of love were as commonplace in movies as, 'You're off this case, it's gotten too personal' or, 'Don't you go die on me, you hear?' or, 'Whatever it is, it's not human', and even now, all the various conventional formulations he'd ever heard were running through his mind on fast-forward – random, stock words and phrases: *worship adore ever since we first met more than life itself can't live without you we belong together think about you every waking moment in my dreams as well you are my rock my northern star the air I breathe . . .*

Clearly none of this stuff would do. Yet he knew that, as things stood, he couldn't compete, didn't stand a chance. Of course the timing was all wrong, and he should wait, and pick his moment, but if he didn't act, didn't say something now, she might go back and see Josh, might forgive him, even. Not initially, of course, but eventually. Stephen had to make his case now, and get Nora to see another, better version of himself, one that was worth sticking with, at least until his luck changed. He had to persuade her that he possessed qualities far, far more desirable than money, success, travel, status, charisma, immense self-confidence, charm, glamour, popularity, sexual virtuosity and physical beauty. Qualities like . . .

Nothing sprang to mind immediately, but he'd come up with something. He would improvise, live in the moment, speak from the heart, not the head. One thing was already clear, though: it was going to have to be quite a speech.

'*You do know I'll have to leave you eventually, don't you?*'

But what if she wasn't there when he got back?

He broke into a run, his breath visible in the air, the bags of shopping banging against his shins, rehearsing potential words and phrases in his head, trying to find a way of expressing himself that didn't feel like bad dialogue, or too conventional, or plagiarised: *ever since I met you more than just good friends really want to kiss you adore you worship you we belong together you complete me love you need you want you etc. etc. etc. blah blah blah* . . . Should he shower first, brush his teeth, in case it led to . . . ? No, keep it spontaneous, stay in the moment. He pounded up the stairs, the words accumulating in his head, ready to make his big entrance and let everything he felt about her flood out. He was just putting the key in the door when, for the second time in twelve hours, he heard a noise that made his chest contract with panic.

His own voice. Singing.

'"The wheels on the bus go round and round, round and round, round and round . . ."'

And Stephen felt all his internal organs simultaneously try to squeeze up into his mouth. He slid the key into the lock, and opened the door.

Nora was sitting on the sofa, sucking on her toothbrush, a blanket wrapped around her shoulders. Projected on the wall, 8 foot by 6 foot was *Sammy the Squirrel Sings Favourite Nursery Rhymes*. On her lap she cradled the severed head of her husband's Best Actor Award. Without looking away from the screen, Nora delved into the folds of the blanket for the remote control, lowered the volume by a couple of notches, then took the toothbrush out of her mouth. 'Hey,' she said, flatly, eyes fixed.

'Hey, there,' said Stephen, as calmly as possible, stepping into her eye-line and the light of the projector. 'What are you doing?'

'Learning 'bout numbers,' she replied, sucking on the toothbrush again, peering around him.

'No, really, Nora – what are you doing?' he said, his eyes fixed on the trophy in her lap, the one with her husband's name engraved on it.

'OK, well, if you really wanna know, I'm just sat here trying to work out what's weirder – you stealing Josh's Best Actor Award, or you dressed up as a massive singing, dancing squirrel. Usually I'd say it was stealing the award. Until I started watching this, that is. Now I'm not so sure . . .'

A new song had started: *'If you're happy and you know it, shout "We are" . . .'*.

'We are,' said Nora, quietly to herself, then smiled briefly at Stephen. He put the bags down, and reached past her to the projector to turn it off. 'Don't you dare!' she snarled, and knocked his hand away with the BAFTA, so instead he came and sat next to her, and gazed up at his own big, red stupid face projected on the wall.

293

'Well – it's a look,' she said, without smiling.

'It certainly is,' he said, weakly.

'If you're happy and you know it, stomp your feet . . .'

Nora stomped her feet.

Stephen decided to go on the offensive, to convert shame into indignation. 'Of course, another question might be, what gave you the right to start nosing around in my stuff?'

'Hey, look, *Sammy* – I understand. You're not happy, and I know it. But I wasn't "nosing around". It's just I was cold, and I was looking in your wardrobe for a sweater, or a blanket or something, and I sort of stumbled upon . . . these.'

'That still doesn't give you the right to— . . .'

'. . . I was going to put them back and pretend that I hadn't seen them, but – well, I'm sorry, but some things are pretty hard to ignore, Steve.'

'If you're happy and you know it, shout "Hooray" . . .'

'You know, most guys would just have porno hidden in the back of their wardrobes.'

'Would that be better, or worse?'

'It's a close call, Steve. It's a very close call. If it was a DVD of, say, you in a squirrel costume having sex with my husband's BAFTA, *that* might conceivably have been worse. You're very good, by the way,' she said quietly.

'It's the role I was born to play,' he said.

She smiled, very briefly. 'I think this is the moment where you say, "There's a perfectly rational explanation for all this."'

'There is.'

'I'm all ears,' she said, then turned back to the screen. 'As, indeed, are you.'

'OK, well, *this* –' he nodded at his huge, burbling red face on the screen – 'this I do partly for the money, and partly because I enjoy—'

'Do?'

'Sorry?'

'You said "do" not "did".'

'I've been filming the sequel.'

'That's what you were filming yesterday?'

'Uh-huh.'

'I thought you said it was a tough indie crime thriller.'

'Set in woodland.'

Nora laughed, and Stephen took the opportunity to reach suddenly for the remote control, but she rapped his knuckles with her toothbrush, hid it under the blanket. Sammy the Squirrel had mercifully stopped singing, and was now struggling to explain the difference between adding up and taking away to Brian the Bear.

'In my defence, I actually think I'm pretty good.'

'You are. But isn't there a scale issue here?' she asked.

'That's exactly what I told the director.'

'That is one dumb bear.'

'That's true.'

'. . . *Four* hazelnuts! You owe him *four* hazelnuts, you idiot . . .'

'Nora, you are listening to me, aren't you?'

'I'm sorry, but I'm finding it impossible to look away.'

'Well, could you try, Nora? Please? You're not making this easy for me.'

'I have no intention of making it easy for you.' She turned to him, smiling again, but still only slightly. 'Stephen, this –' she nodded at the screen – '*this* is fine. *This*, I don't mind. In fact it's actually almost quite cute, in a . . . sinister kind of way. To be honest, I'm a little more concerned about . . . this,' and she pulled the trophy out from the blanket, placed it on the coffee table in front of them. It stared back at them, with its one good eye. 'I mean, it wouldn't be so bad if you'd stolen – I don't know – cash or something.'

'I didn't *steal* anything.'

'So what happened then?'

'OK, well, the thing is, you remember that party, where we first met? Do you . . . please, do you mind if I turn this thing off?' said Stephen.

'Put it on Pause. I don't want to miss anything.'

He paused the DVD. 'OK, well, that party, you know, when I drank a little too much, and had that weird attack, because of those antibiotics I'd been taking. Well, I was in your bedroom, and I saw Josh's award, and I was picking it up, just to look at it, and I was, you know, goofing around in front of the mirror when you came back in the room, to say the cab was there, remember?' She nodded. Stephen took comfort and ploughed on. 'And I clearly wasn't thinking straight, because I sort of stuffed it under my coat, and the next thing I knew I was in the taxi on the way home, and I still had this . . . thing.'

'So, let me get this straight – you stole my husband's Best Actor Award—'

'Not "stole", just . . . misplaced it in my flat. Temporarily.'

'You temporarily misplaced my husband's Best Actor Award in your flat because you'd been taking antibiotics?'

'Well, no, not just because of that. It was booze mainly, but . . .'

'And Josh's affair?'

'Affair?'

'Affair's a stupid word – this woman, these . . . women, he's been seeing.'

Stay calm. Just act. Act well. Perform. 'What about them, her?'

'Did you know about it?'

Shake head, roll eyes to ceiling, laugh in surprise and disbelief. 'No-ho-ho.'

'What was *that*?'

'What?'

'"No-ho-ho."'

'It means I didn't know.'

'You didn't know?'

'No.'

Pause.

'I think you're lying.'

'What makes you think I'm lying?

'Your nostrils flare. And you do this weird "no-ho-ho" thing. I don't know where you picked that up from, Steve, but I have to tell you, no human being has ever made that noise, ever . . .'

'OK. Yes.'

'Yes, you *did* know?'

'Yes.'

'So did you lie to me, or was it just the antibiotics talking?'

'No, no, I lied to you . . .'

'You lied to protect Josh?'

'No.'

'"No"?'

'No, I lied to protect you.'

She laughed bitterly. 'How does that "protect" me, Stephen?'

'I – I didn't want to see you hurt, and Josh promised he'd change, and there were . . . other reasons why I didn't want to be the one to tell you. Also, I thought it was none of my business.'

'And none of my business either, obviously. Well, all I can say is I hope you act better than you lie, Stephen, because as a liar, you absolutely stink.'

'That isn't a lie! I knew you'd find out sooner or later, I just didn't want you to find out from me. It wouldn't have been right to tell you myself.'

'Why not?'

'Because . . .'

'Because what?'

'Because I'm in love with you.'

Pause.

'You are?'

'Yes.'

Beat.

'In love with me?'

'That's right, in love with you. I think I love you, Nora. In fact I know I do. I love you very, very much.'

'For how long?'

'Always. Since we met.'

She sighed. 'How do you know?'

'Know what?'

'That you love me.'

'Because . . . because it's agony.'

She considered this, then turned back to face the projection, the big red buck-toothed face, flickering slightly on Pause. 'I see.'

He reached across to take her hand, but she pulled away, pointed the remote like a pistol, and pressed Play on the DVD, and the image sprang into life again, Sammy the Squirrel and Brian the Bear counting out the hazelnuts. One nut, two nuts, three nuts, four nuts . . .

'Where are you going?' he asked, as she bundled up her dress and coat, and headed for the bathroom.

'Home, Stephen. I'm going home.'

GUNFIGHT AT THE IDAHO FRIED CHICKEN

As love scenes go, it had not been an unqualified success. The location had been all wrong, his timing had been off, and he would have ideally welcomed a chance to run it again, from the top, but it was too late now. Nora was making her exit. With one hand held to her head, as if this was the only thing keeping it on her shoulders, she was stomping downstairs, Stephen following a few steps behind.

'Where are you going, Nora?'

'I told you, Steve – I'm going home.'

'But won't Josh be there?'

'Who knows? Probably.'

'Don't you want to stay and talk things through?'

'Not right now, no.' She was tugging at the front door.

'The door is double-locked; you need to . . . here, let me.'

He opened the door for her, and she stepped out into the street.

'Want me to walk you to the bus-stop?'

'I'll be fine – thanks,' she said, unable to look him in the eye.

'OK, well. Here – you might as well have this, I suppose,' and he handed her Josh's misplaced Best Actor Award in a Price£aver's plastic bag. She sighed, took the bag from him, holding it with distaste. 'Obviously, I'd appreciate it if you could just, I don't know, tell him you found it under the bed or something. It would lessen the humiliation, make things a bit easier for me. But if you have to tell him the truth . . . well, I was going to get it back to him, eventually. I swear, it really wasn't intentional. If I hadn't taken those anti—'

She brandished the bag containing the award, holding it like a cosh. 'Stephen, I swear, if you mention the word "antibiotics" again, I will make you *eat* this fucking thing.'

'Fine. Sorry.'

They stood in silence for a moment, Nora glancing around as if looking for some means of escape.

'You seem . . . angry with me,' he said.

Nora sighed, and finally forced herself to look at him. 'Not angry. I'm still grateful to you for looking after me and everything, and I'm touched that you . . . feel so strongly about me. And I suppose I may have had some suspicions of my own. But, still, you have to admit, well . . . this is all a little weird, Stephen.'

'I know.'

'I mean, I need time to clear my head.'

'Any idea of how much time, though?' She raised her eyebrows in warning. 'Actually, don't answer that. But just so you know, I meant what I said. I meant it very much. I really do adore you. I always have.'

'And what am I supposed to do with that information, Stephen?'

'I sort of hoped maybe you'd give it some thought?'

'You don't think I have enough to think about?'

'I know. I'm sorry. I had to tell you, that's all. It just seemed the right thing to do.'

She reached out and took his hand by the fingertips. 'Freak,' she mumbled, and smiled weakly. 'I should go,' she said finally, stepped closer and hugged him, initially taking care to hold her body a little further away than usual, the very model of a platonic embrace. He put one hand in the curve of her back, and thankfully she moved closer, placing her cheek lightly against his. They stood there for a moment. Looking over her shoulder, on the other side of the road a short distance away, Stephen noticed a low silver Audi TT roar suddenly into life, then pull blindly into traffic. Instantly, he recognised the car, the face at the wheel, and instinctively he tugged Nora back against his front door, just in time, as the car hurtled across both lanes, bucked up onto the high pavement and with an awful metallic crunch, beached itself there, the front wheels still spinning, the bonnet of the car just feet away from the window of Idaho Fried Chicken.

Without turning the engine off, Josh Harper tumbled out of the driver's seat, his leg tangled in the safety belt. He stumbled, fell onto the pavement, then got back onto his feet, and hurtled towards them, towards Stephen. He was dressed, bizarrely, in his costume from the show, and before he knew what was happening, Stephen found himself held high against the glass window, Josh's arm in a puffy white shirt jammed painfully under his chin.

'Hello, Bullitt! Didn't expect to see me, did you, you fucking *traitor* . . .'

Josh's hair was stuck to his face with sweat, his eyes were wide, red and wild, his jaw clenched, he stank of sweat and booze, and a slight frosting of yellow-white powder could be seen around one nostril. Stephen felt something jam into his hip, and was suddenly aware that Josh was wearing his sword too, and that he was being assaulted, in the street, in Battersea borders, by a drunk and wired world-famous actor dressed as Byron, with a sword. It was not a situation that he felt readily equipped to deal with.

'JOSH,' Nora shouted. 'JOSH, PUT HIM DOWN. YOU'RE BEING RIDICULOUS!'

Josh's face was mean and twisted. 'I just want a little word with our friend here, my love, my sweetness, just a friendly little chat with our mutual friend here.'

'Alright, OK, but let's go indoors, Josh,' mumbled Stephen.

'No! I like it out here.'

'Josh, am I meant to find this in some way endearing, or dramatic or something?' scoffed Nora.

'Let go of me, Josh.'

'Or what? Or *what*, Bullitt? What are you going to do about it?' He pressed his hands hard against both of Stephen's shoulders, so that Stephen imagined he could feel the plate glass bow behind him. 'You know, Steve, I may not be perfect, and I may have done some stupid things in my time, but at least I'm not a hypocrite, Steve, at least I'm not a little sneak, at least I don't skulk about like you, acting all friendly, sucking up to me, hanging out in my house, and all the time wheedling your way into my wife's knickers . . .'

'Oh, this is pathetic, Josh,' hissed Nora, standing at his shoulder. 'Grow up, will you . . . ?'

But Josh wasn't listening. 'I asked you last night, didn't I, Steve, *pleaded* with you, as a mate, where's Nora, where's Nora, where is she? No idea, you said, and yet, what a surprise! Next morning, here she is, in this dump, shagging *you* . . .'

'Josh, don't be ridiculous,' scoffed Nora.

'Well, you can forget the deal, my friend. The deal is most definitely *off*.'

'It was never that kind of deal, Josh, you know that.'

'Deal?' said Nora, looking between them, confused. 'What deal?'

'And as for you, sweetheart, you've got a cheek, haven't you? Giving me a hard time, then sneaking off to Bullitt's love-nest here.'

'This is stupid, Josh. We're friends, that's all.'

'I thought you had better taste, sweetheart. You can do better than this . . .' he turned back to Stephen, his face up close, and sneered, with infinite contempt, '. . . this *understudy*.'

Stephen's hand-to-hand combat experience came primarily from stage-fighting classes. Consequently, when throwing a punch his natural instinct was to aim for a point just upstage of the target's head with his right hand, and simultaneously make a noise by slapping his thigh with his left. He suspected that this technique would not have much effect on a crazed man with a sword. Forced to improvise then, he managed to wrap one leg around Josh's ankle and, with both hands, push him with all his strength. Josh stumbled back hard against the side of his car.

'OK, now that's enough, the both of you,' said Nora, arms out, like a referee.

But Josh was standing now, rubbing his back and laughing, and reaching for his sword.

'Call the police,' said Stephen, looking to Nora.

'I am *not* going to call the police.'

'He's got a fucking SWORD, Nora!'

'Josh, listen to me. PUT – THE SWORD – DOWN.'

'Alright, alright, look—' He unbuckled his belt, and threw the sword through the car window. 'No sword, OK?'

Stephen thought he ought to do something, so assumed a defensive stance, one leg forward, fists raised, making him look like a figure from a Victorian circus poster. Josh just laughed. 'I'm a trained martial artist, you little sack of shit,' he grinned.

'Oh God. Please, just get a *grip*, will you? Both of you!'

Josh ignored her. 'Come on then, come on, give it your best shot,' and he assumed an action-figure fighting pose, one that Stephen seemed to recall from the climactic cyborg fight in *TomorrowCrime*, a pose that had seemed striking in Megopolis 4, but looked a little out of place in Battersea borders.

It was Stephen's turn to laugh. He started to speak – 'Josh, do you have any idea what a complete and utter *cock* you look . . .' and then Josh was high in the air, spinning round, his leather-booted foot connecting hard with the side of Stephen's head, and the move that had proved so effective against the cyborg proved equally effective here. Even as the pavement rushed towards his face, Stephen had to admit that it was pretty impressive . . .

An arm came down, grabbed his shoulder, then pulled him

over, and then Josh was sitting on his chest, his face up close, ugly and distorted, his hands tugging on the lapels of Stephen's overcoat. He was dimly aware of Nora, face white, eyes wide with panic, her arm round Josh's neck, trying and failing to pull him off, and Josh reaching back and pushing her away, so that she stumbled back against the window.

Josh's sour breath was hot on Stephen's face as he hissed in his ear: 'I know you called those photographers, Bullitt. I can't prove it, but I know. I worked it out last night. And I know why you did it too – because you're *jealous*, you little shit. You've never achieved anything in your useless, pointless life, nothing worthwhile, and you see someone who *has* achieved something, someone who's got everything *you* want, and so you skulk about and fuck it up for them. Well, d'you want to know why you're the underdog, mate? Why you're the under-study? Because you *deserve* to be. You're nothing, friend, a nobody – no one cares about you, no one even knows you exist, you're invisible, a talentless, mediocre, invisible piece of—'

. . . And before Josh could finish, Stephen felt the air shift, saw something fly past his eyes, and connect audibly with Josh's face. He heard a sound he'd never heard before, the sound of bronze on tooth, and then Josh was falling backwards to the pavement, where he lay sprawled, eyes fluttering, hand clasped to his mouth, felled by his own Best Actor Award.

Stephen stumbled to his feet. Nora was crouched down over Josh, the bronze statue still in her hand, mopping at the red mess with the corner of her coat, and saying, over and over again, 'Josh, I'm sorry, I'm sorry, I'm sorry. Open your eyes, sweetheart, speak to me . . .' And from behind them Stephen heard a first-floor window squealing open, looked around and saw Mrs Dollis gawping down at the scene.

'Bloody hell!' she gasped. 'You've killed Josh Harper!'

Act Five

BEGINNERS, PLEASE . . .

Before you go out on stage, you've got to look in the mirror and you've got to say your three 'S's – 'Star' 'Smile' 'Strong'

Woody Allen
Broadway Danny Rose

If nothing else, there's applause . . . like waves of love pouring over the footlights.

Joseph L. Mankiewicz
All About Eve

A STAR IS BORN

An August day in the long, disappointing summer of 1983.

At the age of eleven, at the public swimming baths in Ventnor, Stephen had sought to impress Beverley Slater, the girl he loved more than existence itself, with his high-diving prowess. Making sure that she was watching, he had climbed to the very highest level, stood at the end of the board, and it was only then, as he stood alone in the high, hot afternoon sun and looked down at the pool and the people many, many miles below, that he realised that he could neither dive nor swim, at least not without the aid of various kinds of flotation device. He was scared of water, of heights, of falling, of the inevitable full-body slap of the water as he belly-flopped in, like a side of meat thrown off a high building. He was completely and entirely unsuited and unqualified to be in this particular place, at this particular time, high up above the clouds, barely dressed in bathers far too small, with Beverley Slater and the entire population of the Isle of Wight watching sceptically from below. The diving board suddenly seemed like a gallows.

And yet he'd chosen to climb the ladder. He hadn't been bullied or pressurised into it. He didn't have to be there at all, but he had chosen to, because he had wanted people to see him do something impressive, something startling and unexpected, something *extraordinary* for a change. Now here he was, finally coming to the awful realisation that diving and falling are not the same thing at all.

According to that year's edition of *The Guinness Book of Records*, it was possible to fit the entire human population of the planet on the Isle of Wight, and looking down, it certainly seemed that a pretty high proportion of them were there that day. Everyone was watching him now. People had stopped swimming and talking, dive-bombing and heavy-petting, and all faces were turned upwards in anticipation of the young lad from Shanklin's spectacular high-dive. Gripping the end of the board with his toes and leaning out, he could just about make out Beverley Slater too, biting her lip and willing him on. Clearly there was only one thing he could do if he wanted to avoid complete and total humiliation.

Stephen took a deep breath, and no one in the crowd could quite believe the extraordinary poise, control and skill with which Stephen turned round and very, very carefully climbed back down the ladder.

Shestooduponthebalconyinexplicablymimickinghimhiccough-ingandamicablywelcominghimin . . .

Stephen C. McQueen sat in Josh Harper's dressing room, staring in Josh Harper's mirror, wearing Josh Harper's costume, and trying very hard to remember how to breathe.

His conventional approach, the in-out rib-and-lung technique he had favoured for more than thirty-two years now, didn't seem to be working automatically any more. He was breathing on manual, reminding himself, step by step – breathe in, breathe out, now breathe in, and now breathe out again – and whilst this would do for the moment, clearly it wasn't going to be practical for very much longer. He felt dizzy and light-headed and nauseous, and with barely enough air in his body to sit and stare in the mirror, let alone stand and move about and do what he had to do. He looked at his watch without seeing it. Ever since he'd arrived at the theatre, time seemed to have lost its conventional chronological quality – instead it was stretching, and stopping, and sometimes even going backwards, so that he had absolutely no idea how long he had until . . .

'Mr McQueen, this is your ten-minute call,' rumbled the Tannoy. 'Ten minutes, Mr McQueen.'

He got up to stretch his legs, then immediately sat down again. Breathing and walking. He could no longer breath, walk or tell the time. What about speaking? Could he still speak? Stephen leaned in closer to the mirror, spoke again.

'*Mad, bad and dangerous to know . . .*'

He noticed his nostrils were flaring. Do it again, without flaring your nostrils.

'*Mad, bad and dangerous . . .*'

Nope, there they go again. It was as if they had a mind of their own, flapping open and closed in time with the words, like something you might find on a coral reef. He tried once more, physically holding them down; better, but clearly not a practical solution, not for a ninety-minute show. Perhaps he should go and tell Donna he couldn't go on. It might be easier. Just go and tell Donna he was sick, he had accidentally fractured his skull or a lung had collapsed or something. Maybe that was why he couldn't breathe. Maybe a lung *had* collapsed, entirely of its own accord.

Or perhaps he should just walk out now, with no excuses, sneak out of the Fire Exit, or climb out the dressing-room window, shin down a drainpipe or knot some sheets together, onto Shaftesbury Avenue and freedom. They couldn't make him do it, after all. They couldn't force him to.

There was a knock on the door, and a sudden surge of hope. It had been snowing fairly steadily all afternoon – perhaps they'd had to call off the show because of the snow. Or perhaps there'd been a power cut, or the upper circle had fallen in, or some other act of God, but no, it was just Michael, the DSM, carrying a bunch of slightly frayed supermarket roses. Michael smiled pleasantly at Stephen from behind the flowers – the kind of gloomy smile more usually seen in intensive care wards.

'These just arrived at stagedoor, Steve.' He glanced at the small envelope, addressed to 'Mr Stephen C. McQueen' in meticulous loopy blue handwriting, a smiley face in the centre of the Q. He knew of only one person who filled every available space with a smiley face.

'Everything alright in here?' asked Michael, a hand on his shoulder.

'Absolutely. Any word about Josh?'

'He's fine. He's at home resting.'

'Alone?'

'No, Nora's looking after him, I think.'

'Good. Good. So – no chance of him jumping in a cab, is there?'

''Fraid not – sorry.'

'OK – just a thought.'

'So – knock 'em dead, yeah?'

'I'll try.'

'Ten minutes, OK?'

'Absolutely. Ten minutes.'

He waited until the door closed, then read the card.

> *Dear Dad. Good luck. I know that your perform-*
> *ance tonight will be truly excellent.*
> *Love Sophie.*

They'd made it. So that was that, then. No backing out now. He slid the card into the envelope, stood up a little unsteadily, and headed down the long, treacherous staircase that led to stage left.

'See you out there, superstar,' said Maxine, in her white dressing gown, peering out of her dressing-room door.

'Thanks, Maxine.'

'And listen, that kiss in the bedroom scene – no tongues, yeah?'

Stephen laughed. 'I thought I was meant to do exactly what Josh does.'

'Only up to a point, lover-boy,' she said, and kissed him on his cheek. 'You're going to be fantastic.'

Donna was waiting for him in the stage left wings, smiling, like a jovial hangman.

'OK – they're all in.'

'They are? Good.'

'Crowd's quite small, what with the weather, but it's friendly.'

'Good, good . . .'

'You're sure you're OK?'

'Oh, absolutely.'

'Because you look very pale.'

'I do?'

'Want me to delay the curtain?'

'For about a week and a half, maybe?'

Donna sighed, unamused. 'If you really want, Stephen, I can always send them home.'

'No, no – let's do it, Donna.'

'You're sure?'

'I'm sure.'

'Because if you don't think you're up to it . . .'

'No, I'm up to it.'

'OK. Obviously there's no one to open the door at the very end, so you'll have to do it yourself. Is that OK?'

'I think I'll manage.'

'You want a glass of water?'

'No, I'm OK.'

'OK, well – do you want to get in position then?'

'I'll get in position'

'And, Stephen?'

'Yep?'

'Break a leg.'

'Probably.'

And Stephen stepped out onto the stage, walking a little gingerly, as if stepping onto thin ice. The safety curtain was down, and he stopped for a moment, and listened to the terrible hush of anticipation coming from the audience.

My motivation, he told himself, is to be strong, charismatic and Byronic. Remember – Sophie and Alison are out there. My motivation is to make them proud.

Then he turned and went to sit in his pre-set position, on the chair at the desk, and picked up the prop-quill, feeling the shirt stick to the sweat on his back as he leant against his chair. The working lights dimmed overhead, and the electric candle-effect candelabra came up. He noticed that the quill was shaking in his hand, and he had a sudden overwhelming need to use the toilet in every way imaginable.

Too late, because the music was starting now, sounding far louder and more portentous than it did when he listened in on the Tannoy. He took a deep breath in, and another in, then a third, out, then two more in, and one out, one in and two out, two in and one out, licked his lips, and ran the first line over and over –

'Madbadanddangeroustoknowthatswhatheycallmemadbad-anddangeroustoknowthatswhattheycallme . . .'

– and then he heard a click and a mechanical whirr and the safety curtain began, ever so slowly, to trundle up, like a guillotine blade being hauled into position. He felt the air of the auditorium mingle with the air of the stage, as if an airlock were opening on a spaceship, and he instinctively held on hard to the writing desk with one hand to prevent himself from being sucked out into the vacuum. Trying not to become aware of the absurdity of pretending to compose poetry with a large white feather, he wrote on the piece of tea-stained prop parchment, in imaginary ink, in a big, loopy Byronic scrawl:

Help
Help Me
Heeeeeeeeeeeeeeeeeeeeeeeeelp
Meeeeeeeeeeeeeeeeeeeeeeeeeee

Then the curtain was fully up, and the music began to fade down. He felt the warmth of the spotlight on his face, and a drop of sweat run down the length of his nose, and in his head he started the slow ten count – 1, 2, 3 – that he knew was always so effective – 4, 5, 6 – when Josh did it – 7, 8, 9 –

When he reached 26, he heard a cough from the auditorium, a get-on-with-it cough, and he realised that there was no avoiding it, he'd have to look up; he'd have to say something. My motivation is to be . . . extraordinary, he told himself, and felt the drop of sweat on the tip of his nose quiver, fall, and splat on the paper, the noise booming around the theatre. He unfocused his eyes, looked out straight into the light, and said his first line –

> 'Bad, mad and dangerous to know. That
> is what they call me in England now.'

He heard the voice in his head, as if played back on a tape recorder at slightly the wrong speed, so that it sounded several registers too high, thin, slightly strangulated and nasal. And hadn't he said bad-mad instead of mad-bad? Had he or hadn't he? That's the title of the play – how could he get that wrong? How stupid could one person be? Should he start again? No. *Doesn't matter, forget about it, say the next line, quick, you're taking too long, you're being too slow, get on with it, and be better this time. Remember – aloof, magnetic, charismatic. What Josh said isn't true. You are* not *invisible, you* can *do this. You are Lord Byron, the most notorious man in Europe. Women desire you, men envy you. Now, smile slightly mockingly, not too much, one side of your face, and speak again . . .*

> 'Or so I am told. And it is, I must
> confess, a reputation that I have done
> little to assuage.'

Not bad, better, but you still sound poncy, lispy, like you've just had dental surgery. Talk properly. Clearly but properly. What now? I know! Why not getup! Walk around a bit. Move. That will get their attention. Try and move with a sensuous feline grace . . .

And he placed the quill down, stood, and caught his hip against the edge of his desk. He remembered that old line, that acting is all about remembering the lines and not bumping into the furniture, and it suddenly seemed that he was incapable of either.

He had also become horribly aware of his arms. It was as if these spare appendages had suddenly sprouted from his shoulders – strange, alien tentacles that he had never seen before, had no experience of, or control over, that just sort of dangled there uselessly like meat in a butcher's shop window. Where did they go? Where could he stash them? Clearly, he would need to get them out of the way, before he could say the next line. He decided to dispose of at least one of them by putting it in the pocket of his breeches.

He tried this four times before he realised that there were no pockets in his breeches. He reassured himself that this was the kind of thing Byron probably did all the time, and instead he slid the arms behind his back, and left them there, hands clasped, until he needed them again. It felt good to get them out of the way. It also felt authentically 'period' too, properly late eighteenth/early nineteenth century, and, eyes still unfocused, staring out into the spotlight, he sauntered downstage, taking one, two, three strides before he remembered Byron's club foot. He turned the fourth stride into a limp, a slightly excessive limp he felt, a Richard III-limp, as if Lord Byron had just twisted his ankle. Best tone it down, best keep it grounded, but too late now, because he was at the front of the stage, as far as he could go. There was nowhere left to limp, and it felt like standing, naked and blind drunk, on the edge of a precipice.

Or a diving board.

What next? The next line.

```
Like all reputations it is simultane-
ously accurate, yet fanciful.
```

He could hear his own voice echo back at him, and it sounded better this time; strong, confident. Professional. In control. What now? He pictured the page of the script in his mind, scanned down the lines, saw the words 'survey audience'. He assumed his expression of wry, mocking amusement, let his eyes slip into focus, looked down into the auditorium, looking around, surveying the audience, taking in the seats . . .

The empty seats.

Row upon row of empty seats.

Hundreds of empty seats.

Close eyes (slowly). Open eyes (slowly). Look again (calmly).

Time slowed, and stopped.

There is nothing quite as empty as an almost empty theatre.

There were, as far as he could tell, six people in the stalls. He recognised three of them – Alison and Sophie and a little further back, absorbed in his programme, Frank. Two people, young, Japanese, sat to one side, their feet up on the back of the seats in front. In the gloom, the sixth member of the audience sat in a seat at the end of the row, got up, hunched over, and scurried to the very back of the theatre, and in the light of the Exit sign, Stephen recognised her as a programme-seller.

Struggling now to maintain his expression of wry, mocking amusement in the face of mounting terror, he looked up into the circle. Two more people, strangers, their heads resting on their arms on the balcony rail, looking at him expectantly. His vision started to blur, and he thought perhaps he might faint; not a good idea, given that statistically the chances of there being a doctor in the house were very slight indeed. Nausea rose up inside him, and he had an intense desire to take a few steps backwards, turn and run, club foot or no club foot, run into the wings, and out of the fire-door and out into the night air, and to keep running, as far away as possible from this terrible place, to run all the way home, and lock the door of his flat, and never, ever unlock it again . . .

And then what?

He scanned the empty rows again, focusing his eyes and finding them, Alison and Sophie, sitting forward in their seats, both madly grinning up at him, Sophie with a wide ecstatic smile on her face, on the edge of laughter. She looked directly up at him, blinked hello with both her eyes, and stuck two thumbs up over the back of the seat in front.

And he remembered that he could do this and, more than that, that he was extremely good at it, and that this was the thing that he'd always wanted, for as long as he could remember. To do good work. Find the thing you love, and do it with all your heart, to the absolute best of your ability, no matter what people say. Make her proud. He smiled back directly at his daughter, a smile that was just about in character, a confident smile, an in-charge smile. Then he took another deep breath and said the next line. And then the next.

And ninety-three minutes later, it was all over.

THE GREAT ESCAPE

'You were *amazing*,' said Sophie, sitting on the edge of the table in the dressing room afterwards.

'Well, not *amazing*,' said Stephen, buttoning up his shirt.

'No, you were amazing, wasn't he, Mum?'

'He was OK, I suppose,' said Alison, grinning broadly.

'That's not what you said. You said you thought he was amazing too. How did you remember *all those lines*?'

'Well, I didn't actually remember *all* of them. Some I left out and some I made up.'

'It didn't show, though, did it, Mum?'

'No, Sophie, it didn't,' said Alison firmly.

'It didn't?' Stephen asked hopefully.

'No, no. Not really. I'm not sure if the real Byron used the word "OK" quite that much, but I don't think anyone really noticed.'

A pause.

'Shame there weren't more people in,' said Stephen, attempting a kind of wry, philosophical tone, as if immune to such trivialities.

'Yeah, yes, it was,' said Alison, attempting reassurance once again, but less successfully this time. 'But everyone who saw it enjoyed it, that's the main thing, isn't it?'

'Exactly. That is the main thing,' said Stephen, not entirely sure if this was the main thing.

And there was another silence, a momentary pause, before Alison leant over, a little stiffly, and punched the top of his arm. 'Well – done – you.'

'Yeah, well done, Dad.'

'Well, thank you, thank you . . .' he mumbled, holding his hand up modestly, to an imaginary, invisible crowd, rather like the one he'd just performed for. 'I wish you hadn't given a standing ovation at the end, though.'

'Hey, it wasn't just us. Other people were standing.'

'Only to put their coats on.'

'That's not true!' insisted Alison. The remark had been intended as a joke, but now he wasn't so sure. Another silence.

'Hey, you should have more champagne,' he said quickly.

'No, I'm alright, thanks,' said Alison, placing her hand over the top of the plastic cup.

'Come on, help me out, I can't drink the whole thing myself.'

'I'll have some,' said Sophie, holding out her paper cup.

'No, Sophie, you're not allowed. You're slurring your speech already.'

'Well, Mum isn't allowed either, are you, Mum?'

'Sophie!' hissed Alison, in a warning tone, stern but unable entirely to stop grinning.

'Why not?' said Stephen, instantly knowing the answer. Oh God, he thought. Oh God, please no. Not that . . .

'Mum's pregnant!' said Sophie.

. . . no, no, no, no, no . . .

'Congratulations!' he shouted, and pushed himself out of the chair, wrapping his arms around Alison tightly, scared of what might happen if he let go. 'That's fantastic news,' he said into her neck.

She pulled her face away so that she could see him, and said more quietly – 'Is it?'

'Of course it is! It's amazing news, I'm so pleased for you.'

'It's only six weeks mind, so we're *not* meant to be telling anyone . . .' and she ruffled Sophie's hair in mild admonishment. 'You don't mind?' she whispered in his ear.

''Course not. Hey, it's not mine, is it?' he whispered back.

He could hear the sound of her smile in his ear 'Wouldn't have thought so. But you're sure you don't mind?'

'Not at all. I'm . . . over the moon for you. Really, I couldn't be happier,' he said.

It was by some way the most convincing piece of acting he'd done all evening.

A little later, he saw Alison and Sophie out to the stagedoor. The snow was falling heavier than ever now, and Sophie gave a little whoop of excitement when she saw it, pushed the door open and went to stand in the alleyway, her face upturned in the streetlight.

'What is it in French again, Sophs?' Stephen shouted from the doorway.

'*Il neige!*'

'Exactly. *Il neige.*'

'I'm sorry about all that,' said Alison, holding both his hands. 'I didn't want to tell you tonight, but Sophie's so excited and . . . you're sure you don't mind?'

''Course not.'

'Because I was worried you'd be upset.'

'Well – it was bound to happen one day, wasn't it? If you will keep sharing a bed with the man. But I'm pleased for you, really I am. You and Colin. Send him my love, won't you?' Alison narrowed her eyes sceptically. 'OK, maybe not love – send him my . . . congratulations.'

A small pellet of grey snow impacted on the side of Stephen's face.

'Sophie – put that snow down, it's filthy, it's got syringes in and everything,' shouted Alison, then turned back to Stephen. 'Hey, and well done again for tonight – you were fantastic. I was very proud.'

'Thank you.'

'And I owe you an apology. For all those things I said.'

'That's OK. I know why you said them.'

'But still. I was wrong. It doesn't happen very often, but in this instance I was wrong.'

'Maybe.'

'No, really – I was. You were . . . extraordinary.'

Another silence followed.

'When's Josh back, do you know?'

'Maybe tomorrow, maybe Monday.'

'Well – enjoy it, won't you? Your moment in the spotlight.'

'I will.'

'And I hope it leads to other things. I'm sure it will.'

'Yeah, well, fingers crossed.'

He kissed her, then lifted Sophie up into his arms and held her tight.

'You were much better than the other man,' she whispered in his ear.

'How d'you know that?'

'I just do.' Then, in her quietest whisper, she said, 'I was really, really proud.'

He held her for a while longer, told her he'd see her on Sunday, then said goodbye again, and they were gone. He pulled the stagedoor shut, turned, and saw that Donna was waiting for him, arms crossed across her chest.

'Enjoy it, did they?'

'Seems so, yeah.'

'Good, good,' attempting a smile, then abandoning it as just too hard. 'So – Stephen, d'you think you could join me for a quick post-mortem? In private?'

''Course,' he said. It was a tone he hadn't heard for some time, her Nurse Ratched-tone. He also couldn't help wondering if 'post-mortem' really was the best phrase to use, but he followed her through from stagedoor to the wings, and realised that he had started to make his noise again, his high-pitched humming noise, his turned-off life-support-machine noise.

On stage, the DSMs were resetting props for the Saturday

matinée. Donna and Stephen found two high stools in the prompt corner and sat.

'So – well done tonight.'

'Oh, thanks, Donna. I was a bit sticky to begin with.'

'Yes, we noticed. But you got better towards the end, and that's the main thing, isn't it?' Once again, Stephen wasn't sure that this was the main thing, but let it pass.

'Well, thanks, Donna.'

'Terence phoned to say he's sorry he couldn't come and see it, but he's directing this show in Manchester and just hasn't got the time.'

'Well, that's OK, maybe he can come tomorrow.'

'Ye-es.' They sat in silence for a moment, before Donna shook herself and said, 'So, look, Steve, I didn't want to talk to you about this before you went on tonight, in case it threw you, but the thing is . . .' Here it comes, looming towards him: The Thing. 'The thing is – I spoke to Josh earlier this evening.'

What was it they always said in war movies? Tell them your name, rank and serial number, nothing else . . .

'Right, OK. And how is he?'

'He's alright. He had just come back from the emergency dentist, and he's a bit woozy from the anaesthetic, so it was hard to work out what he was saying, but he's fine, and his teeth are going to be OK.'

'Well, thank *God* for that!'

Donna narrowed her eyes in warning. 'He's back at his home now, taking it easy.'

With Nora, thought Stephen. At home, with Nora.

'He says he "fell over". In the street,' she said sceptically.

'That's right, yes.'

'Right outside your house, apparently.'

'Uh-huh.'

'And that you were with him at the time?'

'Yes, yes, that's right.'

'Well, look, he admits that he was drunk, and completely out of order, and that you were in no way to blame. He's very, very keen to emphasise that. That's all he wants to say on the matter, and obviously the management are keen to keep our star happy, so we are all prepared to leave it at that. Anyway, you'll be delighted to hear that he's probably going to be back on stage by Monday night.'

'Right. Good. Well, after tonight that's fine by me.'

'However, he did have a message that he wanted me to give you.'

'O-K.'

'He said that he's very pleased that you got your big break, and that he really hopes it went well for you tonight, but when he comes in on Monday, he doesn't want you anywhere near the building. In fact, Stephen, he doesn't want you anywhere near him ever again.'

'Oh. O-K. O. K,' said Stephen. *My motivation is to stay dignified. To keep it together. My motivation is not to fall entirely to pieces.* 'Anything else?'

'Not really. Except he repeatedly asked me to call you Judas.'

'I see. Judas. So – so I'm being fired then?'

'No, not fired. Well, yes, yes, you're being fired. Obviously, we'll pay you right to the end of your contract, for the next two weeks, right up until Christmas, and you're owed holiday pay too. You just don't need to . . . actually come into the building any more.'

'And who's going to play the Ghostly Figure?'

'Oh, I'm going to do that.'

'Well, you'll be excellent.'

'Thank you. I like to think so.'

'And what about the two shows tomorrow?'

'Both cancelled, I'm afraid,' she sighed. 'The thing is, as you'll have noticed from the audience tonight, with a show like this, a star vehicle, the general public really do want to see a star. Anything less, and it turns out they all just ask for their money back. Sorry, but there really is no nice way to say that.'

'I think there might be a *nicer* way, Donna.'

'Yeah, maybe there is.'

They both sat there for a few moments more, both of them smiling tight little smiles that weren't really smiles, until finally Stephen said, 'You've never really liked me, have you, Donna?'

'To be honest, Stephen, I don't feel particularly strongly about you either way,' and Donna pushed herself off the high stool. 'Best of luck with all your future plans,' she said, and slowly walked across the stage, her big bunch of keys rattling against her hip, like a gaoler.

WHITE CHRISTMAS

Stephen packed the contents of his dressing room into a spare plastic bag, and hung up his body stocking in the wardrobe for the last time. He drank down one more glass of the warm, flat celebratory champagne without really tasting it, turned out the light bulbs around the mirror, then the overhead light, and pulled the door closed. Then, as he had done one hundred and twenty-three times before, and knowing that he would never do it again, he made his way down the treacherous back staircase that led to the stage-left wings.

Most of the team had gone home, but he said goodbye to the few of the crew who remained – stage management, the costume department, the crew, the people he genuinely liked and would miss. He took care to avoid eye contact, and thankfully no one asked any awkward questions, or mentioned what had happened, though everyone seemed to know that he wouldn't be coming back. They all shook his hand, said well done for tonight mate, you were fantastic, Steve, good luck in the future, mate, see you around. He even took a couple of phone numbers from people, knowing that he'd never actually be able to bring himself to use them.

He stopped off at Josh Harper's dressing room, and took the stolen *Star Wars* figurine from his pocket, the one he'd accidentally taken from the party, and leant the tiny Han Solo against Josh's door, his gun hand raised in salute, or defiance, he wasn't sure which. Then he said goodbye to Kenny the stage-door keeper, shook his hand, wished him well, and stepped out into the night.

The snow was falling, thicker now, great smudgy grey clumps that hovered in the air as if unwilling to touch the ground. The traffic stood immobile the length of Shaftesbury Avenue, and the crowds shuffled rather than walked through the soupy grey sludge on the pavement. Stephen walked towards the entrance to Piccadilly Circus tube, but couldn't face the wet, steaming, drunken Friday night crush on their way to or from office parties, so instead he crossed the road, and waited outside the Trocadero for a number 22 bus. As he stood in the shop doorway, his phone bleeped, and he opened the text message. It was from Frank.

> well dun tonite you were grate sorry
> couldn't stay til
> end mum is gastro-entiritis
> will call soon. F.

He deleted the message, then sat, immobile, mute, numb and a little drunk, on the top deck of the bus as it crawled down Piccadilly towards Chelsea. On this crowded Friday night so close to Christmas, the snow was having a calamitous effect on the city. People staggered on and off the bus, wet and gasping, drunk most of them, laughing and flirting, but Stephen kept his gaze fixed out of the window, his plastic bag on his lap, watching the snow, and the crowds slipping and shuffling along Piccadilly, Knightsbridge, Sloane Street, the Kings Road.

He sat and thought about Alison, thought about how strange it was that someone he had loved so much could have a child that had nothing to do with him, that Sophie would have a brother or sister who had absolutely no connection with him at all. There wasn't even a term for that relationship; the child's mother's ex-husband; it didn't have a name. He thought about the look on her face when she had told him, the joy apparent behind the embarrassment and awkwardness, and he was pleased with the way he'd reacted to the news, much better, much calmer than his reaction had been when she had told him she was getting married again. At least he hadn't punched any walls this time. He'd been gentlemanly, this time. Generous. Grown up, even if inside he had wanted to scream.

And as for losing his job, he couldn't really blame Josh. He'd deserved it, after all. He felt 'Judas' was a bit strong, perhaps, but still, he hadn't played fair and there was a kind of justice to how things had turned out. He couldn't help thinking it was a shame that more people hadn't seen him, though, because in the end he'd been . . . all right. In his mind, he tried to imagine what the billboard might look like outside the theatre, his own face transposed with Josh, sword drawn, shirt unbuttoned to the waist.

'*More* than Adequate,' screamed the critics.

'Stephen C McQueen *is* OK!!'

'Absolutely *Fine*, Considering!'

'Not Nearly as *Bad* as Some People Expected.'

'He Tried! Really, he did!'

'I've Seen *Worse*!!!!'

Oh, well. Maybe next time.

He decided that there was never going to be a next time.

He decided, there and then, on the number 22 bus, that he was going to give up.

The bus was halfway along the Kings Road now, idling in traffic. Suddenly claustrophobic and panicky, Stephen squeezed out of his window seat, went downstairs and stepped out onto the street, shuffling on frozen pavement south towards the river, and the lights of Albert Bridge.

Of all the London bridges this had always been his favourite; an almost absurd romantic structure, the one most favoured by lovers, and suicides. He stood at the centre of the bridge, his breath hanging in the icy air, and stared east along the Thames. He was suddenly aware of how cold his hands were, and looked down at the plastic bag with all the souvenirs from the dressing room – the good-luck cards, his annotated copy of the script, a chipped and stained coffee mug, the manuscript of the useless, pointless one-man show he'd been writing for years, the flowers Sophie and Alison had brought him for tonight. He imagined the flowers yellowing and wilting in a jug in the flat, and felt a sudden terrifying surge of almost overwhelming despair, a looming blackness that he hadn't felt for many years, and had hoped never to feel again. He felt his head get hot, his eyes start to burn, panic starting to rise in his chest.

He decided to get rid of the flowers, to get rid of it all. Quickly standing a little way back from the rail of the bridge, he started to swing the bag in great swooping circles; then, when it reached the lowest point of the arc, he let go and watched, exhilarated, as the bag sailed high up into the sky, then split, sending the pages of script tumbling out into the air, and falling with the snow into the Thames. He leant as far as he could over the parapet, and watched the paper bobbing on the black water, illuminated by the white lights of the bridge for a moment or too, before being carried away by the river, and to his surprise, he felt a sense of relative calm and relief – the same shaken relief you might feel when a car comes to a halt after an accident, when it stops spinning and tumbling and you realise that you're all right, you're OK, you've survived. He had had his Big Break after all. Giving up, surrendering, stopping, that was the Big Break. The world of show business would just have to struggle on without him, that's all.

He would be a better person from now on. He didn't know quite what he'd do for a living yet, but he would try to be a better person, and live a life free from all that envy and bitterness, spite and regret. He would forget about his imaginary life, the chances he'd never had, what might-have-been, and concentrate instead on making the real thing better. No more Ghostly Figures, no more Dead Guys. Instead, he would be *the* Steve McQueen – not the famous one perhaps, but the happy one.

He'd be caring and friendly to his ex-wife and his daughter, and he'd find a new job that he loved, or at least liked, something that he could do well, and work hard at it; learn sign language maybe, or open a café, or work with kids – hadn't Alison said he was good with kids? Or he could go back to college next September and retrain in something. It was probably too late to become a doctor or an architect, but, that aside, he could do almost anything he wanted. Eventually, given enough time, he might even forget about Nora. It was actually pretty exciting when he came to think about it.

He peered down into the river, watching as the last of the pages drifted off into darkness, and he felt the fear and panic subside a little, as if his luck might finally, finally, *finally* be about to change. It was a sensation that lasted for a good minute and half, right up until the police car pulled up alongside him.

THE LONG GOODBYE

In the end, the policemen were quite reasonable.

They asked him to sit in the back of the car and, once they'd ascertained that he wasn't drunk and disorderly, and that he wasn't going to throw himself off the bridge, they gave him what was, to Stephen's mind, a perfectly reasonable lecture about dumping rubbish in the Thames. Without giving them the full story, Stephen apologised, and they drove him home, Stephen perversely enjoying the ride, feeling quite tough in the back of a police car.

'You live *here*?' said the policeman as they pulled up outside his house, giving him a worried look.

'Uh-huh.'

'Get much hassle from those kids?'

'Oh, nothing I can't handle.'

'Yeah, well, watch your step, won't you? Don't try and answer them back, it's not worth it.'

'I won't – and thanks for the lift.'

'And please use the litter-bins in future, won't you, sir? That's what they're there for.'

'Yes, Officer. I will.'

The police waited in the car until he'd got safely to the front door, then drove off. Stephen stamped the snow from his shoes, brushed it from his shoulders, shut the front door behind him, and wearily climbed the stairs. He let himself into the flat, felt warm air on his face, and noted with irritation that he'd left the electric fire on. He crossed the room and turned it down.

'D'you mind? I'm freezing my ass off here.'

Slowly, Stephen turned round.

Nora lay curled up on the sofa, half asleep, using her coat as a blanket, and Stephen felt a tremendous surge of pleasure and relief.

'I let myself in. I still have your keys – hope you don't mind.'

'I don't mind at all.'

Nora curled her knees up, making room on the sofa, patting the seat next to her. 'You're late back.'

'Well, you know – it's been quite a night.'

'Signing autographs, talking to fans?'

'Something like that.'

'And how did it go? Did you set the show business world ablaze?'

'Uh-huh.'

'Show 'em how it's done?'

'Absolutely . . .'

'Crowds screaming for more?'

'Of course.'

'Groupies?'

'Hurling themselves from the balcony.'

'Waves of love pouring over the footlights?'

'All of that.'

'And was it everything you ever dreamt it would be?'

'Not exactly.'

'Oh. Bad audience?'

'No audience.'

'Ah.'

'Or only a small one.'

'How small?'

'Eleven, I think. To start with, anyway. Down to about eight by the end.'

'Well, maybe it was the weather . . .'

'No, they all got there. It's just not that many stayed, that's all.'

'Oh. I see. Still – small but appreciative.'

'Exactly.'

'And it'll be better tomorrow.'

'Actually, there isn't going to be a tomorrow. Professionally speaking, anyway. I've been fired.'

'Who by?'

'By Josh, I think.'

'Yeah? Me too,' and she nodded towards a small overnight bag at her feet.

'Where is he?'

'At home. I thought it would be a little mean to make him stay in a hotel tonight, so I left him there, groaning and bleeding on his pillow. After I got him back from the dentist, I put him into bed and got the hell out of there.'

'So you're not going to stay with him?'

Nora wrinkled her nose, poked him with her toe. 'After what he did? You know, Stephen, I sometimes think you seriously overestimate the persuasive powers of that man. Even if he wanted me back, which he doesn't, not after what I did to his precious teeth, what possible reason would I have to go back to Josh?'

'So – if you don't mind me asking . . .'

'Why am I here?'

'Why are you here?'

'Well, I know you'll think it's strange,' she said, tucking her hair behind her ear, looking solemnly at the floor, 'but I realised that I could never, ever be happy until I found out what happened to that damn squirrel.'

Stephen laughed, and found himself surprised by his ability to laugh. 'I thought you were still angry with me.'

'Oh, I am, don't you worry about that. You've done some pretty . . . strange things, Stephen. And as for covering up for Josh . . .'

'He told me he was ending it.'

'I know, but still, whatever reasons you may have had, it wasn't especially nice of you.'

'No, you're right. And I'm sorry.'

'And I accept your apology.' Nora swung round and pulled her legs up on the sofa so that she was facing him. 'Also, there were some things I thought we ought to clear up.' She leant forward, took his hand in hers, opened it and looked at it intently, as if trying to read the palm. 'This whole . . . in-love-with-me thing. I have a theory. Would you like to hear my theory? It's a good one.'

'I'd love to.'

'OK, here goes.' She shuffled forward in her seat. 'I think you were lonely, and unhappy, and you sensed that I was lonely and unhappy too, and you thought that might be enough. And I have to admit, I've enjoyed it, us keeping each other company, it's been fun. I've looked forward to seeing you, and I've . . . thought about you. When you weren't there.' She sighed and closed the fingers of his hand over. 'But it's not a particularly healthy starting point for a romantic relationship, is it? Mutual despair.'

'It's not just that, though, is it?'

'Isn't it?'

'No.'

'Well, what else is it, then?'

'For a start, I think you're . . . extraordinary.'

Nora screwed her eyes shut, and pulled a face. 'And why would you think that, Stephen? Why would you *possibly* think that?'

He thought for a moment.

'Because wherever we are, whoever we're with, I always know that you're the best person in the room. The smartest, the funniest, the wisest, the person I most want to talk to, or to be with. The best. By far. Nobody else comes anywhere near.'

She narrowed her eyes slightly. 'And is that from a movie or something?'

'No, that's how I feel. In real life.' Quickly, before he could think about it too much, he leant over and kissed her, very lightly, for a moment or two, and if she didn't respond exactly, neither did she pull away.

They sat, foreheads resting gently together, until eventually Stephen said, 'So – what do we do now?'

Nora sat back. 'Oh, try and get a flight back to New York tomorrow, I guess, spend Christmas with my folks. Give a little time over to comfort-eating. Have my mom tell me, "I told you so". I'm looking forward to it, really I am. How about you?'

'Go back to the Isle of Wight for Christmas. Overeat. Have Mum and Dad tell me, "I told you so".' Nora smiled, then Stephen spoke, quite calmly and plainly.

'I've just realised that after tonight, I have nothing. No job, no plans, no ambitions, no idea what I'm going to do. No money or prospects. Absolutely nothing. I'm going to have to start all over again, completely from scratch.'

'Me too. But that's a good thing, isn't it? A fresh start.'

'Is it? I don't know.'

'We're just starting a little late, that's all.'

'I suppose.'

'You know, I think I should be on my own for a while. That's the sensible thing to do at least. Just go back home, see some friends, work out what I want to do with my life, try and remember who I was before I became Mrs Josh Harper. But I have to admit . . . I will miss you, Stephen.'

Without stopping to think, Stephen said, 'Don't leave then.'

'So what do I do?'

'I don't know, but you don't have to go back to New York. Not just yet, anyway.'

Nora glanced around the room. 'Please don't ask me to stay here. Don't take this the wrong way, Steve, but this place is a depressing shit-hole.'

'I know. I'm going to sell it, I think.'

'Good idea. So. Where else can I go?'

Without waiting to think too hard about it, Stephen said, 'We could always go to Paris.'

Nora laughed. '*Paris?*'

'With me. For a holiday. They're paying me up until Christmas, anyway, so we could both go, me and you.'

Nora looked sceptical. 'I don't know . . .'

'Trust me, it's an excellent idea.'

'You want me to go to *Paris* . . .'

'Yes.'

'. . . with you. Paris . . .'

'You don't like Paris?'

'No, I love Paris.'

'Good. Me too. I spent my honeymoon in Paris.'

Nora laughed loud. 'I'm sorry, Stephen, but isn't that a reason *not* to go to Paris?'

'Well, we won't do all the same things, obviously.'

'Well, *obviously.*'

'But we could get the first train. They leave from Waterloo in about, what, five hours' time. We could be there in time for breakfast. Find a cheap hotel, walk around, sleep. Just for a few days, a week maybe. Get away from here, from all this, just me and you. Escape. What d'you think?'

Nora looked at him in silence. The room was fairly dark, the only light coming from the fire-effect, and the streetlights outside, so it was hard to make out her face clearly, and she certainly didn't smile as such. She just put her head slightly to one side, blinked once, very slowly.

Say yes, he thought. Say yes, and there's still a chance for me, a chance that things might turn out alright.

With one hand, she brushed her fringe across her forehead, and said –

'I don't have my passport.'

THE FIRST GOOD LUCK

EXT. TRAIN STATION. DAY

Dawn. Snow falls on the empty platform.
STEPHEN stands, looking anxious, glancing at
his watch.

>   TANNOY
>   This is your final boarding announce-
>   ment. Ladies and gentlemen, the 7.09
>   train to Paris is about to depart. Last
>   call for the 7.09 train to Paris . . .

One last look down the platform – nothing.
STEPHEN glances at the train – a look of
indescribable sadness passes over his face.
She's not coming. The TRAIN GUARD frowns . . .

>   TRAIN GUARD
>   Sorry, sir – can't hold her any longer.
>   . . . and with a sigh he picks up his
>   suitcase and goes to board the train
>   . . .

>   VOICE
>   WAIT! STOP THAT TRAIN! HOLD IT! WAIT!

He steps back down onto the platform, turns,

and there she is - NORA, passport in one
hand, overflowing suitcase in the other,
running as fast as she can through the snow.
She hurls herself into his arms.

>   STEPHEN
> I . . . I thought you weren't coming!

>   NORA
> Are you kidding? I wouldn't have missed
> this for the world!

>   STEPHEN
> I love you, Nora Schulz.

>   NORA
> Shut up and kiss me.

He does so. The friendly TRAIN GUARD laughs,
their fellow passengers, peering from train
windows, start to whoop and cheer. Snow falls
in thick white flakes. Music up, Louis
Armstrong singing 'It's a Wonderful World' as
the camera swoops up into the air and . . .

Except that isn't quite what happened.

What actually happened was this.

They talked for a little longer, then Stephen put some clothes
in a bag. They brushed their teeth, then lay on the bed back
to back to try to sleep, and within moments Nora was snoring
her trawler skipper snore. Stephen turned and lay on his back,
dozing intermittently then waking and looking at the ceiling
or the back of Nora's head, the short hair on the nape of her
neck. As was his inclination when happiness looked like a possi-

bility, he started to worry. He worried that they might not be able to get a train, that the snow would stop them running, or the seats would be sold out, or they wouldn't be able to find a hotel in Paris this close to Christmas, and the great escape would lose its energy and joy and spontaneity and turn into just another disastrous day-trip. He rolled over to face her back and, as an experiment, placed one arm gently on her hip, and without quite waking, she took his hand, and pulled his arm around her waist. Shortly after that, he went to sleep.

He woke again at 6 a.m. He got up, took the phone into the kitchen, and tried to find a mini-cab office that was open. Finally finding one, he booked a car for 6.30, only waking Nora at 6.25, giving her the smallest possible window of opportunity to change her mind. This was his other great fear: that she might change her mind.

As required by law, the mini-cab was late, and they spent a tense fifteen minutes waiting, with their bags at their feet. Finally, at 6.45, the doorbell rang and they tip-toed downstairs and drove north, very slowly, across an eerily silent, deserted London in the back of a decrepit Volvo estate with a back-seat top-soil of broken cassette cases and old newspapers. The city felt as if it had suffered some calamity in the night, and the only sound to be heard was the dawn chorus of car alarms, Heart FM playing a selection of love songs from the movies, and Nora intermittently humming along to 'Take My Breath Away' and 'Up Where We Belong'.

Finally, they reached Primrose Hill. The cab pulled up outside Josh's house, and Nora and Stephen looked at each other anxiously.

'Want me to come in with you?'

'I don't think that's necessarily a good idea, Stephen.'

'But you're just going to go in, get your passport and leave, yeah? I mean you're not going to wake him up or anything?'

'Just wait here. If I'm not out in fifteen minutes . . .' She started the joke, but seemed unable to finish it.

'What?'

'Nothing. Just . . . wait for me,' and she climbed out of the car, and tiptoed warily across the snow-covered forecourt, and disappeared inside.

The cab-driver – Nigerian, he thought – glanced at Stephen in the rear-view mirror.

'She's a very nice lady,' he said.

'Yes, she is.'

'Your girlfriend?'

'I don't know yet,' seemed to be the only honest reply.

The taxi-driver nodded sagely, then after a while: 'So – what do you do for a living?'

'I don't know that either,' replied Stephen.

'You do not know very much do you?' said the driver.

'No. No, I don't.'

This seemed to end the conversation. Heart FM was playing Bonnie Tyler's 'Total Eclipse of the Heart' now. The driver, clearly a fan, turned the volume up, and they both sat and listened to the song all the way through, neither of them speaking, the cab-driver nodding along solemnly to the music, joining in with the chorus, drumming along on his steering-wheel.

She's not coming, he thought.

They listened to 'The Power of Love', 'I Will Always Love You' and 'Unchained Melody'. Then commercials. Then they listened to 'Love Is All Around', 'Have I Told You Lately That I Love You' and 'The Greatest Love of All', Stephen's finger-nails digging progressively deeper into his palms with each chorus.

Halfway through 'Wind Beneath My Wings', the cab-driver turned in his seat and said, 'You know you must pay me for waiting time, yes?'

'Yes, of course,' said Stephen, peering anxiously out of the misty window. So she's not coming after all, he thought. He's talked her out of it. She's changed her mind. I'll give her two more songs – no, three more songs – then I'll give up and go. I'll leave her bag at the door and go home. Three, four more songs, five more, then the commercials, and then I'm definitely going home.

Music continued to fill the car like exhaust fumes. They sat and listened to 'Every Breath You Take' 'The Greatest Love of All' and 'Endless Love', and by the time 'It Must Have Been Love' started, the tension in the car was becoming unbearable. The sun was coming up now, and the driver had stopped drumming along, and was looking at his watch, and sighing impatiently, and Stephen felt that if he heard one more crash of drums, or one more screaming guitar solo, then he would almost certainly start to scream too. Then finally, just as 'Against All Odds' threatened to make the situation completely intolerable, Josh's front door opened, and Nora could be seen, head down, running as best she could towards the car. She bundled herself into the back seat and Stephen could see immediately that she had been crying.

'Are you OK?'

'Fine, fine,' she murmured, shielding her face with one hand.

'Did you get your passport?'

She brandished it with one hand.

'And did you see—'

'Stephen, I don't want to . . . let's just go, shall we?'

'To Waterloo?'

'Yes, yes . . .' she snapped, impatiently '. . . to Waterloo.'

They drove the rest of the way in silence, Nora pressing herself up against the car door, head resting against the window, biting her nails, Stephen too anxious to talk, and the plan that last night had seemed so perfect and apt and romantic, in daylight now seemed ridiculous, and impractical and fragile.

Finally they crossed the Thames again, and pulled up outside the Eurostar terminal, and Nora turned in her seat and managed a bleary, red-eyed smile. 'Can we agree not to talk about it?' she said. 'No more talking about the past. Only the future.'

'Of course.'

They paid, overpaid, the driver, wished him a Happy Christmas, and Stephen went to buy the tickets for the next available train, anxiously glancing over at Nora every now and then, to make sure that she was still there, that she hadn't run off. Then, not speaking, they went through check-in, boarded the train and sat next to each other, once again, in complete silence. It was only when the doors hissed shut and the train started to move, that they could actually look at each other, and smile.

They rattled slowly out of the station, and Stephen had to admit that, for the first time in a long time, the city where he lived seemed incredibly beautiful.

The train curled away from the Thames and south towards Kent.

'I'm going to try and sleep now,' Nora said, then sank down a little in her seat, and closed her eyes. He watched as she tried to rest her head against the window, her coat wedged uncomfortably between her cheek and the glass, her mouth pressed open. When the make-shift pillow slid down the window, she adjusted it, her eyes still closed, and rested her head once again. When that didn't work, she shifted sides, and leant her head against his shoulder instead.

'What are you thinking?' she asked, very quietly.

'Just that I'm glad you're here.'

'Me too,' she murmured. 'I'm glad I'm here too.'

She lifted her head, looked at him from under heavy eyelids, then leant up and kissed him.

Perhaps this is it, he thought, my first good luck.

'Let's just . . . wait and see what happens, shall we?' she murmured, with her eyes closed again.

'OK,' said Stephen. 'Let's wait and see,' and he closed his eyes too, and did his best to try to sleep.

ACKNOWLEDGEMENTS

Thanks to the following people for their support, their comments, and the kind loan of certain jokes. Camilla Campbell, Sophie Carter, Eve Claxton, Christine Langan, Michael McCoy, Tamsin Pike, Justin Salinger and Olivia Trench. Thanks to Valerie Edmond, for that story.

An on-going debt of gratitude is owed to Roanna Benn, Mari Evans, Hannah MacDonald and Hannah Weaver. For their endless enthusiasm and unfailing judgement, special thanks are also due to Jonny Geller and all at Curtis Brown, my editor Nick Sayers and the fantastic team at Hodder.

AUTHOR'S NOTE

Thanks to the following for their permission to reproduce copyright material:

The Love Song of J. Alfred Prufrock by T.S. Eliot, *from The Complete Poems and Plays of T.S. Eliot, Ready When You Are, Mr McGill* by Jack Rosenthal, *Broadway Danny Rose* by Woody Allen, and *The Apartment* by Billy Wilder and I. A. L. Diamond, all reproduced by kind permission of Faber & Faber Ltd. Material not to be reproduced without the written permission of Faber & Faber Ltd.

42nd Street by Rian James and James Seymour (released 1933) reproduced by permission of Warner Bros. Entertainment Inc.

Exerpt (and chapter heading p53) from *All About Eve* © 1950 Courtesy of Twentieth Century Fox. Written by Joseph L. Mankiewicz. All rights reserved.

Every reasonable effort has been made to contact all copyright holders, but if there are any errors or ommisions, Hodder & Stoughton will be pleased to insert the appropriate acknowledgement in any subsequent printing of this publication.